IRON WAR

THE JACK OF MAGIC BOOK 4

IRON WAR

ALEX LINWOOD

GREENLEES
PUBLISHING

This is a work of fiction. Names, characters, organizations, places, events, and incidents are either products of the author's imagination or are used fictitiously. Any resemblance to actual persons, living or dead, or actual events is purely coincidental.

Published by Greenlees Publishing, contact@greenleespublishing.com

ISBN-13: 978-1-951098-12-4

Cover design by Dominic Forbes

*For those who simply
Do Not Leave Anyone Behind*

Tiny nails scratching on stone woke Portia. She didn't want to leave her pleasant dreams. Her back and hip ached from lying on the cold damp floor for hours. Water dripped down the walls. It smelled bad, she knew, but couldn't tell anymore after spending hours in the dark tunnel that was part of the city's water runoff system.

A chittering got her attention. She sat up, shivering, and pulled the dirty blanket closer.

Red eyes peered at her from the darkness. Many more sets of eyes shone beyond the first, which was less than a length in front of her. Long whiskers twitched below the eyes, the thin white hairs comically wide for such a tiny animal. The bold one in front crept forward. In the dimness, she could see its white furry body, tiny nails, and the two long teeth that stuck out of its mouth. It had a long tail that ended with a poof of fur that it whipped back and forth, dragging the poof through dirty water. Portia wrinkled her nose.

"What are you doing? Can't you feel how disgusting that water is?" Portia whispered to the creature. It twitched its nose at her and then lifted its tail and flicked it back and forth in her direction, sending water flying, some of which ended up on Portia's face. "Stop! I'm up, I'm up." She wiped her face, cursing the creature in her mind, but then stopped herself. It was company, as demanding as it was.

Standing up, Portia pulled a bag off a hook she'd wedged into the stone above her and pulled out a small block of cheese. There were only a few other rations in the limp bag: a loaf of stolen bread and some meat that smelled pungent but was still edible, though just barely.

Portia crouched back down to face the mouse. It stared at her, sniffing, then ran forward and placed one paw on Portia's leg, the white nails appearing to glow in the dim light.

Despite the rumbling in her stomach, Portia broke off part of the cheese and held it in the flat of her hand. The creature's whiskers tickled her palm as it delicately moved forward, placing a paw on her finger and grabbing the cheese with its teeth. It ran back, carrying the piece of cheese nearly as large as its head, followed eagerly by its brethren. The scramble of claws on stone echoed down the waterway.

"You're welcome," Portia said quietly, still listening to the creatures retreating.

The silence left in the dim tunnel after their passage was only broken by the occasional drip of water. Portia shivered. It was safe here but also cold and damp. Facing the outside world was worth it, if only to warm up in the sun. The longer she was down here, the more difficult it was to breathe. Over the last week, a wet, heaving feeling had come with each inhalation. Portia clenched her fists as a spasm gripped her chest. As quietly as possible, she gave a soft cough to clear her lungs.

Portia pulled up the thin layers of linen she used as bedding. She'd hated to get the linens dirty on the damp stones, but she needed something between her and the cold floor. Shaking them out, she hung them from another hook in the wall. They would dry out at least a little by hanging all day.

Checking the leather travel bag she'd lifted from the market earlier that week, she felt her coin purse, as well as a pouch of homemade caltrops. The small metal bits were the easiest way to stop pursuers. Her sword, her most prized possession, was still safely in its baldric wrapped around her body. It hummed a greeting as she placed her hand on the hilt. She put the leather bag on, hanging it securely across her body but still allowing quick access to her blade.

It was impossible to tell what time it was in the tunnel. Almost as a habit, Portia tried to form a fireball with magic, as much for warmth as for light. A tiny flame sputtered in her palm and then flickered out. A wave of exhaustion flowed over her, making it even more difficult to breathe. Ironically, it was easier to do cryomancy in this world, something she did not need in that cold passageway.

Following the small breeze of fresh air coming down the tunnel, Portia walked slowly away from her hiding spot, trying to pick out where the deeper puddles lay. She'd nearly made it to an upcoming turn in the passage when, blinded by the slightly brighter light showing ahead from around the corner, she stepped into a deep puddle and soaked her right foot. Cursing silently, she shook it out and kept going. Hopefully, it was daylight outside. She needed to dry off in the sun.

Blessedly, it was midday when she emerged blinking from the tunnel into a dry riverbed just outside the city walls. The oddly bluish sun blazed down on her. Her skin tingled as the warming rays prickled through her brown and dirty linen robes. Checking the surroundings and finding no one, Portia sighed with pleasure as she pushed back her sleeves and hood and let her skin soak up the light. She lifted her chin to expose her neck and chest, closing her eyes against the intense brightness.

A faraway yell startled Portia. Opening her eyes, she quickly pulled her hood back up and lowered her sleeves. The brown material covered her completely, even her hands. If she was careful to keep her sword hanging more vertically than it naturally wanted to in its leather holder, that too was invisible under the flowing material. It was a bad idea to advertise she had anything of value.

The source of the yell was not visible, nor was anyone else nearby. It must have come from the gate over the hill and further down the wall.

Portia climbed up the dry riverbank and trotted to join the flow of traffic on the road into the city. Hopefully, if anyone should notice her, they would assume she'd been relieving herself in the privacy of the outside shrubs. There were few public toilets inside the walls of the city.

Long strings of carts filled the road, with huge furry horses and even bigger creatures all dressed as she was in long brown robes that covered them entirely. Their faces were not visible, but Portia knew from experience they looked more like walking snakes than men, their faces and bodies covered with large, thick scales. A shudder ran down her back; she was glad to not see them. Even as a tall fourteen-year-old, the top of her head barely reached the chests of most of them. Fortunately, dressed as she was, she could pass as one of their children, even if ridiculously thin by comparison. The creatures were stout and heavily muscled.

The clanking of chains grabbed her attention. Her shoulders stiffened and anger flew into her belly. Slaves. Moving slowly so as to not attract attention, Portia looked behind her. There they were—a long string of humans walking in a line with chains connecting them from neck ring to neck ring, their hands bound in front of them. They stumbled, dehydrated and baking in the hot sun, with just enough linen for modesty but not enough to protect their reddened skin from the unforgiving rays. A looming figure behind them flicked a switch halfheartedly, conserving his strength in the day's heat.

Clenching her fists, Portia forced herself to turn back around. She would do something about those slaves, but now was not the time. It would not help the people behind her if she revealed herself and they added her to the line of humans in chains. But free them she would, and possibly take some revenge along the way.

The growling of her belly reminded her to focus on the day's first task: to get some coin and then some fresh food. The provisions in the tunnel were emergency rations set aside in case she had to flee quickly. Portia chided herself for being so softhearted as to feed the rodent friends she'd made but knew she'd do it again. They were her only companions right now.

Wending through the crowd passing through the tall gates, Portia entered the series of dark alleyways leading to the inner market. She preferred the unfavored alleys to reduce the number of eyes on her. When she'd first reached the city, she'd even slept in those shadowed passages between the larger avenues, or tried to, but after a series of sleepless nights spent mostly watching for bandits, she'd discovered the refuge of the waterway system.

There was a way to her tunnel from within the city, one that did not require exiting through the city gates, but it involved dropping through openings set into the side of the cobblestone streets. It was a tight squeeze. One time, before she'd lost so much weight, she'd been stuck in the narrow opening and given herself deep bruises and cuts in her panicked scramble to free herself. It was not how she would travel if she could help it, leaving it as a reserve for desperate times. In the meantime, she faced the gates to enter and leave.

The inner market bustled with activity. Wooden stands held heavy dark green and yellow produce and fruits. Slaughtered and dressed carcasses hung from racks in other stalls, and live animals of all sorts filled the area.

The air hung thick with the calls of merchants hawking their wares.

The inner market was only open on certain days. Blessedly, it was open today, for it was the best in the city market for begging and stealing—the latter reserved for desperate times, for the stakes were too high if they caught her. Not only would there be the penalty for thieving, of which she did not know, but also the worse charge of being a human on her own. She had not seen an unaccompanied human without a neck ring. It was not a piece of attire that she coveted.

Adopting the limp she'd first had when entering the city, she held out her hand and stepped in front of passersby, wordlessly asking for coins. A few brushed her aside brusquely, but most walked around her. Lowering her voice as much as she could she grunted out the word for "please" in the strange, unpleasant language of theirs. She infused the tone with as much pain and begging as she could.

One especially tall one stopped in front of her. Portia felt its eyes upon her even if she couldn't see them.

"Have some dignity. Go to a bath before you think to eat with this." It snorted derision, but Portia didn't care, for it pressed a silver into her linen-covered palm. Her best days were ones where she earned a few coppers. This creature was generous, and she would have gladly taken its advice about bathing, for she'd not done so for many weeks, but there was no safe place for her to take off her disguise.

She bowed several times in thanks. The creature did not move. It folded its arms. Portia feared it would demand she speak. A trill of fear ran over her scalp, and the hair on her arms lifted. Portia was lucky to know the language it spoke. No humans on her home world had that knowledge except for her. She'd pulled it into her mind with an Elven spell. Still, speaking it remained a challenge. Her throat was shaped differently from the creature's and could not easily form the same words.

More of the creatures jostled nearby through the crowded marketplace. Running would be difficult, but that recourse was not needed, for a friend called to the creature, demanding that it join them at one of the taverns surrounding the market square. The creature pulled its intense scrutiny away and then growled its irritation as it turned in a huff and joined its friends. Portia breathed out in relief.

Portia's eyes followed his path from her when a glint on the ground caught her attention. Waiting until the tavern door slammed behind the group of creatures, Portia ran over to where the object was lying in the dust: a lady's hairpin. Picking it up, she inspected it. It had to be a human's since the creatures had no hair and thus no use for such a tool. Dull gray tines attached to a silver bauble at the end. It was a fine piece. Whoever had owned it was not a pauper and had dropped it while being dragged through the marketplace. Portia clenched her fists and forced herself to breathe. When she recovered her temper, she stashed the pin into her coin bag for safekeeping.

A few more coppers followed from other passersby. It was enough for the day. Portia bought a few savory lunch pies from a vendor with a copper and left the market to explore the city.

She usually meant to follow one of the slave chains when she came in the gates to see where they took the humans, for the groups came disturbingly frequently, but she'd always been too hungry when she arrived to ever do so and would go to find a market first.

Portia was determined to find them today. If she couldn't do so by exploring the city, she'd have to go back to the gate and wait for the next group to arrive.

The sun was already halfway to the horizon. The chances of another group coming in today were low. Somehow, she'd have to wake up earlier in the tunnel. Too bad she couldn't tell her mouse when to stop by. It was not shy about getting her attention.

All too soon, she was licking the crumbs from her fingers. Two pies did not go as far as one might hope. She patted her stomach. At least it had had something.

Gray stone buildings made up most of the city, their doorways tall and wide to accommodate the snake people. There were few animals, really only those belonging to the farmers in the market and used for carts in the city. More often, four of the creatures dressed in short robes and without hoods carried sedans of higher borns, the windows covered with thick dark curtains. The litters raced through the streets, relying on the citizens to get out of the way. Portia had not seen a collision yet, but it had been close once or twice.

The word for snake people in their language meant "well dwellers," though Portia didn't understand what that signified.

Once or twice, she'd glimpsed even stranger beings than the snake people. They were extremely slender with dark, large eyes. They too wore neck rings. *Someone else the Well Dwellers have enslaved*, Portia thought bitterly.

The streets further from the market turned more and

more residential with few alleyways, forcing Portia to walk along one of the larger stone paths. Yards of soft gray moss fronted many of the houses. As the grounds grew larger and more opulent, stone fences walled off each residence, giving the home dwellers more privacy. Up ahead, a patch of green stood uncharacteristically alone in the city. Moving closer, Portia discerned it was a park designed for children, for there were stone blocks to climb on and a rope swing hanging from a hook in a chiseled archway. There were few trees in this land, at least that she'd seen. The creatures constructed everything from stone or metals.

The grunts and yells of Well Dweller children playing in the area of green reached her. They had pushed back their hoods, and one or two had even thrown off their cloaks and ran around in short pants and shirts. The gray scales on their skin glinted in the sunlight. If it weren't for the occasional growl and grunt of their strange language, Portia could have closed her eyes and taken them for human children.

"Who are you?" A small face looked up at Portia, its head cocked to one side. *"I thought I knew all the children here."* The growl of the foreign language sounded even stranger in the small creature's high-pitched voice.

Startled, Portia backed up a half step. *"I'm not a child,"* she blurted out with effort, then regretted it. *"Not really."*

"You're not full age. You're far too small," the creature said, looking her up and down. *"I'm Damon. This is my playground."* He puffed out his chest.

"You are far too young to own this." The language hurt

Portia's throat, especially when she lowered the pitch to disguise herself further.

"*My family does, which is the same thing. I'm the heir.*"

The other noises from the playground had grown quiet. Portia looked around to see all the children had come over to investigate. "*Good for you. It must be good to be rich.*" She kept her tone neutral with just a hint of admiration.

This drew a smile from Damon. "*It is. Come play with us.*"

Portia shook her head.

Damon frowned at that, his scale-covered lips surprisingly expressive.

"*I must meet my sister at the market for...*" Portia did not know the word for humans in their language. It had not come over when she had taken the language from Acrux. "*The new ones,*" Portia said lamely.

"*New ones?*"

"*She means the furry ones. The new servant market.*" A high-pitched voice came from the back. It was the smallest child of the bunch. It grinned at her, but the look chilled Portia, for it looked much like a snake hissing at her.

"*Yes, those,*" Portia said, remembering to keep her voice low. "*I would rather stay but cannot.*"

"*Very well. But if you come back, bring cakes,*" Damon said with the authority of a king in his court.

Portia only nodded. The little one was still grinning at her in what must be a friendly manner, so Portia decided to be bold and speak to her. "*Can you tell me where it is?*"

A cacophony of noise erupted around her as the children

competed to give her directions. Portia picked one child at random to listen to and nodded after she had the information. She waved her thanks and walked off, leaving them calling goodbye after her.

If they were so friendly, why were the parents so awful? Or were they just awful to humans and other species? It made no sense to Portia.

Cutting across the city, she followed the directions they had given. The slave market was further into the city than she'd ever been before. She cursed herself for not having explored all the gates and being more prepared. If she needed to escape quickly, the only exit she knew of was on the other side of a dense and crowded city.

The market was where the children had said it was—in a small cul-de-sac nestled between tall stone buildings with a tall stone fence surrounding it on three sides. It was easy to guard with only one side open to the public.

The slaves themselves were in barred metal pens spread about the space. Guards paced back and forth. A large merchant dressed in opulent robes of deep blue and orange walked through the space, stopping to talk to the less well-dressed customers. Portia stepped out of his sight to stand behind a few others. With any luck, he would assume she was a customer's child if he caught a glimpse of her.

When Portia got closer, she gagged. Foul smells permeated the air. Dirty straw lined the pens, and the open waste pails at the back were not empty. These slaves were not well taken care of and had not been for a long time judging by their defeated and vacant expressions. Most of them sprawled on the floor. They did not look as if they had the strength to stand. The few that did hung off the bars and stared defiantly at the customers eyeing them. Occasionally, a guard would come by and swat a metal rod at the prisoners holding onto the bars. Most of the time, the prisoner would pull their hand back in time, and the clank of metal on metal reverberated throughout the space. Sometimes they didn't, and the sickening sounds of metal on bone sounded, followed by a cry of pain. Portia wanted to kick those guards. Or worse.

Most of the pens were full and surrounded by crowds of shoppers. There was one in the back that did not, having few prisoners in it. Those looked like they'd been there for some time, being especially thin and hollow-cheeked. One of the women in the back stared at Portia with a tear-streaked face. Portia's heart ached at the sight. On impulse, she lifted her hood just a bit so the woman could see her and then shook her head when the prisoner walked towards her. While Portia wanted to reassure the woman, she didn't want a scene that would alert a guard to her presence.

Looking around, Portia saw that no one was paying any attention to her or the pen she was standing in front of. Pulling out the hairpin from her bag, she shuffled to the padlock holding the door shut. It was a simple but huge lock. The prongs of the hairpin were long enough to reach the tumbler, but the metal was too soft, and the tines bent and snapped inside the mechanism just as a howl came from behind her.

"*Get away from there!*" a guardsman yelled in the strange language. Portia shoved the rest of the hairpin into her bag while freezing the lock with her other hand. The guard was several pens over and slowed by the crowd of customers blocking his way. Portia grabbed a loose cobblestone in the street and slammed it down on the frozen lock, shattering it.

The formerly listless prisoners leapt to their feet and pushed out the door of the pen, shoving Portia aside. They scurried out, weaving through the crowds, a few climbing the cage itself and then leaping over the wall behind it.

In frustration, the guardsman knocked over two customers and ran to Portia. Luckily, these creatures had diaphragms, for she placed a high kick right to his gut and he doubled over—gasping—while she ran from the market, silently apologizing to the prisoners she had not freed. Now that the guards were alerted to the possibility of theft, it would be far more difficult to go back and get them.

Portia dodged through the crowd of customers, going in the opposite way of most of the prisoners, hoping to draw some attention away from them. She was better fed than they and had a better chance of escaping. Her sword hummed at her side, reminding her she had other advantages too.

Her footsteps echoed between buildings as she ran from the market. Fewer creatures walked the streets as night drew on, making her flight easier. Looking back, Portia did not see any guards, only a few pedestrians and one slave running after her. It was the woman who had been staring at her from within the pen. She was following Portia.

"Wait," she called out after Portia.

Portia held up a hand to hush the woman, giving a subtle shake of her head. Responding in common would attract attention, and worse, let others know she was human. The woman continued running but did not yell again. One pedestrian turned to watch the running slave but then looked away politely when he saw Portia dressed in the common robes of the city waiting for her. Portia hoped he assumed she was the master of the human slave and would think no more of it.

"How did you do that?" the woman whispered when she caught up to Portia.

Portia shook her head and then grabbed the woman's arm and pulled her into a nearby alley, running around a large pile of refuse and ducking down low to hide. Portia willed her breathing to quiet, holding up a finger for silence. A few moments later, loud pounding footsteps echoed down the main street outside the alley. The guardsmen had made their way through the crowded market. No one stopped at the alleyway though. Portia counted to twenty and then stood and brushed herself off. The woman stared at her.

"Why did you follow me?" Portia asked in common.

"I had nowhere else to go. Why did you rescue us?" The woman looked scared but determined. "Are you going to bring us back to Jukhnovo?"

"Is that where you are from?" Surprised, Portia's scalp tingled, but then she realized it made sense. The creatures had attacked Jukhnovo first. This prisoner must have been here for a long while.

The woman nodded.

Portia bit her lip. She hadn't thought so far ahead. The sight of the pen had so enraged her, all she wanted to do was free the people inside. Getting them home was another matter. Portia didn't know how to do so. It was time to fix that.

The smell of the garbage pile brought Portia back to the current situation. "We have to get out of here first," she said. "Follow me and pretend you are my slave."

Lifting her head and walking with authority, Portia strode to the alleyway entrance, sparing a quick glance to make sure there were no guardsmen about before entering the main boulevard. The slave's footsteps followed behind her.

They passed through the deserted streets unchallenged, reaching the grate to the waterway system quickly. The woman's thinness was an advantage in getting through the narrow opening. To her credit, she only hesitated for a second before jumping through the black hole in the street that Portia indicated. Once she scrambled out of the way in the muck below, Portia slipped through herself, twisting and turning as to not get her sword caught or lose her robes on the rough edges. She landed with a thud in the mud below, moisture quickly seeping into her shoes.

Enough daylight seeped into the small apertures from the street above for them to make their way down the waterway and avoid the worst of the puddles. It had not rained heavily while Portia was here, and she hoped the vast space of the tunnel was not a measure of how much water could pass through and below the city. If she were to be below when water flooded the passageway, she would drown.

"Thank you for saving me. My name is Iva," the woman said quietly. She stared at Portia, who did not respond, instead walking forward without comment. "How did you do magic here? So few here can, even amongst the Dragonoids. I can't feel my magic; it's as if it's gone. It hurts my head to even try."

"I find it harder here," Portia said. Not all her capabilities were equally affected though, which was confusing. Pyromancy, normally so easy for her, was nearly impossible. At least she had some magic that she could do. "Is that the name for the creatures? Dragonoids?"

"It's what I call them. They look like human dragons, sort of."

Portia snorted. "They look like snakes to me. I hate snakes."

"I have no love for them myself, dragons or snakes." Bitterness suffused Iva's voice. Portia glanced at her, but the woman was staring straight ahead at the ground in front of her.

"I've only seen one do fireballs, and that was with a stick with runes on it. That was back in Coverack."

"They're in Haulstatt now too?" The woman's eyes rounded. Coverack was the capital of Haulstatt, the kingdom just south of Jukhnovo.

"They're trying. We rebuffed them from the harbor once. I ended up here by accident when my ship went through the splinter at the Well of Tears."

"I don't remember coming here. One moment, there's a great battle and noise from the center of our village, the next I'm here. My last memory is seeing a creature raise his hand to me. It must have knocked me out. Are we far from Jukhnovo?"

"I don't know. The Well of Tears is far from both kingdoms, and we're beyond even that. Maybe well beyond. The splinter closed when I was there." Portia didn't feel up to explaining that she had closed the splinter.

"Then how are you here?"

Portia grimaced. "It closed with me on the wrong side."

Iva let out a small moan. "Are we trapped here forever?"

I refuse to believe that, Portia thought, but she could not bring herself to make any promises.

They reached the passageway where Portia had been sleeping. She led Iva into the smaller side tunnel and found a dry, or at least a drier, spot and placed the bedding down before motioning for Iva to sit. "Rest here for a bit. I need to buy something for you to wear so you won't stand out. We were lucky to make it down here. Be quiet. If you see some small furry creatures don't scream. They're friendly if a little annoying."

Iva nodded up at her, reminding Portia once again how thin she was.

"Have you eaten today?" Portia asked.

Iva shook her head.

Grateful for having kept some food here, Portia pulled down the sack of provisions and handed it to Iva. "Try to not eat it all at once; you'll make yourself sick."

Portia left the tunnel while Iva dug around in the bag, too excited at the prospect of eating to wave goodbye.

Not wanting to risk the tight squeeze through the grate again, Portia took the long way through the dry riverbed and back up to the outside gate. Luckily, it was still open even as the sun was nearing the horizon. She never tried it at night and had no idea when they locked the city gates, if ever. The high metal and stone structure, and the guards by it, meant there were enemies out there and there was a reason for it. No one would go to all that trouble if all was peaceful.

Trying the clothing shop nearest to the gate, Portia hoped the proprietor was more used to unusual people coming through and would not ask too many questions. Even so, he narrowed his eyes at her and watched carefully as she walked through and looked at his clothing and bolts of fabric. A bolt of coarse-spun brown linen lay on the back table, hidden behind the richer fabrics lining the front of the shop. Her choice did not endear her to the shop owner, for he would make little profit off it.

"*A length, please,*" Portia said in the strange guttural language. The image that came to her mind for length was the height of the creature. That was the definition she had gotten when she had pulled the language from Acrux's head.

The proprietor didn't move.

Portia pulled the silver coin from her pocket and held it out, the metal glittering on top of her linen-covered palm.

"*You're not fooling me. You're a slave. How do you have so much money?*" he asked, a demand and a warning in his voice. The harsh language lent itself to speaking aggressively. He glared at her.

"*How else would I have so much money?*" Portia pulled herself up and returned his attitude. "*My master does not have time for such petty errands. Should I tell him you refused to help me and so he has to come down here himself? He would not be pleased.*"

A flicker of fear flashed across his eyes. He did not want to help her, but sense won out. He grabbed the bolt gruffly and pulled out the fabric, measuring out a section before cutting it and shoving it to her.

"And another set of robes, like mine," Portia demanded.

The proprietor plucked a robe from a stack in the back and put it on top of the cloth in her hands.

He took the offered silver and gave her some coppers in return. When Portia did not move with her hand still out, he huffed but placed more coppers in her palm. *"That is all; now get out,"* he said, growling.

Portia curled her fingers over the change, relieved. Her chest warmed with satisfaction at preventing his cheating, but even more at his having attempted it. If she had a powerful owner who found out the merchant had tried to cheat her, it would not go well for him. He knew that. Now he would be much less tempted to call the guards on her. The chances of things going poorly for him were too great.

Even so, she hurried through the streets to the gate but stopped when she saw more guards waiting there. Other guardsmen walked by in pairs. They were on high alert.

Turning back to the city, Portia went to the street grate entrance to the waterway. She dared not risk the city gate again today.

2

The next morning, Portia awoke to the usual sounds of scratching on stone but jumped when she saw Iva lying next to her, having forgotten she had rescued the woman the day before.

Portia had stopped by the market the previous night on her way back from the clothier, catching the last vendors as they were packing up. There were still stocks of cheese and bread, which the vendors gave a good discount on, not wanting to carry it all back home again themselves. It was good Portia had purchased those supplies, for otherwise they would have had nothing to eat and nothing to share with the mice in the waterway. Iva had eaten everything in Portia's hanging food bag.

Iva watched as Portia fed the animal. "How did you know it was friendly?"

Portia smiled. "Who isn't friendly when you have food?" She remembered how she felt when she'd been on the streets and anyone offered her something to eat. Whoever it was became an instant ally.

"I'm going back to the city," Portia told Iva as she chewed her own breakfast.

"I'm coming with," Iva said, sitting up suddenly. She shoved the food Portia had set in front of her into her mouth and chewed.

"You don't have to," Portia said, laughing. "In any case, slow down. I'm not abandoning you. I just want to check on the markets again."

Iva kept eating furiously, bringing herself up to the balls of her feet, ready to run after Portia.

"Really, I'm not going to leave you," Portia said, her tone low but insistent.

Unconvinced, Iva stared. She swallowed awkwardly and nearly choked on the mass of dried bread. Portia handed her a waterskin. Iva drank from it, never taking take her eyes from Portia.

"Okay, you can come," Portia said, relenting, "but you can't wear that."

Iva looked down at her tattered and filthy clothes.

Iva had been sleeping when Portia returned, so she hadn't seen Portia's purchases. Portia pulled out the new robe and held it up to Iva. It mostly fit. While Iva was thinner than Portia, she was also taller. Portia tied the loose fabric around Iva's waist, using a torn strip of material from Portia's linen undershirt, and then drew the robe over Iva's head, tugging the hood forward to hide Iva's face.

"What's wrong with waiting here?" Portia asked,

adjusting the garments to hide every inch of Iva's skin. "Even covered, going into the city is a risk."

"And stay down here alone? No thanks, once was enough. It was too dark."

"At least the mice won't drag you away by your collar." Portia tried to take a light tone with her voice.

Iva grunted skeptically.

It would be good to have a second set of eyes, even with the additional risk. A small bit of lightness fluttered in Portia's chest.

Fearing there would be extra guards on duty at the gates that day because of the prisoners escaping the previous day, Portia took Iva back to the access hatch that entered the city from the waterway. Iva did not complain about the mud on her feet or the smell of the dirty water in the cold passageway.

It was not a day for the main market, but crowds packed the streets—mostly with guardsmen and patrols. Iva shivered next to Portia as they walked between the tall stone buildings, sticking to the shadows as much as possible.

A line of burly guards faced out from the slave market, checking each customer as they entered and scanning the streets for attackers. Inside, customers crowded the market, blocking Portia and Iva's views of most of the cages. There was no way to get inside without speaking to a guard and revealing themselves as humans. Portia huffed in frustration.

"It's not been like this before," Iva said. "Of course, I've seen no one escape before either." She pointed to the pen in the back. There were just a few humans in it. Not nearly as many as had been there yesterday. Some had truly escaped in the mad rush or had been sold. Or had perished. Pushing away that thought, Portia focused on breathing in deeply.

Chains clanking alerted them as Dragonoids dragged more captive humans into the square. Portia and Iva pressed up against the wall trying to look casual, as if they were having a conversation.

"Are they always bringing in new people?" Portia asked Iva.

"No, not always. There were more prisoners before. When I was first brought here, they had a hard time finding a cage to put me in. Then, later, the prisoners changed and became fewer. The customers were not happy with the new, smaller ones."

Portia looked at her sharply at the word "small".

Misunderstanding her look, Iva rushed on. "At least from what I could tell."

"Small ones?" Portia asked.

"Yes, about half my height and ornery. They fought with the guards until the head guy screamed and got rid of them. It was awful."

"Were they thin? With pointed ears?"

"No. Squat and wide. And angry. So angry. They spit and yelled."

That sounded like no elf Portia knew. Who were these others? "Where do you think they took them?"

Tears welled up in Iva's eyes. "Some they sold. Some... I don't know. One of them bit the one I think of as the owner. He kicked the slave unconscious. Or to death." Iva whispered the last words.

Fresh anger welled within Portia. Her stomach clenched in fury as heat passed from the back of her head over her face. Her fingers twitched into fists. She looked around to see if she could find one of the short ones, straining to look over the crowd of customers waiting in line to get in.

"They were all gone—at least they were yesterday." Iva peered around Portia and motioned to the creature in the fancy robes between an opening in the guards. "That's the owner, I think. He was irate and yelled at them constantly even before he was bitten. He kept motioning how short they were."

"Did you learn where they were from? Did they talk to any of the other prisoners?"

"I heard the word *Morgani* whispered a few times. Someone said that was the name of their land, but I didn't understand anything else they were saying. No one else did either, not that I know of," Iva said.

Morgani! That was the name of the Dwarf kingdom to the west of Lusatiana, just south of her own kingdom of Haulstatt.

She grabbed Iva's arm. "Are they bringing them by boat?"

"Not that I heard. I think they walked them from inland."

If they had not come by boat from the Well of Tears, they must have been transported through another splinter, which meant there was another way to go home.

Home.

Portia's heart raced as she looked around the cul-de-sac, cursing that she had missed these others. They had to find out where that other splinter was. The pens now only held humans. Her stomach thrummed with anxiety and anger.

Shutting her eyes to think, Portia leaned against the cold stone wall. Leaving the slaves was not something Portia wanted to do, but she couldn't get closer to help them now, not without an army. Besides, where would she take them even if she did manage to free them? It would not be a great life to be trapped here, forever away from friends and family.

But she could come back with help and an exit plan. At least with an exit plan to another splinter.

"Do you know where inland they came from?" Portia asked urgently.

"Not exactly, but I've heard it was far from the water. They were surprised to see fish bits on the gruel."

"Close enough." Portia did a mental inventory of everything she owned. There was little food left in the waterway, certainly not enough to waste time going back through the tunnels to get it. The filthy bedding could be replaced, and her sword was strapped to her back. "That's where we're going then." Portia turned away from the cul-de-sac resolutely, pulling Iva with her.

They stopped by the smaller market that was open every day. Portia spent the last of her coin on some fruit and vegetables and a small hunk of cheese. She looked regretfully at the jerky hanging in a vendor's stall.

"Do you know how far away this is?" Portia asked.

Iva shook her head.

Portia looked around the marketplace. There was only one guard on the far side of the market, and he was distracted talking to a vendor who was feeding him pieces of pastry, probably as a way to keep him close by and to discourage thieves.

"Wait for me over there." Portia pointed to the side of the market opposite where the guard was. "Stay out of the way. Don't talk to anybody."

When Iva was safely away, Portia walked through the market, slipping items into her bag—some meat, more cheese, a bottle of mead. It helped that the market was busier than it would've been on a day when the main market was open. The crowd jostled and pushed each other, making it easy for Portia to slip under the arms of the large Dragonoids and slide in between small spaces where they would not fit. They noticed her no more than they would an errant child.

The last stall she visited on her way out was a leather merchant. She grabbed a brown leather bag nearly the identical color of her robes and slipped it under her flowing garments, tucking it against her side and pressed up against other items she'd lifted. She muttered a hope that nothing fell before they escaped the market and she could load everything into the bag.

She walked by Iva, nodding towards the street leading out of the market. They strolled casually, Portia's arms burning from pressing her robes to her body so the goods hidden beneath them didn't slip to the ground.

"How did you learn to do that?" Iva whispered.

"Do what?"

"I *saw* you taking stuff." Iva glared at Portia.

What happened to Iva being friendly and grateful? "Well,

that's disappointing. I thought I was better than that," Portia said with a hint of reproach.

"I don't think anyone else saw."

"For the sake of both our necks, I hope not." Portia knew better than to turn and look around, but she did anyhow. There was no one behind them, and her neck didn't tingle in warning. Still, she felt ill at ease. Only getting out of the city would banish that anxiety.

But how to do so?

If the gates were just as closely guarded as yesterday, they would have to go through the tunnels. At least they could go right to the riverbed and save some time that way.

They managed the journey successfully, not attracting any attention. Portia struggled more than usual with the grate, and Iva had to pick up some things from the wet floor when Portia dropped them struggling through the tiny opening.

Once in the tunnel, Portia packed the new bag with all of their goods, and they raced through the tunnels, neither wanting to linger in the cold darkness, not when they had to make time away from the city. Guilt plucked at Portia for leaving her mice behind, but they surely had as little interest in being dragged to a new world as she'd had in being forced into theirs.

Still, she would miss them.

When they passed by the turnoff to her sleeping spot deep within the tunnels, Portia dropped to the floor and laid out a large chunk of cheese on a bit of parchment. She waited a moment, but the tunnel was quiet. There was no sound of tiny nails on stone. Iva raised her eyebrows but said nothing.

Finally, Portia rose, dusted off her legs, and they set off again, leaving the cheese on the ground.

They exited the drainpipe into the riverbed. Again, no one was around. This time, Portia directed Iva in the opposite direction from the city gate. They walked in the dry riverbed away from the stone walls.

When the city had receded in the distance, Portia handed the bag to Iva. "Can I trust you with this?" She softened it with a smile.

"Of course," Iva said, laying the bag's strap securely across her body. She staggered for a moment under the weight. Portia already had her personal bag and her sword. It would be better to not be too weighed down if she needed to fight.

The dry riverbed made for easy walking, but soon it turned away from the mountains of the inland, and to maintain their direction they had to leave it and cross dry grassy plains filled with a rough standing growth that resisted footsteps, making it difficult to push through. Worse, they were higher than they had been in the riverbed, and Portia was anxiously aware that they were much more visible to anyone who might be looking for them.

The field ended at a large smooth road. The road must have come from a different gate of the city. The smooth stones of the road wound in the direction they wanted to go, inland, away from the sea that was on the other side of the city. On one side was a palm forest with strange tall trees with just a puff of greenery at the top. The other side, the side they had approached from, was all grasslands leading to the hills in the distance.

Portia nudged Iva to cross the road to walk on the forest side. The ease of running to hide from hostile people on the road outweighed the possibility of something strange coming out from between the trees. Birds reassuringly chirped in the forest, and the flutter of wings was occasionally visible as they flew from treetop to treetop.

The road itself was unnaturally smooth, comprised of large flat blocks that locked together. It looked nothing like the small cobblestone streets she'd seen in Haulstatt nor the packed-earth roads that ran through the countryside. She jumped up and down on a large stone to see if she could make it move, but it stayed firmly in place. "This is a strange construction."

Iva's eyes flicked down to the road and then up at Portia again. "There is a road like this in Jukhnovo. It's cut from volcanic rock."

"Like this? Why wouldn't they have the same roads in Haulstatt?"

"Not everyone has them. Only the richest and only the noble-bred. The one I've seen is right in front of the palace. I only know because our shop was close by." Iva's eyes glistened with some remembered emotion. "My Da and I."

"Sorry." Portia didn't know what else to say so just kept walking.

If they had a road like this in Jukhnovo, how did they also have one here on this strange world? The connection made Portia uneasy. Her stomach flipped at the unlikely coincidence.

Despite its mysterious origins, the road made for easy

walking, even if Portia wished for shade. Sweat trickled down her back as the bluish-white sun beat down upon them as high noon approached. Heat waves shimmered off the roadway, rising towards the cloudless sky.

The outside of their robes grew hot even as they protected Portia and Iva's skin from burning, or mostly protected them. Even with the thick cloth, some rays penetrated their cover and pricked at Portia's arms, sending unpleasant tingles into her skin. She doubled the layers of her sleeves for more protection, making her sweat even more, while glancing over to see how Iva was doing. Iva walked with her head bowed, leaning forward against the weight of the bag at her back, but her gait was steady.

The monotonous thump of their footsteps was interrupted by the roar of something. Something large.

The skin at the back of Portia's neck tightened and pulled, and her stomach curdled at the sound. Whatever had made that noise was close. She scanned the area.

A large black creature caught her eye at the tree line. It emerged from the trees quickly, wider and taller than herself, with thick powerful hind legs and large paws tipped with claws in the front, moving along the tree line away from them. The sun glinted off of it, confusing Portia until she realized it was covered in thick black scales.

Blessedly, it didn't seem to have seen them yet. Nor did it look interested in venturing too far from the trees.

Portia grabbed Iva's arm. They stared at the creature. "Do you know what that is?" she whispered.

Iva shook her head, her face ashen. "Do you have any weapons?" Iva asked, a quiver in in her voice.

"Nothing I'd want to pit against that. It's fast."

Standing frozen on the road, Portia pulled Iva down to a crouch. The creature kept moving away from them and then veered back to the tree line ahead. To Portia's surprise, it turned to face them just before entering the woods, roared, and then disappeared into the darkness.

Had it known they were there the entire time?

Portia's heart thundered in her chest while Iva's arm shook under her hand. Portia didn't want to think about what her chances of fighting it with her sword would have been. Its reach, even without a weapon, was more than she had with one. It would have been difficult to survive, much less win, while poor Iva had nothing at all with which to protect herself.

If only Portia had not lost her knives to the sea. She cursed herself for not thinking to steal one at the market.

They had to get Iva a weapon.

Staying crouched for a few more terrified moments, they finally looked at each other and mouthed the word "run" at the same time.

The robes made it difficult to move quickly. Portia hiked hers up and hung on to them as her legs worked furiously. Iva did the same. They ran until the stitch in Portia's side forced her to stop. Checking for the animal behind them, she stepped aside as Iva reached her and stopped, and then bent over, panting.

The animal had not reemerged from the trees. They were the only beings on the road.

Portia marveled at Iva's endurance. She had done well for looking half-starved.

"Maybe the forest is not the safe side to be on," Portia said, stretching as the cramped muscles in her side relaxed.

"Maybe not," Iva agreed.

They switched sides of the road and walked on. To Portia's relief, the forest thinned out and then disappeared entirely, leaving only grassy plains on each side of the road. No longer was there a place nearby for an animal to conceal itself, but this also meant there was no place for Iva and Portia to hide.

Further increasing Portia's unease, the road was now raised higher over the land on either side. If someone came upon them, their only chance of hiding would be to scramble down the hillside and lie in the ditch that ran along the road. Iva nodded agreement at Portia's plan for hiding. It didn't seem wise to confront anyone or to try to bluff their way through an encounter.

"You sure you don't know anything else about where the splinter might be?" Portia asked.

Even if they were going in the right direction, it could be one day away—or a dozen. They only had a few days' supplies with them and then they would have to eat from what they found on the road. Portia was not confident she could recognize what was edible or not.

"No. Only what I told you." Iva gave Portia a sideways glance. "You never did tell me how you learned to steal."

Portia grimaced. "I used to be in a thieving gang. I try to not do it anymore."

"That must've been hard."

"It wasn't fun, but I'd rather be doing that than be here right now."

Iva nodded agreement. "I wonder where the rest of the slaves went to. The ones that got away. Some must have, don't you think?"

"Probably."

Neither one spoke of the possibility the slaves had been killed in retaliation.

THEY TRAVELED for several days without seeing another person. On the morning of the third day, the echoes of metal hitting metal came down the roadway, sounding long before they could see anyone. Portia pulled Iva down into the ditch and they lay pressed up against the dirt, trying to disappear into the rough grass, breathing shallowly and quietly.

Soon, the noise resolved into footsteps. Portia counted four sets of footfalls as they passed by. She held on tightly to Iva's trembling arm, silently willing her to stay quiet. Waiting another twenty count, she then released Iva and slowly crawled up the side of the embankment.

Four Dragonoids walked away down the roadway wearing half robes covered by plate armor. They all carried large metal-tipped pikes with full packs on their backs. Portia guessed they were on their way to the harbor city they had just left.

Iva crawled up the embankment to join Portia. "Those are some terrifying-looking spears."

Portia nodded. "We need to get one of them."

"How?"

"I don't know yet." Portia pulled open her bag. She had a few caltrops. That might work to lay a trap, but it was nearly impossible to make sure the enemy stepped on one unless they were laid thick and wide upon the roadway, and she didn't have enough for that. Even so, she didn't know the Dragonoids' pain tolerance. It was possible the creatures could continue to charge her even while suffering a level of pain that would stop a human.

No, there was no room for error here or for guessing. They had to have a sure plan.

They scrambled into the ditch several more times that morning to avoid running into more Dragonoids, all coming from the direction Portia and Iva were headed. After the third such encounter, Portia began to feel a little ill at what they were approaching. How many of these creatures were there? Were they walking into a death trap?

Except for the first encounter, all the creatures on the road had been alone. Portia might be able to defeat one, especially if she injured it first with a caltrop. Not for the first time, she wished she had the power of coercion to make one of these creatures tell her what she needed to know. Perhaps her sword would be coercion enough.

After the fourth time hiding in the ditch, Portia lay with her head against the dirt, resolve hardening in her chest.

"I'm going to question one of these brutes," Portia said. Iva's eyes rounded.

Pulling caltrops from her bag, Portia climbed the hill and scattered the metal barbs across the roadway.

"I don't think we should—" Iva protested, standing anxiously at the side of the road while Portia worked.

"Don't think. Let's have lunch." Portia finished laying the pieces and then pulled Iva back down the embankment.

"I really don't—"

Portia pressed a finger to Iva's mouth. "I'm hungry. What do we have left?"

Iva shook her head and opened the bag. Shrugging apologetically, she handed over a hunk of softened and sweaty cheese and some stale bread. They were nearly out of supplies.

Worse yet, they had no water, having drunk the last of it the previous night. Portia took a bite of the cheese but was unwilling to try the bread, not without water. Her mouth puckered uncomfortably even thinking about chewing it.

It took less than a candlemark before the echoes of plate mail rang down the road. Prey was coming.

Portia set aside the food and inched her way up the embankment. She wanted to be ready if her trap worked.

Luck was with them. It was a single creature out on its own. A strange feeling coursed down Portia's spine and rose in her chest. It wasn't fear—that emotion she knew all too well. No, it was something else.

Excitement.

Now, after weeks of running and hiding, this was a chance to strike back at one of the Dragonoids. Shoving aside the misgivings that came with her realization, Portia stared through the stalks of razor grass as the Dragonoid approached.

It had the same short robes as the others, with plate mail and the tall pike weapon. It also had something she'd not noticed before. A huge waterskin hung from its belt.

It had water.

Portia licked her lips. Now it was imperative they get it. If she had to, she'd charge after it with her sword and go for the unprotected backs of its knees. If she could just bring it down, there was a chance of defeating it. It had water, a weapon, and information—all things Portia desperately wanted.

Holding her breath, Portia watched as the heavy footfalls came closer. It had only thin leather sandals on its feet, and she watched as the sharp metal prong of a caltrop punctured the sandal and the foot wearing it. Portia pulled back as the creature shrieked and landed with a thud upon the roadway. So much for worrying about its pain tolerance.

Iva whimpered from her place in the ditch, staring up at the roadway anxiously. Portia held up a finger for silence before peering again into the roadway.

The creature was down, moaning and holding its foot, which bled profusely on the roadway, its pike and bag now lying beside it, forgotten. It had not seen her. Indeed, it was facing the other way.

Taking the opportunity, Portia pulled her blade and ran up behind it, pressing the sharp edge against its throat while kicking its pike away. Looking him over, she didn't see any other weapons but kept as far back as possible in case he had a hidden blade.

"Get up here," Portia hissed at Iva in common.

No sound came from the ditch. Sweat beaded on Portia's forehead.

"NOW!"

The creature jumped at the barked yell from Portia. It pulled back as its neck met her sword.

Iva scrambled up the embankment. Portia nodded towards the pike, and Iva ran to retrieve it, staying out of the creature's eyesight as she did so. She stood with her legs apart, holding the pike towards the creature. She shook so much, Portia was amazed she could even hold the pike.

Portia pulled her hood forward as much as she dared in case the creature turned around. Iva did the same with her own hood. It did not need to know they were human.

"*Who's there?*" it said, growling in its language.

"*Not your business,*" Portia said, spitting back the words and ending with an insult for good measure. The Dragonoid curses were even more painful on her throat, but she didn't want it to get the idea she was scared. She pressed her blade deeper into its neck, and a thin line of blood oozed over the damaged scales.

"*Enough!*" it cried.

"*Where's the gate?*" Portia asked. Gate was the Dragonoid term for splinter, the opening between worlds.

"*Who are you to ask?*"

Portia replied by pushing down on her blade. Nausea

ticked her throat at the flow of blood, so she stared at his hands instead.

"Enough! I surrender." He leaned back against her to escape the sharp weapon, but Portia kept with him, allowing no relief.

"Speak!" Portia yelled in his ear. Her arms shook with adrenaline.

"The gate is outside the city, as always. They have broken through twice now. We're getting reinforcements." The creature babbled, talking almost too fast for Portia to understand.

"What city? Where?"

Portia didn't recognize the name of the city he spoke from the maps she had stolen weeks ago, but she did recognize the word for day. They were less than a day from another splinter. It must be on the road if it was so close.

Suddenly, weariness pulled at Portia. Raising her blade, she brought it down hilt first on the creature's head. It stopped talking and then slumped over onto the roadway. Blood trickled from its foot and neck.

"Did you kill it?" Iva whispered to Portia, still holding the pike in defense.

"It should live. We need to get away before it rouses though."

"Why let it go?" Iva asked.

Portia had not taken her for being bloodthirsty, but fear could do strange things.

"Hopefully, they won't bother pursuing petty thieves. The same might not be true for a murderer on the loose."

Portia winked at Iva as she gathered the scattered caltrops, hiding her own anxiety. Iva had enough of her own.

Iva stared at Portia, biting her lip and crossing her arms. "You didn't want to kill it, did you?"

Portia ignored Iva while she looted the dragonoid's pack of food and grabbed the waterskin from its belt.

Soon, they were walking in the ditch next to the road. Between the increasing traffic that day and the unknown time it would take for the fallen soldier to be discovered, it was better to not risk the pavement again. The grass was slow going, but safer.

They walked for the rest of the day, the sharp grass cutting into their footwear. The sun was below the horizon when lights from ahead shone brightly on the clouds above. There was a large city ahead, its skyshine illuminating the surrounding area.

"Let's not walk into that at night," Portia whispered.

Iva nodded.

They slept fitfully that night, taking turns at watch. Portia had a nightmare of the splinter, something she had not had for a long time. When she awoke, she wished she was sleeping again, for in her dreams she had been back in Haulstatt. Now, the daytime was worse than her nightmares.

The next morning dawned cool and crisp. The air was still too dry for dew, but at least the sun was not beating down yet.

The city sprawled in a depression in the rolling grass fields. Like the city they had left, it was surrounded by a stone wall and constructed entirely of stone buildings.

But unlike where they had just come from, where the city abutted a harbor, this one was next to a huge encampment with large canvas tents protected by a fence of metal spikes. The encampment was nearly as large as the city. Soldiers prowled the area, so many the ground was nearly black with them.

A breeze wafted across the fields towards them, bringing the smell of death. Iva recoiled while Portia held her noise.

"What is that smell?" Iva asked, choking.

Portia stared at her. *Could she really not know?* It was a smell of bodies rotting on a battlefield when there were so many dead they couldn't be buried before the soft flesh disintegrated into nourishment for the soil. Or when it wasn't safe to retrieve them.

Something awful had happened here.

A yell echoed across the valley towards them. Perhaps it was still happening.

3

T he yell faded. They waited for more cries, but the silence that followed was worse than any noise had been. Portia began to doubt she had heard it. The smell faded as the breeze died down but did not completely leave them.

"We're going to the city," Portia said.

Iva nodded, her face white.

Portia looked around. There were no soldiers nearby, nor any others, but that would change as they drew closer to the city and the sun rose in the sky. The pike Iva held was not a civilian's weapon. It would invite too many questions.

Waving Iva over, Portia took the pike from her hands and set the base of the metal blade on a rock, then stomped on the wooden pole attached to it, snapping it clean off a hand's width below the metal.

"Wait," Iva protested, too late. She gave Portia a reproachful look. "You could have just detached it." She pointed to where the lashings held the wood inside the metal sleeve at the base of the blade.

"Then how would you have held it?" Portia asked as she handed over the blade to Iva. "This way you have a short handle. Keep it inside your robes." At Iva's puzzled look, Portia lifted Iva's tunic and grabbed a length of the linen strip used to hold the inner fabric length up and tied a loop off, using it to hold the pike head. "Try to not cut yourself. The blood will stain your clothes. We can't hide forever, not in the city, and I don't want to be embarrassed by you." She let the tunic drop down, covering the weapon.

Portia ignored Iva's shocked look as she walked down the road to the city, her lips curved upwards once past the woman.

"Wait, what? What are you talking about?" Iva's indignant voice called after Portia as she scrambled to keep up while holding the blade away from her body.

Portia shook her head but didn't slow. They approached the city, Iva distracted enough to walk past the encampment and the smell of death oozing from it.

The smile left Portia's face as they walked closer to the city. She pulled her hood forward to shield her face even further from prying eyes. The robes covered her hands and every bit of skin. Both she and Iva were dressed as citizens, but they were small and slight compared to even children of the Dragonoids. It was best to not draw any attention, for any who thought too much on their appearance might wonder who, or what, was below the robes. Curiosity in others was their enemy.

It was best to avoid provoking it.

The morning air was cool, but soon enough the sun would beat down on them. The city, even with its unknown dangers, still held the promise of shade. And water. The waterskin they'd stolen from the soldier was nearly empty. Portia cursed that creating ice was so difficult here. The ability to conjure solid water would have solved their problem. She could make things cold with great effect, but conjuring ice had been nearly impossible. She shook her head. It never occurred to her to wonder where the water came from for cryomancy. Did the moisture come from the world the magic was cast in? If so, perhaps the dryness of this place explained her difficulties in creating ice. Mia might know how it worked. The thought of her friend back in Haulstatt cut Portia's heart. It hurt even more to think Mia might not have made it back to the kingdom after their encounter with the Dragonoid ships at the Well of Tears. Portia had ended up on the wrong side of the portal when it closed, with her friends locked in battle with the invaders on the other side.

Portia wiped her face. Now was not the time for memories, not if she wanted to get back to help them.

If they were still alive to be helped.

Other travelers joined them on the road. Portia and Iva walked on the edge of the stone pavement, letting the carts and horses go by without conversation. One driver called a greeting. Portia nodded in return, not daring to attempt a reply in the foreign language. A displeased grunt from the driver followed, but he did not press further and passed by in a cloud of dust. The air was even drier than before now that they were away from the coast.

Any thoughts of slipping into the city disappeared when they saw the gate ahead. Soldiers crowded outside the gate, not just at its mouth, and every approaching traveler was grilled by at least two Dragonoid warriors with chain mail over their half tunics and pikes at hand. Portia halted, nearly knocked over by Iva, who had been looking down to further hide her face.

Portia muttered silent thanks at Iva's wit to keep quiet then fumbled with her bag until the cart just behind them pulled ahead towards the gate. There was no one else close by. When the city guards ahead were occupied with the wagon, Portia pulled Iva down to the ditch by the side of the road, and then walked to the city wall through the dry scrub. Her pulse thumped in her throat as the sharp grass cut her ankles and poked into her leather footpads, while the hairs on her head and neck stood at attention. Despite the feeling of dread and of eyes upon her, no call rang out. They escaped unnoticed.

The wall curved gently around the city. As soon they were out of sight of the gate, Portia slowed down, her breath ragged. She tucked her trembling hands inside her robes, close to her body, so Iva wouldn't see. The lingering smell of death made this city even more ominous than the one by the coast. It was unnerving to feel so much fear.

Working to keep her voice steady and casual, she turned to Iva walking after her. "Hopefully, there is another entrance."

Iva nodded. The hood muffled her response. "No river here."

No, probably not. That would have been way too easy an entrance to the city.

The walls ran smooth and high around the city. The grass had been burned back, and there were no trees or shrubbery to shelter them from prying eyes. They made their way quickly along the wall but only saw one small grated opening in it before the curved path revealed another gate. The wall was too high to climb.

Retreating back to the grated opening in the wall, Portia pulled on the bars. They didn't budge. She tried a kick, which only shot pain up her leg. The bars didn't budge. They were firmly attached to the inside of the opening, with the fasteners out of reach of her grasping fingers. The openings in the grill were not large enough to fully fit an arm for greater reach, not even Portia's slender one. Portia huffed while contemplating the metal structure frustrating her desire to enter the city.

Thinking back on the lessons from the academy on the effects of cold on substances, Portia sent cold cryomancy over the metal fasteners. If she chilled them enough, the metal would turn brittle and she would be able to snap them with a kick.

After several minutes, Portia stood, while continuing to push the magic at the grate. It was hard to judge how cold the metal was, but waves of chilled air flowed down the wall from the metal and passed over her feet, the cold apparent even through the leather of her foot coverings.

Kicking at the grate, Portia grunted in pain as the grate

barely moved. A metallic moan told her the grate was affected by the magic, but not yet enough for it to break. More cold air was needed.

Iva kicked at the grate too, and then, before Portia could warn her, pushed at it with her bare hands. Iva cried out as her palms and fingers stuck to the cold metal, her eyes round with fear. Portia swore and stopped her cryomancy spell.

Quickly, Portia switched to pyromancy magic and set it on the metal bars, conjuring heat and forcing it into the bars and Iva's hands. She had to warm them enough to free them before Iva's hands were permanently damaged from the cold. Casting the pyromancy magic was like swimming through mud. What was so easy back in Haulstatt was nearly impossible here. It took immensely more energy than the cold magic, and she wasn't even sure if it was working. Only the hours of practice she'd done previously guided her as she applied the magic to the bars by Iva's hands, since there was no feedback from the magic itself. Instead of a vibration telling her it was working, there was nothing. Or worse, what she did feel was the sensation of her life force draining away.

Only the subtle change in color on the bars told her it was working at all.

Nausea pushed at Portia, and she wanted to quit, but Iva's fearful whimpering wouldn't let her. Pushing on, she sent what little energy she had left into the magic until Iva was able to pull her hands free, leaving patches of skin on the bars where they had been frozen tight.

"Don't ever do that again," Portia said, panting, dropping the magic.

Iva glared at her while holding her injured hands close. "What, help?"

Portia closed her eyes and sank to the ground as her knees gave way, then she lay down. The ground felt so good. If only she could sleep.

"Portia?" Iva knelt near her head, worry in her voice. "I'm sorry. I'm sorry, please don't die."

Portia forced her eyes open. "I'm not dying... Be quiet."

Iva rocked back and forth next to Portia but blessedly didn't say anything else. Portia let her eyes close again and slept.

THE SUN WAS DIRECTLY OVERHEAD when Portia came to. Iva had had the foresight to pull Portia's hood down over her face, mostly protecting it from the sun and only letting in the rays through the holes in the coarse weave. Portia's eyelashes pushed against the material, and she shoved it aside as she sat up. Iva was lying next to her, her eyes glued to Portia.

"Was I sleeping long?" Portia asked. She looked around. There was no one else close by.

"It felt like forever, but no, not long," Iva said, sitting up. "I thought we might blend in with the dirt with these brown robes, so I laid down too."

Portia's eyes flickered up to the top of the wall towering over them. No faces looked down at them. They were fortunate a guard had not patrolled the top of the wall. At least none that had set an alarm.

Iva followed her eyes. "I don't think they have anyone up there. I've heard and seen nothing."

That was good news, at least.

Standing, Portia went to the wall. It was plaster smooth. Something hard had been applied over the bricks that must form the structure within. There were no handholds for them to climb, nor did she have rope or a hook to toss over the top. They were not getting into the city that way. She kicked at the grate one last time, more out of spite than any hope of actually dislodging it.

"Come on," Portia said, resigned, as she walked back to the road. "We're going in through a gate."

Iva's mouth formed a surprised circle, but she didn't protest as she ran after Portia, still holding the pike blade within her robes to keep it from cutting her. Portia patted her own sword hanging from the baldric beneath her rough linen garments.

There was still a lot of traffic at the gates. Portia halted near the edge of the road, not on it, but not so far off the packed earth as to arouse suspicion. Iva stood next to her. Portia fumbled with a bag at her waist while subtly watching the behavior of the soldiers at the gate. They greeted each traveler but did not go through the contents of each cart, instead merely peering inside covered wagons or a cursory poking with their short swords into those loaded with hay. A few pikes leaned against the guardhouse wall, but they were heavier, and Portia guessed that was why they were not used in favor of the smaller weapons, even if the pikes would have been much more effective at checking the contents of the wagons.

The guards moved slowly in the shimmering heat. It affected them as much as travelers, though they put a better face on their suffering.

"Come on," Portia said to Iva as she walked back away from the city. Luck was with them. It was early enough in the day for wagons to still be approaching the city.

Soon, an appropriately large wagon loaded with hay came down the road pulled slowly by two horses covered in a fine sheen at the load and the heat. Portia hissed in displeasure at the hard usage of the horses as they passed but forced herself to keep looking ahead and not give away her feelings of rage to the wagon driver.

She'd hoped for a covered wagon with more opportunity for hiding, but a look down the road revealed there was none coming. In fact, this wagon just passing them was the only one she saw. It would not do to wait another full day to get into the city, not when they were so short of water and had just a few bits of food left. There was no choice—they would have to cast their lot with this one.

Pulling at Iva's sleeve and holding up a finger for silence, Portia turned just as the wagon passed them and shoved Iva into the hay filling the wagon bed. There were no guards on the vehicle, and the driver did not turn, Portia and Iva having been silent enough to not be overheard from the clatter of the horses' hooves on the hard stone road. Tossing hay on Iva and motioning for her to dig in, Portia leapt up beside her and moved quietly to the middle of the wagon where she lay down and pulled loose hay over herself. She pushed more hay out from beneath her bottom to try to sink deep into the pile. Her hand touched a cold metal pail, which explained why the hay was loose and not tightly wrapped into bales. It was insulating something within the wagon.

Many metal pails were nestled inside the hay. Portia tried to find the center of them and pulled herself to it, grabbing Iva's leg and pulling her close as well. They dug in as quickly and as quietly as possible, stilling as the shadow of the wall fell upon the wagon, visible even beneath the hand's depth of hay they lay under. The harsh voices of the guards reached them along with a cajoling greeting from the driver.

A sword poked into the hay, and its tip banged up against a metal pail, setting off a metallic ringing note. Iva trembled with the impact. Portia held her tight, squeezing even harder to make sure Iva understood she must stay silent. The driver gave an irate yelp at the sound of the struck metal pail and then vented his spleen at the offending guards. He spoke so quickly in the harsh language that Portia understood little of what he was saying, except it had to do with lost coin and the revenge of his master. The guards hushed him but did not send another sword into his wagonload.

The wood wheels creaked as the wagon moved forward again, the driver still muttering curses.

The shadow of the wall fell away as they entered the city. Sunlight pierced into the hay again, warming Portia. Silently, she counted to twenty, listening to the wagon going down the city streets, waiting for a cry from the guards or another check of the wagon bed. None came. Dragging herself towards the edge of the wagon, away from the driver, she peered out. The city street had only a few residents out and about. The main market must be a ways inside the gate. Taking the opportunity, Portia grabbed at Iva's leg and pulled her gently towards the bottom of the wagon, and then they both flipped out, landing on their feet in a cloud of light dry grass.

Brushing herself off furiously, Portia turned to Iva and did the same until they looked reasonably clean. Grabbing Iva's arm, Portia walked off at a good clip in a random direction away from the gate, trying to exude as much confidence as possible. They had to look like they belonged there.

The hair on Portia's neck and arms stood up as she listened for any sound of alarm, but none came. They walked through the streets undisturbed.

The city looked much the same as the last one, though it smelled much different. Instead of the tang of saltwater, an odor of death mixed with dung wafted through the streets. The residents they did see walked along undisturbed, as if they had gotten used to the smell and noticed it no more than the sun or the moon. Their indifference made Portia's stomach clench even tighter.

Portia looked around for a playground or any children on the street. They might be less prone to calling an alarm. Or, if they found the shorter captives that Iva had mentioned, they might be able to ask directly or even follow them to find the splinter's location.

A scratching tickle in the back of Portia's throat surprised her, and she coughed. Then, she was unable to stop coughing, the dry heaving racking her body as it tried to rid itself of the dust in the back of her throat. She grabbed the waterskin from her bag and let the few drops inside wet her mouth, but it wasn't enough to stop her coughing. Leaning over with one hand on a nearby building wall, she let the coughing spasm go on until her eyes watered and enough saliva filled her mouth to soothe her throat. Iva stood by, concerned, trying to shield her from view.

Slowly, Portia stood. Looking over Iva's shoulder, she checked to see whose attention they had. No one was looking except for a large Dragonoid sitting on the ground many paces down the street. No, he was not sitting as much as he had no legs. A begging bowl sat next to him. His eyes burned in their direction, his hood pushed far back revealing his countenance. Portia glanced around for a guard, but he did not leave off looking at her. He did not seem interested in drawing attention to them.

Cautiously, Portia walked towards the legless Dragonoid. His clothing was ragged and dirty. At one time it had been a warrior's half tunic but now more resembled a cleaning rag. Dirty bandages covered the tops of where his legs had once been. A lone coin sat in his begging bowl.

"*Greetings, Warrior,*" Portia began, speaking in the rough language of the Dragonoids. Iva stiffened next to her. Portia gave a small bow towards the Dragonoid and elbowed Iva until bowed as well. Perhaps she was imagining it, but the steely look of the Dragonoid softened. Still, he stared at her without blinking.

"*Greetings,*" he replied so forcefully that spit flew and landed at her feet. His eyes flickered to the bowl.

Portia fumbled with her bag and withdrew several coins, dropping them into it with a loud clink. Portia winced. It took all her willpower not to look around to see if anyone was watching them. She vowed to be quieter next time.

The Dragonoid nodded nearly imperceptibly as the coins landed. He leaned back, shifting to a more comfortable position.

"There is a public well in the main market," he said. *"If you dare go that far."* His eyes settled on the waterskin hanging at her waist.

He knew they were human, Portia realized. And yet he did not call an alarm.

"Thank you, Warrior," Portia said.

This time he snorted at the word "warrior."

"Have I offended?" Portia asked.

"You've only put to shame those of my own kind who will not give me that respect. I have given my body to defend this land." Rage flickered across his face briefly but deeply enough to scare Portia, even as she knew it was not directed at her.

"Yet you sit here, a beggar," she said.

He turned away as an answer. Portia cursed herself for pointing out his humiliation. She dug within her bag for more coins, this time crouching and slowly letting them slide into the bowl, the only noise the soft snick of metal moving on metal.

"My apologies," she said quietly. *"We are only seeking a path home. We're no threat to anybody. Was your battle at the splinter? The portal to the other place."*

He turned back to her and nodded. *"That it was. Threat*

or no, you're welcome to it. I'll show them as much care as they have shown me."

"Who were you fighting? What did they look like?" Portia asked.

"Short like you but wide and stout and violent. They yell a lot. They came pouring out of the hole between worlds, bent on destroying us all. The slavers won't even take the ones we capture." He spat. *"They are too vicious."*

"Too vicious for you?" Portia asked, trying to lighten the mood.

"They took my legs," he said, bitterly, the language well expressing the rage he felt at them and the world. *"And then my own..."*

His own abandoned him. Portia's hatred for the Dragonoids welled within her.

"Portia—" Iva spoke in the common tongue, but Portia grabbed her arm and squeezed to stop her. No one must hear them speaking the human language in this town.

The Dragonoid looked up at them, his suspicions confirmed. As insurance, Portia gave him more coins, leaving just a few in her purse. Hopefully, it would be enough to keep him from revealing them.

"Thank you. Where can we find the portal?" Portia asked.

He flicked his head in the direction of the encampment outside the city. *"It's outside the walls, within those tents. There are siege engines and barriers all around. I doubt you'd live to see it."*

Portia nodded thanks and dragged Iva away. They quickly made their way through the city, following one cart to the market where Portia managed to buy cheese and bread without a word in the crush people in the market, holding up the items she wanted in one linen-covered hand and dropping the coin to pay with the other. It was the last of their money. Luckily, the water was free, and they filled their containers from the city well.

Not wanting to push their luck, Portia turned them towards the gate again. She wanted outside the walls before they were discovered. She hadn't seen any humans, but that didn't mean they weren't there or that these people didn't keep human slaves, even if none were out on the streets openly.

It was late enough in the day that most of the traffic at the gate was leaving the city. The guards were not stopping the exiting wagons nor anyone else as Portia watched safely from the street some distance away. Taking a chance, she grabbed Iva and walked closely behind a wagon, trying to look a part of that group as it approached then exited through the city gate. Portia held her breath as they walked beneath the nose of a guard who seemed more interested in a nearby gambling game run by some other guards than in who was on the street.

Once away from the crush of traffic by the gate, the wagon rumbled off at a higher speed, leaving Portia and Iva to walk on the road alone, only passed by other wagons and more quickly moving Dragonoids. When they were out of sight of the guards at the gate and there was a break in the traffic, Portia pulled Iva down to the land around the road and directly towards the encampment.

The acrid smell of burnt wood and dead things thickened

in the air, burning down the back of Portia's throat. She swallowed down nausea. Iva's arm trembled under her grip, but she did not complain as Portia pulled her forward.

No soldiers ran towards them to challenge them as they approached the tents. There was commotion within the encampment as horses whinnied, and the creaking of wooden and metal gears sounded low and constant along with the shouts and screamed commands of the Dragonoids. No one was looking for a threat from outside the compound.

Iva coughed once, then again, unable to stop.

Portia halted, hanging on to Iva. Grabbing a section of Iva's underfabric where the excess fabric was doubled over, she tore off two strips. Pulling Iva close, she reached her hands within Iva's hood and wrapped the strip around her mouth, tying it tightly in the back. The fabric covered Iva's mouth.

"Breathe through that," Portia said. The smell was only going to get worse.

Iva nodded, her eyes bright and watering.

Portia tied the second strip around her own mouth, forming a crude mask. She wished for finer fabric, but it was better than nothing at all. Breathing through it, the burning in the back of her throat subsided to a low irritation, no longer stinging like fire.

Too late, Portia thought of the waterskin at her side. She should have wetted the material first, but the sounds from within the encampment were increasing in volume. Something was happening—and happening quickly. She didn't want to waste any more time.

Grabbing Iva's arm again, she ran towards the encampment, feeling her sword and bag bounce on her body as she ran. Remembering the pike under Iva's garments, she let go of her arm so Iva could balance with one hand while holding the weapon away from herself with the other. Iva kept pace with her, even so.

They reached the outer edge of the tents and peered around one corner. Portia pulled her sword, holding it ready. Iva held her pike head with two hands around the stubby handle. It was not well-balanced. Portia wished she had left the handle a little longer for Iva's use, but there was no help for that now.

The large ring of makeshift tents surrounded an inner ring of now damaged and half standing tents. A battle raged at the center around what appeared to be a splinter portal rising out of the ground in the middle of the muddy encampment.

This portal was much smaller than the one that had been by the Well of Tears, only reaching up to the height of two men and just as wide. Dead bodies littered the ground in front of it. It was open, yes, but it wasn't large enough for an army to pass through, at least not more than one or two abreast, leaving those entering vulnerable to being cut down by those waiting on the other side. Portia thought she saw dwarf corpses amongst those in the dirt around it, but it was too far to be sure. Weapons littered the ground along with the dead. Iva could get another weapon before they passed through the portal.

If they survived that far.

They had to get closer.

Soldiers were running through the encampment, most

taking positions behind the half-collapsed inner tents and all focused on the splinter. All except for those manning the large machines of metal and precious pieces of wood.

The squeal of metal gears pulled her from that thought. Soldiers cranked on levers attached to gears on the machines, winding the gears around, their feet digging into the ground as they leaned into the work. Several Dragonoids worked at each gear, and even so, it looked to take all of their considerable strength to make the gears go. The machine squealed and groaned in protest. An enormous spear rested with its butt in a cup in the center of the machine, its tip pointed to the splinter. A Dragonoid yelled a command, and the soldier stopped cranking the gears. Another command followed, and a switch was thrown. The spear was let loose with enormous force directly towards the splinter. It passed through the swirling, opaque face of the opening, disappearing from view.

A second later, a bellowing alarm horn sounded from the far side of the splinter, from the world on the other side.

Portia sucked in her breath.

A bolt passed over her head so closely that her hood fluttered. Whirling around, she gasped again as soldiers flooded towards the tents. Where had they come from? Most had their eyes focused on the splinter, but one soldier looked right at her. Portia felt for her hood and cursed when she realized it had fallen back. He could see her face. He knew she was human. He raised his crossbow again, aiming right at her.

Whirling back, Portia grabbed Iva's hand and ran past the inner tents. Iva screamed as they entered the fray, her voice barely loud enough for Portia to hear in the chaos of machines, the hoarse yells from the Dragonoids, and the answering yells and horns from the far side of the portal.

While running, Portia grabbed the last of her caltrops and tossed them behind her. Anything to slow down their pursuers would help. A Dragonoid yelped as he stepped on one, giving Portia some grim satisfaction.

Weaving to one side and pulling Iva with her, Portia grabbed a fallen pike. An arrow sank into the ground where they would have been.

Portia knocked the stubby-handled blade from Iva and then pushed the whole pike into her hands. Iva's face was white with fear, but she grabbed the handle. Another arrow landed just inches from Portia's right foot. Iva jumped, her hands white from gripping her weapon so tightly.

Panic pushed at Portia. She wanted to blow the arrows away from them.

An answering cloud of dirt flew away from her. *Wind magic.*

She could do wind magic here.

Putting as much as she dared into the magical wind flowing away from them, Portia turned to Iva. "We have to get to the other side. Now!" Portia yelled and then took off running, pulling Iva with her.

"Wait, why?" Iva protested. An arrow narrowly missed her. She jumped to the side while running, nearly knocking Portia's grip lose.

Their robes flew as they broke for the portal, weaving between the surprised and shocked faces of the Dragonoids around them. Iva struck one in the face with her pike handle as she ran past. Portia raised her eyebrows at the action. It had been an impressive blow.

Several Dragonoids recovered their wits and took off after Portia and Iva. They were disturbingly fast for such enormous creatures. Portia's heart pounded loudly in her ears, and her lungs screamed as she pushed herself to go faster, Iva wheezing at her side.

The wind magic saved Portia and Iva when they got closer to the splinter. The bodies and weapons that littered the blood-soaked dirt around the portal forced them to stop darting from side to side and instead find a path through the debris—a path visible to their enemies. The wind blew most bolts aside into the dirt around the portal. Only once did Iva yelp in pain, but she didn't stop running.

Another horn bellowed from the far side of the portal just as they reached it. Fear gripped Portia at what it might signify, but there was no time to hesitate. The Dragonoids behind them had nearly caught up.

Together, Portia and Iva leapt through the portal.

4

Portia and Iva landed with a thud on the dirt floor on the far side of the splinter and then stumbled and rolled. The floor was half a foot lower than the bloodied ground they had just come from.

Discordant music flooded Portia's ears. It hurt. The pain was stronger than the stings of the scrapes of her skin from the rough stone floor or the pain from landing with such force. It pressed on her head like the crushing fingers of a giant.

Portia scrambled to her feet. The pain from the music made her feel dizzy. Far away stone walls dimly registered in Portia's eyesight as she tried to take in all around them. Surprised faces looked out over barriers and weapons aimed where they had just emerged. Portia held out a hand over Iva, futilely trying to protect her, as if her hand would stop the gigantic weapons aimed their way.

"Are these like the short captives you spoke of?" Portia

asked Iva, trying to not be overheard by the onlookers. No one had fired on them yet. That was a good sign.

"Yes, I think," Iva said, her voice uncertain.

Portia shot her a look. Iva looked dazed and was having a hard time sitting up. She must have landed harder than Portia.

Turning back to the watching faces, Portia called out in common, "Don't fire!" Any response they might have had for her was drowned out by the alarm horn blaring yet again. Several raised their weapons higher, aiming.

No, no, no.

Portia whirled back to face the portal. She sang the healing song as loudly as she could, holding her hands over her ears to keep out the wailing of the horns. Her hands trembled, and her heart pounded under the onslaught of noise.

The portal responded. The mist swirling on its surface sped up, twirling around faster and faster. Cries rang out from those around her as they noticed the change in the gateway to the other world. They yelled in a language she could not understand. She pushed out thoughts of the defenders and focused on the horrible circle of the splinter and sang and sang.

The only thought Portia spared from her task was the muttered prayer that it would be enough. She waited for a spear to pierce her back, her skin crawling. None came.

She sang on.

The discordant music changed. It stopped shrieking so painfully in her ears. The splinter changed with it, now the entire swirling oval swinging back and forth. They must be connected somehow. She hadn't heard music from the other portal, but she'd only been on the far side a second before it had snapped shut.

A scrambling noise pulled at her attention. Glancing to one side, she saw several of the defenders moving towards her and Iva.

"Keep them away, but don't kill anyone," Portia yelled to Iva, stopping her song just long enough to get the words out, the portal screaming in protest. Fear clenched at Portia as she sang again, getting hold of the magic once again before it destroyed them all.

Iva had gotten to her feet by then. She raised her hands and waved them over the floor, from which rose a dozen small creatures who rapidly grew from the size of small rodents, then to the size of dogs, and finally to human height and size. They looked like oddly melted people made out of mud. The ground there was stone. These creatures were wholly magic.

"Protect us," Iva commanded. The creatures ran between Iva and Portia and the dwarves around them. Portia concentrated on the portal and her singing while stealing glances at the strange creatures pushing back at the defenders. One was cut in half by a sword, and then the two pieces reformed, and *both* ran towards the defender wielding the weapon. Nausea pushed at Portia's throat. At least no blood came from the stricken mud being.

Iva created more of the creatures and sent these into the portal, whose surface was now whirling at incredible speed. It was vibrating wildly, the discordant music ringing out harshly.

Finally, after what felt like an eternity, Portia felt the

vibration of the magic resonating within her chest. Here, her magic didn't have the swimming-through-mud feeling she'd endured on the other side of the portal. Even so, the magic of healing the portal was difficult—and not something she'd always succeeded in doing before.

She must succeed this time.

Pulling off her makeshift mask to get more air, she breathed in deeply and bellowed out the spell with more volume than she had known possible.

The defenders were getting close to Portia. Her arm hairs prickled at the proximity. Their concerned faces looked between Portia and Iva and the splinter, unsure if she was trying to help them or hurt them. Portia guessed they had held their fire because she and Iva were human, but even that was not going to be enough with the terrifying behavior of the splinter and the strange mud creatures running around the floor tripping the dwarves and biting their legs. The smallest mud beings were the hacked remains of the larger creatures Iva had conjured to defend them, having reformed themselves and continued to fight, no matter how small the pieces the defenders had cut them into.

Portia closed her eyes against the activity around her. Pouring her energy into the healing magic, her head felt light and loose. The world spun, but she didn't dare open her eyes. She didn't need to see the portal to feel its wild vibrations. It shook the ground in its desperate fight to not be destroyed.

Clenching her fists and screwing her eyes tight, Portia pulled the music of the spell from deep within as her body was thrown from side to side like a rag doll.

She pushed at the portal, willing it to close.

It shook the ground around them harder.

Portia sang, demanding it close.

It screamed its protest.

Finally, the discordant music from the portal resolved into one high-pitched squealing harmonic that pierced her ears with a shooting pain and then silenced. The splinter snapped shut, only to explode outward in a wave of burning hot air that knocked Portia off her feet as it passed.

As one, the defenders stopped moving and stared where the portal had once been, half of them already knocked to the ground. A tiny mud man ran into the shin of one of the defenders, flopped back on the stone floor, and then disappeared in a puff of dust.

Water dripped on the far wall of what Portia now realized was a cave, while Iva sank to her knees.

Someone dropped their sword with a clatter.

The labored breathing of a defender came from behind Portia. She turned to face him. It was a dwarf. Or at least what she thought was a dwarf.

Suddenly, it came to her that she might have made a gigantic mistake. What if they were not back in her world? Did the portal lead to someplace even worse?

No, she shook her head to clear the thought. There was no place worse than where she had just come from—a world where humans were enslaved.

The enemy of my enemy is my friend, she thought. These were definitely not friends to the Dragonoids.

The dwarf approached Portia. He came to her shoulder

but must have weighed twice what she did, being so wide and well-muscled. He had a paunch and gray hair, as well as a decorative gray braid on his dark blue uniform. If it weren't for the flickering torches lighting the cave and the white in his hair, he would have blended into the dark rocks, the uniform a perfect camouflage.

He stopped several paces in front of Portia and gave her a small bow while Iva scrambled to her feet. A few words in an unfamiliar language rang out from someone in the back, and he turned and spoke harshly back in the same language to them, his face apologetic when he turned back to Portia.

Portia shrugged her shoulders. She could try the translation spell she learned from the Elven librarian but wasn't sure if her casting it on him would be taken as aggression. It had enraged the Dragonoids she had used it on. The dwarves surrounded her and Iva. Offending one would not be a wise move.

He cocked his head for a moment and then spoke again, this time in the human common tongue. "What did you do?"

"I closed the splinter," Portia said, hoping that was what he meant.

He flapped his arms for a moment, looking around, and then faced her again. "Yes, we see that. I mean... who are you? How did you do that? No—" he stopped himself. "There are too many questions."

"My name is Portia, and this is Iva," Portia said, gesturing as Iva came to her side. They both towered over the dwarf, who backed up a step while several of his soldiers came closer. The hair on Portia's arms rose. She continued on in a conciliatory tone. "We mean no harm. We just didn't want them to come after us."

The dwarf rubbed the back of his neck. "That is understandable, even if it might now be a problem. Can you open it again?"

Portia shook her head slowly. Had she done something wrong?

"Ack, never mind. My name is Kerat. I'm the commander of these troops."

Iva pushed forward to get his attention. "Where are we?"

"Morgani," he said.

"No," Iva said, despair in her voice. "No, no, no."

Portia put a hand on Iva's arm and spoke in a reassuring tone. "Morgani is south and west of the human kingdoms."

Iva sucked in her breath and breathed out in relief.

Kerat nodded at Portia. "That it is. And where are you from that you know such a thing?"

"Haulstatt," Portia said, leaving it at that. She didn't want to volunteer too much, and certainly not that she was a Jack of Magic and had special status to her queen and her kingdom. They were in a cave, perhaps deep below the surface, and surrounded by dwarves. Information was the only currency she had, and it needed to be conserved until they were in the safety of her own kingdom.

If Haulstatt was still a human kingdom and not already in possession of the Dragonoids.

Portia's curiosity overrode her caution. "Which kingdoms have fallen to the Dragonoids?"

At his puzzled look, she pointed to where the portal had been. "The ones coming through the splinter."

Comprehension crossed his face. "You mean, has Haulstatt fallen?"

Portia nodded slowly, desiring and not desiring the answer at the same time.

"To my knowledge, Haulstatt still stands, if just barely. Ships attack there regularly. Lusatiana's capital has fallen, and war has overtaken the land," Kerat said.

He watched several of his men checking themselves for injuries and herding the rest of the mud creatures to a central location. The mud beings no longer harassed the dwarves. Portia told herself to ask Iva about them when they were alone, if that ever happened. Kerat motioned another dwarf over, one also with a gray braid on his uniform. He opened his mouth to give a command and then abruptly turned to Portia.

"Will that," he waved his hand to where the splinter had been, "hold?"

Portia nodded, a nagging prick of anxiety in her stomach at that promise. She felt no scar where the splinter had been. It should be gone forever.

Eyeing her carefully, his eyes slid around the room again and considered his men before finally turning back to the dwarf he had motioned over. "Set a guard and a watch, as always. Get the wounded out and that out as well." He motioned to a large spear sent through the splinter by the Dragonoids. It had impaled a dwarf and then continued on to pierce a large wooden shield and catapult directly behind it.

Pulling her eyes away from the carnage of the fallen

dwarf, Portia turned to Kerat. "We would like safe passage to Haulstatt."

"You have to speak to our queen first." His eyes glinted.

KERAT PERSONALLY ESCORTED them through the tunnels, a group of his men following, fanning out behind Portia and Iva, who limped slightly. Pulling Iva's robe from her shin, Portia had found a long gash where an arrow had skimmed Iva's leg.

"I'm fine," said Iva, glancing at the watching dwarves.

Portia nodded and rose from examining Iva's leg. It was a shallow wound, and the bleeding had already stopped.

The dwarves had taken Iva's pike, which would have been difficult to carry through the long tunnels anyway. Portia subtly touched the baldric of her sword, still hidden underneath her robes. The dwarves had not demanded it, either through courtesy or ignorance of its existence. She would not have given it up in any case, not unless forced to.

The vast tunnel the splinter had been in gave way to narrow but tall passages. Portia wondered at the height of the cave until she saw another tunnel high above cutting across the passage they were walking in. An arched stone bridge above them connected the two openings from her left to her right. Ladders carved into the stone wall allowed passage from the lower level to the upper. There must be a network of tunnels crisscrossing everywhere. She had no sense of where they were nor of how deep below the ground.

Suddenly, more than anything, she wished to see the sun

and feel the breeze in her hair. The weight of the earth above her sent a sudden panic down her spine. She forced her eyes to the back of Kerat's head and concentrated on breathing in and out deeply while placing one foot ahead of the other.

Iva shuffled along, seemingly unbothered by the tunnels. She stretched her arms and rolled her neck, catching Portia's eye and giving her a half smile.

"What were those things?" Portia asked, keeping her voice low. "I thought you couldn't do magic."

"Well, not in that other place, but here feels, well, it's home, isn't it? I could do magic at home," Iva said.

"You could've told me," said Portia. She didn't understand why she felt so frustrated by Iva's surprising abilities. It helped them, after all.

"We were a little busy. Those things are golems. They're to protect us. They worked," Iva retorted, her voice defensive.

"Yes," said Portia. "I just was surprised. I've never seen anything like that."

"Had you ever been to Jukhnovo?"

"No," Portia admitted.

Iva shrugged.

Despite having traveled through Haulstatt and Lusatiana, and having survived the Dragonoid land, Portia suddenly felt very small. There was so much she hadn't seen. Did Professor Terfel know about golems? Portia wanted to ask more but was distracted by changes in the tunnel.

The passage ahead widened, the tall narrow way blossoming out into a wide, long galley filled with statues on either side—dwarves carved from a light red rock and set high on pedestals lit with suffused light from glowing golden moss growing on the walls and ceiling. Water flowed and shimmered over the walls, collecting into long channels along the base of each wall. Flat tribute squares lay at regular intervals next to the water, covered with offerings of carved objects that Portia longed to examine closer.

Portia counted a dozen statues as they passed them before finally calling to Kerat. "Who are these people—" At his sharp look, she corrected herself. "Dwarves. There are so many of them."

"Rulers. They are the life force of our kingdom. As is the water."

Looking at the cool water, Portia swallowed and felt for her waterskin. It was gone. Seeing her actions, Kerat motioned her to one of the tribute squares. He pulled a small carved creature from a pouch on his hip and placed it on the wide flat stone near some similar carvings, and then picked up a cup lying next to the square, dipping it into the cool water until it was full. Portia's mouth watered as she watched. He took a small sip and then handed her the full cup with two hands. Unsure, she gave him a small bow and then accepted the cup. He motioned for her to drink. She tipped it back. The water was cool and tasted of sunshine and spring flowers trickling down her throat. Meaning to stop halfway, she lowered the cup and was surprised to find it empty. Portia's face burned red, but Kerat only laughed and dipped the cup again to share with Iva.

The cavern was long, stretching into the distance past Portia's vision, with light from the abundant moss revealing statues as far as she could see. The echoes from their footsteps had died down when they stopped. The silence pushed at Portia, almost feeling like a substantial thing wrapped around her.

"How could there be so many?" Portia asked, under her breath.

"We have been of this land for a long time," Kerat answered practically in her ear, knowing immediately that she spoke of the statues. Portia jumped, not expecting either the answer or his proximity. Somehow, he didn't seem as short in this cavernous place, as if this chamber gave him stature.

"Do you not live... I mean—" Portia stammered, regretting what she had almost said out loud: that she wondered if the dwarves were exceedingly short-lived. Iva silently laughed at her from behind Kerat's back, having guessed at her thoughts.

He stared at Portia with not a hint of a smile.

"Never mind," Portia said, her voice almost imperceptible.

"We live a long time. As long as humans."

That being so, the dwarves had been there a long time indeed, judging by the generations of rulers immortalized by the statues. Portia's mind struggled to comprehend the span of ages the silent carvings represented.

"Morgani's likeness is at the end." He waved to the dim distant end of the cavern.

"Are all the rulers named Morgani?"

He shot her a puzzled look. "No, of course not."

"Well your land is named Morgani, and the ruler's name is Morgani—"

"Our queen."

"Your queen," Portia said, "is named Morgani. I was just wondering if they all were named the same."

"Our land takes the name of our ruler," Kerat said, his tone like that of one explaining to a child.

Iva sucked in her breath. "Isn't that confusing?"

"Not to us," Kerat said.

Iva and Portia pondered that as they continued walking down the corridor. Portia wanted to stop and examine some statues more closely, but she didn't feel the freedom of a guest to do so. The dwarves didn't treat them exactly as prisoners, but Portia wasn't sure they were allowed to explore all the same.

They turned off into a smaller passage before reaching the end of the large cavern. They walked in the narrow cave only briefly before it too opened up into another vast cavern, also with a second level of openings carved into the rock and joined together with ladders from level to level. Some sections of the cavern were three levels high. Dwarves of all ages walked through the openings while others sat on the narrow ledges before the dwellings working on crafts or simply watching the business of others. Portia scanned the crowd for guards but saw no others besides the ones walking with them.

Dwarves nodded at Kerat as they passed. They were all as sturdy and well built, even the women and children. All were dressed in similar garb of linen pants and tunics, a few with woolen cloaks. They passed one barrel that had been propped up over a fire and which was stirred by an older female dwarf. Smoke curled up to a tiny vent high in the ceiling. The smell of wet lanolin surrounded Portia, making her think of green meadows and sheep eating under the sunshine. She looked around, but there were no live sheep in the cavern.

The dwarves they passed pretended a polite indifference, but Portia felt their eyes staring at them after they passed. She twirled quickly and caught several looking. Iva watched her, her eyes wide, and Portia responded with a shrug. It felt good to have some control. At least enough to make those staring look away with embarrassment. Kerat pretended not to notice.

After several turns through the vast space, each turn revealing yet more dwellings and more dwarves, Kerat turned to Portia and Iva. "Do not speak of the king when you are brought before our queen." Portia wanted to ask why, but Kerat had already turned away and walked on. The soldiers behind them crowded forward, forcing Portia and Iva to follow.

The passageway narrowed again. After a hundred paces, it twisted sharply and then revealed a third open expanse that ended at the face of a castle carved out of rock ahead of them. The vast structure occupied most of the far side of the cavern, with soldiers manning each level, carrying long pikes and dressed in full armor. The dwelling only had small slits for windows designed for archers to use and a heavy iron gate guarded by four dwarf soldiers and half a dozen large creatures Portia didn't recognize. One of the creatures growled and stood, revealing itself to be as tall as a soldier next to it and possessing fangs the size of the soldier's head. Iva gasped and stepped back, but the soldier behind her pushed her forward.

"They won't let us be ripped apart before we see the queen," Portia said to Iva, projecting an insouciance she didn't feel. Iva nodded stiffly but stepped forward again, walking so closely to Portia that she almost tripped on Portia's feet. Biting back irritation, Portia gave her a small smile.

The throne room was modest. The thrones were of heavy wood construction, stained dark and polished to a sheen, looking so old as to be of black stone and not wood. One sat empty next to another of the same size where the queen sat. The dwarf queen had long auburn hair tied back in a bun, and she wore a velvet green gown, the first gown Portia had seen in the kingdom. Her attendants also wore gowns, but none so lush and much closer to the dress of the commoners. There were many guards, but no male attendants, nor any evidence of a king except the empty throne.

The queen waited patiently while Iva and Portia were led forward. Portia curtsied and Iva followed, bending low to the queen.

"You may rise," the queen said, her voice surprisingly light. "I have been told you appeared at the portal and did something to it there. Pray explain."

Portia's eyebrows rose. The queen must have some way of getting information much more quickly than their walking on the journey to the castle. Portia had not seen messengers run from the battle site, but perhaps they had, or perhaps there was some other form of communication the dwarves held in secrecy, for the queen already knew what had happened at the battle.

"Yes, Your Majesty. I did do something," Portia said. "I healed the splinter using Elven magic."

The queen looked at her more closely. "But you are human, are you not? Your name is?"

"Portia, and yes, I am human, Your Majesty."

"Then how can you do Elven magic?" The queen gave a small laugh. "Your explanation is sorely lacking, bringing more questions than answers. Do not make me ask yet one more time. Please explain."

Iva shifted uncomfortably next to Portia. They did not know the patience of this monarch and whether the laugh meant genuine amusement or was the signal of misery to come for those causing it.

"Somehow, I can do it. The elves tested me," Portia remembered bitterly the tests they had made her endure, "and found me able. My queen—"

"Your queen?" Queen Morgani asked, tilting her head.

"Queen Lorica of Haulstatt, Your Majesty," Portia answered.

The queen nodded for Portia to continue.

"My queen instructed me to go with the elves and learn their magic for the purpose of healing the splinters. Then, after I had learned the magic, my queen sent me to the Well of Tears to stop the invaders' ships from flowing out."

All Iva let show of her own sorrow at losing her family and her country was a small sigh. If Portia had been sent to the Well of Tears sooner, perhaps Jukhnovo would not have fallen. Her family might yet live.

The queen tapped a finger to her chin and stared at Portia.

"And yet, you are here, through *this* splinter, far inland and nowhere near the Well of Tears."

"Yes, Your Majesty," Portia said. At the queen's irritated look Portia quickly continued on. "There was a problem, and I was stranded in the other place. That was where I met Iva."

"And the splinter at the Well of Tears? Is that healed?" the queen asked.

"I think so, Your Majesty. Truly, I'm not sure. It looked so from the other side."

Portia's stomach twisted in anxiety thinking about what happened at the Well of Tears. It was possible she had completely healed the splinter. It was also possible that Mark, her longest-held friend in her life, had perished in the effort along with her first mate and possibly even her professor and mentor, Professor Aelric Terfel, and those of her Academy house who had accompanied her. All those who had insisted on accompanying her to the splinter.

Her small longboat had been surrounded and attacked and finally destroyed when the splinter snapped shut. She had managed to survive by swimming in the waters on the far side. Those she had left behind not only had the waters to deal with, but also nighttime and the attackers of the two huge invader vessels that surrounded them. It was near impossible to think they lived, yet she could not accept that they were dead—that Mark was dead. She refused to believe it. Her heart wished that he and the others had been rescued by those in the *Dancing Queen,* yet she also wished the *Dancing Queen* had fled to safety instead, carrying all those on it away from the bloodthirsty Dragonoids. Wanting both things at the same time made her head hurt.

The queen cleared her throat, pulling Portia back to the present.

"And can you open it again?" the queen asked.

"Open what, Your Majesty?" asked Portia, her face flushed by her embarrassment at being caught daydreaming.

"The splinter. Can you open it again?" Heavy silence filled the room at the queen having to repeat herself.

Startled, Portia met the queen's gaze. It was not a question she ever thought to be asked.

"No, Your Majesty. That was not something I was taught," Portia said, suddenly uneasy. The eyes of the watching couriers burned even more strongly into her neck. Her answer had not been welcome. "There were so many dead around it. Why..." Portia bit back the rest of the question at the sharp look of the queen.

The queen stared at Portia until Portia lowered her gaze. "I see," said the queen, her lips pressed together. She pulled in a deep breath. "How long were you on the other side?"

"A few weeks, I think, Your Majesty. Maybe more. I didn't think to track the days." Portia stared at her hands with dirt impregnated in her skin and thick under her nails. She'd not had a real bath the entire time she was gone. Her odor must be intense, but her nose could not smell anything as it was so used to it by now.

"That is impressive that you survived that long. Even more so that you returned. We have had few come back to us."

The queen shifted in her seat. "While the portal was still open, we *had* hoped for more."

The hairs on Portia's arms rose. She shifted from side to side and then stopped, forcing herself to be still under the unrelenting gaze of the queen.

After a long pause, Queen Morgani turned to Iva. "And who are you?"

Iva curtsied again. Her hands trembled. "Iva, Your Majesty. I'm from Jukhnovo. Was from—"

The queen waved away any further words. Iva stopped talking. The queen continued. "News of Jukhnovo's fall has reached us even here. Your ignorance of us doesn't mean we are ignorant of you. Were there others with you? Your family?"

Iva shook her head and looked down, unable to speak.

"I see," the queen said.

The throne room waited in silence as the queen considered the two humans. She leaned to one side on her throne and once again tapped her chin with her finger.

Finally, the queen spoke again, "Did you see any of our people there? Dwarves."

Both Portia and Iva nodded. When Iva didn't speak, Portia filled the silence. "We did. There were many dead by the portal." Portia motioned to Iva and immediately regretted it but had to continue on. "And Iva spoke of some prisoners who might have been dwarves."

"You did meet some?" the queen asked, a hint of eagerness in her voice despite her appearing uncaring of the answer. Her look darkened. "You said prisoners?"

Portia stared at her feet and said quietly, "Slaves."

A hiss of displeasure arose from the watching courtiers, which was quickly silenced. Looking up to see who had given the command, Portia saw nothing but concerned eyes looking in the queen's direction. She and Iva were studiously ignored.

The queen's eyes glittered. She stared off into the distance somewhere over Portia's shoulder. The echo of water dripping filled the silence of the throne room. A faint cry from the training yards beside the castle rang out along with the clash of metal on metal.

Queen Morgani's eyes slid to Portia, the monarch's gaze impenetrable. Portia quickly looked down again.

"We will wait to see what happens to the splinter and if it is truly closed forever," Queen Morgani said. "I ask that you remain with us, as our guests, until we know more."

Kerat led Portia and Iva out of the throne room, followed by more guards. Once again, they were surrounded by soldiers. Bile burned at the back of Portia's throat.

5

Kerat led them back through twisting passages deeper within the castle. It was larger than Portia expected, not stopping at the back of the large cavern but actually being carved deep into the rock behind it. She wondered how they defended the structure, having no clear sight of its full surroundings and being vulnerable to whomever came through the passages deep within.

Shaking those thoughts from her head, she entered the small room Kerat pointed at. It was next to an identical room for Iva. Only a small narrow bed and a chest of drawers lay inside. There was no room for much else.

"Is it bad that I closed the splinter?" Portia quickly asked Kerat before he left.

He glanced out along the corridor and then stepped back into the room with Portia.

"Our king led a charge against the invaders. Through the

portal," he said. He tilted his head towards her. Portia's heart sank.

"And he's not returned," she said.

His look confirmed it.

Wonderful. She'd shut the portal and possibly stranded the king on the other side.

His look softened. "You didn't know. They were not negotiating peace when you arrived."

Portia remembered the alarm sirens and the machines of war on the Dragonoid side. They were about to invade in earnest. Only bloodshed was on their minds, not negotiation. The field of dead soldiers—their own and dwarves—was evidence enough of that.

She nodded numbly and went to throw her bag on the bed, pulling back at the last minute and dropping it on the floor. The bag and everything she owned, including herself, was filthy.

Watching from the door, Kerat asked, "Do you need anything? Baths and food will be brought."

"Yes. Do you have a smith?"

"Of course."

"I need some lockpicks and caltrops."

The dwarf laughed at her request. Portia narrowed her eyes at him but let her question hang in the air. Were they truly guests, or were they prisoners who were not allowed such luxuries as the means to open a secured door?

"You are a most unusual human girl. Your request will be given to the royal blacksmith." He strode quickly down the corridor, leaving them to their quarters.

So that was it. They were guests, unless he was dissembling and the requested items would never come.

A COPPER TUB was brought to Portia's room, along with a small army of dwarf attendants carrying steaming kettles and a tray of food. Voices came from Iva's room. She too had been brought a bath and food.

All too soon, the water in the tub cooled. Portia rose. The water had been crystalline and clear when poured into the tub, but now it swirled a murky brown around her shins. She wished desperately for a second bath but didn't dare ask for more water. The still present dwarf attendants wrapped her in towels. They were so gentle she didn't push them away, instead allowing them to dry her and give her clean clothes. None of them spoke the common language, but they had made their intentions known through hand waving and bowing. The only conflict had been when they tried to take her sword and baldric from her. She held on tightly, her fingers white around the grip. They clucked at her gently but finally relented, allowing her to lay the sword next to the tub, within arm's reach, while she bathed. The rest of her clothes disappeared under the arm of a dwarf who scurried out of the room.

She lay the baldric across her chest over the clean garments they'd given her—long trousers, a fine linen undershirt, and a heavier tunic in a gray that shimmered, appearing black one moment and silver the next. The garments were of the right length but were much too wide, having been designed for a dwarf's stout body. The attendants fixed the issue with a rope belt strung through the pants belt loops and pulled tightly. Another belt, this one sewn with pretty embroidery, wrapped over the overtunic and pulled the shirts into Portia's waist. They could burn the brown linen overgarment from the Dragonoid land, Portia thought, for she never wanted to see it again, but her green trousers and linen top would be sorely missed if they were not returned. Hopefully, they were only being washed.

The rest of the dwarves filed out, leaving Portia alone with the tray of food they had brought. It lay on the narrow bed covering the full width with an expanse of filled dishes and bowls.

Chiding herself for not better resisting the theft of her garments, Portia pulled her sword out of the way then sat down on the floor in front of the bed to examine the contents of the tray. Now that she was clean, the growl of her stomach reverberated loudly through her body. One bowl held several red balls with spikes and thorns sticking out of them. They smelled sweet and fruity. Putting the bowl down again, Portia grabbed a handful of nuts from a dish on the tray and chewed, examining the main plate laid out with a thick slice of a brown loaf covered with gravy and surrounded by crisp roasted vegetables. It smelled wonderful but unfamiliar. She poked it with a fork, and then selected a tiny piece that she brought to her nose and sniffed.

"Mushrooms." Iva watched her from the doorway. "The loaf is made out of mushrooms. It tastes wonderful. Like meat, but it isn't."

"Have you eaten already?" Portia asked.

"I have," Iva said, but her eyes didn't leave Portia's plate.

"How do you know what it is made of?" Portia narrowed her eyes at Iva while pulling her tray closer.

Iva shrugged. "It's a common dish in Jukhnovo. They grow the mushrooms in the caves in the inlands."

Taking a tentative bite, Portia chewed. Another bite soon followed, then another, until she lifted her fork for more and realized it was gone. Iva laughed.

"It's easy to do," Iva said. She sat down on the bed next to Portia's tray. "I asked for seconds, but they didn't understand me."

"You should have pointed at it before they left."

"I did. Maybe they just pretended to not understand me." Iva snorted and picked at her pants, finally smoothing the material back down. "How did you learn that magic from the elves? I've not ever heard of that."

"At last. Something I know and you don't," Portia said as she sadly pushed away the empty plate and moved the tray to the floor and out of the way.

Iva crossed her arms and lay back on the bed. Her hair spread out around her, shining in the low light. She looked younger now that the dirt was gone.

Portia poked her leg. Iva didn't look.

"Okay, I'm sorry," Portia said. She was too tired to tease

Iva anyhow. "It wasn't easy. Really, it's just what I told Queen Morgani. They made me take some trials that I might have died doing, and then, after going through all that stuff seemingly having nothing to do with splinter magic, they said I may study it." Portia leaned back against the bed and kicked out her feet on the stone floor.

Iva turned to look at Portia. "It's healing magic?"

"Closing them is. I don't know how they're opened." She put her head back on the bed. An urge to close her eyes overwhelmed her.

"Hallo." A thin reedy voice intruded on the glow in Portia's head. Slapping her hand down on the ground, she opened her eyes and looked to the doorway. A young male dwarf page, dressed in a maroon velvet tunic, stood at the doorway. He had spoken in common. Barely. The accent had been so thick she'd barely understood it.

"Yes?" Portia asked, reluctantly getting to her feet.

"The archmage is requesting your presence." It did not sound like a request. At least they had not sent guards, only the young dwarf.

"Can it wait until tomorrow? We need some rest," Portia said. Iva sat up on the bed, wide-eyed, at Portia's refusal.

He blinked at her. "We do what the archmage wants, we do," the page said.

"I'm not you," Portia snapped. It had been a long day. She'd closed another splinter today, been through battle, and seen a queen. She needed sleep.

The page did not move from the door.

"We do what the archmage wants," he said. "We *do*."

Portia raised herself up to look down at the page and crossed her arms. Dizziness pulled at her now that she was on her feet. Iva looked back and forth between the two of them.

"Maybe the archmage has more food," Iva said helpfully. "Or some mead. Let's go see."

Portia glared at Iva and then back at the page. Neither looked like they were going to budge. Portia closed her eyes and took in a deep breath, uncrossed her arms, and grabbed her bag off the floor, putting it on. The bag's strap lay across her baldric strap but did not interfere with her pulling the weapon if she needed to. The page's eyes widened at the sight of the sword hanging in its sheath.

"All right then. If I have to go, then you do too," Portia said to Iva.

"Of course. You don't think I'd let you leave me alone again? The last time there were *creatures*."

"Very nice creatures. There might be some nice ones here too," Portia said, looking around the room as if expecting to find small furry faces.

"No, no, no. I'm going to grab my bag. I'll be right back. Don't leave without me." Iva ran from the room and into her own room, grabbed her bag, and returned before Portia made it to the doorway.

The page led them deep into the warren of tunnels that was the dwarven kingdom. Between her exhaustion and all the turns, Portia despaired of ever finding her way out again. That fear was a mild nuisance in comparison to her exhaustion, which was so acute her eyes slipped shut even as she walked behind the page. Wringing the archmage's neck when she saw him for not letting them rest first would have been an option if her arms hadn't felt so heavy. Was some rest too much to ask?

Iva trotted along next to her. Portia's skin tingled in irritation at Iva's energy. Even the tunnel seemed darker, as if it was too much work for her eyes to see.

After a full candlemark of walking in the dim tunnels, the page turned to an open doorway revealing a blazingly bright large circular room filled with books and strange devices stacked on tables and piled on the floor, with every surface further covered with large brass candle holders, all holding enormous candles that burned unnaturally bright. Portia shielded her eyes and peered in. A shadow moved on the far side of the room. A squat being dressed in deep blue robes, which were covered with symbols sewn in silver and gold metallic thread that flickered in the candlelight, sat in shadow on the far side of the room. A hand waved away their escort, who bowed and backed out of the room, leaving Portia and Iva alone. The being said not a word. The room was quiet and still except for the flickering of candlelight on the walls. The faint smell of burning tallow and beeswax tickled Portia's nose.

Once her eyes adjusted, Portia dropped her hand and scanned the room. There were many chairs, but they were all covered with books and other objects. The only one available for sitting was taken by the being at the far side of the room.

The archmage. His face was nearly obscured by dingy gray hair that straggled down the front of the robes, and a full beard covered most of his face. His eyes were so deeply set beneath the hair, they appeared as two black holes with not even a gleam of his eyeballs visible.

He stared, the dark holes of his eyes facing their direction. Only the slightest twitch of his right hand reassured Portia that he was alive. Royal protocol dictated that higher rank speak first, yet he said nothing. Pain radiated up Portia's legs from her aching feet and her sore back. Her head throbbed as sleep demanded her attention. Attention she couldn't give because, instead, she stood as a spectacle for this strange dwarf.

"Well?" Portia asked, crossing her arms. The word flew out of her mouth before she even realized she was speaking.

Iva elbowed her and then bowed towards the archmage. "I apologize for my friend, Your High—Your Archmage."

"Why are you apologizing for me?" Portia said under her breath to Iva, even as she uncrossed her arms and bowed, following Iva's example.

"Arch. Mage," Iva said, so quietly Portia could barely hear her. "Do you want to live the rest of your life as a swamp toad?"

Could he do that?

"Too far underground to be a *swamp* toad," Portia retorted under her breath to Iva but then quickly spoke up as gently as she could manage to the archmage. "We are here at your service."

Still, infuriatingly, the archmage said nothing.

A motion caught Portia's eye. It came from outside a window in the room. The room had windows. Something had passed in front of one of the large openings spaced around the circular room. Portia counted the seconds to herself as she stared out the window, but nothing else appeared.

She forced her eyes back to the archmage. The candles burned, sending thin traces of smoke up to the stained ceiling.

Finally, with a groan, the archmage put one arm on his chair and pushed himself to stand. He rose high for a dwarf, even with a deep curve in his back that left his head hanging nearly in front of his chest. Portia estimated he had two hands on her if he stood straight. His gray hair fell forward, further obscuring his eyes.

"Thank you for that," he said, slowly. His voice was clear and melodic. "Please, be seated." He motioned to several chairs in the middle of the room that were nearly buried under books and the heavy candleholders on top. At Portia and Iva's hesitation, he grunted, then hobbled forward until he reached one of the chairs. Pulling on an especially large book resting on the seat, he let the book and all the items on top of it fall to the floor. Portia ran forward, stomping on the flame from the toppled candle that threatened to set fire to the thick rug below. The liquid wax coated her shoe and saturated the rug where she'd tamped down the flame.

The archmage peered down at the burnt spot, grunted, and then repeated his housekeeping with the next chair. This time, Portia caught the candle atop the pile resting on the chair before it landed on the rug and set it gently down on a stack of books. Iva exhaled in relief.

While the archmage pulled a third armchair closer, Portia moved all the closest candles at least a length away, moving swiftly behind his back while he plodded and pulled at the heavy chair. Finally, he gestured for them to sit. Portia sat straight in her chair with her eyes locked on him. Iva also sat uncharacteristically close to the edge of her own seat. No flames were close enough for the archmage to reach, but there were still piles of books and unknown objects next to where he sat.

"You closed the splinter." His words were more a statement than a question.

Portia nodded while examining him closely, looking for any sign that the closure was considered good or bad event by him.

"Speak up," he said, his voice loud.

"Yes, I did," Portia said, once again pushing down irritation. On top of everything else, was she to shout at the archmage to be heard?

"How?"

The weeks of practicing the Elven magic flashed in Portia's head. Sometimes, she felt she barely understood the magic herself, yet she was to explain it to someone else? A dwarf no less? She was the only human that she knew of, that her queen knew of, who could do Elven magic. Were dwarves capable of doing Elven magic?

Portia squinted at the dwarf in front of her. Little had been taught to her in the Academy of the magic of dwarves, nor was she told of any special abilities they might possess. Students had only been told the dwarves had been present before the elves came to their world, just as the elves had been present before the humans. The dwarves had retreated to their kingdoms in the south and the west as the world crowded with newcomers, becoming even more of a myth to humans than the elves had been. Dwarves had been relegated to the fairytales and designed to scare and warn young children, not that her childhood had needed any extra fright.

Portia gripped the arms of her chair while clearing her throat. "It's Elven magic."

The archmage leaned forward to peer at Portia. "You do not look like an elf."

Iva giggled. Portia shot her a glare while responding to the archmage. "I am not an elf, but it was Elven magic."

"If it was elf magic, then you must be an elf," said the archmage stubbornly.

"No, I am not an elf," Portia said, anger edging her voice despite her best efforts of patience.

"Do not lie to me—either you are an elf or it was not elf magic!" He pounded on the arm of his chair, sending a cloud of dust into the air, shimmering in the candlelight.

Portia squinted at him. He knew humans could not do Elven magic, or at least should not be able to. Her ability to do so marked her. A cold feeling sank in her belly. What else did he know? There was a world of knowledge he had that she'd have no inkling of. Awareness of the dangerousness of her ignorance washed over her in a cold wave, leaving the hairs on her arms erect and her scalp tingling. Dinner soured into a cold stone in her belly.

"I am not lying," said Portia. Iva stared at Portia just as

intently as the archmage. "I'm a Jack of Magic. I am human, but I can do Elven magic such as closing the splinters."

"If that is what they call it," said the archmage.

"Isn't that what you call that? Closing the splinter?" Confusion wrapped around Portia.

"That I did, but if what you did was Elven magic and not something new, as I had hoped, then our reprieve is short-lived. We might regain our king but still lose our kingdom."

The faint echo of water falling came from the window, filling the silence as they sat.

"What do you mean short-lived?" Portia asked, her curiosity overwhelming her irritation with the strange dwarf.

He raised his head as if starting a lecture. "Elves... much as they think they can close the splinters, they have learned little from the humans invading this land, and now these strange lizards—"

"Dragonoids. I've named them," said Iva, her chin jutting out. "I claim that."

The archmage tilted his head at Iva. "Dragonoids, vicious as they are, are our newest companions on this world."

"I don't think they have any interest in staying here," Portia said, grateful at least for that.

"No? Perhaps, perhaps not. They have brought a great deal in the way of war machines if they are not planning to stay. Great caravans carry strange metal wagons throughout Lusatiana, and even now fight to decimate Haulstatt."

Haulstatt. Pain gripped Portia's heart. Her home still was there. Were her people? Visions of dead soldiers and decimated cities threatened to overwhelm her. Portia shook her head to clear the images.

"You still haven't explained what you mean by short-lived," said Portia, leaning forward. "I closed the splinter. There was no scar when I was done. It should hold forever."

The archmage shook his head, his hair behaving strangely, not moving along with his scalp. Portia blinked at the weird image.

"And yet it doesn't. It hasn't when the elves have closed them, and if you used their magic, then it won't for you either. I don't understand what you mean by scar, but whatever the reason, where there was once a splinter, there will be one again—if not within a day or a year then certainly within an eon. Nothing keeps them shut forever. It just damages the connection so that when it does open again, a whole new horror is brought upon this world. Elves, humans, and now these," he nodded at Iva, "Dragonoids."

"You're calling humans horrors?" Iva asked, her jaw hanging open. "What have we done to you?"

He gazed at her thoughtfully. "What city did you come from before the Dragonoids captured you?"

"The capital of Jukhnovo, the great kingdom to the north." Pain flashed across Iva's face.

"The great *Dwarf* kingdom to the north. Its true name is Jwason. We found it." He thumped his chest with his finger. "We cultivated that land. We created the fishing villages and serviced our great ships there. We did. Until the elves came and stole it, only to have it stolen yet again by the humans after them in yet another thousand years."

Just as suddenly as his anger had come upon him, it left again, and he sank back in his seat deflated. "Mayhap we deserved it. Do you know the irony of how the elves got to be here? I'm sure not. We were celebrating having found this beautiful world, one we could keep all to ourselves, when our great magicians and archmages, unaware of the great power in this world, set off light shows over the festivals marking the birth of a new king. One especially powerful mage created an explosion of light over our capital city Jwasarel, bright enough to be seen from ships far out in the harbor and upon the rough seas. The light shone so brightly it flew out to the island humans now call the Well of Tears, setting off reverberations across the land. The sea shook and raged. Dwarves huddled and cried in their homes and begged the mages to stop. And they did, not knowing it was far too late. Only weeks later did armies of elves emerge from a newly rent splinter over the dark island.

"The battles between our peoples raged for bloody decades until we retreated south. Our hearts burned with hatred at the elves, but another eon brought their own doom with the humans. This history will repeat with the Dragonoids, and on and on forever, as long as there are splinters in this world."

Iva leaned forward in her seat, clenching her hands. "No, I don't believe you. We must be able to escape that fate. We must." Iva spoke furiously, her eyes glistening. "I won't believe you. I won't."

"I don't believe you either," Portia said quietly, her voice reminding her of being ten and fighting with John in her own gang, before he had discovered how stubborn she was, even after being banished to the attic for taking risks. Taking a breath, she tried again, focusing on keeping her voice low and without a whine. "The elves said that if there was no scar left, the splinter would not open up again. I don't understand what you're talking about."

"Elves may say whatever they want, yet the reality is what we have experienced together on this world. The splinters never stay shut. Not forever. If the elves were so good with this magic of theirs, humans should never have found this place," said the archmage, his voice nearly a growl. "Humans came through their own splinter and have overrun this world after the elves closed it, by their own claims. The elves made the splinters worse—once they touch them, they link up in resonance, so when they do open again, they all open to some new world."

Portia focused on her breathing. If what he said was true, she didn't know which words were worse—that the splinter would never be completely closed or that the dwarves viewed humans as unwanted pests. Professor Aelric's lessons popped in her head unbidden. Reminding herself of Queen Morgani's gracious greeting, Portia managed to dull the rage rising within her, but only a little.

"Tell us how we can fix this," Portia said, her voice rising in pitch even as she fought to control herself.

"It is not fixable," said the archmage, rising in his seat, the arch his back straightening. "You will not fix it. You and all the humans will die from these Dragonoids unless you can defeat them in battle."

"We will fix it." Portia's eyes flashed.

"Do you think you are better than Dwarves?" The archmage rose from his chair, impossibly tall for a dwarf now that the curve in his back was gone. All the signs of advanced age had disappeared, and he stood as a warrior: back straight, chest broad, and his arms full and muscular, the bulk of his limbs showing through the thick blue robes.

Portia rose to face him. Even standing, she had to look up at him. "If you are giving up, then yes, I think I'm better. We are better."

He howled in rage and raised his right arm, sparks flying off his fingertips as he cocked his arm to throw magic at her.

"Portia, duck!" Iva cried. She scrambled from her own seat and ran behind a nearby pile.

There was no easy exit close to Portia, only stacks of items in the way and an impossibly tall and angry dwarf towering over her. She jutted out her chin and pulled ice magic to her, forming a shield between them. It was too thin, she knew. Exhaustion would not allow her to make it as thick as needed, but it was all she had. Fire magic would be easier for her, but flames in that small space would have set off the books and papers like a bomb, and any duplicate of herself she made would have had just as hard time moving freely. Ice magic was her best bet for surviving and for Iva to escape even if she didn't make it.

Tears pricked at her eyes with the effort. If only she'd had more sleep.

The archmage's arm swung down towards her, the sparks from his fingertips brightening and forming a glowing blue ball so bright Portia had to squint. As a spitting mass of magic swung down towards her, the smell of burning sulfur filled her nose. Portia screwed her eyes shut while pouring what magic she could muster into her ice shield, waiting to be decimated by the blue magic.

6

The blue light brightened and burned in Portia's eyes even through her shut lids. Heat seared the skin of her neck while noxious gas filled her lungs, but Portia refused to give up. She would defend herself until no longer able to.

But she was not obliterated in a blue magic explosion. Instead, a rustling came from somewhere on the floor before her, followed by a squeal of pain and a thump that echoed throughout the room as the blue light suddenly went out. Blinking away the spots, Portia tried to see in the darkness.

The archmage writhed on the floor, clutching at his foot and howling in pain. The gray hair that had been on his head lay like a dead animal next to him, while another animal, very much alive, sat up on its rear legs and stared at her, its dark eyes and giant ears reminding her of a playful but enormous and very skinny ground squirrel.

Iva peered around the chair she had been hiding behind.

The motion caught the animal's attention, and it turned to face her. She screamed and ducked back down behind the chair. "No, no, no. No more creatures!"

The animal tilted its head at Iva's outburst and then turned to look back at Portia. She could have sworn it shrugged its furry shoulders. Laughter filled the room. Portia couldn't help it. They had almost been killed by an irate archmage, and Iva screamed over something that rose no higher than her knee.

"It's not funny," a petulant voice came from behind the chair.

"Isn't it?" Portia asked, but she stopped laughing.

The archmage had quieted and now sat up, holding his foot and glaring daggers at both her and the creature. Portia tensed and stayed behind the ice shield she had created, only peering out to see what the archmage was up to.

"Uncalled for," he finally said, staring in the direction of the animal.

"I disagree," Portia said, instantly wishing she had not spoken, for the archmage raised his eyes to her, anger still burning in them. She softened her voice. "I don't think our talk was worth killing us over. And I did close your splinter, even if it is only for the short time of *an eon*."

The creature seemed to agree with her, for it turned to the archmage as she spoke and backed up her words with chittering of its own, which rose in intensity and volume and ending with the rodent equivalent of "so there" just as Portia stopped talking.

"Fine! Enough, the both of you. I won't kill the humans then, is that enough? No more biting."

Portia snickered.

Iva once again poked her head from behind the chair, taking in the scene and controlling herself enough to not scream this time. She pointed to the mass of gray hair laying on the floor next to the archmage. "Your hair ran away."

The archmage looked sheepish, and then stood and grabbed the hair from the floor, tossing it over a pile of books behind him. "Never mind that."

Portia crossed her arms.

When it was clear the tiny animal was not going to run at her, Iva came out from behind the chair and slowly drew closer to the archmage and Portia, her eyes never leaving the archmage's face.

"You're young. Why that old man stuff?"

Out of the shadow of the heavy gray hair that had covered his head previously, his face was smooth and unlined, his skin glowing. He looked barely older than Portia.

"You're not the archmage, are you?" said Portia.

"Yes, I am, thanks to you. You've no idea what you've done." The archmage slumped back into his chair, the rage completely gone. The creature jumped up onto his knee and then lay down, nestled between his thigh and the chair, facing Portia.

Portia and Iva exchanged glances then tentatively retook their own seats. Iva crossed her arms and leaned back. Portia did the same.

They stared at the archmage, who finally sighed and threw up his hands.

"My father was with King Morgani when he led the charge into the splinter. He is, *was*, the archmage. I was the second strongest mage in the kingdom, second only to him, so yes, without him I am now the archmage of Morgani, a title I want not at all. I didn't want you to know my age." He glared at Portia. "I didn't expect you to be so young either. My title is Archmage Vermeil, if you want to address me properly."

Portia nodded, acknowledging the title.

The room they were in was dusty, but certain stacks were clean, and at least one path through the stacks was well used with no dust on the floors. It was a huge repository of information, and well used, even without a staff to care for it.

"How long have they been gone?" asked Portia.

"Near one growing cycle," said the archmage. At Portia's puzzled look, he clarified. "Several of your moons."

That was longer than she expected. It wasn't just his father that used the books in these rooms.

The archmage stared at the creature sitting next to him. He raised his hand to pet it then placed it on his thigh instead. The creature didn't seem to notice, its gaze flicking between her and Iva. It didn't seem hostile exactly, but it was paying attention to their movements. Close attention.

"Your people might still be alive," said Portia. "There were a lot of slaves there. They seemed more interested in capturing slaves and stealing from us than anything else. Iva came from a slave pen in a market there."

A dark look flickered over Iva's face.

The archmage peered at her. "You saw dwarves?"

Iva nodded.

"Even so, you have helpfully closed our portal before we were ready. Many of our people are somewhere on the other side."

Portia pursed her lips. It felt a duty to mention all the dead on the ground before the splinter in the Dragonoid world, but she couldn't bring herself to do it. Without the rage lighting up his face, he slumped in the chair, staring at the ground and rubbing a toe into the carpet.

"I don't understand what you mean by resonance from the elves touching the splinters," said Portia.

"The big splinters the elves have healed all opened together to let in the humans," said Archmage Vermeil.

"Were there only two?" Portia asked.

"Possibly, but not likely. Once a resonance has started again, all sympathetic splinters reopen to the same world. There are at least five that are recorded here," he waved to a nearby stack of books, "and you have closed but two."

"Would they then not all open together to the Dragonoid lands too? If there are still splinters now open to their world, could we not go through them and retrieve your people?" asked Portia.

Hope lightened Portia's chest. They might be able to retrieve those trapped there.

The archmage rose. He paced the room, finding his way through the narrow paths between stacks of books.

The hair on the back of Portia's neck rose as he passed

behind her, but she forced herself to stay seated. The creature had remained on the archmage's chair when he arose. It sat watching the archmage and Iva and Portia but did not move from its half-reclined position. As long as it was not concerned, she would not take action.

"Possibly," said the archmage.

"Isn't that good news for getting back your people?" ask Portia.

The archmage did not answer. Portia and Iva exchanged glances.

"Wait, so you're mad at us because you don't want to go to another splinter?" Iva asked, her jaw jutting out. She twisted to glare at the archmage who stayed behind her, finally giving up and slumping back in her seat, irritated.

More splinters weren't good news for Haulstatt or any of the other kingdoms. Three more possible doors for the Dragonoids to enter their world and decimate their people.

"Even if they are open, getting to them is no small problem." Derision filled his voice. "We would have to transport an army through hostile human lands, or even more hostile Elven ones, all while you're actively closing the routes of escape. If we were to send an army into a splinter to retrieve our people, how can we trust you to not strand them there for their entire lives? It would be one way to steal even more from us."

"I wouldn't do that. Not on purpose," Portia said.

"What does purpose matter if they're out of our reach? You're working against us." His voice sounded distant. He stood at one of the open windows and looked out, not facing her or Iva.

Portia went to join him, Iva trailing after. A flick of fur raced to her left as the creature silently ran to the window ahead of her, placing itself between her and the archmage. Iva shuddered as it went by but kept walking.

"I don't want to work against you. We could forge an alliance. The elves have joined with us," Portia said.

"They have?" Iva said, giving Portia a sour look when she motioned for her to be quiet.

"That is their folly. Tell me how we should trust you?" The archmage snorted.

"I didn't close the splinter to hurt you. I thought I was helping. What can I do to earn your trust?"

"Nothing. You don't even deserve to serve the lowest of us as we open portal after portal searching for our people."

Harsh.

Wait, what?

"You can open these portals? Then why are you so upset? Just open another one here and retrieve your people. I'll close it right after," Portia said in a rush.

He turned and glared at her. "You really are ignorant of how they work, aren't you? It is not so easy to open them back to the place they connected to before. No one in our history has been able to. No one can, ever." He pounded one fist into the other.

"How do you know?" Portia asked, her voice rising in pitch.

He narrowed his eyes at her, then waved to the books around them. "These books say so."

"I'm not in those books!"

He crossed his arms and shook his head.

"After the invasion of the humans, when we finally reached peace with the elves—at least with some of them—our peoples worked together and closed the splinters. They healed them, and we blocked them off for good measure. It is all documented here. They celebrated the end of the nightmares, most anyhow, but they were wrong." He turned back to the window, leaning on the frame. "It wasn't. The splinters resonated and opened again in unison across our world, by some design we know not of."

"The elves—"

"Bah, Elves. Do you know they can't open splinters?"

Confusion clouded Portia's mind. "They opened worlds for me in their tests."

"Those were not worlds. They were little pockets of space, someplace they could play and put scenery and made-up beings, but they are not real. They... They are as my closet is in relation to the lands above. The door may be opened, and you may step inside, but you can never get to the land above through my closet, just as you will never reach another land through an Elven splinter."

"But the dwarves can open them?" Portia asked, her brows furrowing.

"In a fashion. Opening a new one with our magic only brings random results, showing us strange worlds on the other end: those filled with toxic gases or, if we can breathe the air, with blood-thirsty predators. Our ancestors found this world through desperation and sacrifice. They faced the bitter unknown over and over again, and many paid the price, suffering greatly for their daring with death, either rapid or slow. So many died that our race was nearly wiped out from the effort. Finally, they found a hospitable, beautiful land empty of other peoples or races. These tomes are what's left of what we know of those heroic dwarves and of the home we came from." He motioned to the books surrounding them. "If it was so easy, do you not think we would have opened up a splinter and just gone where we wished?"

"That's terrifying. Why did your people—" Iva said.

"Dwarves. We are dwarves, not people." He nearly spat the last words.

"Why did dwarves come here? And once here, why did your ancestors agree to close off the splinters to their homeland?" Iva asked.

"There was something wrong with the Dwarven homeland. I don't know what exactly," said the archmage, unhappy at the last admission. "Their words in our records are less than clear, except to say leaving was necessary and forced upon our ancestors. Going back will never be an option for the dwarves." He let his head hang for a second and then looked back out the window.

Portia placed her hands on the windowsill next to him and took in the view. His eyes flickered to her and back to the view. Heat radiated from his body and warmed her where she was close to him. His breathing was ragged.

If the elves could close the splinters but not open them

again, why would they have closed all access to their own home world? The splinters had been closed after the elves came to these lands, at least as Professor Aelric had taught her. They had been closed for many ages until the humans came.

The creature leapt to the archmage's shoulder and curled around his neck. Its tail twitched as it chittered in his ear.

Iva shuffled behind them, and when neither Portia nor the archmage moved to make room for her, she went to another window to the left, one that shared part of the view of the Dwarven city.

Though it felt like Iva and Portia had only been led along a horizontal corridor from their rooms within the palace, the view from the window was many stories up and overlooked roof after roof of Dwarven dwellings below. Despite being underground, there were creatures flying through the open spaces. The city stretched into the distance.

"I'm sorry. Is that why the elves came here too?" Portia asked softly. "Was their home in danger?"

The archmage snorted. "Elves. You know them better than I. Why didn't you ask them?"

Why hadn't she asked them?

Because they had only told her they alone healed splinters. There had been little time to ask questions while she had been with the elves. She'd been too busy learning the magic to save her people—the magic to close the splinters. The elves had never said it wasn't permanent. Indeed, Lord Fife had drilled her over and over to make the closure as perfect as possible, telling her that it would be sealed forever. Now, not only was the spell not going to endure forever, but there may be reasons to want the splinters open again.

Had Lord Fife intentionally lied to her, or did he not know? Or was this archmage—who had already tried to kill her—lying to her? Suddenly, her eyelids felt unbearably heavy. More sleep would help her decipher all this.

"I don't understand why you can't open them to the same place," Portia said.

Even to her own ears, her voice sounded like a petulant child's. Pursing her lips, she decided to stop asking questions until she could control her tone. Or at least get some sleep.

"Portia is amazing. I bet she could do it," Iva said.

Portia glared at her, but Iva steadfastly looked out the window, biting her nails and then leaning forward to look directly down the side of the tower they were in.

The archmage snorted. "No one can."

"You're wrong. Let her try. I bet *she* can." Iva gave the archmage a smirk while sitting on the windowsill and then leaned out to look down at the houses below. Portia's feet tingled looking at her resting in such a precarious position. She wanted to yank Iva away from the edge. This place was old. Stones fell occasionally from the cavern roofs. The sill itself might crumble away.

"No!" His response was so forceful that Iva recoiled, nearly falling out the window. She dropped down from the edge and into the room, blessedly. Her arms shook visibly.

Rage filled Portia at seeing Iva's fright.

"Why not let me try?" Portia whirled to face the archmage. She was so close, she had to tilt her head up to face him. The creature stared at her from high atop his neck.

He looked down his aquiline nose at her.

"What do you have to lose?" Portia asked, forcing her voice level. "It is located close by, yes? Closer than across the ocean or deep in the lands of other kingdoms. And if I fail, then only a day or so is lost. We can then travel—"

"We." Derision dripped off his voice.

"We," Portia said firmly, "can go to another splinter—one that is open—and retrieve your citizens and ours. If there are more than two splinters, as you say there are, then surely others will be open. I'm the only human who can close them, and the elves are still in their lands. They will not have closed those far from them."

The elves had been in their land of Rocabarra when she had gone on her quest to close the splinter at the Well of Tears. Portia thought she'd only been gone for a few weeks, but even so, armies took time to move, and the elves were not inclined to risk their lives to protect the humans who lived outside their long Eternal Wall. It had taken all of her hard-won political capital within the Elven kingdom to secure even the promise of refuge for the humans who were fleeing their homes in the face of the Dragonoid invasion. The Elven king had risked mutiny of his own people to allow humans within the enormous walls of the Moss Gate, walls that had been constructed to protect the elves from those very humans an age before.

Many of the long-lived elves had not forgotten the time when elves had lived in all the kingdoms of the land, save only those held by the dwarves, only to be driven out by humans. Most of them would never forgive it.

He stared, his eyes burning into her own. Portia's stomach flipped. Suddenly, she felt small. A faint chittering echoed through the room. Jutting her chin, she drew up tall, much taller than she felt.

"Or are you afraid of a human girl who can do what the archmage of the dwarves cannot?" Portia taunted.

The archmage glared at her.

A sticky trail of sweat ran down her back.

"Archmage Vermeil, sir," a tentative voice called from the open doorway.

"What," said the archmage, his voice a growl. His eyes didn't leave Portia's.

"Queen Morgani calls for you, sir, Archmage."

A young dwarf page stood half in the doorway, half hiding behind the frame to address Archmage Vermeil.

"For what matter?" asked the archmage.

The page trembled but finally managed a reply. "It's about the borders. About sealing them, Archmage."

"Now?" Portia asked, alarm in her voice.

"I TOLD you to stay back. The queen has not summoned you," said Archmage Vermeil. He stomped along the tunnel, following the page, in turn closely trailed by Iva and Portia.

"I don't care. We don't consent to being trapped within this kingdom," said Portia, determination in her voice.

"You didn't care about consent when you sealed our splinter."

"Your people were dying," Portia said.

"You asked no one before making such a change in our land. Not one dwarf."

"Okay then, we were going to die. I call the right to protect ourselves, Iva and I."

"You think you have rights in the Dwarven lands?" He hit the wall of the cavern and turned to glare at her.

She stumbled, not knowing what to say to that and not expecting him to stop so suddenly. He stared for a second more then turned and quickened after the page, who had not paused. Iva touched her arm gently. Portia shook her off and continued on after the archmage with Iva following.

They were guests in this land, far from the protections of her own queen and her kin at the Academy. Portia knew little of the dwarves except for what Professor Aelric mentioned in class. The dwarves had once had all of the kingdoms to themselves, only to be driven out by the elves. She had not grown up as a noble with tutors teaching her all the histories from a young age. Nor had she been blessed much in the way of books.

Or food.

Despite the archmage's anger, he had not turned and blasted them nor used any other magic to keep them from following. Portia jutted out her chin as she walked behind him, even as her heart pounded. He would not stop her from following him, at least not without a fight.

Still, she would've felt better if that little two-hand high fur ball that defended her and Iva had come with.

"What was that animal in your room?" Portia asked, refusing to be silenced by his ill temper.

"None of your business," retorted the archmage.

"It seemed to like me better than it liked you," said Portia.

Iva shook her head at Portia. Portia looked away and would not glance at her again.

"Why does it hate you so much?" Portia said, taunting him and determined to not be ignored.

Even the page turned around at this provocation from Portia, his eyes wide. The archmage growled at him. The page quickly turned back to the direction they were walking and moved forward faster.

"It doesn't hate me. It just didn't want me... wasting my time on someone like you." The archmage sped up his pace, nearly overtaking the page in his effort to get away from Portia.

"It had a vicious way of showing it cared," Portia said.

At that, the archmage stopped walking and whirled to face Portia. "Enough!" His voice reverberated down the stone walls.

"Just don't understand why we can't work together. Why won't you at least try? And why is it so awful that I want to speak to the queen before we are trapped here forever?"

Iva exhaled. "Portia."

He looked her up and down. Portia sensed, rather than saw, Iva trembling next to her. She felt bad for making her friend so uncomfortable, but she couldn't back down. There was something they could fix here, but more importantly, they needed to get out of the Dwarven kingdom and back to Haulstatt, and soon, if the dwarves were planning on closing the border.

He pursed his lips then turned again and walked away from her.

"The queen will decide," he called out.

THE QUEEN SAT in her throne just as she had when Portia had last seen her. Had she been seated in the high-backed chair in the throne room this entire time consulting with her advisors? It had been hours.

Archmage Vermeil was announced by the chamberlain. He entered and bowed. The chamberlain turned to Portia and Iva. He raised one eyebrow and then turned to the room and announced them in turn.

The queen looked up from greeting Archmage Vermeil. "You were not summoned," she stated.

Portia shook her head and then curtsied awkwardly. "No, Your Majesty. But we had heard the borders were to be closed and..."

The queen looked sharply at Portia and then her eyes drifted slowly to the page standing by the entryway throne room. The page tucked his chin to his chest and folded his shoulders forward as he shrank under his queen's gaze.

The queen returned her eyes to Portia. "This concerns you?"

"Yes, Your Majesty."

"Do you fear we will not protect you? Abandonment is not the way of the dwarves."

Portia shook her head.

Iva pushed forward to stand next to Portia. "We need to return home."

"Your home is no more," said the queen, her voice kind despite the cruel reality she spoke of.

"Mine is still there. I need to return to fight for it," Portia said.

"Its end may be soon. We've received word that there are additional Dragonoid forces in Haulstatt. Already Lusatiana has fallen. These lands," the queen gestured around the chamber, "have been spared further direct attack only by the hidden nature of our kingdom. If Haulstatt falls, one more access route to our country will be available to the invaders."

One of the queen's advisors stepped forward, alarm on his face at the mention of another access route into the dwarven kingdom. She silenced him with the raising of her fingertips. He worked his mouth to speak then looked down and stepped back again.

"We will protect you," said the queen. "You will be safe here."

"As much gratitude as I feel for that," said Portia. "I can't abandon my friends."

"You cannot help them," the archmage said.

Portia's hairs bristled at his words. She thrust her chin up, refusing to look at him. "I can try."

"We have an army of mages," pain flickered in his eyes,

"and war machines. We have tried. Our people have died for our efforts. You are but a single girl. Nothing but death awaits you."

"I can try," Portia repeated, her words low and firm.

He huffed.

She turned her attention back to the queen.

"If there are more invaders, there must be more splinters to their world. I closed the one at the Well of Tears a moon ago or more. I closed the one here. I, a single girl. Your warriors witnessed it," said Portia, emphasizing the last words for Archmage Vermeil and the whole court to hear.

Archmage Vermeil sucked in his breath.

Before he spoke again, Portia pushed on. "They must be coming from somewhere."

"You know there are more for sure?" the queen asked.

"Yes," Portia said, just as Archmage Vermeil said, "No."

The queen tilted her head questioningly.

The archmage looked at his feet and then up again, speaking in a low voice. "It is possible there are more. There may be many more." His face soured at the admission.

"All the more reason to close our borders. We cannot leave any access open," the queen said.

The court attendants watching the exchange murmured their agreement. The queen raised one hand, about to make a pronouncement. Portia stepped forward to stop her.

"If I can go and close the splinters, we will cut off the invaders' access to all our lands. If we ally with each other now, before even more arrive, we could defeat those left on our world," said Portia. "And even if we cannot get through an existing splinter, we could open a splinter again and return them to their own world, as well as find more of our own peoples and rescue them."

Possibly. Portia forced her head to remain up. The queen could not know of her reservations. Portia had more confidence in her ability to close a splinter than open one to a specific place, especially after what Archmage Vermeil had said, but as long as the dwarves had the magic to open splinters at all, there was the chance of finding that world again.

The smallest of chances was still a chance.

The queen looked to Archmage Vermeil. He shook his head almost imperceptibly.

"You don't know, not for sure," Portia insisted, whirling on the archmage. "You had not known about my healing magic for splinters, at least not cast by a human. That alone is proof you don't know everything."

"No, not by a human. Elves yes, human no," the queen said. "We'd sent word to the elves but have heard nothing in response."

Portia cocked her head. The elves had said they had heard nothing from the dwarves.

Turning to the archmage, Portia held out her hands in entreaty. "I will teach you everything I know. I'm not as skilled as you are in many things—"

Iva snorted.

Portia flicked her hand at Iva to silence her but didn't take her eyes from the archmage. "But I do have the needed magical knowledge from the elves and the ability to use it. I've proven that before the eyes of your people. Let me do what I can. Let me show you all I can." Much good as it would do him.

Portia was the only human capable of doing the splinter closing magic. Dwarves might be able to, in some measure, but after ages of sharing this world with elves and still not fully having the magic, it was most likely because they were not capable of it, no matter how much they tried.

She had not known the dwarves could open splinters, much as the elves had but in different ways. This was magic she had to learn how to do. Her abilities were rare for a human. The same abilities might extend to Dwarven magic. It was imperative to find out. It might save her people.

The archmage considered Portia as the attendants around them murmured. Her offer held some interest for them. Finally, he narrowed his eyes, took in a deep breath, and turned to the queen, who had been waiting patiently for his response while watching him closely.

She nodded for him to speak.

"It is true," said the archmage. "The closure of the two splinters we know of might not be the end of it. It is possible there are more, probably so if the invaders' numbers are still increasing. We might succeed in sending a party into another open splinter, especially if our forbearers blessed us with a splinter gate the monsters have not discovered yet." A strange expression crossed his face, a lightening of the lines on his face. "We might yet retrieve our people." He did not look at Portia, his eyes only for his queen.

The queen's face softened as well.

"Even if they know about all the remaining splinters, we

could still do it," Iva piped up. "We have Portia and your warriors."

Portia could not wait until she got Iva alone after this. They were going to have a talk about court protocol and working together as a team. In the meantime, Portia clenched her fists and breathed in deeply, asking for patience. It took all her will to not kick Iva to quiet her.

Blessedly, Iva said nothing further. Portia held her breath while the queen thought.

"Our duty is to protect the people of this kingdom," the queen said softly. Her gaze dropped to some far distant point behind Portia. No one spoke as she thought.

Portia shifted on her feet and forced herself to stand still, the soles of her feet throbbing and her head light from exhaustion. If they were indeed allowed to leave, she hoped for just an hour, at least, of sleep before they must set off again.

The queen's gaze returned to Vermeil. "There is wisdom in your thinking. We would not be protecting our people by abandoning them so easily. The closure of the splinter within our walls has bought us some time. Let us use it."

The queen rose from the throne, straightening slowly. Suddenly, she looked old and fragile. "You will share the magic you know of the splinters, both of you, with each other. It is in the best interest of our peoples today. We will not lose more to ancient wounds." She looked more closely at the three of them standing at the base of her throne. "Start tomorrow. You need rest first." She left the room, followed closely by her attendants.

The rest of the court filtered out, many walking unnecessarily close to Portia and Iva, craning their necks to get a better look at the two humans in their midst. Their proximity made clear how thick and solidly they were built. Portia looked down at her own slender arm, a twig in comparison to the strongly muscled limbs of the dwarves.

Finally, they were alone in the chamber except for a few servants and a furious, glaring Archmage Vermeil.

7

Commander Kerat had woken them the next morning—late, Portia suspected, though it was impossible to tell for sure so deep underground without a sun above. He had waited patiently while they roused in their rooms and dressed, eating from the breakfast trays that had been brought for them.

Portia had looked for more of the mushroom loaf on the tray resting on the floor near her bed, but there was only a thick white gruel and a dish of dried berries and nuts. Grimacing, she poured the nuts and fruit on top of the white mush and forced herself to eat it. They had run out of their own supplies while back in the Dragonoid world. Thinking would be even more difficult on an empty stomach, fighting more so still. Food was not something to be turned down. She scrunched her nose as she chewed and swallowed the thick paste with difficulty. A pot of steaming black liquid rested on the tray along with an empty cup. Portia poured some brew into the cup and sipped. It was bitter but bracing. She poured, filled the cup, and then blew on it to cool it so she could drink and wash down the mash.

To her pleasure, her green tunic and breeches had been returned to her, freshly washed and pressed, stacked in a neat pile next to her bed. Even her boots had been brushed and cleaned. It worried her a little that she had heard nothing in her sleep when the dwarves had entered her room to return the clothes. She told herself they were exceptionally quiet and that if it had been anyone else, she would have woken immediately.

Even so, she decided to talk to Iva about sleeping in shifts from now on. Until she knew more about the dwarves, and where they stood in relation to the humans, it was wise to be cautious.

She laid her baldric across her chest and pulled her blade to check for signs of dampness. It shone in the dim light. Kerat peeked in from the hallway with interest at the flash of the coppery metal blade within her room but politely turned away when she faced him.

The requested caltrops and lockpicks had not been brought. It had only been a day since she had requested them from the royal smith, so that was not entirely surprising. Even so, she felt vulnerable and underprepared with only her blade and a bag that contained just half a length of rope and some crumbs littering the bottom. Putting on the bag, she made sure the strap did not impede her drawing the blade.

Exiting her room, she nodded at Kerat that she was ready.

The sleep had been more than welcome, but still, Portia

could have used more. Her mind was foggy, even after the black drink. Her back ached with stiffness from laying hours in the bed. She stretched and twisted as they waited for Iva, who was still in her room getting ready.

Iva emerged, beaming in her own freshly laundered clothes. "Good morning, sunshines."

Kerat bowed while Portia grunted. Iva nearly bounced with alertness as she fell in beside Portia as they followed Kerat through the twisting passageways of the Dwarven kingdom. Portia avoided looking at Iva. She needed to wake up more before she could deal with such perkiness.

———

"I DON'T KNOW why you are always so angry," said Iva.

Archmage Vermeil stood with a squad of dwarf warriors, scowling as Iva, Portia, and Commander Kerat joined them.

"We already settled yesterday that you two know nothing," the archmage said, acid in his tone.

Portia crossed her arms. "Not everything is in your books. Don't you ever get tired of being so cranky?"

The warriors around the archmage stiffened, but he didn't change his stance. "Never," he said with a growl, but Portia thought the briefest of smiles flitted across his face. She shook herself. She must have been mistaken.

Iva walked past Portia, briefly gracing the archmage with a bow. She was too interested in the legion of warriors around him. They wore complex but beautiful uniforms. Unlike the garments worn in battle yesterday, these were not covered with the filth of war—dirt, sweat, and blood—but clean and pressed. Embroidery ran along all the hems in intricate patterns of leaves, flowers, and winding vines. The weave was so fine, Portia longed to take a closer look, but she didn't want to offend the sturdy, unsmiling warriors wearing them. From afar, the garments appeared finer than many of the robes the merchants in Coverack had worn. Gleaming blades hung from mounts on their belts, beautiful and ready, the shine of their sharp edges visible even from where she stood. Startled, she realized there were equal numbers of men and women warriors. The women appeared just as strong as the men.

The legion looked fearsome.

And rich.

"Why all the warriors?" Portia asked.

"Splinter magic can be dangerous, mostly because of what, or who, might be on the other side. We risk it, by the wisdom of our queen, for the good of our country, but must take steps to protect ourselves while doing so," said the archmage.

Kerat gave Portia a brief nod of agreement. She exhaled at the lack of hostility from Kerat, a sharp contrast to Archmage Vermeil's countenance, and forced her shoulders to relax. She had only known the dwarf commander a brief time but trusted him enough to relax if he thought nothing was ill, even in the face of the archmage's prickliness.

"So where to?" Portia asked. "I'm anxious to learn how to open the splinters."

"I think it would be safest if you taught me how to close them first," Archmage Vermeil said. "What if you opened one and got hurt in the process? We have our ways of blocking them off, but they are time-consuming and require a skilled mage. We have to be prepared in case you cannot close what you open."

Portia raised one eyebrow at his comment. They would see just how much skill was needed to do her magic. Suddenly, the day sounded like a bit more fun. Nodding, she said agreeably, "As you wish."

The archmage narrowed his eyes at Portia. She smiled back blandly.

"There is a secured zone outside the main commune. We will go there," he said, watching her closely for a reaction. There was none except for a slight tilt of her head.

They walked two candlemarks march past the last residential stone building within the main caverns, following caverns that grew and shrank and crisscrossed each other. There were no markings on the walls that Portia could see, but the archmage and the warriors did not hesitate, walking briskly and turning in unison at the different junctures.

Finally, a single path lay before them, sloped steeply downward. Portia's feet slid forward within her boots. The high dome of the ceiling above them faded into darkness. She imagined the weight of the ground creaking and moaning above her, shifting until it was free to crush the cave they were in and land upon her. Portia shook her head to clear the horrible vision.

Gradually, the glowing moss growing on the walls that had lit their way thinned and then disappeared altogether, leaving the route ahead inky black. Kerat raised a hand to signal a halt. The soldiers lit torches and then the group continued onwards, shadows from the flames flickering and dancing on the walls. The light did not reach the top of the passageway. The skin on the back of Portia's neck crawled. Anything could be up there and they would not know.

After another two candlemarks of quiet marching, the group stopped. Archmage Vermeil stood at the head of the group in front of an enormous wall. The passageway ended there. Before Portia could demand to know what was going on, he raised his hands and murmured an incantation, following it up with the strike of a two-pronged fork on the wall that vibrated and hummed. The pitch coming off the vibrating metal fork was so high it felt like knives in Portia's ears. She clamped her hands over her ears, trying to keep the sound out, but it was futile. The agony was so great, she felt herself doubling over. Running would have been a better reaction, for at least it would have allowed her to get away from the whine echoing through the cavern and down the passageway.

Blessedly, the sound stopped just as Portia thought she could not take it any longer. Turning towards Archmage Vermeil, she gasped. The wall behind him was gone. The passageway continued onwards into a large cavern dotted with glowing moss and large lumps of stone dotted around it.

"Is something amiss?" he asked Portia, his eyebrows pinched together over his dark eyes.

"That noise. I couldn't bear it," said Portia. She rubbed her ears, but it did nothing to help the stinging pain deep within them. His voice sounded fuzzy, as if he was talking from far away. She wiggled her ears, pulling down on the earlobes, and then shook her head. He spoke again, but he sounded just the same odd way.

"What noise?" he asked.

The warriors and even Iva beside her looked at her with puzzled expressions. She stared back at them.

"Did no one else hear that? From that thing," she said, pointing to the metal fork in Archmage Vermeil's hand.

They shook their heads slowly at her.

Portia turned away. The pain combined with their puzzled reactions threatened to overwhelm her. She breathed in deeply. Now was not the time to allow herself to be upset. The noise was gone. Everything would be all right.

"Let us enter. Time is short. We will deal with this later," said Archmage Vermeil, a curious look on his face.

They filed into the room, none venturing too far into the vast, dimly lit space, while the archmage turned back to the opening where there had once been a wall. He struck the metal fork against the stone wall of the cavern and the noise instantly resumed.

This time, the pain in Portia's ears was even worse. The vibrations bounced off the wall and came back to her with both the main excruciating pitch and echoes slightly modified in tone by their travels around the room.

"Stop," Portia yelled.

She ran forward to grab the fork from Archmage Vermeil's hands, but two dwarf warriors stopped her, grabbing her arms and holding her in place, despite her throwing her whole body against them. They wouldn't even allow her to put her hands over her ears. She thrashed in agony and frustration, tears running down her face as the noise continued.

The archmage's back was to her as he faced the wall. He muttered something she couldn't hear and waved once again at the opening, which was soon filled with stone that shimmered translucently and then gradually became opaque. When it looked solid, the archmage made one final motion, and the noise stopped.

They were sealed inside the room.

The two dwarves holding Portia relaxed their grip as she stopped thrashing with the ending of the noise. Iva looked around the room, her buoyant expression from that morning gone and replaced with one tinged with fear.

When the dwarves finally released Portia, she ran forward to the stone filling what had once been the entrance. She pounded on it, cutting her hand and leaving a smear of blood. It was solid. Whirling around, she faced Archmage Vermeil.

"Why are we sealed in here?" Portia demanded.

"To protect the rest of the kingdom," the archmage said, his tone puzzled. "If we open a splinter that is noxious or filled with hostile creatures, or is otherwise ill-suited and dangerous, we could destroy our own lands if we have no way of shutting it off again. Yes, you can heal splinters, at least I have been so told, and I know of a way to seal them—encasing them in stone—but neither you nor I could do anything if we are injured or killed. It is my responsibility, no, it is *our* responsibility," he motioned to the dwarves and commander Kerat, "to prevent such a thing from happening. We will share this magic with you only under safe conditions, and only after you have shown us your ability to heal a splinter."

Portia thrust out her lower lip. The precautions made sense, little as she liked them.

"Wait a minute," Iva said, her hands on her hips. "If you are so careful, how did the Dragonoids get into your land?"

Portia cocked her head, looking at Archmage Vermeil, waiting for his answer. "That is a good question."

"That was a misfortunate occurrence," said Archmage Vermeil while he stared at Portia, his hands twitching. "The splinter that had originally been there was tiny and had once been touched by elves long ago, best I can tell from our records. It had been sealed in stone for good measure since it was so close to the palace. But something happened when the other splinters opened. Just as we had heard word of the attack on Rodaine, the stone around the local splinter shimmered and exploded. A gigantic new splinter arose in the same spot. I think it has something to do with the way the elves sealed it, but I cannot prove it for sure." His hands clenched tightly. Portia wondered if he thought he could squeeze the secrets of the elf magic from her.

Rodaine was the capital of Lusatiana, the human kingdom to the south of Portia's own land of Haulstatt. She had witnessed part of that attack, alongside Mark, her childhood companion. Her stomach clenched at the thought of him. She had last seen Mark while they were being attacked by the Dragonoids outside the Well of Tears. She did not know if he lived or died. That was something she should have been responsible for. He never would have been on that ship if it wasn't for her.

"So, that splinter behaved differently?" Portia asked.

"Yes. From what we learned, it opens to the same world as the beings who attacked Rodaine. Nothing in our records speak of that world. If a splinter had opened to it before, we would have known." Archmage Vermeil scowled.

"The splinters can change, or be changed by someone else, as to where they open?" Portia asked.

"So it seems."

Portia's stomach flip-flopped. It was both confusing and scary. The elves had never said anything of this to her. Was it possible they did not know?

"So, I hope you can understand why we take such precautions," Commander Kerat said softly at her elbow. Portia nodded.

"I suppose we wouldn't have come all this way just so you could kill us," Iva said, looking around the cavern then walking towards the nearest mound of stone. She definitely reminded Portia of someone.

"No, but doing it here means our kingdom would have less to clean up," Archmage Vermeil said dryly. He shrugged when Iva turned to glare at him and then turned slowly away again, weighing whether he was being serious or jesting.

He faced Portia. "What happened to you when I used the magic to open the door?" His question seemed earnest.

"The noise that came from that thing, fork, whatever that is that you were using, felt like knives going into my ears. I couldn't stand it. I wanted nothing more than to make you stop." The two dwarves who had been holding her nodded. She was sure she had left a few bruises on them for their efforts.

"Strange. I did not hear a thing. I've never heard a thing. Honestly, when learning that magic, I wondered what the device was for." The last was spoken almost to himself. After a moment, he shook himself. "The time is short. We must get to work." He motioned around the cavern. "There are many splinters encased in stone here. Several go to empty worlds we have no use for. We could use those for you to show us how to heal them. To show me."

"Or you could show me how to open a splinter, and then I could show you how to close it," Portia countered.

The two faced off. Only the sound of Iva's steps around the cavern sounded.

The archmage widened his stance and crossed his arms while staring at Portia. The soldiers fanned out around him. Even Kerat stood with them, not making eye contact with Portia. Iva paused her inspection of the cavern and exchanged a glance with Portia.

"It seems we are outnumbered," said Portia dryly. "Although wasn't it your queen's express order for us to work together?"

Archmage Vermeil's face flinched at the word "queen." The soldiers shuffled uneasily.

"Perhaps, my most powerful mages, we can find a back-and-forth that would work," Kerat suggested. "Something not too dangerous for us poor soldiers without any magic at all."

Archmage Vermeil and Portia eyed each other. Each gave the other a barely perceptible nod.

Walking to the mound where Iva was standing, Archmage Vermeil held the metal fork over it and then turned to Portia. "Are you ready?"

Portia covered her ears then nodded.

Turning back to the mound, the archmage struck it with the fork and mumbled words. He waved his free hand over it, seeming to wipe away the rock. Iva stepped back as the air shimmered and sparkled where it had seemingly been solid stone just a second before. Portia hummed to herself, trying to drown out the sound of the fork. It was easier this time, perhaps because not as much magic was being used on the smaller stone pile.

Finally, the spell was done. A tiny oval hung in the air where the pile had been. It flickered between silver and black, evading direct gaze, as if it was not really there, or at least not there all the time. A few flecks of sand flew out of the oval and landed on the cavern floor. A second later, a handful of sand fell, landing in a small pile and sending tiny stones rolling away.

Portia looked to Archmage Vermeil questioningly.

"As far as we know, it only opens to lands of sand. There has never been anything else seen there. It is one of the oldest splinters. Our mages use it to practice encasement. It is the first one I learned to use." A dark look crossed his face. He had been taught by his father, the archmage, before him. The father who was now trapped in the Dragonoid world.

Portia stepped towards the splinter. She had never had

the luxury of examining one up close. The two she'd seen had been under war conditions—fending off arrows and blows while also trying to close the splinter itself.

This one looked so harmless. It was small, the size of a maiden's wall mirror. A person would have to crawl to get through it, it being far too small to allow standing or walking. It would be impossible for a Dragonoid to pass through, much less one of their ships or war machines.

Portia reached out one hand and looked questioningly at the archmage. He nodded.

She reached her fingers forward another step and then stopped. Suddenly, she pulled her blade from its sheath at her waist. The dwarf warriors jumped back, startled, pulling their own weapons as they fell into defensive stances around her. She stood motionless until they calmed. Once all was still in the cavern, she extended the blade until the tip of it went into the splinter, disappearing into the shimmery silver air.

Nothing happened.

Portia waved the unseen tip of the blade around. A few more grains of sand fell into the room. Withdrawing the weapon, the air around it shimmered as heat came off it. She gently placed the flat of the blade on her palm. It was as hot as if it had been lying in the sun for an hour.

The archmage raised both eyebrows at Portia. She stood taller, leaving her defensive stance. She pushed her fingers through the shimmering surface to the other side. Warmth enveloped them. The sting of sand hitting her fingers, and then grains coming out of the splinter and landing in her arms and body startled her. She jumped back.

"There is wind there also," the archmage explained.

"What does it look like?" Portia asked.

"See for yourself." A tiny smile graced his face. It made her wary.

She eyed the shimmering oval. Placing her head inside of it suddenly did not seem like the wisest move, but there was no other way to know. Unless... She looked around, but none of the warriors had a seeing glass on them.

"Are you afraid?" Archmage Vermeil questioned.

Iva joined her, staring at the oval.

"Why don't you look?" Portia pointedly asked the archmage

"I have."

Portia glanced at Commander Kerat's face. It was calm and smooth. Making a decision, she stepped forward again to the splinter and this time thrust her face into it.

Sweat immediately popped out on her forehead. The heat was so intense, her cheeks swelled beneath it. Seeing was difficult, for she had to squint against all the flying sand. What she did see was a haze of red skies, dune after dune of red sand, and nothing else. An unpleasant whine caught her already sore ears. What was making that noise on the far side? The wind?

Pulling her head back out of the splinter, she gulped in the cool air of the cavern gratefully. The horrible noise abated.

"At least the air is breathable," said Archmage Vermeil.

Something she should have checked first, Portia realized abashedly. She turned from the archmage so he would not see her expression of chagrin.

She stuck her head back in to be sure. The noise was there. It made the hairs on the back of her neck crawl. Pulling her head back out, she wiped the sweat from her forehead.

"So, you want me to show you how to heal this." Portia affected a nonchalance she did not feel.

"If you are able," said Archmage Vermeil.

"That depends entirely on you," said Portia, her expression making her doubts clear.

"I'm hungry," said Iva.

Archmage Vermeil and Portia turned to stare at her, dumbfounded.

"What? We were walking forever. Now you two are doing whatever this is. Can you hurry up so we can go back and have lunch?" Iva put her hands on her hips and stared at them. As if on cue, her stomach rumbled.

A snicker from one of the soldiers echoed through the room. Vermeil whirled to see who it was, but only sober faces met his stare.

Commander Kerat stepped forward. "As you said, Archmage Vermeil, our time is limited," he said with a conciliatory tone.

"I did say that," the archmage admitted.

Ignoring Iva's glare, Portia motioned to the splinter. "This should be easy. It is music-based." She sang a portion of the spell to him. "Sing it back to me."

He tried, but half the notes were missing.

Portia sang it again to him.

Again, his response was incomplete.

"You're missing much of the song. Sing it all," Portia said.

"I am." He meant it.

Oh dear.

To buy some time to think, Portia pulled the rope from her bag. Unraveling a strand from it, she placed the pieces on the ground and sang the healing magic to it. The rope zipped back together again. Re-extracting the strand, she laid the pieces back on the ground and motioned for the archmage to try.

He sang the same incomplete spell. The strand wiggled a bit and then flopped over and would not move again. The main portion of rope did not budge.

"You aren't singing everything," Portia explained.

"I am singing everything I hear."

Nods from the dwarves surrounding them, and even from Iva, backed him up. They had not heard anything different from what he had sung.

Portia tapped a finger to her lower lip, considered the splinter and those around her before regarding the archmage again. "What did you hear when you looked inside the world?" asked Portia.

"Nothing. Wind, if that," he said, puzzled.

"No, there's a tune there. Maybe not music... A more horrible discordant sound. Do you really hear nothing?" Portia asked.

Iva strode to the splinter and stuck her face in before Portia could stop her. She withdrew her head a second later, her face red from the heat, and shrugged her shoulders. "I hear nothing."

Portia was the only one who heard the discordant music.

A flash of the battle from the day before came back to her. There had also been a horrible noise when they had entered the world through the splinter from the Dragonoid lands.

She turned to face Commander Kerat. "What about yesterday? Did you hear anything around the splinter during the battle? A screeching sound or something like a really bad bard?"

He shook his head no. A few of the soldiers who had also been present at the battle shook their heads as well.

Portia tried to remember what the tune had sounded like yesterday. Beyond the overwhelming sense of discord, there had been a pattern to it. She hummed to herself, trying to reconstruct it. One phrase stood out. It sounded like what she'd heard yesterday, at least part of it. Using more power, she sang the phrase to the small splinter in front of her. The oval itself shimmered, briefly grew bright, and emitted a flash of blue light before again fading back to the silvery blackness. The dwarves around her gasped.

"What did you do?" cried Archmage Vermeil.

"I don't know," admitted Portia. "That's what the splinter sounded like to me yesterday."

The oval swirled in the center of them. It appeared different from how it was before the blue light flashed.

Taking a deep breath, Portia stepped forward and then thrust her face into it, this time taking care to not inhale.

The red sands were gone, the blazing hot air replaced by a more temperate but oddly green atmosphere. Fields of what looked like plants made of thin strands waved in the air. The splinter opened to a different place than it had before. She breathed in without thinking but stopped when the air stung her throat and brought tears to her eyes. Choking, Portia pulled her head out of the splinter and gasped in the cool air of the cavern. She bent over, coughing and sucking in air. After a moment, she straightened and then motioned for Archmage Vermeil to look.

He didn't move. Raising one eyebrow, he looked around at the rest of the dwarves, making sure they were close enough to defend him.

"It looks safe. Just don't breathe in," Portia said, still coughing.

Cautiously, Archmage Vermeil stepped to the portal and gingerly pushed his head through the opening. After a few seconds, he pulled it out again, fear and amazement battling on his face. "What have you done? That splinter went to the sand world for as long as we have records."

"Have the elves ever looked into this splinter? Have they touched it?" asked Portia.

He shook his head. "The elves have only been in this land once, long ago during their civil war when we were shutting off the splinters to their world. The only splinter they have closed in the Dwarven lands was the one they, then the humans, and finally Dragonoids came through. The one you closed yesterday. All our records say that is so. We did not want them touching any others once we realized the elves changing them resulted in linking them to other splinters. These tiny ones," he motioned to the others within the cavern, "we were able to control by encasing in stone. Besides, we were at war at the time, and many of our kind wanted the elves dead. It was a feat of our great General Murat to smuggle those elves into our lands to close the splinter against others of their own kind."

Iva stared back and forth at both of them and then stuck her own face into the splinter and pulled it out again. "That is not the Dragonoid's world."

Portia shook her head. It wasn't the hot stony world she had been on when she had been stuck in the Dragonoid world. It was not their home. Or at least not that home.

"It looked more like the Dragonoid world before," said Portia, frustration pulling her shoulders tight.

"That's great. Just great." Iva kicked the dirt in the cavern and paced rapidly. "But all is not lost. Don't you see, you can move the splinters. If you can move the splinters, you can find the Dragonoid world again."

Portia's eyes met Archmage Vermeil's. "True," she said slowly.

"Maybe you just need to hear that weird tune thing that sounds just like the noise from the Dragonoid splinter and reproduce it to steer the splinter. I wish I could hear it." Iva slapped one fist into the palm of the other hand. "This is all coming down to you."

"I could steer an existing splinter to their world. Or, better yet, open a new splinter to the Dragonoid world in a more convenient place for our armies than deep in the bowels of the Dwarven Kingdom," said Portia.

Archmage Vermeil nodded.

"I DON'T UNDERSTAND how your magic is vibration-based if you can't hear them," Portia said. They had been in the cavern for what seemed half a day. A third of the dwarf soldiers were sitting down with their backs against the wall, resting, while the others stood guard in case anything came out of the splinters the mages were creating. Archmage Vermeil had explained the spell he used to open a splinter, starting with one the dwarves had devised after the elf incursion—a less powerful spell, but also one less likely to form more than one splinter at a time.

Archmage Vermeil had pulled a series of small double-tined forks from a bag he carried with him, all slightly different sized and giving off different pitches. All of them hurt Portia's ears excruciatingly. He demonstrated the splinter creation spells, which relied on the tines to get the vibrations he used for the spells. Portia wondered if it was a similar technique to the vibrations the elves used in their singing. It was puzzling how the dwarves would come to use such a magic if they could not hear the tones themselves.

Portia grabbed the smallest of the forks and banged it on the wall, forcing herself to not cringe as the horrible noise reached her ears. On impulse she sang a brief ditty that merged with the sound of the tines, changing it ever so slightly and making it less painful to her ears. She then completed the splinter spell and opened a small splinter in front of her. Looking inside it, she saw a world teeming with small furry creatures in a blue field. She pulled her head back quickly before any of them spotted her.

Singing the healing song, she closed it up again.

Archmage Vermeil watched.

Portia turned to him. "Are you sure you don't want to try closing a splinter again?"

As easy as it now came to Portia, Archmage Vermeil had not been able to do any better in his attempts at doing a healing spell and closing a splinter than he had done in his initial attempt with the rope. He was utterly unable to do that type of magic.

"No. Not now. I am sure that, in time, we'll find a way with tools of some sort," he motioned to the forks scattered on the floor of the cavern, "to make the sounds needed instead of your singing, but that will not happen today. At least we now know it's possible. We'll figure out more when we have the time."

"If you want more time then you had better stop Dragonoids from pouring into all of our kingdoms," said Iva. She lay dramatically on the ground, holding her stomach. She had asked several times if they could leave to go eat and had finally given up when they no longer responded by even telling her "no."

"I'm sure if I heard the sound of the Dragonoids' splinter again and memorized it somehow, I could open another to their world. That way we could go back any time," Portia said. She wasn't entirely sure it was true, but it seemed reasonable and gave them hope.

Archmage Vermeil sighed. There was no other splinter to the Dragonoid lands within the Dwarven kingdom of Morgani.

"Let's go back," said Archmage Vermeil as he bent to pick

up the forks and place them back in his bag, keeping out only the one needed to remove the stone from the doorway. "You've kept your word to our queen, as have I. We need to report back."

A thought nagged at the edge of Portia's consciousness. "You said the elves only touched one splinter in the Dwarven lands. Was there more than one here to the human world?"

The archmage walked slowly towards the mass of rock filling the way they had entered the cavern.

When he did not respond to her question, Portia ran to block his path. "Is there? Is there another splinter in here that goes to a world of humans?"

His eyes flickered to the left before meeting hers briefly.

He nodded.

8

Portia sucked in her breath. Another land of humans. She looked around the cavern at the small piles of rocks scattered here and there encasing other splinters.

"It's in here, isn't it?" she asked, breathlessly.

"That's what the records say," Archmage Vermeil admitted. At Portia's triumphant expression, he stepped forward into her space, blocking her view of the cavern. "But that was ages ago. Who knows what is there now."

"Can you open it?"

He didn't answer.

"Can you open it? You know how to, don't you, without changing where the splinter goes to? Show me. Show me!" she demanded.

Iva looked up from her spot at the ground at Portia's yelling.

"That may be a poor idea," Commander Kerat said, joining their conversation.

"Why?" she asked. The dwarf commander looked down, uncomfortable.

Passages of the book Portia had read of the invasion came back to her—the bloodthirstiness of the author and their apparent glee in the death and destruction they had wrought. There was fear in the dwarf soldier's faces, much as they tried to hide it with the stoic expression of warriors.

"As you said, that was ages ago. Perhaps things are different now," Portia said quietly.

The archmage snorted. "Perhaps they are worse."

Portia crossed her arms. "We can form an alliance, humans and dwarves, just as the humans have formed one with the elves. We'll go back and help rescue your people and our own, and you will help us fight against these invaders and keep them out. We have to work together. But I want to know where our people came from. My people. Is that too much to ask?"

No one budged.

It was time to try a different tact.

"Are you afraid your warriors here will not be able to defend this kingdom against a few random humans we find if we open a splinter? Is that the issue?" At their wounded expressions, Portia almost felt bad—almost. "Why would humans even want an alliance with those so cowardly and weak?"

Archmage Vermeil shot her a hurt look. The soldiers bristled at Portia's words.

"We are not afraid," said Commander Kerat quietly.

Portia crossed her arms, scowling at the soldiers, refusing to back down. Most looked away.

"They do act afraid," Iva said quietly in Portia's ear, still loud enough for the others to hear. Portia forced herself to not move away from Iva's surprise proximity. She didn't want to give anyone the idea that she could be moved. Instead, she crossed her arms, and she and Iva stared at the archmage. The dwarves around them looked away.

Finally, Archmage Vermeil threw up his hands. "I will unblock the smallest splinter to that land for you to look. But you will not change the splinter in any way. You will not close it nor touch it with the elf magic—nor any other magic. Is that agreed?"

Portia nodded, afraid that if she spoke, he would change his mind again.

"Say it out loud," the archmage said, his tone adamant.

"I agree to those terms. I will not touch the splinter with magic," Portia said.

Accepting her words with a nod, Archmage Vermeil walked to a mound in the far end of the cavern. He struck a tine to the nearby rock wall and said the spell to clear the rock away from the small splinter. The dwarf warriors ran to surround the mound as the rock shimmered away. Not a single one sat against the wall at leisure. Their sleepy looks had been replaced with scowls and tense bodies.

Portia followed him, holding her hands over her ears to keep out the noise from the fork the archmage used. When he finished, she lowered her arms, noticing the way they trembled. She shook them out so no one else would notice and then stepped forward to see the splinter. It was long and low, much closer to the ground than any of the other ones had been. Sitting down, she scooted forward to look inside. She pressed her face forward into the land where humans had come from.

A fragrant breeze pulled her hair, throwing one lock of it in front of her eyes. Birds chirped. A yellow sun shone down on a land of cultivated fields stretching into the distance and ending in a sharp falloff overlooking a huge sea. Buildings clustered along the cliff's edge. She gasped. It was beautiful.

After a few moments of searching the land, the faintest of noises tickled in her ear, growing more and more insistent. It was so quiet that it reminded her of small insects buzzing by her ears, but a shake of her head did not dislodge anything. Slowly, the sound resolved into the strands of faint, discordant music. Pushing her head further into the splinter did not help her hear the music better, rather it only faded away. She only heard the sounds just at the splinter's edge.

Keeping her head close to the opening, Portia listened carefully. There was a pattern to the sounds. After a few moments, the rise and fall of notes repeated itself, as if the splinter was singing a song to itself. She was so deeply lost in concentration trying to memorize the sounds that she jumped up several inches when a hand touched her elbow outside the splinter. Pulling herself back into the room, her eyes met Iva's, who was staring at her in concern.

"What do you see?" asked Iva. "Do you see people?"

"No people, but buildings and land. It looks wonderful," Portia replied.

Iva took in Portia's words, blinking, then edged past Portia and placed her own head into the splinter to look.

"Enough!" Archmage Vermeil roared. "This was risk enough. We must go. There is a war going on."

Portia twisted her lips in distaste at his words but did not argue with him. Of all people, she was well aware there was a war going on.

He glanced down and then around, almost embarrassed at his outburst. For a moment, he looked like a child. Then Portia remembered his father was trapped in the Dragonoid world, along with his king, if either were alive at all. Thinking of Elyas, the closest person she'd ever had to a father, in such a situation would be excruciating. The sooner they got back, the sooner they could get to another splinter and see if they could rescue the others... If they could rescue his father and his king.

More so, they had to stop more invaders from pouring into the land.

And if she learned the unique music of the Dragonoid world from that open splinter, they could open another to it at a time of their choosing and use the new splinter to retrieve their people.

None of those things would happen while they were here in this cavern. They needed to move.

The dwarf soldiers pulled a protesting Iva from the splinter. Archmage Vermeil sealed it beneath a pile of stones. Minutes later, they were outside the cavern, its entrance once again hidden behind a stone wall, and making their way back to the Dwarven palace.

For a while, they marched on in silence, the only sounds

the crackling of burning pitch from the torches and the thumps of feet filling the narrow walls of the cavern passageways.

"Why did your father go into the other lands?" asked Portia. The archmage steadfastly did not look at her, stepping forward in the dim passageway.

Portia frowned. "I apologize... The archmage before you and the king. Why would they enter such dangerous lands when they could have just closed the splinter again?"

He flexed his jaw.

No one else in the group was speaking. Portia sensed more than saw all of them listening to her questions. Even Iva, still dramatically clutching her stomach, hung back a bit to hear if he would answer.

Portia inhaled to try for a third time when he cleared his throat to speak.

"At first," he said, "we had no idea how aggressive they were. When the splinter first opened up, we were entranced by the bright land full of sun and warmth, something in short supply down here. The council was fighting over who would get to enter the new and exotic lands first, who would represent the kingdom. All of us wanted to see it, even if it was hot and dry. Perhaps especially because it was hot and dry.

"I think the council members thought it would be possible to negotiate a treaty, or at least set up some form of trade. They pressured the king relentlessly until he agreed to an initial foray into the foreign lands. But when that first party did not return—not the soldiers, nor any word of anyone else —a larger, better-armed party was sent in."

The archmage walked on. Portia waited patiently, hoping there was more. He shook his head but did not share his thoughts.

"What happened to the second party?" she finally prompted.

"We still don't know. The king and my father were part of the third group. By the time they entered, skirmishing had already broken out around the splinter. The Dragonoid people had set up tents that hid the vast numbers of soldiers. Those soldiers had poured out when our party entered. Our king made the decision to run deeper into their lands rather than retreat. The last command we received from their party was carried by an injured messenger who had run through the battle lines to reach us. It was a short note from the king and only said to "block the splinter until he returned." We had lost sight of them, and then it quickly became too dangerous to even look inside the splinter. They were shooting weapons into our lands through it. We had no idea how to both block it yet also know when the king had returned. That is why it was not closed when you burst through. We were too afraid the king would return to find his exit blocked."

As I had blocked it, Portia thought, kicking a stone in the path. Her face burned red. She had not intended to cause such harm.

Archmage Vermeil continued, not noticing her discomfort. "Days after they disappeared, those huge weapons of war began shooting into our side of the splinter. We had fortified it against their arrows and pikes without sealing it completely, but nothing prepared us for what came after.

One large chunk of metal came in with such force that it went through two caves adjacent to the cavern, pushing through the stone walls in an instant. Those were weapons we'd never seen before. Weapons powered by a strange black powder and fire.

"We had seen smaller versions of those weapons before."

Portia stared at him curiously.

He nodded, abashed. "It was those weapons, as much as the people who had gone in before, that they went in to retrieve," he said, admitting the greed behind the incursion.

Portia had seen the black explosive powder before. The Dragonoids, or more likely humans working for the Dragonoids, had used it to destroy the sea walls protecting Rodaine, the capital city of Lusatiana. They had done so by running long tunnels out beneath the sea, out to the seawall, and underneath the massive structure. Once dug, they filled the long caverns with black powder and finally ignited the lot, creating a massive explosion that cracked and destroyed the stone defenses, bring them crashing down into the sea. Without the sea wall, the city fell within hours to the Dragonoid navy that had been circling beyond it.

Touching the back of her hand, Portia remembered the burning heat and brilliant flash of light that had erupted from a dusting of the substance on her skin getting too close to a candle. The tunnels had been packed waist-deep with it.

The black powder also powered huge cylindrical weapons that spat out balls of metal that smashed everything in their path. The Dragonoids brought those weapons onto their ships, shooting them from their prows, as well as offloading them onto their claimed land. It was those weapons that were marching towards Haulstatt even now.

Or they had been when Portia was stranded on the Dragonoid world.

Portia shivered. Those weapons were so powerful that the most powerful human mages working in concert were barely enough to defend against one such of them. It was as if they were throwing blades of grass in front of a charging bull.

If the dwarves learned how to make the black powder, or source it from somewhere, it would be a formidable advantage over all the other kingdoms, both human and elf. No one understood the secrets of it. No one else had it. King Morgani must have thought it was a risk well worth taking.

Now, though, the dwarves had neither the black powder nor their king, nor their old archmage. What little respite they did have was thanks to Portia closing the splinter, even if that brought with it the problem of retrieving their people.

Another chill passed over Portia. The damp air of the tunnel seeped into her clothes. She hoped the dwarves never got those weapons. Or at least, that all the kingdoms—human, dwarf, and elf—learned of them together and not just one to rule over the rest. It was another reason for her to forge an alliance and bring the armies in together to rescue all their people. No one would be able to go in alone and retrieve weapons and not share them with the others.

A sudden longing for sunshine enveloped Portia, followed by an even stronger longing for a dinner with Elyas. Elyas, whom she would never see again.

Glancing at the archmage, Portia touched his arm gently. His eyes flickered to her before staring forward again.

"We'll get them back. All of them," she said softly.

He grunted.

A few stones skittered on the cavern floor ahead of them. The moss that grew on the walls was still sparse and did not illuminate where the noise had come from. One of the soldiers held up his torch, but it did little to shed more light up ahead of them.

Commander Kerat surged forward and motioned for two soldiers to join him. Portia held her breath as they ran into the darkness, the torch held by one soldier lighting a tight circle around them, bouncing as they ran. A dark shape loomed up in the dim corridor ahead, hanging over the trio of dwarves until it abruptly dropped straight down on top of them. The dwarves completely disappeared under whatever it was.

Iva yelped as the dwarves around her circled and some ran forward to help the first three. Whimpering beside her, Iva emanated fear. "What is that?"

Portia shook her head. She did not know. Her stomach clenched. Raising her hand, she conjured fire magic and threw it forward, hoping it would help more than hurt the dwarves ahead of them.

Flame from her magic flew over the running dwarves and then ran along the corridor floor, licking up along the sides of the walls to the left and the right and then racing to meet on the ceiling far above.

Iva screamed.

Gigantic spiders swarmed on the ceiling and walls. The

thick-limbed massive creatures crowded together and peered at them with clusters of shiny black dots for eyes. The largest amongst them crawled on the dwarves ahead, its limbs dripping in mucus and jabbing at the dwarves' feet and legs.

Bile rose in the back of Portia's throat. She focused on her fire magic, bringing it together in a thick stream directed at the spider ahead. The room dimmed as the fire came down the walls and focused on the spider attacking the dwarves.

Fire poured onto the black creature's head. It stopped attacking the dwarves and spun unnervingly fast to face them. Portia pushed the fire towards its eyes as it ran in their direction faster than any human could, closing the distance between them quickly. Too quickly. Sweat beaded on Portia's forehead and down her back. Beside her, Archmage Vermeil pushed Iva behind him and pulled out a sword.

Keeping one hand focusing the fire on the spider, she pulled out her own sword. Her attack on the animal had roused all the watching spiders, and they were running towards the party, their legs clicking on the walls as they squealed in their attack.

The dwarves held their weapons at the ready and formed a circle. Iva whimpered but also pulled her dagger and stood back-to-back with the archmage, crying and stabbing the oncoming spiders at the same time. The sickening sound of metal hitting their softer bodies rang out around them.

Finally, Portia's spell broke through the thick outer shell of the oncoming spider and reached its soft brain, incinerating the part controlling leg motions until it slid into a heap at their feet. A hideous smell of musk, burnt hair, and mildew filled the surrounding air. Portia coughed and choked.

Several of the dwarves ran forward to rescue the three soldiers downed in the first attack. Kerat yelled "swords up" when one soldier bent to grab his arm, but it was too late. A spider ran in and grabbed the soldier by the waist, carrying him off towards the darkness of the far passageway.

Portia growled and shot a ball of ice at the retreating spider, afraid fire magic would kill the soldier it carried. The spider slowed, wobbling in its steps. A dwarf ran to it and cut off the legs holding the snatched soldier.

The rest of the battle was intense but brief. The spiders had little appetite for prey that fought back so viciously. In the end, several dead spiders lay on the cavern floor along with a few wounded soldiers, but there were no fatalities.

Portia had to pull Iva off a dead spider's body, her arms covered in muck, as she kept stabbing it over and over again. Iva collapsed on the ground, shaking and crying. On impulse, Portia grabbed Iva tightly, wrapping her arms around her in a hug. Portia held on for several minutes until Iva's breath evened out.

"Thank you," Iva whispered, before pushing Portia away with a small nod.

"Is she all right?" asked Archmage Vermeil, walking towards them with a limp. An oozing black wound ran across one thigh, covered in thick mucus.

"She is. Are you?" Portia said, eyeing the wound.

He looked down at it. "I won't die, but it is rather repulsive."

"Is it poisonous?" Portia looked closer at the mucus and then wished she hadn't.

"No, but we should wash it off. There is a stream just some paces down the cavern, if there are no more spiders between us and it."

The group walked to the stream with several dwarves ahead and behind as lookout. They washed as a group, taking turns, carefully getting all the black muck off of them and out of their clothes. Portia carefully bathed her arms and feet. Her clothes were soaked, but she was able to get most of the substance off herself without having to remove them. The cave seemed even colder after emerging from the fast-running waters.

Several of the soldiers were bleeding, as was Archmage Vermeil.

Portia approached the archmage as he was sitting by the stream and pressing a cloth to his wound to staunch the blood. He nodded at her motion to the wound and her questioning look. She took the rag from his hand and let the wound bleed for a moment to clean itself before singing a healing song. The archmage moaned, first in pain and then in relief, as the flesh on his thigh came together.

"Thank you," he said.

She nodded in reply and then stood and moved to the next wounded soldier.

Later, Portia sighed as she laid back by the stream, exhausted, letting her back stretch out. The coolness of the cavern floor was welcome, even if was most likely filthy. She closed her eyes.

Above, a thin voice spoke as if in a dream. "She needs food," said Iva.

Portia smiled. She didn't need to open her eyes to know Iva was standing with her hands on her hips, more than likely scowling at the archmage and anyone else close enough for her ire.

"I told you we should have eaten. If you had known we were traveling so far, why didn't you pack a lunch?"

"We could eat spider bear sandwiches. They are a delicacy," suggested one of the soldiers. A few muffled laughs broke out.

Iva gasped. "No. N. O. Never. Horrible. Horrible. She saved you, and you joke like that."

Kerat stood next to Iva and bowed deferentially. "We did not mean to offend." There was a hesitation, as if he was considering whether to say it before he continued. "Truly, they are a delicacy."

"I'm not talking to you," Iva said, but her voice was softer.

Even in the dimness of the cave, Portia sensed a shadow falling on her face, blocking the light from the glowing moss in the walls and the flickering of the few remaining torches the dwarves had hung on mounts in the wall. She opened her eyes.

Archmage Vermeil looked down at her. "She's right. We should have brought food. My apologies, and embarrassment, in light of how you have healed us all. Let's return to the palace for food and rest." He stuck out a hand towards Portia. She grabbed it and used it to pull herself up to her feet.

Once again, Portia and Iva were shown to their tiny rooms, and once again copper bathtubs were brought and filled with hot water and trays of food laid out in the beds. Portia had insisted on cleaning her sword carefully before she allowed herself to be bathed and her back massaged by the hovering dwarves. In the neighboring room, Iva was not shy about calling out directions on where she wanted her back scrubbed next, the trauma of the spiders forgotten.

Portia laughed and blew the bubbles in her tub and slid deeper into the water.

All too soon it was time for her to rise. There was a state dinner that night. Archmage Vermeil had forwarded the invitation, along with a note from himself. He mentioned casually that there would be many advisors there and to be sure to wear a pleasing gown. He knew she had no gowns. The note was not about gowns at all. It was his way of telling her important ears would be present, and if she wanted an alliance, tonight was her opportunity to make a case for it. Morgani took seriously the words of her counsel. The entire council would all be present that night.

The dwarves had brought her a shimmering gown of violet with diaphanous folds of the silky thin material for sleeves and an even fuller skirt. She let them put it on her. It fit surprisingly well. Checking the seams, Portia found new stitching in the waist in a different colored thread than was used in the rest of the gown. It had been taken in recently. No dwarf could fit in such a narrow dress, so the modifications must have been for her. The fine quality of the material made her wonder if the gown had been one of the queen's own.

Iva entered her room, dressed in an equally splendid red gown with long fitted sleeves. Her hair had been washed and styled and threaded with ribbon. Only the faint swelling under her eyes gave away the exhaustion of the long day.

"That is a wonderful dress," Iva said, eyeing Portia.

Heat rose to Portia's cheeks. She felt ridiculous as it was.

"It's hard to walk in." Portia glanced around and immediately regretted her comment. "Still, it is quite beautiful. The most beautiful I've ever worn," she said a little too loudly, wanting to make sure the attendants would take her words of praise back to the seamstress and to the queen. It would curry no favors for her to complain of such a beautiful gift.

The dwarf who was pinning up her hair stepped back, signaling that she was done, and Portia nodded her thanks. She rose and strode to the bed to pick up her sword, halted by a loud throat clearing by her door.

Commander Kerat stood in the archway, one eyebrow raised.

"Good evening," Portia greeted him.

He bowed. "Good evening to you, young human." Portia flushed yet again, this time the heat reaching her ears. That greeting was familiar. Mixed feelings flooded her heart. She pushed them back. Now was not the time to deal with feelings.

"Do humans always turn that color?" he asked, his head tilted.

Iva, who had been arranging the folds of her dress, looked

up sharply and spied Portia's blush. She giggled behind her hand.

"Not on purpose," said Iva, before another giggle emerged. She went back to arranging her dress.

Lacking a witty comment, Portia turned back to grab her sword.

"There are no weapons at state dinners," said the commander.

"This is... I can't just leave it here," Portia said, flustered. She had not let the sword out of her sight since Rodaine. Even in the heat and misery of the Dragonoids' land, she always found a way to keep it with her.

"It will be safe here," he said. "Nothing will hurt it, or you, tonight. It will be waiting for your return. My word."

Portia stared at him, bit her lip, and gave a sharp nod. She put the sword back down and then, after a moment's hesitation, tucked it underneath the bed and drew the covers over the edge of the bed to hide it as much as possible. It was a pathetic attempt at concealing the beautiful copper sword and its green leather scabbard, but there was no other place to hide it in the tiny room. Commander Kerat graciously said nothing, nor did he laugh at her anxiety about leaving her prized weapon behind.

He motioned for them to exit the room. Commander Kerat was dressed in a fine detailed tunic—one delicate enough that it would never have been appropriate for the daily use of a warrior. Even the maids who had come to bathe them and bring trays of food were dressed in brightly colored soft gowns, a change from the normal tunic and pants they wore. It appeared the whole palace was wearing its best for a celebration.

"How do we rate a commander for an escort?" asked Portia, realizing now that they seemed to only be led through the palace by Commander Kerat, with the singular exception of their time following the page to Archmage Vermeil's tower.

He turned to her and raised his eyebrows and then looked forward again without speaking nor breaking his pace.

"I see," she said.

He was both escort and guard.

Yet he wanted her to trust him about her sword. She growled, startling even herself. At his surprised glance, she gave him a smile. "Sorry, something stuck in my throat."

Iva followed behind, still distracted by her dress. She twirled and made the bell of the skirt fly open. Portia was grateful for the silence.

"So, what about those lockpicks and caltrops? I suppose those are not allowed at a state dinner too?" Portia asked, wanting to see just how far the dwarves had set the boundaries around her.

"No, I'm afraid not. But they will be there for you tomorrow. The royal locksmith sent word this evening." This time the commander's smile came easily.

Finally, she would have something for her empty bag.

THEY JOINED the rest of the guests standing about and milling in a salon outside the large dining hall, while waiters passed through and served drinks. A cluster of dwarves stood in the corner and whispered, giving Portia occasional glances. Some of the group had completely silver hair while others were younger. All wore heavily decorated uniforms, whether male or female. Other clusters of dwarves dotted the room, though none with as much military insignia.

Portia stood in the center of the room along with Iva and Commander Kerat, awkwardly holding a glass of dark ruby liquid and glancing about while trying to not look as if she was doing so. Even Iva shifted uncomfortably on her feet. Only Commander Kerat stood at ease, conversing easily with the two of them as if no one else was watching.

But the others did watch them. It seemed the entire room watched them.

Two footmen opened the double doors to the salon wide, followed by the entrance of the chamberlain who announced Queen Morgani. The quiet conversation ceased as those in the room turned to face the queen as she entered, the men bowing and the women curtsying. The queen acknowledged their greetings, and the room rose as one.

Conversation started again, but this time the looks towards Portia and Iva were more circumspect.

Portia's discomfort grew as the queen made her way to their group. Portia curtsied again and elbowed Iva to stop the words from coming out of her mouth. Iva gave a hasty curtsy.

The room quieted as others turned to watch the conversation.

"I've had Archmage Vermeil's report this afternoon," said

the queen, her voice level. "Congratulations are in order, I think, on your ability to open a splinter."

"Thank you, Your Majesty. I hope to be able to control it, I mean, where it goes..." Portia said. Her words came out in a rush.

The queen held up a hand, silencing Portia. "That would be useful, indeed." The queen's face gave away no expression, no betrayal of her thoughts on the possibility of retrieving her husband, the king of Morgani.

"Yes, Your Majesty." Portia hesitated and then spoke again. "I'm sorry I was not able to teach Archmage Vermeil how to heal them with Elven magic."

The queen studied her.

The glass felt awkward in Portia's hand. There was no tray nearby to set it down. Holding a glass of wine in front of the queen felt disrespectful. She raised and lowered the glass, finally settling on holding the glass low in front of her, clasping it awkwardly in her hands.

The queen summoned a waiter with a glance and took a glass of the same ruby liquid Portia held. She slowly sipped it, her eyes meeting Portia's over the rim, then lowered the glass again. "Never apologize for someone else's challenges. We assure you, the kingdom has full confidence Archmage Vermeil will overcome the difficulties he encountered today. An honest evaluation of the shortfall is the key to that, indeed. We have the utmost faith in Archmage Vermeil's judgment."

A furious whisper, quickly quieted, echoed from the back of the room. The queen did not react.

Portia nodded, unsure if she was being reprimanded or

encouraged. She wished for a spell that would have told her what the archmage had said to his queen.

"My counsel urges me to close the borders quickly," said the queen. Her gaze flicked to several of the groups in the room. "They felt strongly on this issue as to *demand* a meeting before our celebration of the splinter closing tonight." The queen paused, letting the awkward silence take over the room. Finally, she took another sip, and then spoke again to Portia as if they were the only ones in the room. "It seemed wisest if they met you first. Before any decisions were made. Don't you agree?" The queen addressed the last question to the room at large.

Was the whole dinner party her counsel? Portia stole a look around the room, examining the details of the clothes the dwarves around her wore. Far more formal uniforms graced their bodies than light dresses and evening suits. The closed looks and narrowed eyes on many of their faces chilled Portia. They endured this meeting for their queen, but few had an interest in what Portia might say.

"Yes, Your Majesty," said Portia, focusing on the queen. "I do hope you'll consider my request to leave your lands so I may travel to close the splinters in the far kingdoms." She spoke more loudly than necessary, hoping all the advisors would hear.

The queen raised one eyebrow but replied, also louder than before. "It is a danger to our kingdom to leave our borders open, even for the short time for you to leave."

"That is true, Your Majesty, but would it be a greater

danger to allow the Dragonoids to invade the other lands unhindered, bringing in their fearsome weapons?"

A red-faced dwarf rushed forward from behind the queen, inhaling to speak. Without pulling her eyes from Portia, the queen raised her hand and stopped him. He huffed, looking back and forth between the queen and Portia, and held his counsel.

"We do not have the numbers to prevent such a thing happening," explained the queen.

"But in an alliance with others, there would be enough—"

"Not with humans!" spat out a voice from the back. Others muttered about elves and taking care of their own. Portia forced herself to not look for the speakers, instead focusing on the queen in front of her.

"Alliances can be difficult," said the queen, as if they had not been interrupted.

"I understand, Your Majesty, that the protection of your people is your first concern. There is hope for the success of an alliance. The king of the elves did not seem entirely opposed, and my own queen, Queen Lorica, has agreed to work with the elves. The addition of your strong warriors might be enough to defeat these invaders. Any spoils won from them would be shared equally." Portia paused, trying to memorize who was paying the closest attention. "Including any weapons found."

The word "weapons" echoed around the room in a dozen whispers. Somewhere in the back of the room, a glass fell to the floor and shattered.

"Weapons?" a meek-looking dwarf echoed and then looked down at the queen's glance.

"The black powder weapons," Portia said, affecting an innocent tone.

Now that Portia had closed the single portal in the Dwarven land, the only splinters accessing the Dragonoid world were in the human lands and over the seas beyond them. All out of easy reach of Morgani. Those splinters remaining open did pose a danger to the populations around them, yet they also were an opportunity to the most ambitious and those unafraid of those populations—those willing to fight for new advantages. Only those races close to those open splinters—now the humans and the elves—had the opportunity to steal technology from the new world. Or more worryingly yet, form an alliance with the invaders in exchange for the coveted arms.

Portia frowned, thinking of the lack of loyalty already shown by the corrupt humans in Rodaine who had willingly sold their own people, and their city, for a few pieces of gold from the invaders. What would they be willing to sacrifice for weapons that would allow them to defeat all the other kingdoms in the land? If the Dragonoids truly only had an interest in stealing slaves from this world, then any race that worked with them could remain on these lands and rule over them with brutal efficiency using weapons they bartered from the Dragonoids.

The faces of the surrounding council members worked as these thoughts and calculations filtered through their brains. The queen sipped her wine and waited.

In the end, Queen Morgani let herself be convinced that it was un-dwarf-like to abandon the humans and the elves in their lands to the brutal invaders. It was only right that their kingdom should join the united Elven and Human kingdoms in their fight against the invaders and have the honor of protecting Portia as she closed the splinters. Of course, with their vast experience in battle, they should take their destined role supervising any rescue parties that had to be sent into the Dragonoid lands, the land from whence the black powder came and the strange weapons that used it.

A battalion would leave with Portia and Iva in the morning.

9

Portia stifled a yawn as she sat on the bed and leaned over to tie her boots and then picked up her blade and a cloth laying on the floor nearby. The dwarves had never brought back the filthy brown linen garments she had fashioned into concealing coveralls in the Dragonoid world, but her green pants and shirt and tunic had been returned, mended and washed. They had even brought a vial of oil for her sword, and Portia rose early that morning to wash and oil it. She had dried the blade and scrubbed it with sand to avoid corrosion in the Dragonoids' land but dared not risk thieving oil for it on top of stealing her own supper.

Iva poked her head in the doorway. She wrinkled her nose at the pungent smell of the oil.

"We should get you a knife," said Portia, continuing to wipe down the blade with a linen rag, removing the excess oil.

"I have a dagger," said Iva, entering the room and sitting on the bed next to Portia.

Portia stopped wiping the blade and stared at Iva. "That's right, I forgot. How did you get that?"

"Commander Kerat must have ordered it, I guess. It came on the top of my pile of clothes from yesterday." Iva frowned. "My pike blade has not been returned."

"Maybe the knife was payment for it. I'm glad you had it yesterday though. Have you cleaned it?" asked Portia.

"A little. Yesterday."

"That's not enough. It will rust unless fully dry and treated," explained Portia as she bent over her sword again, applying pressure to polish the metal with the oiled cloth. "Bring it here."

Iva scrunched her face in complaint but rose to get her dagger.

As she reached the door, Portia called after her. "Wash it in your bathwater first if they haven't taken it away."

Iva glared over her shoulder at Portia. "Ew, it's probably still full of spider guts."

"Whose fault would that be? That blade prevented the spiders from taking your life; it deserves better care."

A few minutes later, Iva returned with a clean cloth and a dripping wet blade. Portia had her dry it thoroughly first and then showed her how to pour a thin stream of oil on it and wipe it from hilt to tip, careful to not cut her fingertips on the sharp edge.

"I'm glad we're leaving today," said Iva.

Portia nodded. When she had been stranded on the Dragonoid world, Haulstatt was fending off the Dragonoid attacks, but at a huge price. She needed to return to help them in their battle.

Commander Kerat collected them from their rooms. They walked through the long winding caverns of the palace and then exited the huge structure, emerging into the cavernous Dwarven city around the palace. High above them, the roof of the cavern arched out of sight. It felt early to Portia, but without a sun above, it was impossible to know what time it was.

They reached a large, low structure. The smell of hay permeated the air as animals shuffled within the building. Several soldiers waited outside, holding the reins to tall, sleek horses, firmly muscled and sturdy enough to carry the heavy dwarves. The horses' coats shone.

Iva walked closer to Portia, almost tripping her. Portia held up a hand to keep her from coming even closer. "Let me guess, creatures?"

Iva nodded then stepped closer to Portia, ignoring her efforts to get some space.

"You're going to have to ride one of these creatures. You might as well try to become friends with it."

Iva turned to Portia, her eyes huge and her mouth a tiny circle.

"They are nice, I'm sure. Not walking is even nicer," said Portia, not as kindly as she could have.

Archmage Vermeil entered the cavern around the barn from a different direction. The weasel creature rode his shoulder, chittering a greeting when it saw Portia and Iva. Iva recoiled from that as well. Portia glared at Iva, her hands on her hips.

"Now that one *did* save your life, so you will be nice to it," Portia said, pointing to the weasel.

Iva nodded.

"I don't understand how you can be scared of such a tiny thing. You, who came from the Dragonoids' land," said Archmage Vermeil, laughter in his voice. Despite his mirth, he was careful not to come close to Iva with the curious creature on his person. It was staring at Iva, its head tilted, as if she confused him.

"They're just so... furry. And they can get into such spaces, like my clothes and my hair," Iva said. She made an exaggerated shiver.

"I think the fur is nice," said Portia. Her fingers itched to touch the creature, but she wasn't sure how it would react to her taking such liberty. She shoved her hand in her pants pocket.

Commander Kerat disappeared into the barn, leaving Portia and Iva with Archmage Vermeil.

"I won't be going with you," said the archmage. "My queen thinks it's best I stay here and monitor the splinter that you closed and then meet you with our ship later. If there is another splinter on the waters between the land and the Well of Tears, that will be our best bet for rescuing our people. We can bring our forces to bear much faster by water.

"Ship?" asked Portia. "How can you have a ship when you're landlocked?"

"Finally, something I know that you don't," said the archmage with a smile.

Iva snorted. She tried to make her face serious when Portia turned to glare at her. "What? It just sounded... familiar?"

Turning back to the archmage, Portia stepped so her back was to Iva. "I just don't understand where you would keep a ship?"

"That I cannot tell you without risking our security. Just trust that we have one, and we will meet you," he said.

"Thank you for everything." Warmth flooded through Portia. With help from the dwarves, they might yet defeat the Dragonoids, and they also had the possibility to find other humans, relations not even thought possible before the opening of the splinter in distant lands. Their could find their human ancestors.

He nodded, clearing his throat and looking uncomfortable. "Well, then, you're welcome. Take care of this one." He pointed to Iva. "Keep away the furry ones, or I think her heart will stop."

"I might stop it for her if she screams much more," Portia replied, ignoring the kick in the back of her calf from Iva.

Commander Kerat emerged from the barn leading three horses.

Portia turned to Iva and gave her a wicked grin. "Look, one for each of us."

Iva narrowed her eyes at Portia and then looked at the horse and at Commander Kerat. She drew in a deep breath and slowly stood straighter and pulled backed her shoulders. She walked to the commander and gave him a nod.

Portia watched, her mouth hanging open.

The commander placed Iva's left foot into the stirrup and motioned for her to swing up and on the horse. Iva glanced around at the other mounted soldiers, checking to see how they sat, and then turned back to the horse. She looked down for a second and then back up, launching herself up onto the horse. Or trying to. The horse was so high, she only made it halfway before having to drop back down to the ground, nearly falling backwards because her left foot was still caught in the stirrup. Commander Kerat caught her before she fell. Iva hopped on her right foot, positioning herself again before trying once more. This time, Commander Kerat lifted her by the waist to give her a boost while she leapt up with one leg. Her right leg swung over the saddle and Iva perched on top of the horse, a surprised look on her face. Her expression relaxed into a grin.

Then she started to slide off the right side.

"Put your foot in the stirrup. The *right* stirrup," Portia yelled.

Iva felt around with her right leg, startling the horse with her quick movements, until she found the stirrup and used it to stop her slide, pushing to right herself in the saddle. The horse pranced and huffed until a dwarf soldier grabbed the reins and held its nose close. Once she rebalanced herself, Iva sat stiffly in the saddle, her back straight, looking forward and not moving a muscle while the horse breathed more slowly and calmed.

"It's a little disconcerting when others surprise you, is it not?" Archmage Vermeil said quietly to Portia while they both stared at Iva. Portia shut her mouth and nodded.

"Impressive. First time in the saddle?" a voice behind them asked.

Portia turned. A dwarf wearing the dark blue uniform of their army stood behind. A set of stars decorated one sleeve, but otherwise the overcoat was plain. The dwarf stood confidently, weight on one hip, an intelligent appraising eye on Iva.

Archmage Vermeil cleared his throat. "General Seren, this is the mage I was telling you about."

The general's eyes moved from Iva to Portia. "Not the brave one on the horse?"

Portia involuntarily backed up a half step under the gaze of the general. She forced herself to stop, her stomach unclenching when she realized the general's eyes were sparkling with mirth. Still, she felt she must defend Iva. "She does have some magic."

"So I've heard. Terribly persistent mud people. It took a while to clean that off." The general laughed.

Portia flushed. Had Iva left some magic running loose?

As if reading her mind, the general said, "Don't worry, we understand. It was chaotic. Archmage Vermeil was kind enough to assist us." She stuck out one hand. "I'm General Seren. I'm leading the battalion that is escorting you today. Or at least this part of the battalion."

A general leading the expedition?

"I'll also be coordinating our forces and doing advanced planning. We don't really think you need a general to protect you." Again, General Seren grinned at Portia. She had deep laugh lines in her face. Portia shook her head slightly, confused. Most generals she had met, few as they were, had been much more serious.

The general spotted someone coming out of the barn and walked past Portia to speak to them, slapping Portia hard on the back as she passed, nearly knocking her to the ground.

"Stand with your feet apart for a little more stability," Archmage Vermeil suggested dryly.

Portia shook her head again.

They set out soon after, leaving Commander Kerat and Archmage Vermeil behind. General Seren placed Portia and Iva in the middle of the battalion and rode ahead of them. A lower rank mage was amongst the army, also dressed in the blue and gray uniform, but carried no visible weapons. The horses plodded along the caverns but then picked up their pace naturally as the floor ramped upwards. The animals were eager to go this way.

Most of the passageway was wide enough that they were able to travel in pairs side by side, only occasionally having to narrow to single file as a horse-drawn wagon filled with hay came from the other direction.

After several hours, the slope of the path increased even more. The air in the tunnel smelled fresher. Portia thought she smelled summer flowers and pollen. The roof of the cavern increased in height and soared upwards even as the passage ended in a set of tall double doors five lengths high. That many horses, each standing on top of the one before it, could have passed through those doors. Portia craned her neck to look upwards.

Two guards stood at attention at the base of the doors. They saluted as the general approached. Portia, Iva, and the rest of the group waited behind. The horses tried to move forward but were kept back with their reins.

At a word from the general, the two guards picked up thick blue ropes attached to the door above. Blue light shimmered along the ropes, starting from the guards and running up the thick twisting fibers to mountings high up in the middle of the doors, then spreading over the surfaces of the dark wood of the doors themselves. A faint humming sound echoed. Stepping towards the passageway, the guards pulled on the ropes. They leaned heavily into the task and dug for purchase on the stone floor with their boots. Finally, the heavy doors swung slowly open.

Sunshine streamed ahead, its brightness blinding the entire party. Portia shielded her eyes and looked away, as did the others. The doors fully opened and came to a halt. No one moved except to blink their eyes rapidly and peer out the door.

"Don't worry, we have scouts out there now," General Seren said, having returned from the door and drawn her horse next to Portia and Iva. "Word was sent last night that we'd be leaving this morning, so they extended their range further than normal to check for invaders and spies. The persistent Dragonoids have not reached our mountains, at least not yet." The general nodded at Portia, her persistent smile replaced by an intense seriousness. "If I have my way, not ever."

Once everyone's eyes were acclimated enough to see, they

let the horses walk out the double doors and into the mountain pass beyond. The air was chilly and dry in the heights of the mountains, even in full summer, but the sun reaching around the peak was warming.

After the entire battalion exited the doors, they halted in a narrow strip of sunshine and waited while the doors closed again behind them. Portia lifted her face to the sun and pulled back the sleeves of her tunic to expose more skin to the precious rays. The horses seemed similarly entranced, each trying to get as much of their body into the warm light as possible, the smaller horses whinnying as the larger ones would not make way for them, leaving them to have their rumps or forelocks left in the shade. Their riders patted them on the shoulder, reassuring them there would be enough sunshine for all in a few moments.

The group did not move immediately after the doors finished closing. Puzzled, Portia looked around, trying to see what was happening. The military mage stood next to the general in front of the double doors, the reins of their horses held by other soldiers. At a signal from the general, the rest of the soldiers moved several paces down the trail and then stopped. Portia craned her neck back to see what they were doing by the doors.

The mage struck a tuning fork, the sound cutting into Portia's ears, then lifted his hands and motioned in complex patterns while reciting not quite audible words. The blue magic, still crackling across the dark wooden surfaces, flared and shimmered once again and then faded. The doors turned translucent then morphed into dark gray lumps matching the surrounding rock. All that was left was a scrub-lined goat path trod into the rock of the mountainside. Any evidence of doors or stonework cut into the mountainside was gone. Portia gasped at the strength of the illusion—if it was an illusion.

"I wish I could have hidden my kingdom that way," said Iva under her breath, staring at the goat path where the entrance had been. "Hey, where are you going?" she called as Portia slid down from her horse and walked towards the general and the mage.

"Nowhere," Portia called back.

Rather than stopping by the mage and the general, Portia kept going to where the door should have been. The ground rose up below her, forcing her to climb a steep ascent. It felt just as it looked. She jumped up and down—the ground was solid. She grabbed a bush alongside the path, only to quickly pull back her hand and wipe the blood from her thumb that had found a thorn. This was not like her duplicate magic. It was solid. She could make the illusion of duplicates, but they were like smoke—a hand could pass right through them.

"Hey!" the mage said behind her. He drew in breath to launch a tirade, but the general clapped him on the back. They looked up at Portia, whose feet were now at their eye level.

"She's mighty impressed with your work, I guess—had to see it up close." The general's smile was contagious, and the mage's indignation melted. His shoulders relaxed, and he gave out a soft huff instead of yelling at Portia.

Portia climbed back down the goat path to the mage and the general. "I am impressed." Her face flushed red, realizing how the words might be taken as arrogance on her part. "Not that I'm an expert, of course. But I've never seen that before. Could you show me how you do it?"

The mage's face softened at Portia's praise. The general, her arm still around the mage, answered for him. "I'm sure that is possible, but it will have to be around our campfire tonight. We have a schedule to make." The general pointed to their horses. "Shall we?"

They rode down the mountain path single file, the path down looking as much like a goat trail as the path behind them. The horses were surefooted. Iva hung onto hers with almost affection as the horse walked down the steep rocky path.

A lush green forest spread out before them. In a few moments, the path opened to show the ground below the mountain. Puffy clouds raced over the land, leaving shadows on the greenery as they were pushed by the high winds above.

The lower they went, the warmer and more humid the air became. The greenery increased. Finally, the path widened and dumped them down to a lush forest that pushed up against the base of the mountain. Birds called in the trees. Sunlight dappled through the leaves onto the bare forest floors far below.

They walked some distance along the road that ran along the base of the mountain, skirting the forest, before the general called a halt for lunch.

Portia dismounted gratefully and stretched.

Iva slid down from her own animal and then straightened. "Ouch, ouch, ouch," she said.

"Wait until you sit down to eat," said Portia, unable to stop the smirk on her face. This was far too enjoyable.

Iva sent her a sour look, but rather than going through her packs for food, she took her horse's reins and led it forward to the stream where soldiers were watering their own animals. Portia watched, eyebrows raised, as Iva then took the animal to a patch of grass and tied its reins to a tree so it could eat its lunch in leisure. Only then did Iva dig into the packs on the animal to find the meal wrapped in linen the dwarves had packed for her.

She walked back to where Portia stood. "What?"

Portia shook her head, unable to answer.

Portia cared for her own animal before returning to where Iva sat. She dropped onto the grass in front of her. The soldiers had grouped themselves apart from Iva, except a few soldiers who were arming themselves with additional knives and crossbows from their packs and then standing before the general.

"I wonder what they're up to?" Portia nodded in the direction of the soldiers and the general.

"Something about a scouting party and a nearby village," said Iva around a mouthful of sandwich.

"I should be a part of that," Portia said, rising again and going to the general, ignoring Iva's call to come back.

"I volunteer to be part of the scouts," Portia said to the general, flushing as she realized she had interrupted one of the soldiers making a report.

General Seren held her hand up to the soldier, requesting a moment, and turned and gave Portia a gracious smile. "That is much appreciated, but for now please wait here."

"I know how to sneak," Portia said, thrusting out her chin. She had survived for years on the streets as a thief when many would have liked to punish such wrongdoing with physical harm, all while in a crowded street. She had also found her way through Rodaine as a spy. It would be so much easier in an empty forest.

The general spoke firmly. "No. It is safer for everyone if you stay behind. Our scouts have protocols that we've no time to teach you." She couldn't have said it in a kinder manner, but Portia's stomach flipped.

The general's tone softened. "This protects everyone, including you."

Portia wished she could disappear into the ground on which she stood. Instead, she nodded stiffly at the general and the other scouts and walked back to Iva. She had to go around the other soldiers sitting in the grass eating their lunch. She hoped they didn't notice her flaming red face. She didn't check if they were looking at her. Her neck felt too rigid to move.

Sitting down heavily by Iva, she grabbed the sandwich she had dropped earlier. "They don't want me," Portia said, roughly unwrapping the linen.

"I'm sure that's not it. What did she say to you?" Iva asked.

"Something about not knowing protocols. But that doesn't matter. I... I'm really good in dangerous situations. I'd be a help."

Iva chewed, considering what Portia said.

"You are good. But if you don't know how they operate, you might put them in danger. You can't do everything, you know," Iva said and dug around in her bag for a waterskin to take a drink of water.

Portia narrowed her eyes at Iva when she wasn't looking but didn't say anything. What did Iva know? Portia had not asked to be a Jack of Magic, but somehow, she was one. There was so much responsibility with the role. She was supposed *to save humankind*—she was created to do it by magic. Didn't that sound like doing everything? It surprised her to realize she felt like crying.

How nice it would be to not have to do everything.

Instead of allowing tears to fall, she took a bite of her sandwich, and then, in three more bites, ate half of it. She had not realized how hungry she was until she started eating.

And she hadn't had to make the food or steal it. Perhaps it was okay letting others help.

There had been another sandwich in the pack, along with some nuts and a strange fruit she'd never seen before, but she'd decided to leave it uneaten for now in case they couldn't find any game or other foraging on the road. They were still several days' journey to the kingdom of Haulstatt.

———

GENERAL SEREN WAS LOOKING at a map spread out upon a stump when the scouts returned. They looked haggard and panted as if they had run the entire way.

"General, sir, the village is gone," the scout leader said.

By then, Portia and Iva and the other soldiers who had been resting under the trees had gathered around. A murmur of unhappy reactions greeted that news.

"What do you mean, gone?" General Seren asked, her characteristic smile replaced with a tense jaw.

"Gone... All the people and animals. Most of the buildings were flattened into rubble. We didn't find a single resident. The smith's shop was as if it had never been—the anvil gone, the bellows too, the wood of the walls... Even the ground where it had stood was swept clean." The scout leader squeezed his eyes shut and opened them again and continued with a shaking voice. "I've never seen the like before."

"Could you tell when this happened?" asked the general.

The scout shook his head. "Not exactly, but the hearth stones we did find were cold. Bone cold. There'd not been a fire in that village for days."

"Those were Dragonoids, those who did that," said Iva. She shook, rubbing her hands rapidly up and down her arms despite the warm air. "That's what they did in Jukhnovo to the fishing villages before they invaded inland. Our king thought the destruction was done by Haulstatt bandits, at least that's what they told us. We only found out later what had happened to the fishing villages, how they had been razed. No human bandit would do such a thing."

She turned away from the skeptical look the dwarves gave her. They did not share her opinion of humans.

"The Dragonoids are in your lands," said Portia.

"This land is Lusatianan, but yes, they are closer than we

thought, or at least have been so," said the general, her eyebrows drawing together. "We must hurry."

If they were in the human kingdom of Lusatiana, they had traveled much further east than Portia realized before emerging out of the Dwarven caverns into the land above. The hair on Portia's arm rose at the thought of the Dragonoids so close.

Continuing down the road, the group went north and further east, bringing them close to the capital city of Rodaine. It seemed like a lifetime ago she and Mark had traveled to that city to see if his suspicions were correct about his employer teaming with the invaders. They had barely escaped with their lives.

The general allowed the group to use the main road to make speed, but they traveled at night and in the clear hours just after dawn and just before dusk, when it was possible to see especially far. The scouts continued to look for any Dragonoid encampments but saw none. There were no fires in the distance, nor signs of war wagons dragging their weapons down the dusty country roads.

Portia knew the Dragonoids were out there, somewhere. The jumpy looks of the others betrayed their same thoughts. Not knowing the whereabouts of the dangerous forces was almost worse than seeing the war machines. Almost.

A crossroad leading directly east into Rodaine met up with the road they were on, while their road turned sharply left to go north to the border with Haulstatt. The juncture sat at the top of a large hill that afforded a view of the surrounding countryside and down into the valley holding the city of Rodaine nestled up against the sea. Or where the city had been.

The group rested on horses and stared into the valley as soon as they crested the hill. They looked down the long slope to the burned foundations and scattered debris of the city, and then to the sea and crumpled piles of stone—what remained of the seawall peeking up through the waters. Despite Portia having watched the seawall's destruction, along with the attack on the city, the sight was still unnerving.

The city was just as the scout had described the vanished village—gone. The crowded buildings that had ringed the harbor before were gone. The warehouse district to the north, gone. And the residential houses to the south, gone. Here and there, smashed piles of lumber lay, giving notice to where especially large houses had once been. Those piles were the largest structures of anything left.

"What use is it to them to destroy a city so completely?" asked the general, almost to herself. "Burning the fields, that I can see if they were trying to avoid our following them in a retreat, but they're not retreating. It required much effort to completely flatten all that." She waved to the brutal scene below. "What could they gain by that?"

No one had an answer. The tight pit in her stomach told her that intended or not, one of the results was terror.

The Dragonoids had whisked away the city as if it had never been.

Following the general's order, the battalion turned the horses to the road going northwest and resumed their journey in silence.

THEY REACHED the border to Haulstatt the next day. Portia exhaled when she saw the town that marked the border between the two kingdoms was still there. There were tents and caravans around it, but not nearly as many as she'd seen when the populace of Rodaine had been fleeing the invaders. Where were the Dragonoids? There were a few roads leading into Haulstatt. The invaders were not in Rodaine, and last she had heard, they had been heading inland. That had been many weeks ago, before her stay on the Dragonoid world. Much might have changed since then. It was too much to hope for that the invaders had retreated back to their own lands.

But when they got closer, the scars of the battle lay etched and burned into the ground. Marks of fire ran up the stones of the city's walls. Something had happened here, but the town hadn't been razed. If the Dragonoids had attacked, they'd been pushed back.

Smoke rose from the land on the far side of the town, its long brown tendrils winding up into the sky. They'd seen the smoke from afar, and while no one had said anything, it was clear all were expecting to find the smoky ruins of an outpost town.

When they reached the city gates, one of their scouts returned to them, running through the fields next to the road, having gone ahead earlier that night. He stopped, bent over, and sucked in air. He'd not taken a horse for fear of breaking its leg in a hole in the muddy fields in the darkness of night.

The general waited patiently. Finally, the scout straightened and saluted the general. "There's a full army at the far side. I'd have been back sooner, but they," his face red even in the dim light, "almost caught me. It took some doing, but I am here."

"An army?" The general tilted her head, waiting for details.

The scout went into details of what he found. What lay on the other side of the town was a regiment of Haulstatt soldiers along with ragged remains of the Lusatianan soldiers. Those were the flags that had been visible, and the accents of those sitting and talking around the fires matched. Soldiers of both armies patrolled the wall before them. There were many wounded and far fewer horses than the scout expected for such a large force, both facts pointing to the forces recovering from deadly prior engagements. Together, the forces defended the town ahead.

"We are glad to have you back. Find your horse," the general ordered.

The scout saluted again and then wound his way back along the line to where the reins of his horse were tied to the pommel of a fellow soldier's saddle. Portia watched him wearily go past.

The guards above the front gate stared at the dwarf battalion as they approached the gates. More guards from inside came to look through the bars of the gate. Children from the caravans ran around them and then towards the gate to stand waiting with the guards. The children's shouting drew more onlookers.

One especially daring child ran up to a dwarf soldier mounted on a horse and grabbed the ankle of his boot, dancing around to avoid the hooves of the horse. The child stared at the soldier, who in turn glanced at the other dwarves and then down back at the child, shifting uncomfortably. He tried to pull his foot free, but the child held on tightly.

"You look weird," said the child with no malice, only curiosity in her voice.

"I... don't mean to look weird," replied this soldier.

Iva giggled in her saddle next to Portia. They were right behind the soldier, watching this interaction.

"He's a dwarf," called out Iva.

The child swiveled to look at Iva and then back up at the soldier she was still hanging onto by the foot.

"What's a dwarf?" asked the child.

Iva shrugged and pointed at the soldier. "That's a dwarf. They're like humans but different."

A growl rose from a soldier in the back ranks at the comparison between dwarves and humans, but a few others chuckled, mostly because of the innocent and persistent behavior of the child.

"Okay. Hello, dwarf," said the child.

"Hello to you, too," said the soldier, who then looked up to see a concerned mom running along the road, trying to get her child's attention. "I think your mother is calling you."

The child swiveled to see her mother and instantly let go of the dwarf's foot, stumbling back and avoiding the horse's steps. Her mother swept her up in her arms, squeezing her tight and burying her face into her child's hair.

The fear in the mother's face was matched in many of those lining the road watching the dwarves walk to the city's gates. They had never seen dwarves before, despite the kingdoms being so close. For the first time, uneasiness settled in Portia's stomach at what might happen in this human city. The dwarves were here at her behest. She didn't want anything to happen to them.

A TRUMPETER CALLED ALARM, and the people along the road vanished, returning to their tents and makeshift shelters. The swiftness of their disappearance took away Portia's breath. Ahead, the gate to the town was shut. Soldiers lined the top of the walls. A second trumpet call rang out, and the troops standing on top of the wall raised crossbows and aimed them at the dwarves on the road. A cloud passed over the sun, sending the entire landscape into deep shadow.

General Seren raised an arm, bringing the troops to a halt.

Not even insects made a noise as the two sides appraised each other. At a signal from the dwarf commander, a white banner was raised and flapped in the cold breeze that blew from the fields. Nothing from the town's soldiers showed acknowledgment of the signal.

The clattering of armor reverberated in the air as additional troops came around the walls of the town on either side and positioned themselves facing the dwarves on the road. A few soldiers stood with crutches, ready to defend the border even while injured.

"Seems we are not welcomed," said the Dwarven commander quietly. She turned to look at Portia. "Come join me. Slowly."

Portia signaled her horse to move forward. The strike of each hoof on the dirt road reverberated in the air. The hairs on Portia's arms and neck stood up. She feared making a wrong move and sending the armies into action.

"Any suggestions, young human? We are here for an alliance, but there might be too much fear here for that. Do you know any of these people? Can you vouch for them or for us?" asked General Seren, speaking low while keeping her eyes on the armies ahead.

A second to the commander held out a spyglass to Portia, extending his arms slowly and held high so the opposing army saw that it was not a weapon. Portia took the cold instrument and held it to her eye, scanning the soldiers. Dark circles ringed under the soldiers' eyes and fear showed on their faces. Their arms shook as they held the crossbows at ready, holding the heavy weapons in ready position.

The faces were all unfamiliar to Portia. A motion caught her eye on the far end of the wall, and she moved the spyglass to that location. An older woman in uniform stood, also with a spyglass held to her eye, staring at the Dwarven army in the road. The woman lowered the glass. Portia recognized the face. It was General A. Bancrot. What was she doing here, so far from the Elven wall? What had happened?

An arrow skittered along the road ahead, shot from the wall of the town. It missed badly. The soldiers around Portia jumped, hands flying to swords and their own crossbows.

"Halt!" called General Seren.

Another command rang out from the other side.

A hiss of disapproval rang from the Dwarven soldiers around them, and the air smelled of fear, but they did halt. Portia held her breath as all motion ceased again as the two sides eyed each other, waiting for the other to take the opportunity to attack.

"I know their commander," said Portia quietly. Her voice shook. Her hand shook on the pommel of her saddle, and she grabbed it tightly to hide her trembling. "I don't know if she'll remember me."

"Let's hope so, or this has been a death mission for us," said General Seren. The commander nodded at Portia and then motioned to the front of the line with her head.

Portia nudged her horse forward, her heart lodged in the back of her throat, making it difficult to swallow or breathe. The troops parted for her, leaving an open path to the road ahead. When she reached the front of the Dwarven line, Portia stopped her horse and held both hands up for the armies to see. Slowly, she reached back with one hand and unbuckled the baldric that held her sword to her body. When the leather straps slipped from the buckle, she let the sword and holder slide down her body to the ground, landing in a crumple. Putting the hand back up so both were visible to the far side, she nudged the horse forward with her knee. To her relief, her horse slowly stepped forward as directed and avoided stepping on her sword.

Thoughts of her sword were soon lost as she approached the gates and the weapons held by the guards on the wall came into clearer focus. They looked as afraid as she felt, though it was more hidden in clenched jaws and scowls under the metal helmets. More weapons were aimed at her through the metal bars of the gates.

"Stop!" a woman's voice rang out.

Portia looked to see General Bancrot staring down at her.

"What is your business here?" demanded the general, her tone unfriendly.

"I brought friends," said Portia slowly. "They would like to help."

At the use of the word "friends", the general's eyes flicked up and over the array of dwarves behind Portia on the road.

"Well-armed *friends,* I see," General Bancrot said, leaning over the wall to get a closer look.

"Perhaps we could discuss it over a meal, as you so generously did with me once," said Portia, trying to keep her voice calm and friendly.

The general stared at Portia, squinting her eyes, and then stepped back a half step. "You, from Rocabarra."

Portia nodded and exhaled in relief. "Truly, they are friends."

The general hesitated for a second and then raised her arm to signal her troops. "At ease."

The troops around the general lowered the tips of their weapons but did not stow them.

At least I am no longer one finger-slip away from death, Portia thought. Even so, her heart raced.

"Wait there," the general called.

To Portia's surprise, the general herself stepped through

the gates as they slowly opened. She walked to Portia with a single aide at her side. Both held their hands up high. The general gave a brief nod to General Seren when she drew close to Portia.

"It is you. You are a most unusual child. Are these really dwarves with you?"

"They are."

"And do you have a letter from their king and queen as well?"

"I do, from their queen. May I show you?"

General Bancrot nodded.

Moving slowly, Portia reached behind herself to open one saddlebag and slowly withdraw a letter. The general did not move to take it from her.

Her legs shaking, Portia slowly dismounted the horse and slid down to the ground, the gravel beneath her feet feeling strange after hours of riding. Portia patted the horse, willing it to step back, but instead it trotted back to the dwarf battalion, nuzzling up to another horse of the group. Portia stood alone in front of the general and her aide with the weapons of both sides still at ready for a false move from any of the three of them.

The general took the letter from Portia's outstretched hand. She broke the seal and scanned it quickly. "This proposes an alliance," the general said, wonder in her voice.

"I told you, they are friends."

The general handed the letter to her aide, who scanned it himself. His mouth dropped open, and the look of disdain he had worn while walking out with the general disappeared. He stared at Portia as if he could find some secret within her countenance.

"I do not have the authority to make such alliance, nor do I have the authority to allow a foreign army within these gates, or beyond into the kingdom of Haulstatt. I'm here to assist Lusatiana."

"I understand, but we need to get to Coverack. The queen expects us, or me anyhow. I need to get back to close the splinters."

The general's aide shook his head and sneered at Portia. She ignored him. To the aide's surprise, the general nodded. "I am coming to expect as much when I meet you. We will send word to the queen."

At some signal Portia did not catch, the command was called out from the wall behind. Within moments, a shadow lengthened from the gate ahead, as if the sun itself was moving from behind the town and casting a long, dark trail ahead of itself. The shadow resolved into a hooded person dressed all in dark gray standing feet from the general. Portia recognized the uniform as the spy house of Coverack.

"Yes, General, you called," said the shadowy figure to General Bancrot, giving a bow.

"Yes, send word to the court of Coverack of what has happened here and ask for their command," the general said.

The figure nodded once. "I will have an answer within a day." It was many days ride to the capital and many days ride back. There was magic involved somehow. Portia wished she knew how it worked, but word of such magic was not even breathed in the Academy she had attended in the capital city. Some secrets were held close to the state.

Just as quickly as it had come, the figure faded away again and was gone.

As if on cue, the cloud bank overhead passed away from the sun and light streamed down in the group, warming Portia's back.

"If your friends are anything like you, I'm sure they're starving. Come, I can't let you inside the gate, but we can share a meal out here." The general held out her arm, a smile on her face.

———

THE ARMY from Haulstatt generously cleared a spot close enough to the creek behind the city that the dwarven soldiers felt comfortable enough to bathe in twos and threes while still in sight of the others from their battalion. The dwarves set up camp and put cook pots over fires with wood provided by Lusatiana and soldiers of the town. A deer was gifted to the dwarves from the soldiers of Haulstatt kingdom. General Bancrot herself brought a sack of fruit from the orchard in the bishop's yard in the town and came to eat with them. Conversations were carefully guarded and focused mainly on the game available and preferred cooking methods. Nothing of the strategic use of the forces was spoken of. Those close enough to Portia to hear circled around and listened intently as she described her experiences in the Dragonoid's land to General Bancrot.

The campfires were just dying down as another shadow stretched across what was left of the red coals. Grania, the spymaster of Coverack in the kingdom of Haulstatt, appeared. Portia jumped, as did others at the old woman's sudden presence.

"Greetings, young Jack. You were thought lost. The queen and king consort will be much pleased," said Grania. Her eyes fixed intently on Portia, who squirmed under the examination. As always, in a way she couldn't explain, Portia felt that Grania wanted to take something from her.

"I'm happy to be back," said Portia, straightening and forcing in a deep breath.

Grania glanced at the dwarves around the campfire and then tilted her head questioningly at Portia.

"This is General Seren, of the Dwarven kingdom Morgani. Queen Morgani has agreed to an alliance to fight off the Dragonoids," said Portia in a rush.

Grania raised her eyebrows. "Only the queen and king can agree to an alliance. You overstep your place with any promises you have made."

Portia got to her feet so her eyes were level with Grania's. No one else rose. Instead, they sat and stared at Portia as she faced the spymaster. "I made no promises, at least none to our disadvantage," Portia said, trying to recall exactly what she had said. "Jukhnovo has fallen, I know that, and I've seen Rodaine with my own eyes. Nothing is left. The remainders of Lusatiana's army is around us. If we don't band together, Haulstatt will be next, and the people of our kingdom will be slaves to these invaders. The dwarves have agreed to come help, and they will send more to meet us so that we may retrieve our people from the Dragonoid lands and not just shut the splinters against them. They are our best hope."

An ember flicked up from the fire and drifted off in the breeze as Grania considered Portia and her words. General Bancrot cleared her throat and then slowly stood. Spymaster Grania acknowledged her with a nod.

"Portia speaks the truth of the matter. You know it. I would not be here if it was not so, for they still need my help up in Rocabarra and the Moss Gate, but this was even more urgent," said the general.

"I see," said Grania. "How many are there?" She gestured to the dwarven soldiers.

"One battalion," answered Portia.

"One company of a battalion," said General Seren, gently correcting Portia.

"One company?" asked Portia, confused.

"A battalion is usually somewhere between four hundred to eight hundred troops," General Bancrot said to Portia under her breath.

"That is correct," said General Seren. "The rest of this battalion will be meeting us at sea outside of Coverack."

The shocked faces of General Bancrot, Spymaster Grania, and Portia shone in the low light of the fire, while Iva let out a long low whistle.

10

"I see," said Grania. "And this force is to help us." The spymaster faced General Seren over the fire. Soldiers in the dark behind them shifted as they watched.

"It is to help Portia, so since she says so, then yes, to help you," said General Seren, an edge to her voice. "She has worked hard to earn such help."

Grania narrowed her eyes at Portia. "Then the kingdom is in your debt."

Unsure what to say, Portia nodded.

"This dwarven company may enter the kingdom of Haulstatt and journey to Coverack. General Seren, you will need to come and discuss this alliance with the queen and king."

"Of course," answered the general, her tone polite.

"You will be escorted by General Bancrot and her army. The general has other business in Coverack," said the spymaster. "And you, young Jack, no more alliances without talking to the queen and king first." Grania scowled in Portia's direction.

A retort died on Portia's lips as she staggered from a kick to the calf that Iva delivered from behind her.

"Why does she keep calling you Jack?" asked Iva as they lay under their blankets in the small tent the dwarves had given them.

"It's my title, Jack of Magic," answered Portia, her eyes shut.

"Title, huh?" said Iva, gently teasing. "You didn't tell me you were so fancy." She poked Portia with one finger.

"I'm not fancy. It just means a lot of work. And pressure," said Portia, pulling her blanket up higher under her chin.

"And armies following you."

"Goodnight, Iva." Portia rolled over so her back was to Iva, who grunted and crossed her arms before elbowing Portia's back. Portia shifted a few inches away and pulled the covers over her head.

Mark haunted her dreams that night. She hadn't seen him since their battle outside the Well of Tears. He and the two others on their longboat had been fighting off the arrows and torches from two huge vessels that towered over their tiny craft so that Portia could concentrate on closing the huge splinter that was the portal to Dragonoid world. The soldiers on the enormous boats had known that whatever Portia was doing was endangering their escape route, and their weapons and flames had rained down on the humans' tiny craft from above with desperate abandon.

She hadn't intended to leave Mark and the others. She hadn't intended to go through the portal at all. But by the time she knew what was happening, she was already through, and her spell was complete. The portal had snapped shut, slicing through the boat and leaving her portion in the Dragonoid land while the other section remained behind. She could only assume the section Mark and the others had been on had sunk just as quickly as her own little corner of the boat. At least where she ended up, no one was trying to kill her, and it had been daylight out. The others had been fighting for their lives in the blackness of night.

The longer she stayed away from Coverack, the longer it would be before she would hear that he was severely injured, or worse yet, dead. For as long as she could remember, he had been her closest family, her only family after John had died. As amazing as it had been to find her mother, that still didn't feel real. The woman was a stranger to her.

Mark was a different matter.

For the hundredth time, she dreamt of the wood boat shuddering as the splinter snapped through it, closing off the passage between the two lands. Ice-cold water flooded her legs, lapping up against her abdomen and covering her head in a rush. Portia jerked awake, panting in the darkness. Undisturbed, Iva snored next to her.

Not only was there Mark to think about, and Sawyer, the second-in-command, but also Professor Aelric Terfel and all the other students who had insisted on going with them to the Well of Tears. The others had stayed back on the *Dancing Queen*, as Portia had insisted before the longboat had set out, but she knew they were talking of plans to rescue the small attack party, despite her insistence they not do so. It would be horrifying to return to learn that the entire party had perished in a suicide mission.

Portia shook her head to clear the vision of all those dead faces. Somehow, it had to have worked out. But thoughts of John and Elyas, who had both perished, reminded her that those she loved were not immune to dying.

A chill ran over her, and she rubbed her arms. Iva groaned in her sleep, and Portia exited the tent to walk off her anxiety. The rest of the camp slept, except for the night watch, who nodded as she passed.

It took an hour of pacing before she was able to return to the tent and sleep again.

THEY MADE quick progress through the countryside of Haulstatt, heading north towards Holne, a town on the road on the way to the capital city of Coverack. Most of the soldiers camped outside Holne for the night after obtaining permission from the local commander, but Portia and Iva were able to go into town for dinner at an inn. Grania had been tightlipped about any information from the kingdom, no matter how many ways Portia had asked. Portia clinked the silver in her bag she planned to use to buy drinks and loosen tongues.

Iva walked quietly alongside her, her head bowed, as they made their way into the town square.

"Are you okay?" asked Portia.

Iva shook her head no, then yes, then no again. "It's harder to see everything here so normal. It doesn't seem right when my kingdom was so devastated."

Portia squinted at the streets filled with soldiers and weaponry and horses. Gone were the women and children in the market square. True, the buildings still stood, but it did not look anything like she had remembered the last time she saw. Still, seeing Iva's watery eyes, she decided against mentioning the changes.

One of the barmaids recognized Portia when they entered and gave her a glad smile. Portia struggled but couldn't remember her name, and the maid unhelpfully did not offer it. The young woman did give them a good table in a quiet corner and a huge helping of bread while they waited for their meal. A few jealous eyes stared at them. Portia looked away, feeling uncomfortable being served before the few army men who had made it inside the inn. But soon enough the maid brought bread and drink for all, and the looks subsided.

Iva perked up when a huge bowl filled with stew arrived. The barmaid lingered for a moment, brushing invisible crumbs off the table in front of Portia.

"Are you really a Jack?" she finally asked.

Portia's face flushed red, the heat extending to her ears.

"I'm not sure what you mean," she said, her tongue feeling thick on the lie.

"Just that you're something special. You're gonna help us."

"We're all going to help." Portia waved to the soldiers and herself and Iva.

"That's not what I meant," said the barmaid.

"Well, I'm not sure what you're talking about," said Portia, grabbing a spoon to dig into her meal and then stopping herself. "But we've been gone a long time. We know nothing of what has happened here."

"You're lucky to have missed it. We were blessed here. The invaders were in Valencia and never made it this far."

Portia's throat felt thick. Valencia—her hometown.

"Does it... Does it still stand?" Portia asked, forcing the question out. Iva stopped eating, listening for the answer as well.

"That it does, but only for the fierceness of those gangs," said the barmaid, a mixture of shock and pride in her voice.

"Gangs?" asked Portia, disbelief in her voice. It couldn't be her old gang and the others, could it?

"The Brown Hares and some other things, all animals or something. They were a bunch of kids with magic."

Portia's scalp tingled. *Were?* The gangs she had been a part of were gone?

When Portia did not respond, sitting and staring forward, her spoon dangling from her limp fingers, Iva leaned in to get the barmaid's attention. "What happened?" she asked, prodding for more information.

"They drove off some Dragonoids and held the rest until most of the people fled. It was a mess here as the retreating townspeople passed through. Queen Lorica insisted the refugees move on further inland. Some were really pissed. Others tried to go back to get their stuff, but the soldiers wouldn't let them. It seemed like everyone was fighting each other. Most of the refugees moved on, though I've heard of a few hiding in town. The captain here drives 'em out when he finds them. Says it's a mercy." The maid looked around the soldiers at their tables and lowered her voice further. "If I could leave, I would too. It's far too close to Valencia being in this town and all."

"And the gangs?" asked Portia quietly.

"What about them?" the maid asked.

"Are they okay?" Portia enunciated the words carefully, using the remainder of her control.

The barmaid shrugged. "I hear most escaped. Didn't get too many slaves that time; at least that's what I heard. That happens to those they capture... They're dragged off and enslaved. I'd rather be dead."

"No, you wouldn't," Portia said reflexively.

"Ha! You know nothing." The barmaid wiped their table one last time before walking off.

"That's some good news," said Iva, digging into her food.

"Yes," Portia answered, moving her food around with her spoon and staring at it glumly.

Iva stopped chewing and stared at Portia. "What's wrong? Do you want the Dragonoids to come here?"

"No, of course not."

"Then why? Is that the town where you were from? Valencia?" asked Iva, realization settling on her face.

"Yes. For as far back as I could remember, before I went to Coverack, that's where I lived. I knew those gangs." She lowered her already quiet voice even further. "I was *in* one of those gangs."

Iva's mouth hung open. "You? In a gang? Did you stab people?"

"What? No, of course not," Portia answered before realizing that yes, actually, she had stabbed people, but only when she had to in self-defense. It was one of her rules to avoid such fights, a rule she usually followed.

"I don't know. If I was in a gang, I think I'd stab people," Iva said, paying attention to her dinner again.

"No, you wouldn't. You're afraid of mice," said Portia. "You didn't like stabbing that spider."

Iva scrunched her nose. "No, you're right. That was gross. I only did it because they were attacking us. It's not like if I said 'spider, please go away' it would have."

"How do you know? You didn't even try."

Iva shoved a piece of her bread in her mouth and just pointed at Portia, who snorted. "Seriously," said Iva, around her mouthful of food, "what was it like being in a gang?"

"Scary. It wasn't fun." Portia looked down, away from Iva's intense gaze. "The gangs are there for survival. If you're not in a gang, it's bad. You got no one to watch your back, and even sleeping is dangerous. But if you can get in one, then you have a gang house with a guard and sometimes a cook. People can go out with you. Even if you have to steal to make your dues, it's still safer than sleeping on the street."

"You pay dues?" Iva asked, her brow wrinkling.

"You work. You have to bring money into the house," said Portia.

"So, it's a job."

"Sort of."

"A really dangerous job."

"Yes," said Portia. "If you have to steal for your dues, then yes. Some find other ways."

"Did you?" asked Iva.

Portia shoved the rest of her dinner away, half-eaten, then picked up her dinner knife and banged the base of the hilt on the table repeatedly with soft taps. "No."

"You—"

"Yes. Are you almost done?" Portia asked. Iva shook her head and started shoving food into her mouth quickly, chewing while wrapping a protective arm around her dinner plate.

Portia snorted and picked at her food while waiting for Iva to finish.

———

LATER THAT NIGHT, after finishing their meal at the inn, they wound their way through the army camp to find their tent. Some guardsmen had found kegs of ale, and loud singing rang through the camp in celebration of their return to Haulstatt. A few men stumbled drunkenly before them but got quickly out of the way when they saw Portia and Iva coming. The commander had warned everyone to take care of the young girls and impressed over and over again the value they were to Queen Lorica and King Consort Aldis. They were to be protected at all cost. Iva watched in amazement at the soldier's deference, staring after as they walked away after bowing low to the girls.

"Life is good as a Jack," said Iva, turning to look at Portia again. "I know that was not for me."

Portia shook her head. "It's better to not be noticed."

Iva bit her lip thoughtfully at that.

They walked in silence for a few moments, the rowdy singing growing further away. Here the tents were dark, lit by low fires with soldiers in front of them sharpening their blades and cleaning their armor. Not all the soldiers relieved their anxiety by drinking. Here, anxiety was honed down with every honing stone stroke and every wipe of polish on already shining armor. The men at work over their tools nodded in acknowledgment as Portia and Iva passed them.

"Do you know what happened to your gang in Valencia?" asked Iva.

Portia shook her head. "Only what that maid told us."

Iva hesitated and then asked in a rush, "Why did you leave? If the gang was your safety, how did you end up in Coverack so far away from it?"

"It didn't stay safe. The old gang leader, John, who had brought me and Mark and most others in, died." Portia swallowed then shook her head again. "His replacement was not so caring, at least not for me. She had the magic of coercion."

Portia kicked at a rock in the path, sending it flying down the packed dirt. "I didn't realize I was the only one resistant to it until it seemed the whole house was turned upside down and nothing was what it was before. I couldn't understand what was happening. If I had been quicker thinking, she might not have ever figured out that I could resist her. I was foolish and said no to her." Portia stared at her feet while she walked. "She did not like it."

"You couldn't spend your life a mindless slave for someone," said Iva, protesting.

Portia kicked another rock. "No, not a lifetime, but I could have been smarter. I could've played the game and bought myself some time to figure out what to do."

"What happened?"

"She turned the gang on us," Portia said bitterly, thinking of all those she had thought were her friends, or at least her allies, pointing and jeering at her and calling for her death. *Her death!* She had almost fainted that evening with Mark at her side, their entire lives forfeit in just a few minutes from the only place of safety they had ever known. She felt a little faint just thinking about it.

"Us?"

"Mark. He's like my younger brother. I found him on the street, soon after his parents... soon after he lost them. John said I could take him in if I'd be responsible for him. And I was." Until she hadn't been. Until she'd left him behind.

Again.

A pit of nausea and bile clenched in Portia's stomach. He had to be okay, but thinking of the fierce attack they'd been enduring outside the Well of Tears, she couldn't see how he would be. Still, somehow, she thought she'd know if he was dead.

"Wasn't there anyone else there that was your friend?" Iva asked quietly.

"Some of them were okay. They weren't mean, just... preoccupied. One of the enforcers would have rather been a scholar. All he cared about was his books. I know he did his enforcer duties just to survive. Still, when a person holds your life in their hands, it is little comfort to know they only are doing it because they have to."

"True," Iva said, glancing at Portia's morose posture. "Tell me about this scholar."

"All he wanted to do was read. He stole so he could buy books. Can you imagine?"

"I can," said Iva, drawing Portia's look. "Books are expensive. We only had one in our house, and Pa didn't let me touch it much. Told me I never cleaned my hands enough. Guess no one's worried about being clean now that the book's probably a pile of ash. Along with Pa."

Portia squeezed Iva's arm as they continued to their tent.

That night, Portia dreamt of the gang, not just Mark.

They were back in the Black Cat house in Valencia, everything just as she remembered it: the guard at the door, the dim living room, the delicious smells emanating from the kitchen, just slightly stronger than the curses and foul language of Cook, who had always shooed everyone away before dinner time. All the faces of her old gang members passed by her, even tiny little Tonya, with her golden hair and tiny little pink bows, who they had used as a decoy when robbing mothers in the market. Tonya looked sweet, but inside the house and away from the eyes of marks, she packed a strong punch if anyone tried to take her food.

The only strange thing was in the living room. Peter was in a cage, hanging and swinging from a gigantic hook in the living room ceiling while Merwin held out a book just out of Peter's reach. Peter swiped at it, sending the cage rocking back and forth while Merwin laughed at him and told him he made the wrong bet. Peter cried out in frustration as Merwin slowly rubbed his fingers around the outside of the book. Peter never let anyone touch his books. He threatened violence and gang expulsion to anyone who thought of it. As an enforcer, it had not been within Peter's power to remove anyone from the gang, but no one had ever been brave enough to test that rule.

Merwin winked at Peter and opened the book, his ink-stained fingers poised over the clean vellum. Peter moaned and then yelled at Merwin, who only chuckled with delight at Peter's discomfort.

Portia looked around wildly. This made no sense. Merwin was Peter's friend, or at least as close to being friends as orphans in a gang got.

Then Portia saw her.

Deyelna sat in a chair at the back of the dark living room, watching the scene with a smirk on her face. She was the new gang leader with the magical power of coercion. Deyelna flicked several fingers in Merwin's direction, and he lowered his head, his dreads falling in the crisp pages as he read a few sentences out loud from the book, his tone singsong and mocking. Another flick of Deyelna's fingers and Merwin grabbed a page between his thumb and index finger then slowly tore it from the book, the page jerking free as each stitch of the binding was broken through. Peter screamed, his eyes wild, as the book was desecrated. His scream rang out, going on and on, rising in pitch until Portia shoved her hands over her ears.

She woke with a start. The screaming noise was the metal axle of a wagon dragged sideways over a rock by an agitated horse. The camp was up and packing. She had overslept. Pushing the sweat soaked bedclothes aside, she stood and quickly dressed. Iva was not in the tent.

Portia's hands shook as she shoved her belongings into her bags and pulled the tent rope free from the stake that held it tight. Dreaming of Deyelna unnerved Portia. Deyelna was not a threat to Portia any longer, nor to anyone else.

Deyelna was one of the people Portia had stabbed so she would survive.

***

THEY RODE HARD TO COVERACK, making the journey on the second day. The foot soldiers slowed them down, and the commanders had them camp for the night rather than push on into the evening. Portia shifted uncomfortably on the saddle on her horse, thinking longingly of the hot baths they had had in the kingdom of Morgani. Except for the occasional dip in an ice-cold stream, none of them had much chance to bathe, and the army was an aromatic group.

As the capital city rose up on the horizon with the sea

shining behind it, Portia exhaled loudly. Iva looked to her and then back at the city.

"As if nothing has happened," said Iva.

"As if," said Portia. "They were attacked; I saw it. I was there. But somehow, it looks as it always has."

"Wait until we get closer," said Iva quietly.

Closer inspection did reveal the scars from fires in the harbor and the whiteness of fresh wood on the walls of some buildings. The city had not been decimated and, indeed, was well on its way to repairing itself. The castle on the hill was unscarred, at least from the distance they could inspect it.

A scout came down the road to greet them, the hooves of his horse galloping loudly on the gravel and packed-earth road stretching out before them. Portia looked around the country-side, trying to catch a glimpse of the spies that must also be watching. An occasional shadow looked suspiciously dark, but she couldn't be sure if she had seen anyone.

More changes were apparent the closer they got to the city gates. The sprawling tents and outer market were gone, only bare patches of dirt revealing where they had been. All brush had been burned back from the walls of the city. There was no place for a spy or an invader to hide.

Tall pikes revealed the location of soldiers on the wall, while thin slits in the brickwork provided access for archers. Goosebumps rose on Portia's arms as they drew closer. Before, the entrance to the city was almost joyous. No one was smiling now.

Once General Bancrot and General Seren called out their credentials alongside Portia, the gate was raised, and they were allowed inside. There, the smiling faces of Queen Lorica and King Consort Aldis greeted Portia. Queen Lorica wore a thick green embroidered brocade gown and King Consort Aldis a matching doublet. A crowd gathered behind them and continued down the sides of the road to the castle. Soldiers lining the street herded curious kids back to their parents while the crowd craned and peered at the newcomers.

"What's going on?" Iva said under her breath to Portia.

Portia shook her head. She didn't know. Sliding off her horse, she handed the reins to a waiting soldier and curtsied to the queen and king.

"Stand," said the queen. "We are here to welcome back our Jack."

"Since our spymaster has testified to your identity," said King Consort Aldis, giving Portia a wink. "It would not do to have our city give such a welcome to an interloper."

"Why wouldn't it be me?" asked Portia, confused.

"The story we heard makes it hard to believe you could be in front of us, and yet, here you are," said Queen Lorica. "For that we are grateful, make no mistake. The whole city is grateful. Word was leaked of your arrival, and we acquiesce to our citizens' desire to see you celebrated."

"After we verified it was you, of course," said King Consort Aldis.

"It is me," said Portia. "I'm sorry about Mark and Sawyer and the rest of the *Dancing Queen*."

"Mark?" asked the queen.

"I mean, leaving him to..." Water filled Portia's eyes. She

forced herself to breathe slowly and deeply, willing the tears to retreat back into her head and not run down her face.

The queen tilted her head at Portia. "If you have amendments to make up to Mark, you may do so in person. He now lives in the palace. We have become quite taken with him."

Portia's mouth fell open, and she stared at the queen, until Iva, who had curtsied alongside Portia, gently nudged her with an elbow. Portia closed her mouth and looked down, her mind racing.

"He's alive," she finally choked out.

"Oh, very much so," said the queen with a laugh. "He can be an energetic young man. Luckily, we have found a use for such."

"But how?"

"We will discuss this later. Our people are waiting," Queen Lorica said gently.

The queen was assisted into an open carriage by a finely liveried footman, followed by King Consort Aldis. The carriage slowly rumbled away, and the second one, also open and just as magnificently painted as the royal carriage, pulled up from behind it. A footman opened the door and motioned for Portia to enter. Portia grabbed Iva's hand and pulled her in alongside her.

Iva pulled back, resisting. "They're not here to honor me."

"I don't care. I'm not riding in this thing alone," Portia said, not taking her gaze from the crowds ahead of them. The last time she'd been in the city, her existence as a Jack had been a secret. What had changed? What did these people know about her, or think they knew about her? The warmth of

Iva sitting next to her reassured Portia, as did the knowledge that General Seren and General Bancrot were in the next carriage back. She had turned to stare until she saw them get into their vehicle. Only then did she relax and face the city people.

Some cheered, some stared. Most looked happy, but an occasional dark scowl on a brow startled Portia. If Mark was indeed at the castle, she hoped he could tell her what was going on in the city and why some folk would not be happy to see her.

"Oh my, this is all for you?" said Iva, wonder in her voice.

"I don't know why," Portia said, her voice coming out more petulant than she intended.

"Perhaps because you closed the splinter."

"One or two, which apparently comes with its own problems."

Iva stared at Portia then gave her arm a gentle punch. "These people are happy and grateful. Accept it. You helped them, and they love you for it."

Portia rubbed her arm and then stared at the crowd, slowly raising her hand to wave back at them. They let out a cheer. She couldn't entirely hide a hint of a smile on her lips.

KING CONSORT ALDIS put down a glass of mead in front of Portia. She looked up, startled. After the fanfare and pageantry of going through the city streets, the royal retinue had retreated to meet in one of the smaller rooms behind the throne room.

Portia, the king consort and queen, and several guards and advisors had been ushered into this room, while Iva was led to the banquet hall. Iva's protests of being separated from Portia died down after Portia's nod and a graphic description from the chamberlain of all the delicacies awaiting her from the royal cook. Portia laughed under her breath as Iva's concerned stare entreating Portia to do something had turned into fascination at the officious palace official as he described stuffed wild boar, rare field greens with fresh berries drizzled in exotic oils, and trays of flaky pastries. His voice droned on in a monotone as he led her away, still listing dishes, sometimes repeating himself at Iva's request.

Advisors lined the back of the small room, seated at desks with parchments in front of them, quills ready, while the main group occupied a round table that took up most of the room. The king consort himself poured drinks and served them, even to General Bancrot and General Seren. General Bancrot shifted uncomfortably in her seat at the break in protocol but managed a polite "thank you" as a drink was placed in front of her.

"We are most grateful to see you here alive," said Queen Lorica, once the king consort had taken his seat beside her. "Although we are somewhat concerned with these treaties you have attempted on our behalf."

"I have not promised anything except that we will work together," said Portia, unsure of what the problem was.

"Our resources are stretched rather thin. Our first priority is protecting our people," said Queen Lorica.

General Seren cleared her throat, drawing the queen's eye. At the queen's nod, she spoke. "We are not here to retrieve forces from your kingdom, but rather to offer our own in assistance."

The queen stared at the commander. "I see. And what is the price for such assistance?"

"It is not one without benefit for yourself," said General Seren. "Some of our own are trapped in the Dragonoids' lands, as many of your people are, I daresay. Your young Portia here has convinced our archmage that she might be the key to retrieving them if she can learn the melody of one of the still-open splinters. We have two possibilities. One is to go through an existing splinter and rescue our folks through force."

After speaking, General Seren looked down. All in the room knew the difficulties of fighting the Dragonoids head-on. The cities of the kingdoms below and above Haulstatt were decimated, flattened shells of what had been. The fact that Coverack and the underground kingdom of Morgani still stood was due in no small part to Portia's ability to shut off the splinters and the access the Dragonoid forces had to their lands.

"And the second possibility?" asked the queen.

"Portia learns the tune of the splinter to that land and can replicate it in a different place where the Dragonoids will not be expecting us," said General Seren quietly.

The queen tilted her head in understanding. "Opening up the possibility of surprising them."

General Bancrot nodded agreement with the queen's assessment.

"Or simply sneaking in and moving around them because they do not know we have come." General Seren gave a wry smile. "I am not above skulking through the night to retrieve my liege, if it increases my chances."

"Your liege?" the queen asked.

General Seren nodded. "My king."

The queen raised one eyebrow and looked to the back of the room where the advisors were sitting at their desks. A shadow lengthened, and Grania appeared, bowing to the queen. Portia shook herself. She was never going to get used to that.

"Apologies, My Queen. I had not yet acquired that information," said Grania.

"It is not something we would freely share," General Seren admitted.

"Things do not usually escape our spymaster," said the queen.

The commander shrugged.

"No matter. That does make some things clearer. Grania has briefed us on the forces coming. We had wanted to meet you in person first," said the queen.

Portia straightened up hopefully in her chair.

"We will agree to the alliance, to the terms that were offered in the document sent ahead with our spymaster, with one caveat: that our Jack of Magic be protected at all costs.

We nearly lost her once. We cannot afford to do so again." The queen picked up her glass and sipped it, waiting for the commander's response.

"Of course," said General Seren. "We have our own selfish reasons for wanting her continued good health and presence."

"Then it is agreed," said the king consort, a cheerful note in his voice. All around the table, voices echoed assent, while the scribes in the back furiously wrote, documenting the meeting. "There are more details to be looked to, but I'm sure we can find agreement on all of them." The king consort looked up at a door opening in the rear of the room behind Portia where a servant stood in the doorway and bowed.

"The visitor you requested is here," said the servant.

The queen looked up.

"By all means, let him in," said the king consort, smiling as he turned to look at Portia. "Portia, I think this is someone you've been waiting to see."

Portia looked to the king, confused, and then back to the door. Mark stepped inside the frame. His hair was overgrown and shaggy, and he was several inches taller than she remembered, but it truly was Mark, the boy she had grown up with, now looking so unnervingly like an adult. And alive. He gave her a wicked smile before bowing to the company in the room.

The last time she had seen him, he had been struck with an arrow and was under attack with no seeming possibility of escape. Yet here he was. Her mouth went dry and her stomach flipped, bouncing around until she thought she would no longer be able to breathe. Gripping the armrests of her chair, she forced herself to stay seated.

"How are you alive?" she asked him.

"Are you disappointed?" he asked, good-naturedly mocking her.

"Of course not. I just... We were so outnumbered. How could you possibly have survived?" Portia asked, incredulous.

The king consort quietly cleared his throat. Portia turned once again to the round table with all the dignitaries.

"I apologize, Your Majesties, I am just so surprised," she said.

"No apologies needed, our Jack, but we know the story and you do not. Go with him and learn it. We have further business here," said the queen.

Portia wanted to protest. If they were going to do more negotiations, she felt she should be involved. Perhaps that was far too presumptuous. Who was she, a former street thief and mere student at the Academy, to think she had a right at the table of leaders?

Part of Portia flared in rebellion.

A voice inside her screamed that she was the Jack of Magic. It was she who had convinced the Elven kingdom to allow the fleeing humans shelter. It was she who had brought a Dwarven army to their lands. She was the one to close the splinters.

But Iva's words suddenly filled her head. She could not do it all alone. She must trust in her leaders who served her and allow herself a rest. Portia glanced back at Mark. He gave her another mischievous smile.

Placing that trust would also allow her to leave and spend time with her friends.

The queen gave Portia a gentle look. Portia's misgivings faded away. She rose and then curtsied at the queen and king consort.

"Yes, Your Majesties. Thank you, Your Majesties."

Walking with more restraint than she felt possible, she exited the room with Mark.

THEY WALKED along the palace hallway, their footsteps echoing down the empty corridor. Portia wanted to ask Mark more questions but knew her words would drift into the room they had just left. She bit her lip to force herself not to speak.

Finally, they made it to the entry hall and out the door into the bright sunshine, servants holding open the door and then clicking it shut behind them. Portia turned to Mark and grabbed both his arms, shaking him a little. He laughed and backed up.

"Whoa, are you okay?" he asked.

"Of course I am. How are you okay?" Portia asked, exasperated even through her gladness.

"I might ask the same of you. One moment you were there, the next you were gone. Sawyer had to drag me away. I feared you had been yanked up into one of the boats above us. He had been watching and saw you disappear into the portal. That convinced me," he said ruefully. "That, and the sheared-off corner of the boat that sank before my eyes."

"Drag you off to where? If the boat sank, weren't you drowning as well?" Portia asked, confused. He made it sound so much less chaotic than it had been. They'd been under full attack with weapons raining down on them, hugely outnumbered by two gigantic ships full of Dragonoids.

"Ah, but we had a secret escape," Mark said. He grinned at her, offering nothing more.

"Well?" She crossed her arms.

"Well, what?" he said, echoing her, and crossing his own arms before dancing back out of her reach.

Her fingers twitched in irritation. As happy as she was to see him, he also infuriated her faster than anyone else she knew. "How did you escape!?" she yelled.

He laughed again. Portia slapped her thighs and whirled around in frustration.

"Okay, I'm sorry. It's just so good to see you again," he said, his voice dropping. "We had a secret weapon. We weren't to tell you and distract you. It was from Professor Aelric. He gave us these balls. I don't know what they were, but when we smashed them, they formed an air pocket around our heads. I had one for you too."

"Air pockets?" asked Portia, even more confused. "How is that useful? Why wasn't I told?"

"Because you," Mark pointed at her, before motioning for her to follow him down to the carriage waiting for them, "had other things to concentrate on. Like closing the splinter. Which you did."

Portia stepped into the open door of the carriage and flopped down on the seat while Mark followed and took the opposite seat, leaving the liveried servant to shut the door and tap on the wall of the carriage, letting the driver know they were ready to go. A flick of the reins rattled outside, and the horses jerked the vehicle into motion.

"You still haven't explained air pockets," said Portia, once again crossing her arms and slouching down in the carriage seat to stare at Mark.

"It was rather terrifying, to be honest. The plan was if the boat was sunk, to let them think we had drowned with it. We put the air pockets around our heads and let our bodies fall into the waters. We had to cling to our weapons to have enough weight to sink into the waters. Some of us needed more help than others. That soldier, he dropped like a stone, while Sawyer and I had to hold on to the soldier's shield to keep under the waters." He chuckled a little at the memory.

Portia had tilted her head at Mark. "Are you insane? When people want to live, they try to keep to the surface, not to fall down into the deep depths of the water."

"True. But then most people don't have arrows and torches pitched at them while they are in the water."

True.

"Well?"

"Are you impatient?" Mark teased.

Portia's right foot twitched. His kneecap was within easy reach.

His eyes dropped to her swinging foot and then back up to her eyes. "No need for that." He shifted to the side of the carriage, putting more distance between him and her foot, before continuing on quickly. "The plan was to drop out of sight, for me to use my light beacon underneath the waters so the second longboat would know where to drop a rope. We all had to stick together. I was the only one capable of the light magic. We managed that. That was why we couldn't leave unless we were sure you were beyond our reach. It was one shot—and our only chance to make it out of there."

Portia's foot stopped moving. Her mouth hung open. "A second longboat? Who was on it?"

"Who do you think?" Mark asked, a gentle smile on his face.

Professor Aelric, Liam, Richard, or maybe even Mia and Ella.

"My classmates," Portia whispered.

Mark nodded. "I'll be honest though; I don't remember much about who was there exactly. After we grabbed the rope and were pulled up, I passed out in the bottom of the boat. We had tied Sawyer to me, he had so many injuries. The air bubbles could have been a little larger." His tone was nonchalant on the surface, but the tiniest crack in his voice gave away to Portia the frightening experience he was describing.

"I could have helped," Portia said.

"No, you couldn't have," Mark said gently. "If you'd been distracted from your task, the whole mission would've been for nothing. Closing the splinter was more important than our living, maybe even more important than your living. The air magic was only a last-ditch life preserver just in case we ran into problems. Thank goodness we had it. I am rather impressed with your professor."

Portia nodded, swallowed, then looked out the window,

suddenly uncomfortable with the truth of Mark's willingness to die for the mission. She hadn't thought it probable they would run into such terrible odds. Her bravado had been more a denial of reality than true courage. How had he known and she hadn't?

"It's okay. We're all fine, for the moment. Your classmates aren't bad, not even Ella," Mark reassured her.

She turned back to him and raised an eyebrow. "Even Ella?"

"Aside from the threats and vague ominous sayings, she's not that awful. Except for when we returned without you. Then she was livid. It was actually quite frightening. She held me personally responsible. Unfair, you know. I wasn't the only other person on the boat." Mark picked at imaginary lint on his immaculate trousers. Despite his scruffy hair, he still had the perfect outfit and persona he had cultivated in Rodaine, as that of a son of a rich merchant. Perhaps the messy hairstyle was the new fashion. "It was hard to keep her from stowing away in the carriage to come meet you."

Her classmates! Now that her fears of Mark's death and the deaths of her old classmates had proven to be unfounded, the tight coil around Portia's heart, one that she had not even realized was there, slowly unwound, letting her heart lift in her chest. She would see them again. All of them.

It was all of them, wasn't it?

"No one... No one, died, did they?" she asked tentatively.

He shook his head. "Not on our voyage. When we got back to the *Dancing Queen*, Sawyer and Professor Aelric decided we should head back. News had to be brought to the queen and king consort of the closure of the splinter. And your disappearance. Professor Aelric took it upon himself to deliver that news in person. Not a job any of us envied."

THE TRAINING LAKE on campus was still there, along with the field of obstacles and magic practice targets made of paper and hay. Gone were the expanses of dark green grass.

Students crowded into the fields, training in groups. Some ran from target to target while others aimed magic at distant bundles of hay that exploded into clouds of golden dried grass when struck. Mixed in amongst the students were city guardsmen in uniform. Guard leaders called commands to the students. Weapons training echoed across the lawn, the ring of sword on sword a constant background to the yelling and pops of magic going off.

Portia stared out the window of the carriage, fascinated. The only constant to the school she remembered was the unique blue stone of the campus buildings.

She leaned back to stare at Mark. "What's going on here?"

He leaned forward to stare out the window at the training, his expression serious. "They're preparing for war. Somehow, when you were lost, it sank into the people that they had to save themselves. For the short time they had known of the existence of a Jack, of you, it had kept them in a bubble of security. After the attack we fought off, and your disappearance, everything changed. The queen and king consort commanded a different mission for the school for the duration of the war. The protection of Haulstatt is to be its only aim until further notice."

On a far field, a soldier yelled clear, and people scattered to each side of the long grassy knoll. A flash of smoke went off by the soldier, curling in a black greasy plume up into the sky. An object burst from the smoke and flew down the field, landing in a shower of thrown up dirt and grass. Portia turned back to Mark.

"Did they figure out how to make the black powder?" she asked.

He shook his head. "Not yet. That was all magic. It still takes too much magic for each strike, but at least now we can manage to throw things with only two people and not four. If we could make that black powder, our precious magic could be used for more complex things."

The carriage pulled to a stop in front of the main building. They exited, and Portia stretched, twisting her back and her neck, appreciating not being on horseback or in the bouncy stiff ride of the wooden wheeled carriage. With a guilty start, she remembered Iva back at the palace. She hadn't meant to leave her there.

"I left someone at the palace," she said. "I probably shouldn't have. She doesn't know anyone, and her family's gone."

Mark barely gave her a glance as he looked for someone on the campus grounds.

"Don't worry. I have a room there now as a reward. I'll find her for you." Mark patted her on the back.

"You what?" Portia asked, she but was distracted when she was grabbed and knocked sideways by a blonde whirl.

"Portia!" a voice shouted in her ear.

Portia staggered back but was squeezed and held up by the arms holding her. She turned to see Ella's face inches from her own. Ella released her.

"You're back! You're alive! Roomie! Savior!" Ella said in a rush.

Portia laughed at the enthusiasm but couldn't help herself retorting, "I thought I was a lazy bum who got out of classes."

"I don't care! Skip them all, as long as you come back," Ella said, laughing herself. More people surrounded them, and hands clapped on the back of Portia's shoulders. A shadow fell over Portia's face.

"I don't think you have the authority for that, Ella Schulz, but you are right that all is well as long as Portia comes back," a deep voice intoned.

Ella turned and looked up to see Professor Aelric staring down at the group, and behind him stood a smiling Professor Hilda Griffiths—her two main teachers in the school and the first to know of her Jack of Magic status. Professor Aelric had been the one responsible for saving Mark when she couldn't be there. Tears welled up in Portia's eyes. Professor Aelric awkwardly cleared his throat and motioned the students away.

"Go, catch up," he said. "But Portia, make no mistake, you're expected in classes in the morning. Now more than ever."

Professor Hilda nodded at her over Professor Aelric's

shoulders and then turned away with him, leaving the students to crowd around Portia. She wanted to talk to them, but the constant questions from the friends around her pulled her attention down, and when she looked up again the two professors were gone.

"Look at you," said Liam, his hair a wide rainbow Mohawk. "Back, but from where? Somewhere warm, judging by your tan," he added teasingly. Nothing about Liam's appearance was ever an accident, but he knew most others were not like that.

His twin, Richard, with plain brown curls and an embarrassed, pained expression, elbowed Liam and then waved at Portia. "Welcome back."

He didn't have a sling on his arm, and Portia was glad to see he looked recovered from the Dragonoid's attack on the city. She wondered how long she had been gone. She had not had a chance to ask Mark that yet, and none of the royals or soldiers had volunteered the information for her.

"Hello, Portia," a warm feminine voice said over the chatter of her friends.

Portia looked up. It was Cecilia, the woman the red mage said was her mother. They did look similar. Suddenly, Portia felt exhausted and went to share an embrace with the woman she had lost once and never thought she would see again.

11

Even though Portia had not known the woman most of her life, the earthy smell of lemongrass and flowers that came up from her kirtle was oddly familiar. And comforting. Cecilia pushed Portia back to see her face but didn't let go of her arms.

"You're really okay," said Cecilia, her face serious.

Portia nodded, wiping tears from her face while smiling and laughing uncomfortably. She turned her face away from her classmates, her voice cracking when she answered. "I am. And so are you. And you're here—at the school."

"That I am. I like it very much here. They've given me room and board in exchange for working in the Academy. Mark checks up on me often."

Portia turned to see Mark whispering conspiratorially in Ella's ear while Ella giggled. Liam looked uncomfortable, his eyes flickering between Mark and Ella. Richard put an arm on Liam's shoulder, pulling him back.

Portia turned back to Cecilia. "Things do seem different here."

Mark loped up to join them. "They are different. After our time on the *Dancing Queen*, I think they have a better appreciation of what it takes to survive on the street as a thief. Or at least my skills. I'm helping teach some stuff."

"You?" asked Portia, incredulously.

"Well, isn't that a little insulting? I did survive, didn't I?" Mark buffed his nails on his shirt.

"Yes, but..." Portia noticed the gazes of her friends as they surrounded her and addressed them all. "Well, that is fantastic news. He learned everything from me."

Ella laughed. "You are such a joker, Portia. Mark's told us all about you. We had no idea you used to do such *funny* things."

Portia huffed and squinted at Mark. She didn't remember much being funny about their time in the Black Cat gang back in Valencia, but the way Ella giggled and laughed made her think Mark might have made something up—something rather embarrassing for her. She took a deep breath and exhaled, purposely looking away from him and centering herself. Perhaps there was a reason. She would have to get him alone to ask him, but for now, with all the others around, there was no chance to talk. It was best to not say anything further. If there was something nefarious going on, he would tell her. And if not, he had found a place, and she should be happy for him.

She *would* be happy for him, she thought as she uncurled

her fists. Portia plastered a smile on her face. "You're right, Ella, I'm always joking,"

Liam came up next to Ella and put his arm around her shoulders. "Nearly dinnertime," Liam said softly into Ella's ear while he stared at Mark.

Ella perked up. Eating was her favorite thing of all, except of course for people. "It is! Oh, Portia, I am so glad you're back," Ella said, as she grabbed Portia's hand and led her towards the dining hall. Abruptly, she stopped and looked around. "Where's your stuff?"

Portia started. Not only had she left Iva at the palace, but she had also left all her gear. Reflexively, she felt for a sword strapped to her side. It was still there.

"Don't worry," said Mark, as he walked with the rest following Ella and Portia. "Everything else will be retrieved."

THE NEXT MORNING, Portia woke before Ella. The sun was just turning the horizon pink outside their bedroom window, but stars still shone in the mostly dark sky. Ella was snoring on her back. They had stayed up late the previous night, talking of all their adventures in the house kitchen. Ella could barely contain her enthusiasm at her own daring while also exclaiming that Portia could not possibly be telling the truth about all that had happened to her. Portia had sorely wished for Iva's presence and her words of confirmation. She told herself that her classmates would meet her soon enough.

Professor Griffiths, or Hilda as Cecilia called her, had

allowed Mark and Cecilia entrance to the house so they had been present as well. Apparently, they had been coming to the house for meals for some time now, being allowed entrance through the portal doors on campus, even though they did not live in the house and had no rooms there.

Mark had left the previous evening along with Cecilia, going back to the campus and then taking a waiting carriage to the palace. Uncomfortable pangs of jealousy pricked Portia's stomach when they took their leave. She knew she should be happy for them but somehow felt she should be the one going back to the palace. There were important meetings in the morning, and she intended to be there.

Moving slowly, Portia eased out from underneath the covers and treaded quietly to her wardrobe. She eased open the door, wincing as the right hinge squeaked. Ella snorted in her sleep and flipped over to her other side. Portia exhaled and opened the left door, trying to not touch the right one again. She was pleased to find her old clothing neatly washed and folded. She'd left in such a hurry for their journey on the *Dancing Queen* that she knew she had left a mess of clothes, both dirty and clean, in the bottom of the wood shelving. Someone had taken great care to wash and mend her old fighting outfits.

Briefly, she held the red kirtle she'd worn when she had first entered the city of Coverack, then discarded it in favor of an older but still serviceable set of breeches and tunic with a matching overtunic. The skirt of a kirtle would not do with her sword. She had been able to hide knives with special slits for access within the red garment, but there was no hiding her copper sword. It was far too large for stashing in a hidden spot. It had to be worn openly, both an advantage as a warning to others and a disadvantage in that it eliminated her ability to hide her armament and surprise any would-be attackers. Discarding her nightgown, she pulled on the chosen clothes and then took the leather baldric with the sword attached from atop her trunk and laid it across her chest. The sword thrummed as if a cat when it settled into its place nestled on her side. She gave it a pat.

Sparing a glance for her trunk, which appeared still sealed, Portia left the room and slowly closed the door behind her. She would verify its precious contents were still intact later, after the morning's business was done.

None of the other students in the house were up yet. Only the distant banging of a cook in the kitchen pulling a large kettle from the back storage room and swinging it over the fire rang through the house. Portia waited by the open archway leading into the kitchen, until she heard the cook once again swing open the door into the back storeroom and go inside, before running across the archway into the doorway that led to the portals to the campus.

The campus itself was eerily quiet. Even in the dim early morning, city guard patrols walked through the grounds nodding at each other. This was a new addition. Previously, only the school's own guard patrolled the grounds. Now, the campus guards looked on sullenly as the city guards proudly marched through. A few of the city soldiers gave her a curious glance, but none challenged her. Making her way to the front of the campus and looking up the hill towards the palace,

Portia was chagrined to find no carriage awaiting her, nor a horse. She chided herself. Why should there be a ride waiting for her as there had been in other times? No one had sent for her. Portia considered trying to take a horse from the campus stables, but she did not have a Letter of Need from any professor, something the ostler in charge of the stables would want from her. Students were not allowed to just take horses at their whim—unless they owned their own, like Magisend Lucy. Portia snorted at that. She would not ask Magisend for help. Not for this.

Checking her waistband, Portia realized she had a purse full of silver with her. It was one of the things she wore without thinking, along with an interior belt where she kept more silver and a few pieces of gold.

It did not take long to find a merchant with a tired horse standing outside his storefront, willing to hire the horse for twice the silver it was worth for a ride to the castle. Taking a look at the horse's gaunt frame and protruding withers, Portia purchased an additional bunch of carrots and extracted a promise of an extra bag of oats for the horse for its efforts from the bemused merchant. She promised a return visit to check up on his word, upon which the merchant's smile disappeared, but he did not cancel the transaction, and she was taken to the palace in the back of the merchant's wagon.

The sun was streaming down by the time they reached the castle gates, having crested the horizon during their journey up the hills of the city. The beams of light shone warmly on Portia's back. It was early summer, and even though the sun was fully up, it still was early in the day for most folk of Coverack, who were just now rising to break their fast. Even the guards at the castle gate seemed a little sleepy, perking up and standing at attention while peering curiously at the wagon approaching.

"Halt," one guard said, holding out one hand and stepping imperiously in front of the wagon. The other guards made no motions to open the gate.

Portia had never seen the castle gate closed before. She had always been invited or escorted by someone else and brought up from the city in a royal carriage with servants and a driver. The merchant seated at the front of the wagon twisted in his seat and eyed her before turning back and studiously staring ahead, staying still so as to draw no attention from the guards.

Looking back and forth between the gate and the guard, Portia bit her lip and then jumped out of the wagon. Both guards outside the castle gate jumped back and lowered their pikes at her. An alarm was called from the top of the castle wall.

"No, I'm no threat," Portia said, backing up and holding up her hands. "You know me. I'm the Jack of Magic."

The merchant turned again and looked at her more closely, squinting as he looked her up and down, and then shook his head. As much as Portia longed to address his dismissal, now was not the time for it. Forcing her eyes away from him, she focused on the guards.

The guard furthest away from Portia kept his pike down and circled around her to provide cover for the other guard, who straightened and advanced on her to take a better look.

After careful inspection, he nodded and waved the other guard at ease. A second horn sounded from the top of the gate. More guards ran along the top of the wall. None pulled back their crossbows aimed at Portia and the wagon driver.

"Welcome, Jack of Magic. You can appreciate we must be careful," the nearest guard said.

Portia nodded. "I can hardly look like a Dragonoid, can I?"

The guard gave a bitter laugh. "Not all those on their side look like them. We've had unhappy news of betrayals and spies. And you are here without anyone to testify you are who you say you are. You do look the part though."

"I am the Jack. I'm Portia," Portia said, feeling a little confused and disgruntled.

"Appearances can be imitated," the guard retorted.

That was true. Appearances could mean nothing at all. She had just started to learn about magic at the Academy, and there were more types than she had even known possible. Portia could do any kind of magic just by watching someone else and other sorts of magic that other humans could not do at all, like the magic of the elves and the dwarves. What she had seen while growing up had been what the orphans in the gangs could do, and the few other instances of people revealing magic in the city of Valencia. It had been frowned upon so often those that could do it hid it from all others.

The orphans in her gang had been able to work light magic, fire magic, and the creation of illusions duplicating one's self. When she'd come to the Academy, she'd learned ice magic along with wind and portal magic, even the magic of the truth cube—an incredible spell that forced anyone to tell the truth. The one kind of magic she had not learned, had not wanted to learn, was that of coercion—of forcing another to do her bidding without any choice of their own. That was a magic too toxic for Portia to even want to attempt. She'd witnessed the bloody harvest of that sort of effort and wanted nothing to do with it.

However, none of those types of magic precluded using magic to imitate another person's image. The guard was right to be cautious. Just because she had not seen it or been taught it, did not mean it didn't exist. If it did, she could easily be someone else. The only way to verify it was with another mage who had the power to reveal the truth. Scanning the wall above revealed no mage standing amongst the guards above her.

"That is true, but I am who I say I am. There are important meetings today with our queen and king consort about negotiating an allegiance with the elves and the dwarves. I should be there," said Portia.

The guard remained unmoved. Portia stepped forward to plead her case, which was greeted by the notching of arrows into the crossbows above and the warning creak of a weapon ready to discharge.

Portia quickly stepped back before speaking again. "Surely someone inside can verify who I am. Isn't the red mage there? Or Grania?" Portia was grateful her voice did not crack.

"It is too early for us to send for anyone," said the guard. "We have our orders for who is allowed entrance and who is not. You are not listed. Even if you were who you say you are, the Jack of Magic, you are not listed to be allowed inside the castle grounds today."

"Then call for someone who has the authority to allow me in," Portia said, demand creeping into her voice despite her best efforts to be calm.

The guard with his pike still pointed at Portia gave a low growl deep in his throat. Her request had come off too much as a command, and that did not go over well with him. The rustling of armor plate and metal hitting metal gave way as the soldiers above agreed with his assessment.

The merchant shifted uneasily in his seat at the front of the wagon. He hunched forward, and Portia could almost envision his wishful thinking that he would disappear on the spot.

The soldier in front and closest to Portia gave her a warning look. He motioned subtly with his head to the guards above. In the silence, the merchant cleared his throat and twitched the reins in his hand, readying himself to leave despite having promised Portia to stay and wait for the extra silver she had promised him.

Portia blew out a puff of air and then shook her shoulders and arms while the soldiers watched closely.

"My apologies, good sir, I would never want to risk even the appearance of putting our queen in danger. I will come back later. Please leave word of my visit to my queen," Portia said, bowing to the surprised guard.

She jumped onto the back of the wagon and thumped on the wooden wall of the bed around the hay she sat on, signaling to the merchant to leave. He flicked the reins and the horse leaned into the harness and drew the wagon away. They turned a wide circle in front of the gate and then went back down the road away from the palace.

The guards watched them leave, only lowering their weapons just as the wagon turned the corner at the base of the hill from the palace. When they were out of sight of the guards, the merchant whistled a long, low whistle. "I thought you were going to get us killed there, miss."

Portia chewed on a piece of hay, not bothering to answer. Her heart was still pounding from the confrontation she had not expected. It probably only meant security was increased because of their ongoing war, but she still felt unease at the hostility and unwelcome from the guards.

Leaving the horse happy with his extra carrots and bag of oats, Portia thumped him on the hindquarter and left the merchant, still disgruntled but much happier with the extra silver she gave him, more than she had even promised initially.

The students were up and about on the campus grounds now, mixing in with the soldiers patrolling the grounds. She had to pass a checkpoint at the main building, describing who she was, but this time her word was accepted, and she was ushered onto the grounds. Perhaps because the campus was full of mages who would see through deception, it was easier for the guards to trust she was who she said she was. Her stomach growled, but she had already missed the breakfast bell. There would be no more food available until lunchtime, at least on campus. She might as well go to class.

Trying to remember her old schedule from what seemed like a lifetime ago, she thought it might be time for history class with Professor Aelric. She had questions for him anyway, so even if there was no class, it would be good to see him. She owed him some thanks for saving Mark and the others, even if he had thought it best to not tell her his plans. Grimacing at his duplicity, she climbed the stairs to his classroom on the second floor of the history building. It galled her to not know everything that was going on.

Portia walked down the hall to his door. It was open. He was lecturing at the front of the hall, writing in chalk on the big blackboard while the students sprawled in the desks behind him.

"It was the confluence of disease, new weapons, and blight on the crops that fall that led to the downfall of the free Phriestine era," Professor Aelric said while scribbling on the board. Something in the room alerted him to a change, and he turned to see Portia standing in the doorway facing him and the other students. Her desk was still there, empty. It felt surreal to be in the classroom after having been gone so long and spending time in the Dragonoid world and under the lands in the Dwarven kingdom. It was as if nothing had happened at all.

"Welcome back, Portia," Magisend Lucy said, a slight drawl in her tone. Portia nodded at her, unsure if it was a true greeting or sarcasm.

"Someone has to keep you on your toes, Magisend," answered Portia. She wove her way between the outstretched legs of the students to reach her desk and slide behind it.

"Yes, welcome back, Portia. Although you are late," Professor Aelric said.

"She does seem to get lost quite often, only to find herself in some exotic land. Perhaps it was a treacherous journey from the breakfast hall to here," said Magisend Lucy, her cronies around her tittering.

"I see that saving your life was not enough. What does it take to get on your good side, Magisend?" Portia asked, feigning politeness she did not feel.

"You—" Magisend started to say.

"Enough." Professor Aelric held up his hands. "We all worked very hard in the battle. I am disappointed in this behavior in my classroom. You will stop now, all of you. Is that understood?"

Both Magisend Lucy and Portia nodded slowly and turned to face the front of the class, sliding down in their seats in nearly identical slouches. Someone in the back of the class giggled. Portia's face turned red, but she refused to turn and glare at whoever it was.

"I will talk to you after class, Portia," said Professor Aelric before he resumed his lecture.

Portia slumped down even further in her seat and stared out the window at the campus grounds and the soldiers walking by as Professor Aelric droned on, the whole day feeling unreal. The classroom was so far away from the real world she had just been in—the world where people were struggling for their homes and their very lives while others were trying to kill and enslave them.

Portia thought of the historical figures Professor Aelric

was lecturing about. Had they had to sit in lectures while their world was burning down around them and all was being changed without their desire or their will? She doubted it. But here she was, Jack of Magic, in history class while the queen and king were up in the castle making history of their own with the visiting dwarf commander.

PORTIA KICKED at an empty chair before sliding into another one next to it and slumping down. "I don't understand. Why would I be stopped at the castle gates?"

Professor Aelric sat at his desk watching Portia and tapping the end of a quill to his chin, considering her words.

"Can the queen do the magic that you can do?" he asked Portia.

"No, of course not," said Portia and then reconsidered her answer. "At least not that I know of.

"She cannot heal the splinter, something that is most critical to our survival?"

"No, not that I know of.

"And we cannot risk her on a boat out in the middle of the ocean to go to battle for us?" asked Professor Aelric.

"No! Why are you asking me these things that surely you know the answers to better than I?" asked Portia, exasperated.

"Because I am not the one who needs the answers," said Professor Aelric as he set down the quill and then tented his fingers, tapping them together in front of his face, staring over the tips of them at Portia.

Portia scowled and looked down. She examined the toes of her boots, turning each boot one way and then another before tucking her feet back underneath her and sitting up straighter.

"I understand your point," she said, sullenly.

"You sure?" he asked.

She nodded, finally making eye contact.

"They will contact you when they are ready for your assistance. Is it not too much to ask to trust your own queen and king that they might do what is best for our kingdom?"

Portia didn't answer, instead rising from her chair and going to look out the window, turning her back to her professor. He sighed and pushed his hair back from his face.

"It is so hard to not do something," Portia said, finally.

"Then do something."

She turned from the window to stare at him.

"From what you told me today, you have learned something very important about these splinters—how they can be steered by sounds—but you have not solved the mystery completely. Why does the Elven magic make them resonate together? Why is the Elven healing magic for the splinters not as permanent as even the elves themselves think?" ask Professor Aelric.

Portia thought over his words, staring off to the side and leaning against the windowsill behind her.

"Have you not learned how to deal with questions in this Academy?" he asked.

Shooting him a glare, Portia crossed her arms then shook her head as if clearing cobwebs and uncrossed her arms.

"Okay, this is a lesson; I can tell by the way my head hurts. Can you not just say it straight?" she asked.

Professor Aelric sighed. "Might there be more you can learn from our libraries on specifically why some splinters link together, and why many, if not all, the splinters have a strange melody that only you can hear? Answering those questions is a better use of your intelligence and attention, Portia. You are the only one who has heard these things—there is no one better to investigate this," he said gently. "I will help, of course, and search the libraries the best I can, along with the other staff, now that we know there is a question that needs to be answered, but in this, you are the expert."

"There isn't time for that!" Portia exclaimed, the urgency pushing at her again, feeling almost a physical pressure behind her eyes and on her arms. "We don't have time to sit in the classroom and talk about theoretical things when people's lives are at stake."

"No, we don't have the luxury of time," said Professor Aelric, his eyes implacable.

Portia stared back at him, blinking. With a rush, she waved goodbye as she went out the door and ran down the hallway back to her room at the pyromancy house.

ELLA WAS LONG GONE to class by the time Portia got back to their room at the pyromancy house. She ran into the room and pushed her travel bags off her trunk on the back wall next to her bed. Flipping it open, she found the little green book that described the past invasions from the point of view of an invader. It was a translated copy of an old book she'd found in The Building of Mages, the special library that students were not normally allowed into but that had been opened up as part of the war effort to find a solution against the Dragonoids.

It was not an easy read. The descriptions of war were graphic and heartrending, especially since the author of the book seemed to enjoy the war even more as blood was shed and people died. She hoped to never meet anyone like that in real life. Or perhaps they were exaggerations put down for the benefit of glory and not truly how the author felt. She hoped that was so.

Thumbing through the book, she finally found the passage she was looking for. It was a description of the invaders' retreat from the elves who were defending their lands. The city she was in right now was built by elves, or perhaps even by the dwarves before them, but at the time this book was written, elves lived in it. The elves had chased invaders back to the island called the Well of Tears, named for all the misery that seemed to come out of it from the splinter that would open up outside of it.

Portia scanned the passage describing the splinter and the invading humans' retreat. The elves had altered the splinter, and then a different set of humans had emerged, compounding the problems the author was having in the book. Not only were they fighting the elves who already lived in the land, but now their retreat was blocked by other tribes of humans. Putting down the book for a second, Portia stared off into space, thinking about the described events. They were terrible. World ending. And yet, somehow, this book survived. Was this all a true account written by the original author, or could it be some made-up story meant only to entertain?

She thought back to the original volume she had found. It had been handwritten, bound in odd purple leather completely unfaded despite its obvious age, given away by the brittleness of the pages. The preservation spell on the book had somehow missed the sheets of vellum, though the ink upon them was as dark and black as the day it had been written.

Only one line in the book gave away that there was a particular sound associated with the splinter. The author was describing the Elven healing magic that closed the splinter and mentioned, in just a few words, a strange line about an "ear burning sound." Could that have been the discordant music she had heard from the Dragonoid splinter? Archmage Vermeil had not been able to hear anything at all, nor had Iva. Perhaps dwarves couldn't hear it, but only some humans could. Like herself.

That must be it, Portia thought. There was something to do with the sound as well as the visible scarring. If a sound was added to the splinter when the elves touched, then it might explain why different humans had come out of the portal than the ones the invaders came with—the elves had inadvertently changed the destination of the portal.

Portia put down the book and looked out the window, deep in thought. At least one other human had heard that sound: the author of the book. That meant there were prob-ably others who could hear the sounds as well. She had always wondered why music had been taught at the Academy. Could that be another reason that even the current professors did not know about? Tradition often carried forward habits long after the original reason for doing them was forgotten.

Portia slid off the bed where she had been reading. She stuffed the book into her bag and left the pyromancy house. Her growling stomach reminded her that she had one hour before lunch. That should be plenty of time to make it down to the healing house to see if she could speak to a healer in person. She would have rather spoken to an elf, but there were none in the kingdom that she knew of, and even if there had been one, there was no guarantee that particular elf would understand the magic of Elven healing, the magic used to seal the splinters. Not all elves could do that magic. Very few, actually. The closest magic Portia knew of to the Elven healing spells was the magic used by the human healers. She needed to speak to one of them.

Maybe a music teacher too.

The healing house was busier than Portia expected. The main lobby was full, and an open doorway at the back revealed a long cavernous hall filled with beds, all filled with patients, while healers walked in the space between the rows checking the patients as they went.

The rest of the campus might look recovered from the attack by the Dragonoids, but there were still victims healing, Portia realized with a start.

"Can I help you?" an elderly woman dressed in the long robes of a healer asked Portia.

"I need to speak to someone about healing wounds

without scars," Portia asked.

The healer stared at her, her eyes widening a little before she gave a bark of laughter. "Right now, we are dealing with more serious issues than scars." Her voice was unfriendly.

Portia blinked at the unexpectedly harsh words. She looked back at the ward full of patients and then to the incredulous face of the healer in front of her. Finally comprehending, she shook her head and blushed.

"No, no, not for me," Portia said, trying to explain. "I mean yes, for me. I need to understand, but it's not about getting rid of a scar on me but more understanding how healing works with and without scars. It's for our war effort. Truly."

The healer looked skeptical but finally gave a small nod, holding up one finger for Portia to wait a minute, then walking off to get somebody.

A few moments later a very young woman, younger than Portia even, with the half robes of an apprentice healer, came up to Portia. She was out of breath but still gave Portia a smile.

"I hear you want to learn about scarless healing. You did get Eugina quite puffed up, but then it doesn't take much. I like you for that already. I'm Geniette. How can I help you?" the young woman said to Portia without any embarrassment for her own words mocking her elders.

"Can you talk like that here?" Portia asked, looking around to see if anyone else was glaring at them.

"Do your ears need healing too? I did just say that, didn't I?" said the Geniette teasingly.

Portia shook her head, suppressing a smile as the tension

in her stomach relaxed.

"She said something about the war effort? This is some-thing to do with the Dragonoids?" the young woman asked while she motioned for Portia to come join her down a quiet side hallway.

They entered a small room with just a few chairs pushed up against the wall and a desk in a corner. It looked like a consultation room, long disused, with a faint odor of dust hanging in the air. Portia sat on one of the thick leather chairs and waited while the young woman shut the door and sat in a chair opposite her.

"Yes, I'm trying to figure out..." Portia struggled with her question. What was she trying to do? "There is this healing magic I can do on objects, including portals, but what I've been taught seems to be missing something. It concentrates on not leaving visible scars. If I leave a scar while healing an object, the magic is unstable and the object itself can explode or worse. Yet, some objects are visually healed but still open again later. There is something I am missing."

Geniette looked at Portia, her smile replaced by a serious expression.

"You're talking about the splinters to the invaders' world, aren't you?" she asked.

"Yes," Portia said, surprised. "How did you—"

"Know that you are Portia? The school is not so large for you to escape all notice. Just because Eugina didn't recognize you doesn't mean others won't. You're our Jack of Magic."

Portia nodded.

"Is there any other sign the portal might open later?" the

young woman asked, prodding when Portia appeared lost for words.

"I can hear music, at least now that I've started listening for it. It often sounds discordant."

"Discordant?"

"Like some notes don't belong there—as if the music is fighting itself. I'm doing a terrible job of explaining this, I think," Portia said.

"Why do you think that has something to do with scarring?"

"The music gives me the same sensation I have when casting a healing spell and I know there will be a scar, and the spell might backfire on me." Portia's palm twinged at a memory of one of her past failures and the resulting explosion when she had failed to cast the spell correctly. "Also, the magic is Elven magic. Elven magic is done through singing. There is some connection there between the sounds and the scars and why the healing won't take, either immediately or later."

Geniette raised both eyebrows. "Would the music instructors be of some help?"

"I had been given some instruction on healing here, so I thought perhaps this group would be more helpful. My musical skills have never won me any friends in the music hall," Portia said with chagrin.

It was true, Portia was not skilled when it came to music. Her lack of ability had frustrated more than one teacher. It had been a nightmare to realize she had to do better if she was going to be able to do the Elven magic.

"I see. Let me think a moment," said the healer.

Portia sat in silence and then leaned forward and placed her elbows on her knees and stared down at her boots.

"Okay, so what do you know about healing?" asked Geniette. "I mean, we all know you can do some since you have saved the city from the Well of Tears splinter."

"Not much more than what I've told you. When I'm seeing the spell, sometimes I can feel when it is going correctly, almost like a vibration in the song," said Portia. "I concentrate mostly on getting the right notes and then looking for the visual confirmation. If I can't see what I'm doing, then I have to listen."

"Do you concentrate on one side of the healing first over the other?"

"I don't understand what you mean. Aren't you joining both sides at once?"

The young woman held up her arm in front of Portia and took her other hand and pinched the skin, pulling up part of her forearm. "When you're healing something, say the skin on an arm, there are two parts: the inside and the outside. The outside is the skin. The inside is the blood and flesh. When they are not both healed perfectly, the inside and the outside mix and you are left with the scar. If you concentrate on healing the inside first and then the outside, mixing doesn't happen. There is no scar or very little."

"I'm not sure how that works for a splinter. There are our lands—"

"Which could be the inside," the young woman said.

Portia stared at her. "That would make the outside the

Dragonoids' land." She blinked slowly and leaned back in her chair. "That makes sense. It is not how I've been healing them though. If your example is one to go by, I've not been paying any attention to whether I am mixing up the two layers. It also says nothing about the music."

"Does it sound like someone is trying to play a tune in the wrong key?" Geniette asked.

"Yes, it does," Portia said, surprised. Her mouth dropped open. "Like playing one land's tune in another world's key! Blessed! That's it! How did you know?" Portia jumped to her feet and twirled around in excitement.

The young woman laughed, the sound like glad bells. "I didn't—it was a guess. You should hear my father yell when the musicians don't tune first at the tavern! That is a piece of knowledge I never thought would be useful."

"It is so useful. Thank you! I'll be back. Maybe," Portia said as she ran out of the room.

PORTIA WAS so excited she wanted to run to the music hall right away to talk to a teacher, but her growling stomach finally demanded her attention and forced her to admit that eating lunch first would be a good idea. She was amongst the first of the students to arrive for lunch after morning classes. Loading her plate up high with roasted vegetables, roast fowl, and three servings of bread pudding, she finally carried her heavy tray to a long table in the back of the dining hall. Her massive lunch seemed reasonable considering she had not had breakfast, and with all that she had to do, it was possible she would miss dinner.

"That's where all the pudding is!" Ella said, sliding her tray down next to Portia's and stepping in front of the long wooden bench to sit next to her. Mia, Liam, and Richard followed, each putting down their own tray and sitting to join them. Only Ella's tray came close to having as much food piled on it as Portia's had, and even then, there were only two small bowls of black bread pudding. Ella pointedly stared at Portia's tray with its three bowls of pudding. Portia pulled her food closer and shot Ella a warning look, which made Liam laugh.

"This could get ugly," said Liam as he leaned to put his head on Ella's shoulder. "I've not seen anyone stand between Ella and her food."

"*My* food. This is my food. My tray. Stop staring at it," Portia said with a warning tone. She wrapped an arm around the outside of the tray to form a physical barrier. She had forgotten Ella's obsession with food. Had Ella not had enough to eat while living under some foreign city? Had Ella been starving on the street as an orphan? No. Portia had, and she still remembered the hunger.

"There is more up in the buffet," Richard said, raising his eyebrows.

"Not bread pudding," said Ella petulantly.

"Leave mine alone and you will live to eat it another day," said Portia.

"Fine," Ella said with a huff and picked up her fork.

Portia wouldn't have done anything to Ella, but Ella didn't

need to know that. At least not until lunch was over.

Mark appeared at the doorway with a wide-eyed Iva with him. Portia jumped to her feet and walked to them, leaving a surprised table full of classmates.

"Iva, I'm so sorry I left you at the castle," said Portia.

Iva grabbed both of Portia's hands in her own and shook them. "Sorry? Are you crazy? I have never eaten so well in my life. You should be sorry you weren't there." Iva looked around the room at all the students. "Were you here?"

"Yes, and to class, and the healers—"

"Are you sick?" asked Iva, concerned.

"No, no. I'm trying to find out more about the splinters and how to heal them better," said Portia. "Come join my friends and meet them. Wait, how are you here?"

"Professor Griffiths thought you would want to see Iva again. Things are tense at the palace right now."

Portia stopped pulling on Iva's hand and turned to squint at Mark. "Were you in the talks this morning?"

He laughed. "They like me, but not that much. No, I wasn't in the talks. There was word of elves coming to join the negotiations. Advisors were running up and down the halls and someone gently pointed out I would be better off on the campus grounds. Or not so gently." He rubbed his left upper arm with his right. "I grabbed Iva on the way to keep her from being confined to her room."

Iva turned on Mark. "I didn't mind my room. It came with room service. Many trays of room service."

Portia turned to stare at Ella. Now she knew who Iva reminded her of.

Once Mark and Iva had gone through the line and helped themselves to lunch and joined them at the table, Portia made the introductions.

Mia, whose lunch was long finished and who was sitting quietly, spoke. "Were you really there in the Dragonoid land with Portia?"

Iva nodded, her mouth full of apple puree. "I was."

"Was it as bad as she said?" Mia asked. The rest of the table leaned in to hear Iva speak.

Iva swallowed and then looked at the intent faces all around her. Only Portia continued to eat. "I don't know what Portia said, but it was terrible. I feel lucky to be alive. Being a slave wasn't the worst thing that could happen in that land."

No one said anything, their thoughts churning on the possibilities of what would be worse than being a slave. Everyone at the table knew Jukhnovo, the kingdom to the north of Haulstatt, had fallen to Dragonoids, and that Iva was from Jukhnovo and had lost her home and family. What happened to Iva could easily happen to them if they lost their war with the Dragonoids. As much as Mia and Ella complained of their families, they were still families, and still a place to return to if they so chose after the Academy. Iva had no such choice.

Portia swallowed and stared down at her plate. "I think I learned something important about the splinters today."

Her friends' attention turned to her from Iva. They waited while Portia toyed with the remaining beets on her plate. "I think I've been healing the splinters wrong. Well, not wrong, but maybe not as good as I could have. I've been treating the splinters like a single object, and there might actually be two things there—an inside and outside. That might explain why they open up again."

"Is there any way to find if that's true?" asked Mia. Portia looked up to Mia and raised one eyebrow. Of all the students, she'd had the best education as a young child.

"Maybe you can help me figure that out," said Portia.

Mia nodded. Portia imagined a dozen books open on Mia's desk that very afternoon. If there was a task for Mia to do, she would have it done as thoroughly and quickly as possible.

"I told you all about the music last night, about how some splinters sounded different, and usually they sound pretty bad," said Portia. "The healer I saw this morning suggested that perhaps there was a song for each world, but they sounded out of tune where the two worlds met, as if one was playing its tune in the wrong key of the other world, or something like that."

"As if you would know," sneered a voice behind Portia. Portia turned in her seat to see Magisend Lucy standing behind her holding her own tray of food, surrounded by her cronies. "I've been in your music classes. It was a miracle you somehow passed. I've never seen anyone with less musical ability."

The girls around Magisend giggled. They, like Magisend, were also cryomancy students. Eating in the dining hall was one of the few places the students of the different houses saw each other, besides in the rare shared classes.

Portia's face burned red. Magisend Lucy was not wrong

about her musical ability. Her lack of natural talent had made learning the sung Elven magic that much harder.

"As if you would know," said Portia, her retort halfhearted.

Everyone quieted. Richard and Liam looked down awkwardly while Mia dragged a fork across her already empty plate. Only Iva was oblivious as she scooped mashed turnips into her mouth. Even Mark looked away.

Magisend Lucy gave a small sniff, raised her nose, and then left. Her cronies followed with their noses held high.

Portia looked around at her classmates who were looking in any direction but hers.

"What?" Portia asked, bewildered.

"While you were gone," Ella said, explaining, "Magisend Lucy gave a concert. We never heard her play the three-tier harp. She was amazing. It was both magic, true magic, and a lifetime of practice. No one knew she had that ability or where she worked on her skills without anyone having heard before or known of them."

Magisend Lucy?

Portia stared at the retreating back of the tiny girl, Magisend's straight black hair matching her ramrod-straight back. And she had thought Magisend's only talent had been in tormenting her.

"She's a musical genius," said Richard softly.

Great, just what Portia needed. The one person who could help her figure out the music between worlds hated her more than anyone else in the world.

"There's a huge ship in the harbor!" a young man yelled from the doorway. "It's as big as the palace!"

12

The ship was so large that it had not even attempted to enter the mouth of the harbor where enormous boulders lay partially submerged on either side of the entry channel to narrow it and protect the city from a concerted attack. Instead, the ship had kept back and anchored in the deeper waters just beyond. It lay faintly visible in the fog that still hung over the waters even at noon. It was not a sunny day, which meant the fog might linger until the morrow.

The students ran to the upper wall on the edge of the city by the harbor. This was the place where the annual festivals were celebrated, a large open field abutting the city but still within the city walls. Standing at the top of the wall, there was a clear view down the cliffs to the harbor and the sea beyond it.

Down in the harbor proper, smaller vessels plied the relative safety of the protected inner waters. A row of three warships edged the harbor mouth, facing the enormous ship outside of it They looked like ants at the foot of a large animal. A large, dangerous animal.

The enormous ship's look was unique. Instead of large white sails rigged from triple masts, as the local merchant ships were fashioned, the sails on the towering vessel were of the same dark blue as the Dwarven uniforms. Its wood was a deep and brilliant red, unlike the sun-bleached wood and paint of the ships. It looked both old and pristinely new at the same time. The water shimmered around it as if it gave off magic.

"Morgani," Portia said under her breath. She stood at the wall along with the other students. Mark, standing further down between Ella and Liam, heard her and turned to face her.

"The Dwarven kingdom?" he asked.

Portia nodded. She looked around but did not see General Seren. Not that the commander should be at the city wall along with the common folk. She was probably still at the palace having a meeting with the queen and king consort. Portia did not see General Bancrot either.

A trumpet called faintly from the enormous ship and was answered by bells ringing in steeples of churches in Coverack, in the towers of guardhouses, and from the palace itself. The entire city sounded the alarm. People on the walks below that ringed the harbor ran into nearby buildings while sailors on docked ships raced to raise their sails and cast off their lines.

Some students ran back to the school. Portia's friends looked to her, and when she did not move, they stood their ground, letting the crowd around them buffet them as they left.

"It looks like the rest of the battalion has arrived," Portia said. She hoped it was true that the ship was from Morgani and not a new design of a Dragonoid ship.

"You're telling me that enormous ship is full of dwarves?" asked Liam, running his hand through his hair, making its artful messiness even messier. Liam, who normally joked about everything, had a look of concern on his face. His brother, Richard, stood closer to him.

"Wait, that makes no sense," Richard said, turning to peer at Portia. "Morgani is a landlocked kingdom. How would they have a ship? And why?"

"They were not always landlocked," said Mia, reminding them of the history of the dwarves losing their kingdoms and lands close to the sea.

"They've been landlocked for a very long time," said Richard, arguing his point.

"Maybe it's a very old ship," said Mia unperturbed.

Still, thought Portia, if that ship was from the time when the dwarves ruled the lands next to the sea, where had it been all this time? And why had they never used it to attack the elves or even the humans who had taken these lands so roughly?

Portia shook her head to clear her thoughts from it. She had enough to worry about with the splinters. Someone else could worry about where the ship came from. As long as the ship truly was full of dwarves, that was enough. They had come to help them. That was their promise to her.

The ringing of the bells finally died down. A caravan of brightly colored carriages wound its way down the hillside from the palace, preceded by two horses running at full speed bearing the banner of the kingdom of Haulstatt.

Out in the harbor, the royal ship of the queen unfurled its sails, revealing matching insignia. From its decks rang out an answering trumpet to the call of the Dwarven ship.

"They're going to meet the ship. I want to be there," said Portia. She ran along the wall towards the road that ran down the hill to the harbor. The other students shrugged their shoulders and followed her.

Mark had come with them to the wall while Iva had stayed behind in the dining hall to talk to Cecilia, who'd shown up looking for Portia.

It turned out Iva was not just afraid of furry creatures. She also blanched at the mention of the sea and quickly cried off that she still needed to eat more from having not had enough during their time in the land of the dwarves. Cecilia had gotten Iva a cup of tea and sat down to keep her company, waving the students to go on without her.

Despite many of the townsfolk of Coverack hiding in their houses once the bells started ringing, there was a good number brave enough, and curious enough, to want to know more about the ship outside their harbor. The crowds thickened the closer they got to the harbor until they were so closely packed it reminded Portia of the farmers' market in Valencia where the poorest of the city came out early to get the best prices on what limited food there was available. Or to get the food at any price. The hairs on her neck tingled uncomfortably at the press of bodies against her. It was not a feeling she wanted to remember.

"Clear the dock!" the soldier called, holding his pike horizontal and pushing the people to back up. Portia fought against the crowd to reach the line of soldiers. She waved at the nearest, hoping to get through, but he shook his head at her and looked away. He had recognized her, she was sure, but would not let her through.

"Portia," a voice called from behind. Portia turned to see Professor Aelric Terfel and Professor Hilda Griffiths standing behind them. They were out of breath and panting while they pushed through the crowds.

"We've been looking for you," said Professor Hilda. "The queen wants you at the palace."

Portia scowled. "I was there this morning. They turned me away."

"The queen?" asked Professor Aelric.

"No. The guards," said Portia.

He nodded. "There must have been some miscommunication."

"Is that where you went so early this morning?" asked Ella.

Portia ignored Ella's question, turning her face away from Mark's watching eyes. He had been in the palace that morning while she had been turned away. For some reason, that humiliated her more than anything.

"No matter," said Professor Aelric. "Things are moving fast; we need to get you to the queen." He waved to the nearest guard, who at first shook his head and then took a closer look at Professor Aelric's Academy robes and came closer. The professor and the guard spoke in low whispers, and the guard ran to a cluster of soldiers standing on the walkway that ran alongside the water.

A few minutes later, the guard returned with three other guards. Two held the line of people back while the original guard and one other pulled Portia and the two professors from the crowds. Portia tried to pull Ella with her, but the guard was adamant that no one else could come with, and Portia was forced to release her grip on Ella's arm. Mark and the other students were quickly swallowed up in the crowd as Portia and the two professors were pulled along the road towards the harbor and the queen's ship.

At that moment, a cry rang out followed by a cheer as the crowd was parted for the queen's carriage. The carriage was the beautiful lacquer it always was, but the horses were missing half of their livery and it was clear they had been harnessed in a hurry. Haste had been chosen over pomp. Even the servants riding on the high back seat outside the carriage looked disheveled and dusty from the speedy journey down the city streets.

The carriage pulled to a stop, and then one of the liveried footmen jumped down from the back bench and hurriedly opened the door for the queen to exit, followed by the king consort. They both looked impeccable, as if not rushed at all. Or perhaps it was the queen's expression. The queen surveyed the crowd impassively and raised one hand in greeting. The crowd responded with a cheer.

The guard brought Portia and the professors to the queen and king consort. Portia curtsied deeply.

"It seems this is your handiwork, Portia," said the queen.

"Yes, Your Majesty," said Portia, biting her lip.

"Have no fear, it appears to be a good thing, better perhaps than could be expected, but we shall see," said the queen cryptically.

A second carriage pulled around the first and stopped. This time, General Bancrot and General Seren exited and joined the group gathered around the king and queen.

They stood waiting on the harbor walk while three longboats slowly rowed in from the far side of the harbor. The longboats fought the choppy waves at the boundary of the waters from the harbor and the sea, and then they slowly made their way past the guarding warships in the calmer waters of the harbor. The sailors in the boats were dressed in the same dark blue as the sails of the gigantic ship. A flag flew on a long pole held up by a sailor in the first longboat. It depicted a black profile of Queen Morgani set against a field of deep red.

After many moments, the longboats finally reached the dock. Sailors on them threw ropes to the waiting city soldiers. Not only was Queen Morgani herself on the third longboat but Archmage Vermeil as well. Gladness overcame Portia. If she talked to the archmage about the magic of the splinters and what she'd learned, perhaps he'd help her figure out what she needed to do.

"Queen Morgani, of the great kingdom of Morgani," announced a dwarf in a bellowing voice. The two queens nodded their heads at each other, the acknowledgment of one equal to another.

Queen Lorica stepped forward. "Welcome to our land, great Queen Morgani. We have heard much of you and your wondrous people. This is a pleasure to have the honor to meet you in person."

"It is our pleasure. It has been many generations since we have sailed upon the sea. Only the most exceptional circumstances would bring us so. May we be victorious in our joint efforts," said Queen Morgani.

Portia swallowed and then looked to see Queen Lorica's reaction. Queen Lorica gave Portia a quick glance with one eyebrow raised before smoothing her expression and walking to Queen Morgani. She offering her arm. "Indeed, let us speak more of that. We have prepared rooms close by, so you needn't make the journey to the palace just yet, though we do hope for the pleasure of hosting you there at your convenience."

A liveried steward led the queens and king consort away to a nearby inn that had been emptied of patrons by guards and whose entrance was now flanked by the same guards. More guards walked the roof of the wooden structure. Portia had not been invited, nor had been Archmage Vermeil, for which she was grateful.

Portia gave the archmage a smile.

"I couldn't remember if you were coming or not. Did you tell me?" Portia asked him. He didn't answer immediately, instead staring at the crowds and the city on the hill topped by the glittering purple stones of the palace high above them.

The crowd was equally entranced with him and the other dwarves, some yelling out for them to come closer so they might take a better look. Elves only occasionally came to this worldly city. Dwarves never did.

"I may or may not have told you," he said finally. He pulled his eyes from the crowd to look at her.. "Having all this sky and city out in the open like this is a little disconcerting. How do you get used to this?"

Portia laughed. "You just do. How was your journey? I have so much to tell you, so much about the splinters."

The word "splinters" got his full attention. "You know more about how you might open one to the Dragonoid world?"

"Perhaps," Portia answered. She went on to explain what she had learned from the healer of the possible dual inner and outer nature of the splinters and how they might be steered. The professors stepped closer so that they might hear this as well. Portia pretended not to notice.

"So, the sound does have something to do with it, but maybe in a more complicated way," Portia said.

Archmage Vermeil shifted his weight back and forth as he thought about her words.

"But you haven't tested this yet?" he asked. "I mean you were able to move a splinter before, but that is not enough. We need to control its location much more exactly."

Portia shook her head, unease plucking at her stomach. "We haven't been here long. There might be others who can help, but I haven't yet had a chance to ask them." Portia thought of the professors in the music hall and more uneasily of Magisend Lucy and her unexpected musical ability. "There are those here who might have skills that will help us."

Archmage Vermeil nodded. He noticed Professor Hilda and Professor Aelric standing close by and jumped. Portia laughed.

"Do not worry, these are my professors. Magic professors," Portia said, turning to Professor Hilda and Professor Aelric while motioning to the dwarf. "This is Archmage Vermeil."

Despite attempting to hide it, a hint of surprise showed on Professor Aelric's face. He bowed respectfully to the dwarf. "Welcome. I am most pleased to meet you. I am Professor Aelric, and this is Professor Hilda."

The archmage regained his composure, smoothing down his robes and drawing himself up tall before giving the professor a nod in return. "I've heard of you. Most wondrous things."

Portia stood awkwardly between them. She looked to the inn where the royals were still meeting. There was no indication from the guards outside that they would be coming out soon. General Bancrot and General Seren came to join them and introduced themselves.

"As much as we need the manpower," said General Bancrot, motioning to the gigantic ship, "that vessel is most welcome. There is a splinter over the waters on the way to the Well of Tears. We've managed to get some intelligence off it while the fog still holds, but the season is changing, and that opportunity is going fast. It will be far too easy to spot our spy ships on the open seas when the sun has burned away all our cover. Our ships cannot stand up to theirs, not in force, and they are guarding that splinter well." The general's expression went dark. "Frankly, we don't understand why they are waiting there. We fear there is an unpleasant surprise coming our way."

General Seren only grunted in reply, examining the city and the harbor with a critical eye. "You are exposed here."

"Yes. Attack from sea has not been a concern—until now," admitted the general.

"So that is where their forces are," said Portia under her breath.

General Bancrot turned to her, tilting her head in surprise. "You were expecting something different? Perhaps you expected them to run over this land already?"

"I didn't mean to offend," said Portia in a rush. "It's just that I saw them attack Rodaine, and before I left, I'd heard they were traveling overland with weapons. Then, I was gone for so long. Things were much changed when I returned."

Pursing her lips and nodding, General Bancrot looked to the city beyond Portia and then back to her. "You are well informed. I keep forgetting how traveled you are for someone so young. And it's true, we lack even a seawall such as Rodaine had, and here the city still stands. In part, thanks to you, if the words I've been given were true."

Portia blushed even as she felt pride blossom in her chest. "I was just one of many."

"A true soldier there," said General Bancrot before giving Portia a wink. The general turned to General Seren. "That then is the rest of your battalion?"

"It is," said the commander, pride in her voice.

"Is the ship included?" asked the general.

General Seren considered the ship. "That is a question for my queen. I do not even know the weapons that are upon it. The captain is the child of the captain before him, who in turn was the child of the captain before him, and so on. That is the one who has true knowledge of the ship. That knowledge is handed down from generation to generation, even if they only visit the vessel and never experience it on water." The commander looked at the questioning faces around him and hastily added, "Or so I've heard. I admit a desire to speak to the captain myself."

"You don't know the details of the ship?" asked the general, surprised.

"Security," General Seren said.

The general nodded. "Ah, I see. Very smart. Very smart."

At Portia's puzzled expression, Professor Hilda leaned in and said quietly in her ear, "The fewer details people know, the smaller the chance the knowledge will reach the ears of someone who should not have it."

Having heard Professor Hilda's words, the commander nodded the truth of them.

"It does look like a considerable number could board that ship," said General Bancrot, unwilling to drop the subject of using the ship.

"You mean soldiers?" asked Archmage Vermeil, concern furrowing his brow at the human commander's frank appraisal of the dwarf ship.

"Oh, not just soldiers, but mages, Jack of Magic, and her guardians. You know, an attack party." The general did not take her eyes off the ship. The furrow on Archmage Vermeil's brow pushed down and turned into a scowl.

Portia stepped in between the two of them. "Or we could just sneak in on a small boat like we did last time."

"No!" said Professor Aelric, the words coming out more forcefully than he expected. All eyes turned to him. "That is what we did last time, and we nearly lost everybody. Let us keep it as a last resort."

The others nodded and slowly looked away. The sun beat down on them as they waited for the rulers to finish their meeting.

THE SUN WAS DIPPING on the horizon by the time Portia returned to campus. She sat in the gravel in front of the cryomancy house door in the Courtyard of Doors while the guards circled around it and through the campus. Only students were allowed in the gravel courtyard. Each door was marked by a symbol of the magic house that it led to. The houses themselves were secreted far away somewhere outside the city to protect the lives of the students who lived within them.

Portia's own door, the door of pyromancy, had the symbol of a flame on it. It stood on the other side of the courtyard.

Shifting uncomfortably on the gravel, Portia wished for a bench. The Courtyard was a transition space—students did not normally linger there.

Students passed Portia, some clicking their tongues as

they walked around her. A few whispered and pointed, knowing who she was. Student after student passed her by, but not the one she was waiting for, until at last a shadow fell over her, blocking the sun. Portia looked up to see the irritated face of Magisend Lucy scowling down at her.

"This is not your house door," said Magisend, her voice dripping with contempt.

Portia sighed. "How astute of you."

"What are you doing here, commoner?"

"Jack of Magic."

"Pardon me, commoner?"

"Jack of Magic," Portia said, repeating herself as she stood up. "That is my title. If you cannot be so kind as to use my name, you can at least use my title."

"I was using your title," said Magisend.

Portia's fingers flared, and a circle of fire puffed out around Magisend's feet and then just as quickly went out, leaving behind a circle of smoke that floated up around the girl. Portia closed her fingertips together slowly, and the smoke around Magisend crowded in until it closed around her head and then drifted up and away.

Magisend gasped. "I'll have your head for that."

"Get in line, though I don't think you'll have much assistance from the Academy until our nation's war is over."

Magisend looked around at the staring guards who had been drawn by the fire. They looked away and would not meet her eye, instead resuming their patrol walks.

"See?" said Portia. "Things are a little different right now. Busy. Something about a war."

Magisend Lucy grasped her hands into tight fists, her face reddening.

"Oh calm down, Magisend. I came to talk to you, although you make it difficult to have a civilized conversation," Portia said. Portia felt as if she was watching herself from the outside. When had she lost her fear of Magisend Lucy, the bane of her life at the Academy for the first year?

Magisend's shoulders tightened. She raised one hand to cast magic.

"I wouldn't do that. I really wouldn't," said Portia, her voice quiet.

Magisend halted. She considered Portia's words.

Portia smiled.

With a pained expressed, Magisend deflated, dropped her hand, and then shook her hair as if not caring what happened.

"Thank you," said Portia quietly, gratitude in her voice. "I need your help, Magisend. We all do."

Magisend squinted at Portia, trying to discern if she was joking or not.

"There is some music of the portals—the splinters—that I need help with." Portia motioned to the portal doors in the courtyard. "None of the mages that created these doors knew anything of music. They didn't even believe me when I told them what I knew. They were less than helpful. But I have reason to believe music is very important. Your housemaster let it be known to Professor Hilda that not only do you have the musical talent from the concert I missed, but you have a perfect ear and a perfect memory for music—a photographic memory of sorts for sound. You only need to hear something once and can repeat it, pitch-perfect."

"It's not your place to talk about me," Magisend said, even as pride glowed from her at the words that had been spoken about her by her housemaster and the professors.

Portia waited. Tired of standing, she sat down in the gravel again and motioned for Magisend Lucy to join her. Magisend sniffed and then looked around. When she saw no one staring at them, she wiped away some blown leaves on the ground and slowly sat down in front of Portia.

"We need your skills," Portia said, gently.

"For what?"

"For opening a portal to the Dragonoid world."

"What! Have you lost your mind? We do not need that." Magisend Lucy glared at her.

"We do need that. We've lost people we need to retrieve." Portia looked up from the ground where she had been playing with a piece of gravel and fixed Magisend with an intense stare. "Have you lost no one in your family to this war? Has no one you known been taken?"

"No, no one has. Our house is within Coverack. We are whole."

"Will your house's business stay whole when your customers disappear and your suppliers can no longer supply? Your family's house is a noble house, yes, but it is also a merchant house. It will not survive without trade," Portia said.

"We will survive," Magisend spat back.

"It won't. You know it. Your father has spoken of the difficulties."

Magisend gaped at Portia who smiled weakly back.

After a moment, Magisend closed her mouth. "How is it that I may help... you?"

"Help the kingdom."

"The kingdom then."

"I need help remembering a tune. Perfectly. Not one note must be off. It will only be heard once," explained Portia.

"That's easy," Magisend said with a scoff.

"The tune will be played in the middle of the battle while the enemy is trying to kill you."

Magisend blinked back at Portia.

"I STILL DON'T UNDERSTAND why you had to be the one to go get her. Why do we even need her at all?" asked Mark as he hefted a heavy canvas roll up the plank of a clipper in the harbor.

It had been decided that not only would the huge Dwarven ship be taken to the splinter as the point ship in battle, but all the navy ships from the kingdom would accompany it. The local merchant vessels had been conscripted to defend the harbor in their absence. It was a gamble by the royal house that no other Dragonoid ships would appear to attack the city during their action at the splinter. Even the city guards were uneasy with the queen's boldness. Tempers flared within the guard, amongst the townspeople, and at the Academy.

Mark, Portia, her friends, and even Iva—though she

refused to go anywhere near the water, instead helping by packing supplies on the campus grounds—had been recruited to help load the clipper. The main group of mages, along with Portia and the other students coming to assist her, would ride on the *Pearl*, the Dwarven ship out just beyond the harbor. In the interest of speed, a clipper would bring them out there instead of hand rowing all supplies out to the huge ship.

Magisend Lucy had shown up at the harbor an hour previously in her own house's carriage, the house of Riddlepit, with two of her most dedicated cronies with her. She'd insisted her friends be allowed to come. Everyone was too busy to fight her on it, and Professor Aelric had simply thrown up his hands and walked away after she had stomped her feet while demanding her way, which Magisend had taken as permission. Another Riddlepit carriage had followed Magisend's first, this time loaded with tents, trunks, and supplies, along with two servants to carry them on the ship for her. The captain of the clipper had forbidden Magisend's personal maid from boarding, which had sent Magisend into a rage, and she had stomped off. She and her cronies sat at a table outside a harborside inn and watched everyone else work.

Mark growled every time he had to pass the three of them. "We don't need her," he said to Portia for the twentieth time that morning.

"We do need her. Stop, you're just making yourself upset," Portia said.

"No, you're making me upset. Just tell them to go."

Portia bit her lip to keep from saying anything.

"Oh, you're so cute when you're angry," Ella said, waving her fingers in Mark's direction as she passed Portia and Mark, carrying a large duffel bag of her belongings.

"I'm not angry!" Mark yelled and then stomped off to get another load from the wagon. Ella giggled and Portia shook her head.

Liam and Richard followed Ella closely, also carrying supplies, a scowl on Liam's face. His hair was pure white tipped with sky blue. It would blend in with the sky perfectly.

Portia's housemates were all coming to the battle with her. Neither Professor Hilda nor Professor Aelric could dissuade them, and Queen Lorica had granted them the right to come if they so chose because of their bravery in the previous mission to close the splinter at the Well of Tears.

A faint trumpet sounded, an alarm from the palace, followed by the ringing of bells that once again echoed through the town. Sailors and soldiers loading the ships ran to get the last of the bundles in their arms on board and stowed. Portia and the other students followed. There were no ships in the harbor. A lookout with a long glass scanned the horizon but did not call out a sighting.

A second faint trumpet sounded the triple note of stand-down. It was not an imminent attack. An audible sigh of relief came from those around them. The panicked running footsteps slowed to a fast walk as people scrambled to finish their tasks. The town bells did not stop ringing.

In less than an hour, all was loaded and the carriages sent away empty. The bells had finally died down. No word had come as to what the alarm had originally been, and the guard captain watching the harbor kept looking to the hills, waiting for a signal.

A cloud of dust signaled a rider coming down the hill from the far gate of the city. Several riders, judging by the size of the dust blowing out around them. Portia stood and watched, fascinated, and soon her classmates joined her to see who was approaching. The dust settled as the horses made the cobbled streets of the city and left the dirt roads from the gate. The green flag of elves shown on the first rider's standard.

The elves were here. Portia's heart leapt into her mouth. Help was here! Selfishly, she wished that Lord Fife, the ancient elf who had taught her Elven magic, was with the group, but she knew it was not possible. He was far too old to travel, which made his training of her even more important. They all needed her to be able to do the elf magic and heal the splinters.

Portia recognized many of the faces when the group drew nearer. Sergeant Lyren rode next to Lady Harper along with several soldiers from the Elven army. The group on horseback wended their way through the city and down the cobbled streets to the harbor while the students watched. A second group had peeled off and ridden up to the palace.

When they arrived, Sergeant Lyren leapt off her horse and threw the reins to Lady Harper, who laughed and dismounted her own horse. Lady Harper wore a complex and beautiful outfit of blue silk that floated around her while also revealing strong leather armor pieces that could fend off any knife.

"Young human, we are not too late! That is good to see.

We've come here to join you on your boat," Sergeant Lyren said as she approached the group and came and slapped Portia on the back as an old friend. "It's so good to see that you are not dead yet." She beamed at Portia.

"Yet?" Portia asked, nonplussed.

"Yes, yet. We all die. Not today, that would be good, so yes, yet. Do not look so serious, young human; it does not suit you," Sergeant Lyren said while rubbing her hands and looking around the harbor. Her uniform sleeves had more gold braid than Portia remembered.

Portia's classmates circled around, their jaws hanging open while they stared at Sergeant Lyren. They then parted and made an opening for Lady Harper to join them. Most of them had seen elves before, but none had known of Portia's close relationship to these particular elves.

Archmage Vermeil exited the nearby inn carrying a bag of provisions and spotted the group around Portia. Seeing the elves, he hurried over. He slowed when he got closer and peered at them. Feeling his eyes on her, Lady Harper turned to look at the dwarf. There was a moment of silence as the elf and the dwarf eyed each other.

Portia swallowed. It was one thing for the elves to have forgiven the humans and forged an uneasy alliance to fight off their joint enemy of the Dragonoids, but the elves had long ago driven the dwarves out of these lands in a bloody battle that cost the dwarves sunlight itself to this day. She had no idea if there was any peace between the two groups.

"Greetings, Archmage," said Lady Harper, giving Archmage Vermeil a bow.

His eyebrows shot up in surprise—and some satisfaction. He stood taller.

"Greetings," he said, his voice rising in an unspoken question of her identity. She answered it.

"Lady Harper, and this," she gestured to Sergeant Lyren, "is General Lyren."

Portia sucked in her breath. *General Lyren.* What had happened since she had been in Rocabarra?

General Lyren caught Portia's surprised expression. "Yes, that's correct. I'm a general now." General Lyren beamed at Portia. "I suppose I owe that to you, young human."

"No way," Ella said. "Do not tell me my roommate—who never goes to class—has done some other awesome thing." Ella looked pleased and also exasperated, blowing her bangs out of her eyes.

"Actually, it was me that did the awesome thing. The young human here just told me about the problem." General Lyren turned to Portia. "That cult that was causing us so many problems? They were indeed connected to this invasion. How they thought they would end up as anything other than slaves themselves is beyond me, but they were doing a lot of damage in their efforts to assist the enemy and bring down their own fates. I just helped them take a shortcut—for their fates anyhow. They can thank me for spending their prison time in their own lands and not slaving on Dragonoid soil." General Lyren winked at Portia. "Perhaps they can thank you too. Would you like to meet one in person?"

Portia shook her head.

General Lyren laughed. "Just kidding, young human, just kidding."

Lady Harper appeared at Portia's elbow and touched her arm softly. "It is good to see you again. Lord Fife and Merit send their regards."

"They couldn't make it?" Portia asked, already knowing the answer.

Lady Harper shook her head and spoke as if she could read Portia's mind. "You know what you need to know; do not worry."

That is easy to say but not to do, thought Portia. She looked over the group planning to go into battle and risk their lives so that she could close a splinter and save them all—after taking a moment to memorize the sounds of the lands beyond. Past their group lay the city and the kingdom full of people that were depending on her. A shiver ran down her spine. Lady Harper noticed and rubbed her back quietly and then stopped, giving Portia a quick smile before stepping back.

"Our forces are lagging, but we didn't want you to leave without us. Our ambassador is up at the palace as we speak with a letter from King Magnus and Queen Ceola. We can't let you have all the fun without us," General Lyren said as she folded her arms and rocked back on her heels, excited for the adventure ahead. Portia wished she felt that enthusiasm and not the deep pit of dread in her stomach at what lay ahead. At least they had help. More help.

Maybe even something close to enough.

Archmage Vermeil watched both elves closely, having

said nothing after their introduction. Lady Harper noticed and turned to face him.

"Archmage, would you do us the honor of a drink? We've been riding a long ways. The company of a distinguished dwarf such as yourself would be a glad reward," Lady Harper said.

Archmage Vermeil stared at her. She returned his gaze with a sunny smile. Finally, he nodded and motioned to the inn where he had just exited. "I have many questions for you as well."

"And we will gladly answer them over a drink," answered General Lyren while hooking her arm inside Archmage Vermeil's and ignoring his outraged look while dragging him to the inn. Lady Harper gave an exasperated sigh and followed after them.

"Portia," an unsure voice behind her said. Turning, Portia found Cecilia, her mother. She'd not had much time to spend with her since coming back. Near every moment had been spent preparing for their mission to close a splinter. Guilt pulled at Portia's heart, along with a longing have a home with a hearth and soft chairs by the fire—the sort of leisurely evening with a mother she'd never had as a child.

"Cecilia... Mother. You're here. Did you pack a bag?" Portia asked.

Cecilia shook her head sadly. "No, battle is not for me. I fear I would be of no use and only a hindrance to those brave enough to go. I wish—"

Portia didn't want to hear what Cecilia wished. She knew Cecilia did not want Portia to go, but there was no choice.

"There is no other way," Portia said before Cecilia could finish her sentence.

The students around Portia politely backed up and drifted in the direction of the buildings along the harbor wall, giving Portia privacy with her mother. Most knew Portia had come to the Academy as an orphan, never expecting to find her mother on a mission in Jukhnovo to learn more about the invading forces. Cecilia's appearance had shocked even the queen and king consort of Haulstatt, for reasons not even Portia understood. It had something to do with the house of Portia and her mother—the house of Callac. That house had been the former rulers of all the human lands before the splitting of the kingdoms.

Portia wanted to hug Cecilia but wasn't sure how. It felt so awkward, this woman who was her mother yet also a stranger to her. Portia wanted to stay, but her responsibility lay elsewhere.

"Portia," Cecilia said again.

"Please, don't," Portia said, pleadingly. It hurt enough to have to leave without directly going against her mother's wishes. Cecilia nodded and wiped at her bright eyes before opening her arms to offer Portia a hug.

Portia walked into her arms and let her head rest on Cecilia's shoulder, the scent of lemon grass tickling her nose. Cecilia squeezed her and kissed her on her head.

A horn sounded from the palace as carriages exited the main gate. Those at the docks cheered. The royals were coming down to see them off to their battle at the splinter to the Dragonoid world.

13

Magisend Lucy shoved the other girls' packs out of her tent and on to the sprawling deck of the *Pearl*. Ella stood on the deck, her hands on her hips and her lips pursed in a frown, watching Magisend.

"You're kidding, right, Magisend? We all have to stay in there," said Ella, exasperated. Her normally bright eyes were red with exhaustion. It had been a long day bringing everything out to the gigantic ship and loading it before it pulled anchor. They'd not been allowed to go back to their houses nor to rest.

Mia and Portia flanked Ella, their arms crossed. Magisend and her two cronies exited the tent and stood facing them. It was an even match, three for three, but that was assuming a fair fight. If Portia knew anything, it was that Magisend would do anything to win. She had her own scars to prove it.

On the deck above, Liam whistled and called, "fight!" He didn't sound entirely unhappy about it. Soon, the rail above was crowded with sailors, students, and mages. Guards moved on the deck above that one. Portia pursed her lips, hoping the royals would not be notified of this confrontation.

"This is my tent," said Magisend.

"And we are grateful for your contribution," said Ella, "but there are not enough tents for everyone to have their own."

"It's not just for me." Magisend waved to her two friends.

"That tent," Ella said, pointing to the tent behind Magisend, "can sleep six people at least, maybe a dozen."

Magisend raised one shoulder nonchalantly. "Why should we be crowded?"

"Because," Ella said, stepping forward only to be blocked by Mia, "we all need to sleep somewhere. The boys have their tent over there, and they are accommodating some mages from the Academy as well. They are very crowded in that little tent."

"That is not my problem," said Magisend, unrepentant.

Portia stepped forward. "This mission addresses a problem that belongs to all of us—the Dragonoids. Causing a problem for some of us causes a problem for the mission." She glared at Magisend, willing the girl to understand she had to cooperate.

Magisend eyed Portia and then looked to the crowds on the rail above. She closed her eyes then opened them again, and then she fixed Portia with a stare. "Fine. We'll share, but if you get my tent dirty, I will make you lick it clean," she warned.

A chorus of "Ooooh" came from the railing above them.

"I'd like to see you try," said Ella as she picked up her pack and walked around Magisend to toss it inside the tent.

"So would I!" a voice from above yelled, setting off a round of laughter that broke the tension around them. Portia looked up but could not pick out who had said it.

Portia forced her hands to relax. She hadn't realized she had clenched them until an ache ran along her forearms. She grabbed her own pack, and Mia's as well, and followed Ella to toss them into the tent. They would deal with their packs, and Magisend, later.

They had left the shore for the ship as soon as the royal carriages had arrived at the harbor and orders had been called. Much to everyone's surprise, the royals were coming on the ship along with the rest of them—despite the risk of battle and against the pleading advice of their advisors. Queen Morgani would host Queen Lorica and King Consort Aldis. The Dwarven ship, the *Pearl*, was large enough to host a small city. Half the mages of the Academy were on board, as well most of the Elven contingent. The rest were left in Coverack to defend the city in case more Dragonoid war wagons appeared. Portia regretted not having Professor Hilda Griffiths or Lady Harper with them, but she understood the needs of the city.

On the main ship, the interior cabins on the third deck were reserved for the royals and their advisors and their servants. The captain and the crew occupied the cabins of the other decks, while Portia and the other student mages camped out on the deck itself along with many city guards and the Elven and Dwarven soldiers. The deck was high enough from the water that most spray did not reach it, but the wind cut across its surface. Clouds muted the glare from the sun, but on cloudless days there would be no protection from its beating rays except for the tents they had been allowed to bring on board. Everything had been done in a scramble, and only now were things getting sorted out so that dinner could be served to not just the sailors but also the soldiers and students.

Accompanying the vessel were several clippers from the royal navy of Haulstatt. They were dwarfed by the large ship, their masts barely reaching its deck high above them. The size difference reminded Portia uncomfortably of the massive size of the Dragonoid ships they'd seen outside the Well of Tears. There had been several of those enormous ships. At least the humans and dwarves and elves had one ship that size on their side, but a fleet of them would have been better. A fleet with weapons using black powder would have been better than that.

The mages had still not yet figured out the magic of the black powder. A sample had been brought back from Rodaine, pulled from the remains of a metal ball buried in a building in the harborside. The dust had exploded and singed them just as it had singed Portia when she got some on her skin and then got too close to a candle. The city mages were scrambling for more samples to study, but without capturing an enemy ship, or an enemy weapon with a large amount of powder inside it to test, it was unlikely they would discover its secret. There was just not enough for them to examine in detail.

The Dwarven captain and his crew were concerned about

the metal hulls of the ships of their enemies, as well as their ability to throw metal balls far across the sea. Portia and Professor Aelric and all the students who had been present on the *Dancing Queen* had explained the defensive technique they had used of sending alternating heat and freezing cold to the Dragonoid ships to weaken the metal of their hulls. It was a labor-intensive effort to fight even one ship that way, and their mage firepower was limited. Magisend and her friends were walking the deck when they overheard the discussion happening around the captain on deck.

"Why don't you just make some rocks explode at them?" Magisend Lucy asked.

Portia whirled to stare at the girl. Below deck was a chamber full of boulders and studded metal balls to be used in the ship's giant catapults to throw at the enemy ships. The catapults' range, described by the captain, was not as far as the Dragonoids' with their black powder weapons. Right now, the group was trying to plan how to use magic to extend the natural range of the catapults so they could strike at the Dragonoids without having to bring their own ships within range of the enemy weapons.

An explosion of one of their own missiles would propel some of the missiles further, even if other bits bounced back into the ocean. Portia's mind thought furiously. They had both cryomancy and pyromancy mages on board. Professor Hilda's lessons on heating metal and other substances came back to her in a flash.

"Oh, you're a genius, I could kiss you!" Portia said, grinning at Magisend Lucy, who recoiled back in mock horror. At least Portia thought it was mock horror.

Portia had turned back to the others, who looked at her curiously. "If we put little bits of water inside our missiles, we could chill and warm it to make the missiles explode." At their puzzled expressions, she explained in more detail. "Freezing the water would expand it, cracking the rocks. Superheating the water right after would blow the pieces out. The bits of the rocks would shoot even further to the enemy ships. It might be the extra firepower we need to strike at them. And we'd do it all remotely with magic from the deck of our ship."

She purposely did not look at Richard, whose magical power was breathing fire. Of all the students, he was the only one unable to do magic at a distance, and that lacking on his part embarrassed him severely. She did not want to make it worse.

Archmage Vermeil was with the group trying to figure out how to modify their weapons. He was the first amongst them to understand what Portia was talking about and nodded agreement. At the others' murmured questions, he did his best to explain to those nearest to him while Portia did the same to those around her.

The captain decreed it be done, but it would require immediate work to prepare their payloads. Mages and crew were dispatched to the decks below to get to work immediately. Portia went to join them, but Professor Aelric held her back with one arm.

"Not you," he said, a bit of sadness in his voice.

"I want to help," Portia said, staring down at his arm in her way.

"And you have. But you must conserve your strength. Of all of us on board the ship, you are the only one who can heal the splinters. Your duty to us all is to do no magic, say, except for perhaps the most minimal amount of practice needed to keep up your skills. Beyond that, do nothing. It's for the best of our mission." At her skeptical look, he spoke lower and more intently. "No magic. Nothing extra beyond our mission. Without you, this would be a meaningless exercise in death for us all."

Portia's mouth hung open at the stark terms Professor Aelric used. Death. Was she the only one who did not think about these missions as suicide missions? Surely, the royals two decks above did not think of it so. They would not risk their own lives. They had a duty to their people.

Professor Aelric refused to move. Portia stepped back and snapped her mouth shut. Perhaps the royals thought their duty was to do what it took to protect their people, no matter what the personal risk was to themselves.

Giving a curt nod, Portia backed away. Professor Aelric turned and followed the others down below decks to work on the catapult payloads.

The wind was dying down on deck. Now was as good a time as ever to get some sword practice. She might not be able to do magic, or at least not much, but she could at least practice her skills with her sword. Unable to part with it, she had brought it on board as she always brought it with her everywhere. She ran to the tent to retrieve it from her pack.

Mark found Portia several hours later, sweaty and resting with her feet over the edge of the deck, staring out at the waters. She was wiping down the blade with her extra overtunic, making sure it was clean of sea spray and any sweat that may have dripped on it. The copper of the weapon shone in the dim light of the setting sun.

"That really is a beautiful weapon," Mark said as he dropped down to sit next to her. "Is it truly an Elven blade?"

Portia looked down at the copper blade. She thought it vibrated in response to her gaze. "It came from the Elven lands. I did not get the true story of where it came from."

"It came from the king and queen," Mark said.

"No, where it came from before then. How it came to be in their armory. I was in such a hurry to get back to Haulstatt that it wasn't the time to try to find out more."

"I wouldn't care where it came from if I had such a fine weapon." Mark turned to stare out at the horizon. The land behind them had disappeared hours ago. Only sea stretched out in all directions. It was disconcerting to be so far away from solid ground.

"We should be coming upon the splinter soon," Mark said. They were about halfway to the Well of Tears. This was the spot where their information had described another splinter. They should be upon it at any time.

Portia glanced up at the lookout in the crow's nest. She had been on edge waiting to hear a call out all day, but none had come. The dwarf high up on the mast had seen nothing.

"Staring won't make him see anything sooner," said Mark, not even checking where her gaze was pointed.

"I know, but it worries me to not know where the Dragonoid forces are," said Portia, dropping her eyes once again to stare out at the horizon.

"I know. I agree. How they didn't just rampage through Lusatiana and onward to Haulstatt is a mystery. If Grania is such a great spymaster, how can she have no answers for that?" A hint of disbelief surfaced in his voice.

"She isn't like the cult or those companies you worked for," Portia said, defending the spymaster without even thinking and almost instantly regretting it.

"I stopped working for that company," he said defensively. "And how do you know she's not like them? Does she tell you what she's thinking or doing? She just appears and talks about her intelligence and spies to the queen and king." He looked around suddenly, as if he expected the spymaster herself to step out from a shadow nearby. When no black shadow lengthened to reveal a woman, he relaxed and turned back. "I don't trust her."

They sat in silence for a few minutes, contemplating the mystery of where the Dragonoid forces had gone after Portia had closed the gigantic splinter at the Well of Tears that had allowed their enormous ships to pass into their lands. The Dragonoid they had captured at the attack on the harbor at Coverack and forced to talk had mentioned another splinter being created. There might even be more than one if the Dragonoids had the ability to make new ones. Portia hoped it wasn't so, but rather that they were pushing open an already existing portal that was somehow weakened. If the Dragonoids could create splinters at will, it would be near impossible to defend their lands from portals that could open anywhere, at any time, especially if they were so overpowered by the strange weapons of the Dragonoids.

The wind whistled over the dock, picking up in speed and making the lines above them sing and vibrate. Portia shivered, her sweat now chilled. She yanked her spare overtunic over her head and pulled her arms inside, rubbing them vigorously to warm up. The clouds whirled on the horizon, spiraling up into a tall vertical column that rose higher into the sky than she thought possible. It didn't look natural.

It wasn't natural.

Portia jumped to her feet and pointed at the cloud column. "Splinter! It's right there!"

Mark followed the direction of her finger and gasped when he saw it. There had been nothing there a moment before. Just then, the lookout in the crow's nest called out the alarm and rang the bell over and over again. The soldiers and sailors on the deck sprang into action, running and churning like an angry bees' nest.

Orders were called out in the ships below—the human clipper ships—which fell into formation to the sides and behind the *Pearl*. Flagmen at the front of each ship waved signals, directing the action and communicating between the ships for their captains. Portia cursed herself for not having learned the flags yet. She had planned to do so but then forgotten and practiced her sword instead. It was a stupid mistake.

She ran back to the tent where her pack was and dug through it to find the pieces of body armor she had: the stiff leather guards and the chain mail neckpiece that fell down over her chest. It wasn't as protective as the heavy plate armor many of the soldiers had, but she could move quickly in it. Ella and Mia were there as well, pulling on what pieces they had and strapping daggers to their belts. Portia hoped they would not get close enough to need the knives in direct combat, but it was better to be prepared.

They exited the tent to find Magisend and her cronies already dressed and ready for battle. Portia nodded acknowledgment of their being so well-prepared. Magisend's look of contempt and boredom had been replaced by an intense set of her jaw, and her eyes gleamed as she looked to Portia.

"I'm ready, anytime you are, *partner*," Magisend Lucy said.

Portia raised an eyebrow at the respectful term.

"I can call you commoner again if that would make you feel more comfortable... commoner," Magisend Lucy said, perfectly understanding Portia's surprise.

"I wouldn't want to strain you too much by asking you to change your habits," Portia said, dishing out sarcasm even while adjusting her baldric and her sword.

"No strain. A perfect memory, remember?" Magisend smirked.

Portia wished she could forget. Of all the people to have the skills they needed for this mission, it had to be Magisend Lucy. She shook her head and beckoned Magisend to follow her by way of response.

The captain had already called out the orders for the catapults to be loaded. His second echoed his orders for the crew further down the boat, and they were yelled sailor to sailor. Despite the ship having been stored for generations, the crew worked in perfect synchrony. They must have drilled somehow, Portia realized, deep within the bowels of the earth in the Dwarven kingdom of Morgani. It took immense discipline to work so hard to be prepared to sail on a ship one might never see in one's lifetime. Portia's respect for the dwarves rose in a leap. They worked seamlessly as a team.

Running to the edge of the deck, Portia saw that the other ships had fallen far behind the Pearl. It must have been by design. Mark joined her at the rail, pushing between her and Magisend Lucy.

"I overheard them talking," he said, looking down at the ships with her. "They're going to try your technique with the catapults. The wood of this craft is magically reinforced. It's not as good as metal, I guess, but better than what the clippers have."

Portia looked down at the deep red wood of the hull. It shone and had depth, like there were several inches of water over the wood. It was beautiful. And apparently strong. The clipper ships behind them look like painted matchsticks in comparison.

"We need to get to the splinter," Portia said.

Archmage Vermeil joined them, staring out at the fast-approaching squall of clouds. "If there are enemy ships there, we have to disable them first. Our queen is not willing to underestimate these Dragonoids again. For that I am grateful. I've seen firsthand the damage they've done."

Portia nodded, thankful they were not immediately facing hand-to-hand combat with the Dragonoids. It sometimes seemed so unreal that she and Iva had survived in their land, as if it had happened to another person. The horrific battle at the splinter within the Dwarven kingdom was still a fresh memory.

The squall of clouds continued to puff out and up, a space opening up from beneath them to the waters below. Three smaller Dragonoid ships sailed out towards them. Even from a distance, it was clear they were not as big as the ship upon which they stood. Portia cautiously exhaled, hopeful that there were no more vessels deep within the clouds ahead.

A flash of fire rose up on the deck of the middle ship and just as quickly disappeared, followed by a boom that rang out over the waters.

"Duck!" Portia yelled.

She grabbed Mark and Archmage Vermeil by the sleeves and pulled them back, scrambling to get around the far side of the captain's overlook structure. If the shot from the enemy ship had the range to get as far as they were, the three of them were on an open deck with no cover. They were completely vulnerable.

Luckily, the shot had been premature. An enormous splash jumped up from the waters between the ships as the cannonball from the Dragonoid vessel fell far short of its mark.

"Set!" a sailor yelled, the command having come down

from the captain to fire. The gigantic catapult high on the deck creaked and moaned as it was cranked tight. The wood of it squealed and screeched in agony. The hair on Portia's arms rose, and the skin on the back of her neck and scalp tingled. There was enormous energy stored within that catapult, and if anything went wrong and it did not fire, all that energy had to go somewhere. Suddenly, she was afraid of the weapons on their own deck more than she was of the Dragonoid ships across the waters.

But the catapult did fire. When the command was given and passed down the line to the chief weapons officer at the catapult, his arm came down to signal its release. The gigantic arm of the catapult swung free and its basket flew high over the deck, flinging the payload forward, just missing their own mast in its trajectory towards the Dragonoid ships.

The payload arched high in the air above them, racing towards the enemy. It started its descent. Portia yelled in frustration—it was not going to reach its target. But just as she thought they were doomed, the gigantic rock payload burst into several large pieces, two of which hit the ships ahead of them. The impact rang out with the echo of a metal cup hitting the ground. It was a good strike. The Academy mages at the railings cheered while still throwing fire and ice magic towards the enemy ships, following up on what the catapult had started. The decks glowed red and then faded again as Portia recognized the series of strikes Professor Aelric had first designed in their mission on the *Dancing Queen*. The second catapult on deck creaked and complained as it was cranked back and readied for firing, while the first was reloaded. The deck was a hive of activity.

Portia moved to get closer to see what was happening to the ships ahead, but Mark held her back by one arm. She whirled on him. Both he and Archmage Vermeil faced her.

"You can't go there. Stay here where you are safe," Mark said, refusing to let go of her arm despite her pulling on it. Magisend Lucy watched from over Mark's shoulder.

Portia stared at the two of them. "You were sent here by Professor Aelric, weren't you?"

"What if we were? Wouldn't it be better if we weren't needed to be here to stop you? We need you to be ready to go to the splinter," Mark said, standing up to her in a way he had never done before. A sudden feeling that she did not know him at all overtook her.

Archmage Vermeil nodded agreement with Mark's words.

She growled under her breath but could not deny that he was right. "Fine. But Magisend stays too. We can't lose her," Portia said.

Magisend started to say something when Mark and Archmage Vermeil turned to her, but she shut her mouth again and gave them a curt nod.

Satisfied, Portia turned to watch the other students rush to help the academy mages while the battle continued. It seemed like an eternity of strikes firing from the catapults against the three ships who had increased their speed towards them, returning their own fire of whistling metal balls. The enemy ships were pushing to get into range so their payloads would hit their targets instead of landing futilely in the sea. It was a race to see if they could do it before the damage from the Dwarven ship was too much.

The middle Dragonoid ship had not made it, having sunk after too many direct strikes, but the two flanking it continued on, one aiming straight for the *Pearl,* the other veering in the opposite direction. The Dragonoid ship had made several direct strikes on the *Pearl.* The *Pearl* creaked and moaned with each hit and the decks vibrated with the impacts, but blessedly, none of the strikes tore through the walls of the ship. They only sent small fragments of damaged wood to fall down into the waters below. To Portia's horror, she saw several soldiers swimming in the frothy seas below the ship, having been knocked from its deck with the force of the impacts.

The other Dragonoid ship had sailed to the side and away from the *Pearl.* Portia didn't understand what it was doing until it turned its cannons and fired at one of the clippers behind them and to the right. The cannon found its target and tore through the wooden clipper ship like it was a child's toy, the wooden beams and sails exploding outward and spreading across the water like so much painted debris. Men screamed. The hull of the ship took fire and burned on the water. Bile rose in Portia's throat.

Another cannonball landed in the water of the remains of the ship, warding away the other clippers that would have come to the rescue. Rage clouded Portia's vision. Her hands clenched; she wanted to strike out at the enemy ship. Mark grabbed her hand and shook it, making her look at him. Over his shoulder, she saw Magisend Lucy with a strange expression on her face as she stared at Portia and then at the ships in the water and all the damage being done. It took Portia a minute to realize the expression on Magisend's face was concern.

Finally, with the mages at the rail redoubling their efforts and the two catapults on deck whizzing their payloads overhead, the second ship was sunk and then the third chased and finished.

Portia couldn't bear the thought of all the Dragonoids on board drowning. She had to turn away as the ships sank into the seas.

Even as they had caused the destruction of the ship of their fleet, she could not be glad of their own deaths. Why had it come to this? Why couldn't it have been a peaceful meeting from two different lands?

Her thoughts went back to the ancient book written by one of the early human invaders. They had been no better. Her face flushed red at the memory. She turned so no one saw her and looked back out over the waters at where the three ships had been, now only holding choppy blue waves.

The smaller, more nimble clipper ships below raced to rescue the men in the water from the sunken ship behind them while everyone on board the *Pearl* stood tense and watched, waiting to see if another ship would emerge from the clouds ahead. None did. The sun was setting, sending its rays stretching underneath the heavy hanging clouds and illuminating what was below them. The faint shimmer of a portal splinter shown over the water, but there were no other ships.

Professor Aelric came running up to them. "Hurry," he

said, motioning for Portia and Magisend to run to the side where a longboat stood in its harness waiting to be lowered to the waters. "We can get close, but we don't dare let any part of this vessel drift inside the splinter. We know the splinters can pull a current—at least the other splinter did. Who knows what would happen when such a large vessel comes into contact with too small a splinter."

Portia looked up, confused. "If it's small, how did those larger ships we saw at the Well of Tears disappear?" Those huge, Dragonoid ships had been stuck on the Haulstatt side when she had closed the splinter and trapped herself on the far side, in the Dragonoid's land.

Professor Aelric shook his head. "We don't know, but they aren't here. And something else might come out of that splinter any moment, so we must hurry." He glanced at the setting sun. "We don't want to be doing this after dark. Let's go. We'll be providing cover from here."

Mages and students lined the rail closest to the splinter, all at the ready in case anything appeared from within it.

Portia nodded at Professor Aelric.

Portia, Magisend Lucy, and Professor Aelric ran towards the longboat. A full crew of sailors waited for them. As soon as Portia and Magisend were loaded onto the small craft, it was dropped with stomach-churning rapidity down to the waters below, the lines clanking as ropes raced through pulleys. The boat landed with a thud on the choppy waters. The pacer called out immediately to start the rowing. The boat jerked forward with each stroke of the rowers.

Between the moans of the men in the water behind her,

the choppy waves, and the jerking rowing, Portia thought she was going to be sick. She leaned forward and put her head down by her knees, not caring what Magisend thought of her. Blessedly, the girl said nothing, and Portia concentrated on her breathing in and out.

Portia was soaked through from the sea spray by the time they rowed under the swirling clouds and reached the location of the splinter. Her wool cloak still held warmth even as water dripped down her back and along her arms.

The portal was much smaller than the splinter over the sea at the Well of Tears. The oval of the splinter rose up above them and down into the waters, but it did not extend nearly deep or high enough for a large ship to pass through completely, nor even one of the clippers behind them. Portia tried to think if one of the three Dragonoid ships would have fit through the splinter, but it was difficult to concentrate with her nausea from the rough waters. She looked to the top of the oval above her.

"We have to get closer!" she yelled to the sailor in charge of the prow of the ship, struggling to be heard in the winds and rough water. She pointed to Magisend Lucy, who was huddled in her own cloak. "She has to hear the splinter. She has to put her head through," Portia said.

She looked up and glared at Portia. "If I'm putting my head through, so are you," Magisend said as she grabbed Portia's arm and dragged her up to the front of the boat.

The two of them crouched at the front, leaning forward and gripping the gunwale while the pacer moved back to give them room. The rowers behind them rowed carefully to bring them closer without going so fast as to send them shooting through it into the other world. It was a nerve-racking balancing act, all the while fighting the sea and the storm. Portia's ears stung from the wind cutting across them. She hoped the howling gales would not interfere with their being able to hear the music of the worlds at the edge of the splinter.

They drew closer and closer, but there was no sound from the splinter. Magisend turned to glare at Portia, the threat clear in her eyes that she would kill Portia if this was all for nothing and there was no music. Portia steadfastly refused to look at her, feeling Magisend's eyes burning into her cheek.

Just as Portia thought she might be wrong and there was indeed no music, a faint tune reached her ears. Magisend heard it too. She whipped her head around, staring at the splinter and trying to hear it better.

"Closer!" Magisend yelled. She half stood up and leaned forward even farther to hear better. Portia grabbed her by her belt and leaned back to keep her from falling overboard. Magisend was even smaller than she looked.

The sailors behind them swore in their struggles with the waters and then quieted themselves when Portia turned to glare at them. Both Portia and Magisend concentrated, listening intently. Portia heard it too, even from behind Magisend. It sounded as if there was a repeat of the pattern of note. Finally, Magisend turned around and nodded at Portia. She'd heard it. All of it.

Pulling Magisend back into the boat and pushing her back into one of the seats between two of the rowers, Portia took her place at the front of the boat and faced the splinter. She sang the song of healing to it, forcing it closed. Closing her eyes against her nausea, Portia concentrated on the song and feeling the splinter itself. She tried to separate the music she had heard from it, from both sides, and heal one side first and then the other, but it was like feeling around a burlap bag to separate two kittens—all fuzziness and fur and sharp claws and uncertainty in what she was doing. But she did it the best she could, forcing the two sides together to heal without any explosions or missteps. Just as the splinter had done at the Well of Tears, once it started to close, the edges pulled together faster and faster until the oval finally compressed down to a circle and then disappeared with a pop.

Only the sounds of the waves breaking against the gunwale of the boat and the wind howling over the sea were left.

Darkness crowded around Portia's vision as her head suddenly felt light, and she fainted forward towards the dark swirling waters.

14

The bed below Portia rolled to one side and moved her face into the beam of sunlight streaming into the tent. She opened her eyes and scowled at the bright light then sat up, confused.

"The commoner is awake," Magisend Lucy said from behind Portia.

Magisend was sitting in the back of the tent with her legs out in front of her while eating from a tin bowl. Her cronies' bedrolls were empty and made, and Ella's bedding was rolled up in a corner along with Mia's.

Magisend Lucy watched Portia's gaze. "They're at breakfast," she said after swallowing her last bite and setting down her dish. "I've been up early, working, so had already gotten mine. Lucky me, I got to watch over you. I think I missed my chance to rid myself of you permanently."

Portia tilted her head and gave a sharp look at Magisend. Magisend laughed. It was actually a pretty laugh. Portia had never noticed before. Or maybe it was a different laugh than she'd ever heard from her before.

"I'm only kidding," Magisend said. "I have no intention of having anything bad happen to my house, which means working with you, commoner."

"My apologies for the torture. I hope it hasn't been that bad," said Portia.

Portia pushed back the bedding and found herself in a thin nightgown. Looking around in a panic, she saw her sword and baldric atop her bag. Her clothes were nowhere to be seen.

"I've been told to tell you that your clothes are hanging to dry on the aft line, and your sword was cleaned and dried by Mia. She said you would ask right away," Magisend said, a hint of amusement in her voice.

Portia breathed a sigh of relief and gratitude to Mia, for surely that was who had left the message as well. Ella, her roommate, could be counted on for questions of gossip and hair, but seemed to forget the daggers at her side needed her attention and care as well. But now she had another problem. She needed to get her clothes and didn't want to ask Magisend to go and get them for her. Nor did she want to walk across the deck of the *Pearl* in front of the Dwarven sailors and the soldiers of all the armies. Not to mention the indignity of not being properly dressed in front of the royals that were on board. Hopefully, her housemates would come back so she could send them to run and get her clothes, even if she had to beg.

Ella loved to talk over any meal, so it might be a while.

Magisend had not moved from her spot after setting down her bowl. She crossed her arms and stared at Portia thoughtfully. "How do you feel?"

Portia's head hurt and was fuzzy of memories of how she had gotten into the tent. The last thing she remembered was being on the boat with Magisend and the others. Magisend had never before asked her a kind question, and that change, too, added to the sense of unrealness. "Not well."

"I imagine not. I suppose we are lucky you're not coughing and feverish. Of course, I am not either, and I got just as wet as you, having to be the one to fish you out of the brink."

Portia looked up in surprise.

"Yes, me. I was tempted to leave you there, but we have a task to do together. My house depends on it. Besides, the sailors would have seen me leaving you to drown. If I'm going to do something like that, I'll be more skilled than to do it in front of witnesses," Magisend Lucy explained. Her voice was perfectly even, but somehow, even through the fog in her head, Portia sensed she was kidding.

"Then I owe you my eternal gratitude," Portia said.

"Yes, I think some good linens too."

Despite her throbbing head, Portia laughed. The first time she had met Magisend Lucy, it was in the young noble's richly appointed bedroom. Portia had snuck in the window to steal the fine linens on Magisend's bed. The tiny girl had nearly killed Portia for her pains. It had been a horror to make it into the Academy only to realize she would have to go to class with the girl who hated her so badly. And perhaps,

Portia had to admit even to herself, she might have deserved it.

"I can't quite see you pulling me out of the waters," Portia said.

"They spared me no dignity, I'll tell you that. I had you by the waist and they had me by the ankles, and I held on to your sorry hide until they had dragged us both over that rough boat edge. I think I'll have bruises for a week. I'm sure you'll have some too," Magisend said, some of her old haughty tone coming out.

Portia patted her arms and her legs and indeed did find tender spots. Her throat was also scratchy and sore. She must have swallowed some of the acidic seawater.

"But you're awake, I have finished my work, so I think our mission is on track," Magisend said as she rose.

She walked along the back wall of the tent, only having to bow her head a little despite the tent's shortness, to retrieve a large sheet of paper resting atop a small trunk she had brought along. Bringing the paper to Portia, she laid it on Portia's lap and retreated to sit back along the back wall of the tent again.

Portia looked down at the paper. It had sets of long black lines written across the page, with small black dots scattered along the lines. Below it, there was writing in a beautiful cursive script. She gave Magisend a questioning look.

Magisend raised her shoulders nonchalantly and let them drop. "It's the music. I know you were talking about inside and outside and all that, but I only heard one tune, in one key, and that was it." Magisend pointed to the paper on Portia's lap. "I have perfect pitch. It must be that melody, in that key."

Portia looked back down at the music. This was the key to the Dragonoids' world. She read sheet music a little, painfully. Mia had taught her some of it while she was teaching her about cursive. But she wasn't fluent and had to sound out the notes to herself.

Singing softly, she tentatively tried out the melody written on the page. It was familiar. This was what she remembered hearing, but there were some additional notes, things she hadn't heard out on the boat.

"Are you sure this is correct?" Portia asked.

Magisend crossed her arms and glared at Portia. "Perfect. Pitch. And a perfect memory."

Portia looked back down at the sheet. She knew of no reason for Magisend to write the tune down wrong. Still, it was hard to trust the girl who had tormented her for a full year and nearly took her life, even if by accident.

"It's not for you. It's for my family. You're welcome," Magisend Lucy said. She stood again and exited the tent, not giving Portia another glance.

Suddenly the tent felt very lonely. Portia turned to see where Magisend had gone, but all she saw was empty deck to the prow of the ship where a few sailors were sitting, huddled, working over a thick rope line.

She stared at the music again. Her first priority had to be memorizing this. She hated depending on Magisend Lucy. Still, getting the music written down was more of a boon than she thought she would get.

Voices echoed over the wooden deck as the other students returned from breakfast. Ella walked between Mark and

Liam, laughing and flirting with them both, first touching Mark's hand and then Liam's. Each boy glared at the other when Ella wasn't looking. Portia snorted. If Ella had been anyone else, she would've thought she was doing it on purpose.

Archmage Vermeil walked behind with Mia, the two of them in deep conversation. Richard and Professor Aelric turned off from the group to join the sailors at the front of the ship. The sailors were showing them something with the rope. Portia wanted to know what tactic they were discussing and rose to join them but then sat down quickly again, remembering she was only wearing a nightshirt. She cursed under her breath, feeling helpless. Ella did not look like she was carrying anything near large enough to be her bundle of clothes.

Suddenly, Mia ran around the group ahead of her and to the tent where Portia was sitting. She threw in a bundle of Portia's clothes. They were mostly dry, with only a few damp spots where the cloth was doubled over around the waistband.

"Hurry, before Ella brings the guys right into the tent," Mia said.

Portia did not need encouragement. She quickly donned her britches, threw off her nightshirt, and put on her shirt and tunic. She instantly felt better.

Exiting the tent, the warmth of the sun on her face and the fresh air blowing across the deck completed her sense of well-being. She was surrounded by friends, and it was only the soldiers scattered around the deck and the guard on the upper deck where the royals were staying that reminded her that they were on a war mission. If it weren't for those things, this could be a great adventure. Being on a ship like this was beyond even her wildest dreams from her days of being a street orphan in Valencia. She remembered looking longingly at a royal ship in the harbor then and realized with a start how tiny it was in comparison to the vessel she was on now. No, she never could have imagined her future life when she'd been living in the hovel of the Black Cat's house.

Loud footsteps rang out from the stairs leading up to the deck above their tent. Portia looked up to see General Lyren running down the stairs towards her.

"Young human, you're okay," the tiny elf said, grabbing Portia by both shoulders and shaking her. "We saw you getting dragged out of the water. Lord Fife would not be pleased to see his student falling over from such a simple spell." General Lyren beamed at Portia, despite her ribbing words.

"Yes, I'm okay."

"Excellent, excellent. Our mages want to talk to you. One, at least I know of, is a bit perturbed that a human has the healing spell of the elves and they do not, being elves themselves." General Lyren let go of Portia and put her hands in her belt and looked out over the deck.

"Um, I'm not sure..." Portia started but then didn't know what to say. She was not in charge of who learned what spells.

"No worries, no worries. If Lord Fife was not able to get through to them that they couldn't learn the spell because, well, they couldn't do it, I don't think you'll be able to either. But we must try, mustn't we, young human?"

Portia nodded unsurely. "Okay."

"Excellent, excellent." The general turned to look at Portia, this time critically looking her up and down. "You have not been eating enough. I can tell. Have you had breakfast yet?"

Portia shook her head, feeling slightly dizzy from the rapid change of subjects.

"Go eat then! What are you still doing standing here?" General Lyren said before walking away and climbing the stairs again to run across the deck above them and then climb the second set of stairs to the royal decks above. Portia watched her go, feeling vaguely like she'd been run over by a horse and cart. It was good to see Sergeant, no, General Lyren again, if not exhausting.

SEVERAL HOURS later Portia was summoned to the top deck of the royals. Her friends below had been happy and enjoying the sunshine, but on the upper deck all the faces were grim. She had not seen much of Archmage Vermeil nor Professor Aelric that morning. The feeling hung over her that she was missing something obvious, but her growling stomach and her aching head distracted her. By the time she was truly worried there was something amiss, the courier had come to find her and brought her immediately up to the reception room.

Queen Lorica and King Aldis sat with Queen Morgani around a wooden table fastened to the floor of a back meeting room behind the more ostentatious reception room, which was now empty except for some soldiers huddled in groups over maps laid out on long wooden tables.

Portia curtsied when she entered the room. Queen Lorica waved her forward. She noticed with a start that Archmage Vermeil and Professor Aelric were standing in the back of the room, along with several advisors. No one smiled.

"Portia, our Jack of Magic," said Queen Lorica, "we have need of your assistance."

"Anything, Your Majesty," said Portia.

She searched the faces in the room for some reassurance, but all expressions were grim, and few met her eyes. Neither Archmage Vermeil nor Professor Aelric would do so, instead looking past her at the wall behind. Portia shoved down the urge to turn around to see what they were staring at. It would not do to turn her back on her queen.

"We have something to show you that most students will not see. It is something most of our citizens would never see. But it is a necessary part of war. We must ask for both your secrecy and your strength. Is that understood, Portia, Jack of Magic?" Queen Lorica asked.

Portia nodded. King Consort Aldis, who always smiled, now had a frown and pinched brows, scaring Portia more than anything in that room.

Queen Lorica, Queen Morgani, and King Consort Aldis stood. A servant led the way, opening the doors for the group as they went into another room and then down a long set of stairs, deep into the bay of the ship. A mage held aloft a burning light that cast rays ahead of the main group without the risk of an open flame on a boat.

Inside a dirty room along the curved hull of the ship sat a Dragonoid. He slumped over against the curved hull, breathing shallowly. His uniform was torn, and gashes along his face and missing scales were crusted with blood. One arm was within a sling, bloodied and crushed fingers sticking out the end. He stared at the group entering the door, his eyes shiny and not seeming to focus.

The smell in the room was terrible. There was a bucket in the corner, but it was empty. The Dragonoid had either been unwilling, or unable, to use it. Its clothes were dirty with night soil and still damp with saltwater. Nausea rose up in Portia's throat.

She turned to look questioningly at Professor Aelric. He shook his head subtly. She bit back her questions.

As if reading her mind, Queen Lorica turned to Portia. "We did not do this, not directly. Not as torture. But unless we force his hand, he will not let us help him. Nor can we communicate with him without him learning our language as well, something we are unwilling to do. It is too dangerous."

Portia looked around the room, taking in the heavyset guards posted both inside and outside the prisoner's door. It was hard to imagine the injured creature on the floor a danger, but it was a possibility, no matter how remote.

A small elf mage Portia had not realized was with them pushed out from the group of people behind her and nodded the truth of the queen's statement of there being no work-around when it came to learning the Dragonoid language without sharing their own.

That had been Portia's experience as well—it was impossible to extract a foreign language from a living creature without sharing her on language with it in return. It had not been an outcome she had wanted. She had discovered that unhappy truth when she had applied the ability with languages the elves had given her to a Dragonoid prisoner in Coverack. The ability had worked to extract the Dragonoid's hissing tongue from the mind of the Dragonoid, but much to Portia's horror, the Dragonoid had learned Common in return. It was small consolation that it was true for all mages, not just for Portia.

"But we know you can speak the language already," said Queen Lorica.

Portia nodded.

Professor Aelric withdrew a small cube from his robes. It looked like the truth cube, a form of magic that measured the veracity of the speaker's statements, but this cube had a strange silver sheen on it. Portia stared at it. Professor Aelric looked uncomfortable holding it.

Finally, he explained, "This is the truth cube, but it behaves a little differently than the one you experienced in the Academy." He hesitated, as if not wanting to speak, but then forced himself to continue. "It has direct feedback to the subject. It causes... excruciating pain if the subject lies."

Portia's mouth hung open. She looked around, and again, no one would meet her eye. "You're torturing this prisoner." It wasn't a question.

Archmage Vermeil stepped forward, and after a nod of permission from his queen he spoke to Portia. "It's not torture if he understands the consequences of lying and willingly does so. No one is forcing him to lie." In the shadowy dim light of the room, Archmage Vermeil looked much older. Dark circles fell below his eyes, making them look even sadder than they usually did from their slight droop.

"It is not an ideal choice, but many lives of our citizens depend on finding out what we need to know," said Queen Lorica. "Its use is only authorized in times of extreme need. This is an instance of extreme need."

Portia's stomach roiled. She didn't want to be there. Gripping her hands into fists, she looked down and forced herself to concentrate on her breathing. Letting out an especially large breath, she relaxed her hands, looked up again, and nodded to her queen.

Portia sipped a mug of hot mead on the deck, willing her shivers to go away. She was sitting in full sunlight, a cloak wrapped around her shoulders, but she couldn't get warm. She shivered, icy cold shooting through her body. Her ears burned from the inside out. The screams of the prisoner still rang within them. She shook her head and pulled the cloak tighter around her shoulders.

Ella and Mark came to her bearing a bowl of food. It was a hot meal of meat mush and a precious tiny orange. Portia reluctantly put down her cup of mead and took the plate. They sat down facing her, cross-legged on the deck, leaning forward to look down. Portia was grateful they did not stare.

Ella was white-faced. Her normally bubbly demeanor was

gone. The prisoner's screams had echoed through the enormous boat. The afternoon for those on deck had been an anxiety-ridden trial of listening to someone else's suffering. No one had asked Portia what had been going on when she returned to the sunlit deck, her eyes still blinking from the darkness below. They had only shot her covert glances and whispered amongst themselves.

When Portia had first emerged from below, Mark had gone to sit next to her, shrugging off the hands that tried to keep him away. He had not asked any questions, instead sitting in silence next to her and staring out over the waves. After several hours, when the dinner bell rang, he had stood up and walked away. Dinner was still going on below decks when he returned with Ella.

Clearing her throat, Ella finally spoke. "The captain announced we are heading to a large splinter. They think that is where the rest of the Dragonoid fleet is."

Portia nodded, staring down at her bowl as she took a small spoonful and raised it to her lips. She didn't want to think about how she had heard the prisoner scream out the location of the splinter, how he'd pissed himself some more, and how she had been the one to ask over and over again in its hissing tongue for him to speak or else. At the thought of what "or else" had been, Portia put the spoon down, the food untasted. She pushed the bowl away.

Mark reached forward one hand and pushed the bowl back to Portia. He kept his hand there so she wouldn't move it away again. "Eat. You must," he said.

Portia shook her head.

"Eat, or all that creature suffered for today will pay for naught," he said, an edge in his voice she had never heard before. Looking up, she saw his eyes bright with concern for her, but also an anger that burned behind them. "Is that what you want?"

"Of course not."

"Then eat."

Reluctantly, Portia pulled the bowl back into her lap and raised the spoon to her mouth, putting the food inside her lips and chewing the tasteless mass. Tears welled in her eyes. Her skin tingled. Sadness at the way of the world washed over Portia. She had not wanted the Dragonoid to be hurt, but if they did not act, hundreds of her kinsmen would die. The queen's citizens would die, and more kingdoms would fall.

When she had been an orphan on the streets in Valencia, she thought there would be a safe place somewhere in this world, someplace where there was love and happiness for all. She hated learning that no place could have happiness without being willing to pay the price for it—the willingness to fight for it, to sacrifice, and to do the unbearable. She thought of all those who had fallen already in Rocabarra against the cult, deaths she had witnessed herself, and news she had heard about Jukhnovo from Iva and how she lost her entire family.

"I don't know what you've done, but Magisend Lucy was almost bearable today," a voice above Portia's head said. Mia was standing over her, her hands on her hips. Of all the students, she looked the most composed.

"I think she's realized we're all in this together," Portia mumbled around a mouthful of food.

"I doubt it. Still, she's been nicer," Mia admitted.

"Maybe it was all the screaming. Sorta adds to the atmosphere," Liam said, joining them and attempting a light tone but not quite managing it. He too was slightly gray-faced.

Richard came and joined the group sitting around Portia. They talked quietly amongst themselves or just sat companionably while she finished her meal. Out of the corner of her eye, Portia saw Magisend Lucy and her two cronies sitting by the railing watching the group with narrowed eyes. Portia considered asking them to join the group, but exhaustion held her back. She didn't have the energy to verbally spar with the girls from the cryomancy house right now. They would still be there tomorrow.

Thumping footsteps came towards them across the deck. Portia recognized the heavy walk. Archmage Vermeil stood in front of her, his arms crossed. "Can I have a word with you?"

"Sure," Portia said.

"Alone," said the dwarf.

Portia swallowed. She was exhausted and just wanted to rest with her friends, but Archmage Vermeil had a stubborn look on his face. She might as well get whatever he wanted over with.

15

P ortia and Archmage Vermeil walked along the railing on the edge of the deck of the enormous ship. It skirted around the entire circumference of the ship, only a few feet wide as it passed the buildings that comprised the upper-level decks and expanding out of the fore and aft, giving the sailors' workspace a clear view to the horizons. Above them, a stiff wind whistled through the sails and the rigging, throwing the ropes against the mast and snapping the sails whenever the wind faltered and then resumed again. Portia had somehow thought the sea would be peaceful and quiet, not the cacophony of sound and wind this ship had.

Portia grabbed and then released the chain railing strung through posts that lined the very edge of the deck as she walked. Archmage Vermeil clasped his hands behind his back as he walked, mostly looking down at his feet and occasionally looking up to make sure they were not going to walk into anything. He needn't have bothered. When the sailors and the guards saw them coming, they carefully drew out of the way of the pair. Portia's skin crawled at the deference. Everyone was careful to give them space. No one could have mistaken them for being part of a larger group.

"Are you okay?" Archmage Vermeil asked.

Portia shook her head. Who would be okay after the day they had had?

"I'm not too well myself," he admitted. "I know this is for my king, my people—"

"Your father," Portia said.

The archmage glanced at her, and then back down. "Yes, for the archmage... my father. It doesn't make it any easier."

"I wish we had another way."

"If we had more time, if not so many depended on us, if they had not had the cleverness to open another splinter."

Portia stopped short. "At least we know they didn't open a new one, just pushed open a weak one that was already there."

The archmage stopped to face Portia. "That's what he said."

Portia looked at him, surprised. "You don't believe him?"

"It's possible he was telling the truth. It's also possible he was not."

"No, we had the truth cube. He was telling the truth," Portia said, turning to resume her slow walk along the railing.

"There are ways to play with language, to tell a half-truth that can be taken as a full one," the archmage protested.

Portia shook her head, and then she grabbed the rail more tightly this time and swung the chain that was hanging strung along it with all her might. It rattled all the way down its length along the deck, startling two soldiers behind them who were polishing their swords in the afternoon sun. They stared at Portia and Archmage Vermeil, concerned. She waved apologetically at them, and they lowered their heads slowly back to their tasks.

"No, not their language. It is too direct in everything. Much like the Dragonoids themselves. He was telling the truth," Portia said bitterly.

"Well, then we can be grateful for that and for you having their language."

"Do we have any more of them?"

"Languages?" Archmage Vermeil asked, confused.

"Prisoners. Did we rescue any more of them from the waters in the last battle?"

After a moment of silent walking, Archmage Vermeil answered. "Yes. Quite a few, I believe."

"And they're below decks?" Portia asked.

"Some. I'm not told everything."

They continued their walk, turning around the front of the ship and now walking into the sun along the far side. Portia squinted and then turned around and walked backwards, the wind whipping her hair around her face. Archmage Vermeil pulled his hood down further and kept going forward, leaning into the wind to keep his balance.

"Speaking of things only you know," he said in a deferential tone. "Would you consider writing down all your magic and putting it in a book for us?"

She turned and squinted at him, drawing a lock of hair out of her eyes. "For the dwarves?"

He nodded. "Yes, for our people and for Queen Morgani and... for our king who shall, with all our hopes and efforts, return."

"Your king who went to go get weapons for the dwarves?"

He shrugged.

Portia turned away and stared out over the seas as she walked backwards. They continued onward past another group of soldiers who scrambled away, this time elves. She wanted to grab the elves who shied away from her and tell them it wasn't her fault the prisoner was hurt, but they wouldn't even make eye contact with her. She grabbed the railing even tighter, feeling the chain links pinching her skin when the chain moved.

"It would be good for there to be a record of all that you can do," he said.

"Maybe. I think it depends on who gets that information," Portia said. "I don't know how useful this book would be since I am the only one who can do much of this magic. You can't even hear the splinter music. Humans can't do Elven magic, and even most elves cannot do the splinter healing. Who would this book be for?"

"History. And the next Jack after you who desperately needs this knowledge. Do you really think you will be the last one?"

Portia looked at him in alarm. *The last Jack of Magic.* There were two ways that could happen: one would be for humans to never have another crisis that would need a Jack of

Magic, or two, for humans themselves to be no more. She was too cynical to believe humans would never have another crisis, but even she was not so hopeless as to think humans would disappear from their lands entirely. So, there would be another Jack. For that Jack—and for those that would depend on that Jack—she would write the book.

She should write the book.

Portia looked away, and then resumed walking forward with Archmage Vermeil keeping pace.

After several minutes, Portia finally spoke. "You have a point there, my friend. I will do it." She looked out over the waters, avoiding his face. "I will write this book for you, but there will be copies also for the Elven kingdom, who has shared their magic with me already, as well as for the human kingdom. All should have this knowledge."

Archmage Vermeil grimaced then nodded. "Very well."

Portia stopped walking to look out over the sea. The waters shimmered and reflected the red sky of the setting sun. "I want to test opening another splinter. We listened to the music from one splinter—and Magisend Lucy wrote it down —but I want to try opening a splinter with it before we close the one the Dragonoid spoke off. I must know the music is correct. To not verify it is to risk not being able to ever open one to the Dragonoid world. We would be abandoning all our people trapped on the other side."

"What would you do if the music was wrong and the new splinter didn't open to the right place?" the archmage asked.

"Close it. Then listen to the splinter the Dragonoid spoke

of, the one that opens to his world. We have to know the music exactly before we cut off all those people."

The archmage didn't look convinced.

"Morgani is not the only kingdom that lost people," Portia said, pushing her point.

"No. It's not me you'll have to convince." He glanced up at the royal deck high above them.

"I'm most likely our only hope of opening a splinter to their world and rescuing our people. What could be more important than that?" Portia asked, exasperated. "There is no other than me. The last Jack was half an eon ago. If we wait for another, our people will be long dead."

He shrugged, and then nodded again to the royal deck.

"I hate politics," Portia finally said when no other words came to her. She refused to directly criticize her queen.

"As do I," said Archmage Vermeil. "We must trust they know what they are about."

She squinted at him. *Did they?*

The wind whistling through the rigging did not have an answer for her. Looking around the deck and the soldiers scattered upon it, Portia brought herself back to the present.

"If those large Dragonoid ships are at the last splinter, we probably can't defeat them with a direct battle," she said, almost to herself. "We'll have to do something sneaky like last time. We barely sank their three smaller craft."

"Don't talk too loudly," the archmage warned, glancing about. "You might scare off the sailors that have to go into this battle."

Portia folded her arms and considered their armada of one

enormous Dwarven ship and the much smaller cutter ships of the Haulstatt navy.

PORTIA CROSSED and uncrossed her legs, unable to find a comfortable position. She was sitting inside the tent, using the top of the trunk Magisend Lucy had loaned her, as well as some parchment and ink. The sheet of music Magisend Lucy had written lay next to her. Portia grimaced as she looked down at her own shaky writing and then Magisend's beautiful script. Stretching her writing hand, she shook her head; there was nothing to be done for it. She dipped the quill into the inkpot and slowly scratched out the next line. She hadn't been sure where to start in writing the book, so she started with her ability to imitate other people in doing different sorts of magic. She could do anything she saw others do, just about, and that was the main difference between her and others. A fire-breather like Richard could watch others create ice all day and yet still be unable to do anything but breathe fire.

Stopping her writing, she cocked her head and listened. The ship had changed course towards the coordinates given by the prisoner. He had turned out to be a navigator, by luck or by astute observation of the soldiers who had grabbed him off the sinking ship. He had been huddled in the captain's overlook of the Dragonoid vessel. Perhaps he had been the captain of the enemy ship too. If he had been, he had not volunteered that information to his interrogators.

While the ship was rushing through the waters towards

their destination, the mages and students were on the deck practicing their magic to use in striking at the enemy vessels. If there were many Dragonoid ships at this new splinter location, they would need all the firepower they could muster to help support the two catapults on the Dwarven vessel, as well as the smaller catapults on the human ships. Some mages who were adept at cryomancy were also practicing dousing the deck with water just barely cold enough to freeze. This was to be used on their own ships if the enemy struck at them with fire. The chilled water would help put out any burning wood.

Professor Aelric was working with two advanced mages from the Academy to create a decoy version of the *Pearl*. It took a tremendous amount of energy to create the illusion, and the phantom ship itself did not look quite solid, but at first glance it would fool the enemy. Their fleet would not look quite so outnumbered to their foe if indeed there were two enormous Dragonoids vessels waiting for them, just as there had been at the Well of Tears.

For Portia, the writing was slow work. She paused, taking a break from her work to look down at the sheet music Magisend had written out and hummed the tune, trying to fix it firmly in her memory. Still, something clenched at Portia's gut every time she got to the middle passage. Something about it did not seem quite right. Her mind wanted to skip some notes through that strain. The notes felt superfluous, as if they didn't belong. It took all of her concentration to force herself to sing those notes. Her brow pinched as she thought of Magisend Lucy's adamant words that it was correct.

No matter how much she tried to talk herself into

thinking it was, it didn't feel correct.

Stretching her neck, Portia put the music down and addressed herself again to her task of writing down her book. She decided she would write five more pages and then allow herself time to get out and stretch and practice her sword. She looked over at the weapon sitting on top of her pack and patted it.

"Do you need a moment alone?" Mark asked from the open tent door with a smirk. He jerked his head in the direction of the weapon.

"Stop," Portia said.

Mark motioned to the inside of the tent. "Can I?"

"Yes, please." Portia waved him in.

He sat down next to her and leaned forward to look at the parchment sheets in front of her filled with her shaky handwriting. "I never knew you were one to have a diary," he said, picking up a sheet and pretending to squint at it and turn it this way and that in an effort to read it.

Portia grabbed the sheet from him and put it back down on the trunk. "My writing is not that bad."

He raised both eyebrows at her. "You sure?"

She pointed at him in warning. He shrugged and leaned back, crossing his legs out in front of him. "What are you doing?"

"I'm writing a book of my magic to give to the dwarves... and the elves, and—"

His nonchalance disappeared in a flash. He sat up and grabbed the sheet from her again. "You're what? Are you crazy?"

Portia grabbed the sheet back from him, irritated to see it had creased where he had been careless. She carefully smoothed it on the wooden trunk's lid.

"Look what you did. What do you think you are doing?" she asked.

"Stopping you from making a huge mistake, I hope," he said, eyeing the sheet but deciding not to risk her wrath by grabbing it again.

"It's not a mistake to pass on knowledge," she said.

"It can be depending on who you're passing it to. They're not exactly our best buddies." His voice was beginning to rise.

"And whose fault is that?"

Mark shook his head, not having an answer. "They're not humans," he said, stubbornly.

"So? Maybe that's a good thing considering how we acted towards them."

"That was a long time ago."

"And you're saying we're so different now, our enlightened race of humans? That's why you and I had to beg in the streets and steal and fight for our lives," Portia said, more anger coming out of her voice than she expected.

"That's different."

"How?"

"It just is." Mark leaned back as if he was going to cross his feet again and then changed his mind and leaned forward intently, resting his body on his elbows over his crossed legs and scowling at Portia. She scowled back at him. "I'm just worried about you, that's all. Can't a brother worry about his sister?"

The line in Portia's forehead relaxed, and her breathing evened. It was hard to be angry at him when he wore that earnest expression he had when he was worried. And he was worried. That much was clear.

"How are things with Ella?" Portia asked, trying to distract him.

"Who? Ella, oh fine, she's fine." The continued scowl on his face did not match the attempted lightheartedness of his tone. Portia imagined Ella was outside practicing her magic with Liam. The whole thing confused Portia. She thought Ella hated Mark and Mark hated Ella. They were always at each other's throats but still always together, except for when Liam was there. It was like watching three gangs face-off for a fight where the rules were unclear, and sometimes they shared cakes between the veiled threats to each other. Ella was a touchy subject. Portia tried to think of a safer one. She didn't want to lift her quill to write in case Mark tried to grab the parchment again. It had taken her a long time to write out a single sheet.

"When do you think we'll get to the splinter?" he asked, finding the new subject for both of them.

Portia shrugged. "Another day or so, I think. You could ask our navigator; he has the coordinates."

Mark shook his head. The dwarf ship's navigator was up on the royal deck in the captain's overlook, which was on the same level as the royal cabins. Despite having stayed in the palace, Mark kept his distance from the royalty. He had little trust for those more senior to him or higher in a hierarchy.

Portia waited for him to say something else, but he didn't.

Instead, he looked down into his lap. Hesitantly, she lay the sheet back down on the trunk and grabbed her quill, then paused to see if he would move again. He did not. She dipped the quill into the pot of ink and brought it down onto the paper, slowly scratching out the letters of each word.

She was lost deep in thought of how to use the magic of duplicates, the magic she was writing about at the moment when Mark's soft voice reached her ear.

"You're making a mistake," Mark said. "If you won't listen to me, at least ask our queen and king." His brow furrowed, hating to invoke their authority.

Portia paused her writing and stared at the top of his head while he still looked down into his lap. Closing her eyes for a second, she thought and then opened them again.

"If I do that, will you leave me to work in peace?" she asked.

"Yes.

"Then I will, I promise."

"Before you give the book to the dwarves," he insisted.

"Yes, before," she agreed.

He rose to go, standing as tall as he was able in the short tent and brushing off his pant legs. At the entrance, he paused and turned to Portia again. "I think you're wrong about Magisend too. Her and those two simpering idiots she hangs out with were whispering something and shut up the moment they knew I was coming by. They have too many secrets; I feel it. If we were back on the streets, I'd never have let them in the gang."

He didn't wait for her response, instead stepping outside

the tent and letting the flap swing back down again.

Portia bit her lip, thinking about their old gang in Valencia. For the most part, John, the leader when she had joined, had done a good job in keeping out the bad seeds, but even his excellent judgment had let a few in, or at least one very bad seed. For a moment, she wished intently John was there to help her figure out what Magisend was up to. Staring ahead, she realized what she was looking at—Magisend's trunk. It had a large padlock on it, its metal face with a keyhole swinging right in front of her, hanging from a large hasp and nearly hitting her knees. It was one of the simpler padlocks. Picking it open would take little time, especially with the fine tools she had finally been given by Kerat as they had left the kingdom of Morgani. She had shoved the tools in her bag in her rush to pack and not thought of them since. The same bag she had with her now.

Leaning towards the flaps of the tent swinging in the breeze, she looked to see if anyone was close by. Her view was partially obstructed by the tent itself, but she didn't dare go any closer to the opening. If someone saw her looking around, it would look suspicious.

There was no one in her view. Cocking her head, she listened. There were no footsteps approaching, only the distant shouts and bangs of magic going off from the mages and students standing by the ship's rails practicing their magic. Sailors ran along the decks and the lines hummed above her, but no one was close by.

Grabbing her bag, Portia pulled out the pick set and made short work of the lock. Holding her papers on top of the trunk, so if someone just looked in it would not be so apparent the trunk was open, she eased the top up and glanced inside. On top of piles of luxurious clothes, there was a sheaf of paper, more paper than Portia expected a student to have. Some of it was bundled together in a folio held together with a fine ribbon. Still holding the trunk lid with one hand, she slid her other hand into the trunk and pulled the folio towards her. She loosened the ribbon and tried to lift the flap to see what the paper said. In the dim shadows of the trunk, it was hard to discern words, but one item stood out to her—a large stylized diamond. Portia's breath caught in her throat, and her heart pounded, suddenly racing in her chest. She felt dizzy. A noise outside the tent startled her and she shoved the folio back deep within the trunk and quietly shut the lid as quickly as she could. With a curse, she saw the open padlock sitting on her lap.

Magisend Lucy appeared at the doorway of the tent. She looked in and gave Portia a sweet smile.

"How is the writing coming?" Magisend asked.

"Good, good." Portia stretched her arm out with a yawn while leaning forward to let her tunic drape over the lock in front of her. "It's exhausting doing so much writing."

"You're lucky, commoner; most of us had to spend our childhood doing that while you were free to roam the streets." Magisend gave her the smile of a viper.

"Yes, lucky, I guess. I'll be out soon," Portia said.

"Good. I've heard your sword technique has improved and thought maybe we could spar."

Portia raised her eyebrows at the invitation. "Um, sure,"

Portia agreed, not able to think of an immediate reason to refuse Magisend's offer.

Magisend waved her fingers goodbye and disappeared from the tent front.

With an exhale, Portia quickly shoved the shank of the lock into the eye on the trunk. She pressed the top and bottom of the lock together and was about to snap it back in place when she, the trunk, and everything around her floated up into the air and then to one side before violently slamming back down onto the deck. A deafening explosion rang out, and the walls of the tent vibrated with the noise as much as with the jolt of motion from the ship itself. For a moment, Portia couldn't hear anything and the world was silent, and then, with an excruciating sharp pain in her ears, sound came back to her: the screaming complaints of wood bent too far too fast, shouts of men, dwarves, and elves, commands, and alarm bells incessantly ringing.

Dazed, Portia pushed the trunk aside, and without thinking, donned her baldric and sword, pulling the thick leather strap over her head and across her shoulders. She grabbed the sheet music, folded it and stuck it inside her tunic. The deck of the ship began to tilt, the front of the tent rising higher than the back. Portia and all the tent's contents started sliding towards the back of the tent. The tent itself was not nailed to the deck, only tied to the masts at the top and with the bottom corners attached to anchors on the deck with long ropes.

As the deck tilted further, the items along the back tent wall pushed up against it, bulging out the bottom of the canvas wall, then slipping out from underneath it and sliding away one by one across the deck. With all the chaos, it was impossible to hear if there was a splash of the items going into the water. She couldn't remember if there was anything between the back of the tent and the edge of the ship. Cursing, Portia decided to not risk it. Looking up, she saw the front of the tent stretched tight between the ropes holding it to the mast. The tent itself, at least, was attached to the ship.

Portia lay flat on the slick wood while she shimmed up the deck to the swinging flaps of the tent opening. It took painful minutes to make a few hand lengths of progress, and all the while, the noise around her continued at a maddening volume. She was almost to the top when the ship itself jerked, and Portia slid halfway back down the tent, her nails trying to dig into the hard wood and only breaking, leaving red bloody trails behind her. The wind from the opening below her whipped her hair around her face, blinding her.

Finally, she stopped sliding. Portia shoved back a sob. If she cried, she'd be blinded. She could cry in the afterlife if she did not make it.

Slowly moving again, Portia shimmied her way up to the opening of the wildly billowing tent. Finally, she was able to grab a swinging tent flap. She pulled hard on it with both hands and watched to make sure the door itself didn't rip from the main body of the tent. It held. She used it to move forward and grab the main body of the tent and flop over the end of it, panting. Looking back, she saw nearly all the items that had once been in the tent were gone. The bottom of the tent swung free in the wind.

Outside the tent, the deck was oddly tilted against the

horizon. Sailors swung from ropes tied around their waists while others crawled in the rigging above her, and yet more ran along the deck, their sticky shoes giving them a grip on the slick surface. On the side of the ship that was highest, mages hung over the rail using the chain that hung from post to post to mark the edge of the deck to secure themselves to the ship. They faced down over the edge of the ship and towards the water. They waved their hands in odd signals until Portia realized they were using magic. Something was down below them.

Taking a step onto the slick deck to the other mages, Portia's foot slid on the angled deck and she landed face down on its surface, nearly losing her grip on the tent. Cursing, she unlaced her soft leather boots and tucked them under a line by the tent. Hopefully, they would not be lost. Her bare feet gave her a much better grip on the deck.

Using a running start from the tent she quickly scrambled up the surface of the deck, letting go of the tent at the last minute and running up to the railing and grabbing the chain tightly. She almost overshot the edge of the ship, but luckily the railing was intact, and she felt the chain push up against her thighs.

The barrier against her lower body brought her head down as her body stopped. The side of the ship was visible from her tenuous perch. She gasped. The mages were responsible for the ship tilting so wildly. They were using enormous amounts of magic to lift that side of the ship up, holding it out of the water, frantically working to keep the sea out of the gigantic hole in the side of the ship.

16

G uards were visible within the hole in the side of the *Pearl* along with some chained Dragonoid prisoners and a few terrified looking elves.

On the railing of the deck above, Professor Aelric was mumbling under his breath while casting magic, sweat running down his brow while his hair whipped around his face. Portia didn't even know what sort of magic he was doing, or how it was even possible. There were two unknown mages next to him—perhaps the magic was from them and he was just lending his strength. She'd seen him do that before for the truth cube back in the Academy and the much nastier truth cube they had on board the ship.

What the ship needed was a healer. The same magic that closed the splinters would fix the wood of the hull if she could find enough of the original wood left. A large piece of the dark red wood hull was bobbing in the water below them. A few smaller pieces drifted away behind the path of the ship.

Feeling eyes upon her neck, Portia turned. Queen Lorica and King Consort Aldis were standing on the edge of the royal decks along with Queen Morgani. They were all pale. They couldn't see what was happening with the side of the ship, but it was unmistakable that the ship was in trouble. The captain came out of his command cabin and ushered them back inside to relative safety. At least inside his command room they were no longer in danger of sliding down the deck and off into the sea.

Everyone on board would perish if this was not fixed. There were not enough life rafts for all of them. Portia had only seen a few longboats they used for bringing supplies in from the harbors. The boats would hold at most twenty or thirty—just a fraction of all those on board.

Even a single healer would help. Portia noticed one healer dressed in the healers' distinctive red robes within the group of mages. She was working frantically but had only managed to heal a small corner of the open gaping hole in the side of the ship. It would never be enough. Portia knew she was only supposed to use her magic for the splinters, but there would be no chance of doing that if they all came to their mortal ends now.

Shifting her weight back a little so she wasn't so precariously perched on the edge of the ship, Portia started singing the healing song. It took so much more energy than she was used to using to have to drag the missing pieces of the ship's hull over the water, bring them alongside the ship, and then magically lift them to the right height. Only after those steps were taken could she sing the tune in earnest to match the main body of the ship and the piece punched out of it, merging them back together, whole, as they had been before.

When the first wooden piece came back over the water towards them Professor Aelric whipped his head around until he spotted Portia. He narrowed his eyes but did not tell her to stop. Portia ignored him but was still relieved when he turned his face back down to concentrate on his own tasks.

It seemed to take forever, but Portia kept singing, despite the scratching sensation in her throat that soon turned into a stinging pain that went down her lungs and up and out through her ears. She sang when she thought she had not another breath in her, forcing the melody out in a whisper.

The other mages were failing. Their magic was not pouring out as strongly, and their bodies starting to droop in place and collapse below the railing on the edge of the ship. The ship sank lower as the magic holding it up faded. Portia tried to hurry, but she had little energy left and was grateful she could continue at all.

Finally, she had healed all the wood pieces she found, missing only some small splinters and other bits blown especially far out to sea and out of her magical reach. She stopped, and as if on cue, the other mages stopped as well. The ship, now so much closer to the water, finally dropped the last few feet, landing with a splash and rocking drunkenly back and forth. The chain railing at the edge of the deck kept the mages from slipping overboard, though one swung wildly out over the sea before swinging back and being grabbed by the desperate hands of the others.

Darkness crowded around the edge of Portia's eyes. The

exhaustion she always felt after using so much magic came upon her. She carefully wrapped her hand in the chain marking the edge of the deck and positioned her body against an upright post set into the deck for the railing so if she lost consciousness she would not accidentally slip off the ship into the swirling waters below.

Sailors ran by calling commands and carrying pitch and repair materials. The job Portia had done was not perfect, but it was enough to prevent immediate disaster. The sailors raced below decks to finish the repair job and pump out the water that had made its way inside their vessel.

PORTIA SAT in the long mess hall of the Dwarven ship, a blanket wrapped around her shoulders. Mark came to the table and set down a steaming cup of broth in front of her then climbed over the bench to sit next to her. Others were huddled under blankets as well, scattered around the room, also being tended to. A medic walked from group to group, asking questions in a low voice. Some of those wearing the blankets were the mages who expended themselves near to death to save the ship, while others were the students, sailors, and guards who had not been so lucky as to stay on board and had been flung off the *Pearl* with the initial explosion. After it had been determined that there were no enemy ships nearby, the captain ordered a rescue operation and longboats had been dropped down into the sea to row after those floundering in the waters. Only an Elven soldier was still missing.

While the captain had ordered the rescue mission without reservation, he had paced the deck nervously the entire time they were gone, with triple lookouts up in the masts, scanning for any possible additional traps that might be waiting for them. No one had seen what had originally struck them, except for one student claiming they saw a strange-looking fish swimming up to the ship. Whatever it was, it had nearly taken them down entirely. If the trap had hit one of the smaller clipper ships in their wake, the clipper ship would have sunk near instantly. Their enemy was close by, even if not in visual range yet.

Conversation in the mess was muted—low whispers that didn't carry and furtive glances at others around.

"Are you feeling better?" Mark asked solicitously.

Portia nodded, breathing in the wonderful smells of the hot broth in the cup in her hands. A commotion by the door drew everyone's eyes. Magisend Lucy walked in, soaking wet and wearing a blanket over her shoulders. Her eyes flashed fire. She stomped down the aisle and then sat down on a bench, saltwater dripping from her clothes to form a puddle underneath her. One of her friends, perfectly dry, ran to the kitchen to get Magisend a cup of hot broth, which Magisend took from her roughly. Her friend looked down and backed up slowly, sitting a ways down the bench from Magisend.

"That looks like fun," Portia said.

"What? The helping or the soaking wet?"

"Both."

Mark shook his head. He moved closer to Portia and away

from Magisend, who was further down the same extremely long bench he was sitting on.

Another commotion started from the opposite end of the room. This time, it was the queens and king consort. Everyone scrambled to stand and show their respect.

"Please, everyone, sit," said Queen Morgani. "You've been through enough today, all of you. Which is why we are here."

Without giving any further instructions to the wide room, Queen Morgani nodded at everyone and waved for them to go about their business. Slowly, with even quieter conversations, people sat down in their little groups. Queen Morgani, Queen Lorica, and King Consort Aldis made their way through the crowded seats and tables to Portia and Mark. Professor Aelric and Archmage Vermeil followed in their wake along with several advisors and the commanders of all three armies. General Bancrot gave Portia a warm smile over the shoulder of Queen Lorica.

Portia tried to stand. Again, Queen Lorica motioned for her to remain sitting.

"Our being here is to protect you, not to make you stand when you are so weak," said Queen Lorica.

"Yes, Your Majesty," said Portia.

Queen Morgani gave Queen Lorica a meaningful look. Queen Lorica nodded in return.

"We have not much time, so I will be blunt. Can you still close the splinter when we find it?"

Portia nodded.

"This is not an idle question. Think carefully before you

answer. Can you, if even asked in a few minutes, muster enough energy to do what needs to be done?" asked Queen Lorica insistently. "We have some control now of our approach. We can husband more time if needed."

Portia looked down, considering how she felt and how much healing the boat had taken out of her. She must be honest, both with herself and with her queen. If the splinter appeared now, could she close it?

"Your Majesty, I fear I would falter if I don't get some rest," Portia said, the admission curled and stinging in her stomach. She raised her eyes to Queen Lorica and then quickly dropped them again, her face burning red from what had come from her mouth.

"It is as we thought," said King Consort Aldis. He motioned for the generals to come forward. "We can buy some time, but we should use it to make a plan. Our strategists are hard at work, but you are the key, which is why we had to speak to you. We understand what you did to save the ship, and no one blames you for it, but it cannot be allowed to let us lose this war."

Lose the war? Portia stared at him, her jaw hanging down. They couldn't lose the war. Portia refused to believe it. It certainly would not be because of her.

"Do not misunderstand," Queen Lorica said, her voice gentle. "We understand you saved our lives, but we must plan carefully. This is about more than just our existence. We must care first for our kingdoms and our people above our own lives. Always."

Portia glanced to Queen Morgani, whose husband and king was stranded on the Dragonoid world, if he lived it all. The queen returned her gaze impassively.

"Yes, even my husband, King Morgani, must come after our people. We are here to lead and protect."

"I'm confused, Your Majesties. Should I have done nothing? I could have dropped a boat to escape, but there was no promise I'd have found the splinter on my own," Portia said.

No one spoke for a moment.

"You are correct, Jack, there was no guarantee that would have been a better plan. But you must put closing the splinter as higher priority than our lives," Queen Lorica said gently.

Her queen had said she did not blame her, but still shame pricked at Portia as if she had made a colossal error.

"Does that include the people stranded on their world as well? Those on the Dragonoid world?" Portia asked.

"Of course it does," said Queen Lorica. "We must, however, prioritize the ones that are here—there are so many more of them."

The queens looked on while Portia sat staring at her hands, hunched underneath the blanket.

"I apologize, Your Majesties, but I do not understand why you are here."

"We told you, we are here to impress upon you that our first priority is closing the splinter," said Queen Lorica.

Portia looked up questioningly.

"Even if we can never open another again to the Dragonoid's world," said Queen Morgani. "Ever."

Portia locked eyes with Queen Morgani, whose gaze was both sad and resolute. She glanced at Archmage Vermeil. He gave her a brief nod and then looked down, shifting on his feet.

"Can't I even try to check to see if the music is right?" asked Portia, a plea coming into her voice as she thought of all of those stranded on the other world.

"No, child, my Jack of Magic. You may not. Not because we don't care, but because we cannot risk your ability to close the splinter. What happened with the *Pearl* here was unfortunate, but we suspect," Queen Lorica glanced at Professor Aelric before returning her gaze to Portia, "that it was intentional to sap your powers or to kill you specifically. We do not know how—perhaps it was from the battle of the Well of Tears—but we believe the Dragonoids know of you and your worth to us."

"And of your threat to them," said King Consort Aldis.

Portia stared up at the serious faces around her. Finally, she nodded. "Yes, Your Majesties."

"You will work with our generals for the battle plan to close this large splinter, hopefully the last one in existence to their lands. May you be blessed in your journey," said Queen Lorica before rising and walking away, followed by King Consort Aldis, Queen Morgani, and several attendants, leaving Professor Aelric, Archmage Vermeil, and the generals behind.

General Lyren walked to the bench in front of Portia and sat down. "Okay, young human, now we plan."

The other leaders—General Bancrot and General Seren—took their places on either side of General Lyren, while the Archmage and Professor Aelric took seats at either end of the group.

Mark brought Portia another cup of broth and a large bowl of food, which she ate while the group discussed and planned for the upcoming battle. Couriers were sent with instructions for the commander of the *Pearl*, as well as for the other vessels in their fleet.

After Portia had finished her bowl of food, she turned to set the empty bowl on the table behind her and her gaze lifted to see Magisend Lucy staring at her with narrowed eyes from down the table. Knowledge of Magisend's duplicity flooded back to Portia, and she glanced at the generals behind her.

THE HORIZON GLOWED pink where the sun was hiding, shining elsewhere in the predawn hours. The wind whipped Portia's hair into her face, and she brushed it away and tucked it behind her ear while looking down the shadowy deck of the *Pearl*. Mages and sailors worked in groups, lowering long-boats, coming and going, sending some mages to the smaller clipper ships, as well as bringing back sailors so the smaller ships would not be overwhelmed. Their plan depended on magic coming from all the ships at once in a coordinated manner. They could not risk concentrating everything on the *Pearl*. It was too easy a target for the enemy. They had fought that way once—with the *Pearl* doing all the work. They couldn't afford to repeat that tactic. No one knew for sure where those in league with the Dragonoids were placed as spies. The prior day's attack was too convenient to be just by chance.

Mia, Ella, Magisend Lucy and her two shadows, as well as Liam, Richard, and Mark were in with the other mages, moving catapult loads and helping the mages inject them with the water they would need to explode with their magical spells. Senior mages did most of the work and directed the students to help. Even Magisend bent her back and worked as hard as the other students. Perhaps even harder. She had not lost her bad temper since the previous night when she had been fished out of the waters.

Finally, after what seemed to be long hours and too much noise, all was settled on the deck of the Pearl, as well as on the clipper ships that now spaced out alongside them. Two clipper ships over was a large space where a ship the size of the *Pearl* could sail. It was left open for the duplicate of the *Pearl* the mages would create. The tactics the generals had come up with accounted for that space with no firepower where the phantom ship would be.

Sailors and mages sat at the ready as the sails above them flapped. As the sun rose, the breeze died down. Blessedly, the sun was behind them and not ahead, sending long rays out over the waters. They would be spared having to squint into the brightness to see what lay before them. The destination coordinates they sailed to had been checked and double-checked with the stars against what the captive navigator Dragonoid had said. The splinter should be in front of them. Now, there was nothing to do but wait as the ships sailed forward into the danger awaiting them.

Despite it being the obvious target, the decision had been made to keep Portia aboard the *Pearl*, along with the royalty and the commanders. Its flags were visible to all, and it offered the best location to communicate to all ships should any changes in strategy have to be made on the fly during the battle. Mark was with her. The other students had been split amongst the clippers so they might coordinate with the catapults on each ship, exploding the payloads at the correct moment, as well as defend the ships from any boarders and use direct magic against the enemy vessels when they got into range.

Suddenly, as if fading into existence, a long line of ships appeared ahead, the rays of the sun sparkling off the metal hulls. At first, it appeared just to be water glinting in the sunlight, but the glints were too persistent and too constant. The reflected light was not from moving water but from the stiff unyielding metal of their enemy's ships.

Portia sucked in her breath sharply. It was as they feared. There were two tall enormous Dragonoid vessels—the ones they had seen at the Well of Tears—along with a fleet of smaller ships. At least there were not more of the enormous vessels. Glancing over, Portia saw their own phantom vessel appear over the waters. They had waited until the last minute to place it, not wanting to drain their mages unnecessarily. Hopefully, it had been soon enough, and the enemy had not seen a ship materialize out of nowhere.

The fleet ahead of them had a strange look. Portia squinted until she resolved the smaller ships. They were so close to each other they appeared to be touching, more like a wall than a series of ships.

The captain of the *Pearl* yelled out the first commands. Sailors went to ready position and the catapults were cranked back and readied. The ships sailed on forward to the enemy.

Portia held her breath until the first catapult launched the exact moment they were within range. The payload arced high above them, and a second after hitting its zenith it arced down and exploded, fragments shattering into the line of enemy ships. One particularly large fragment hit a smaller vessel square on. The stone should have sunk the enemy vessel, even with its sturdy metal hull. Instead, the vessel dipped below the water with the impact until the rock slowly rolled off its prow and sank into the waters, leaving the ship to bounce back up again like a child's bathtub toy. The ships next to it bounced up and down as well.

Cries of dismay rang out across the deck of the *Pearl*. The captain yelled more orders. More catapults launched. All ships on their side shot their catapults as quickly as they could, doing what damage they could before the Dragonoid ships got in range to use their cannons on the wooden clippers. They made many direct hits, but again, instead of going down, the Dragonoid ships merely shucked the stones and bounced back up. Portia stared at the boats but couldn't see anything to explain what was happening. Looking up at the main mast of their own ship, she saw a lookout in the crow's nest, his spyglass trained on the enemy.

Cursing, Portia grabbed the mast and climbed it rapidly, using her soft leather boots to grip the shallow notches put there for climbing access. Every time the ship fired a catapult, the mast vibrated, and she held on tight, fearing she would be knocked off and smashed onto the deck far below. Finally, she reached the crow's nest and hopped over the rim, much to the startled look of the dwarf seated there. She grabbed the spyglass from him and aimed it at the water line between the enemy ships. There were chains running from ship to ship.

The Dragonoid ships were connected.

That was how the struck ships stayed up. The Dragonoid ships that should have gone down were being held up by their neighbors, by the chains run between them.

Portia's heart thudded in her ears. She lowered the glass. The two facing sets of ships were noticeably closer. If the *Pearl* and the clippers with it did not eliminate any of the Dragonoid ships soon, cannons on each one of the enemy Dragonoid vessels would be able to reach the human fleet and decimate them. Even the *Pearl,* with its magically reinforced wood, would not withstand such a barrage. There were too many Dragonoids ships with too many cannons.

The commanders on board had minutes to do something. Once they got closer and lost the advantage of range they had over the Dragonoids, they'd fall under the returning superior firepower of the black powder weapons. The humans, elves, and dwarves alike would perish if they did not pull back and flee first—if it were possible to flee the armada ahead of them.

"Does the captain have one of these?" Portia asked, holding up the spyglass.

The dwarf nodded, still stunned. Portia shoved the eyeglass back into his hands and then jumped out of the crow's nest, holding loosely on to the mast as she slid quickly down. Splinters burned her hands, but she gritted her teeth and kept going.

Reaching the deck with a thud, she took off at a run to the stairs leading up the two decks to the captain's lookout. She took the stairs two at a time. Guards outside the door were startled but did not stop her when she nodded at them and then burst into the room. The captain and the commanders were arrayed in front of the open window that looked out at the battle. The queens and king consort sat in tall chairs just behind them.

"The ships are connected!" Portia yelled, trying to get the commander's attention while also curtsying to the king and queens. She nearly fell over with the effort. The captain stared at her, puzzled.

General Lyren was the first to understand. She grabbed the spyglass on the table in front of the captain and pulled it out, setting her eye to the eyepiece and training it on the enemy ships.

"Look just below the waterline between the ships," Portia prompted.

General Lyren moved the spyglass slowly until she stopped and stared for a few seconds through it. "She's right. We should have figured that out when the ships weren't going down."

The general handed the eyepiece to General Bancrot, who checked. Swearing came as the eyeglass was handed from commander to commander and each saw the truth for themselves.

"How many damaged ships can a single intact ship hold up?" asked Queen Lorica.

The captain of the *Pearl* considered her question. The other commanders looked to him, waiting. Of all of them there, he was the one with the most experience with sea vessels.

"If they're all the same size, I can't imagine they'd even keep up a single other ship. They must be suspending the damaged ship between two whole ones. If we can hit more than one ship in a row instead of scattering our shot evenly along the line as we have been, then we might be able to damage enough ships close together to pull a group under."

General Lyren looked out at the ships thoughtfully. "If we managed to sink several in one end, would not the rest fall like dominoes?"

General Seren, the normally quiet dwarf commander, spoke, drawing everyone's attention for the rarity of it. "Perhaps. It depends on the strength of the chains. But what we're doing now is not working. Try this now, or we should turn and regroup."

A hiss of disapproval came from General Lyren. The expressions of the others matched the commander's. No one wanted to run.

"Change the focus then. Pick a spot far from one of the larger ships. If we can sink their support ships, we might have a chance against the other two," commanded Queen Lorica.

"Make it so," agreed Queen Morgani. "Now!" she added when the generals and the captain did not immediately spring into action.

A quick map was drawn out of the ships and the commands for the flags were dictated and then run off by messengers to the flaggers at the front of the *Pearl*.

No one told Portia to leave the command center, so she stayed and watched the battle unfold. A few seconds of unusual quiet caught her attention. None of the catapults were going off on their side. A lone Dragonoid ship set off a cannonball with a puff of black smoke from its deck. The metal ball whizzed through the air and landed just a few ship lengths in front of the *Pearl*. The Dragonoids were close to striking distance, and both sides knew it. Portia thought she could even see the enemy ships ahead of her increase their speed, trying to get to their targets. She pleaded under her breath for their side to be successful while she squeezed her hands tight, feeling powerless. If they failed, the consequences would be upon them soon enough, either through the sea swallowing them whole while their ship sank or facing hand-to-hand combat with the enormous Dragonoid soldiers. This warfare through shooting things at one another was agonizing in a different way than she'd ever experienced before. She wished she could strike at them directly with her sword.

And then, as if cotton had been pulled from her ears, noise exploded around her as all the catapults on the *Pearl* and the cutters around them went off at once. The payloads flew overhead, arcing together. They were aimed at the middle three ships of a long line of smaller vessels. When the payloads got closer to their targets, the mages exploded them in a cloud of rock and steam and fire. The pieces rained down on the ships, rocking them with their hits and then bouncing off, some strikes blowing holes in the sides of the metal hulls while other rocks broke open holes in the tops of the decks. The middle ship bowed first under the assault. Instead of bouncing back up as the rocks slid off it, as they'd seen in previous attacks, it stayed down and slowly took on water.

The focused attack had worked. The nose of the vessel dipped lower under the sea as the ship sank into the waters, pulling on the chains taut on either side of it. The two ships connected to it had not been struck as hard but were still damaged with holes in their hulls. The additional pull from the sinking ship was too much to overcome, and they too took on water. All three ships sank down towards the seafloor.

The chains connecting the damaged group of ships to those on either side grew tight and pulled, tipping the unstruck ships in towards the center. It appeared they would be going down too, and cheers broke out from the deck of the *Pearl* and reached the captain's lookout. The cheers were choked out when one after another the chains between the ships snapped and broke, and the undamaged ships bounced back up.

"Still, that is three fewer ships to shoot at us," said Queen Lorica.

Her general, General Bancrot, nodded. The commands

were given for the next target. If they were lucky, they could do this two more times before the Dragonoid ships were close enough to strike them with their cannons.

They were successful with the second strike, watching three more ships go down and a fourth, severely damaged, turning in circles as if possessed, but by the time they tried it a third time, the Dragonoid commanders had figured out their tactic and the chains were dropping between the ships. The struck ships still went down with the third volley of catapult payload, but they lost their opportunity to damage the ships on either side.

The crack of a cannonball hitting the deck of the *Pearl* and bouncing along, hitting screaming men and ripping the rail from the ship on one side, announced the Dragonoids' cannons were now within reach and firing upon them.

A second hit knocked out the glass in the captain's overlook, sending everyone ducking while the shards exploded into the room, and the queens' and king consort's attendants checking the bodies of the royal highnesses for injuries. Queen Lorica pushed them away as the sudden wind within the room swirled papers and other objects everywhere.

The rest of the battle was a blur to Portia, seeming to drag in slow motion yet also going too fast. Shots fired on both sides, men screamed, and wooden ships crumpled on themselves. The two sides lobbed their fire at each other until the ships themselves met, grinding together in a roar of splintering wood and twisting metal.

One of the taller Dragonoid ships met the *Pearl* in a nearly head-on collision, glancing stern to stern. Dragonoid sailors were ready at the prow to leap onto the *Pearl* and board. Their numbers seemed unending as the mages and sailors fought them back, sending many to their death below in the crashing seas.

Mark was amongst the mages and warriors at the frontline beating back the Dragonoids. Portia wanted to go to his aid—only the strong hand General Lyren gripping Portia's forearm so tightly Portia's hand went numb held her back. Weight pressed upon Portia's chest as she watched Mark fight off a much larger Dragonoid with a long curving sword.

Mark danced back and to the side, jabbing his ridiculously small knife at his opponent. The Dragonoid, tired of playing with his constantly moving opponent, lifted his sword with both hands for a death blow, the force of which would be able to split Mark in two.

Mark dropped to the ground and rolled forward underneath the Dragonoid, leaping up again in one motion behind his opponent's back and stabbing him in the neck, in the small opening between the Dragonoid's breastplate and his helmet. General Lyren whistled under her breath.

"I do not think your young friend needs your help. Stay here; we cannot lose you," General Lyren said in her ear, barely audible above the howl of the winds around them.

Portia nodded numbly, staring after Mark until she lost him in a crowd of fighting bodies and ocean spray.

Explosions rang out all around them. Messengers came running with reports from the lookouts and from the flaggers. The generals sent out more commands.

The battle raged on.

Bile rose in the back of Portia's throat as bodies lay on the deck of the ship, now tripping those still fighting.

The sky darkened as thick dark blue and black clouds gathered above the fighting ships. The sun disappeared as the air grew darker and darker. Soon, it was difficult to even see others within the captain's overlook, and only the occasional flare of fire magic shot up over the battle made things visible, reflecting off the white sails of their ships and the black metal of the Dragonoid vessels.

One final flash of light burst forth over all the human ships and the *Pearl*, shining down on the battleground like daylight and then fading just as quickly as it had arrived. Immediately after, bolts of lightning came down from the sky and hit every single Dragonoid ship. And kept hitting each ship. The lightning went on so long, it seemed to suck all the air from Portia's lungs, and the strange smell of burnt atmosphere permeated everything.

Then, the lightning stopped. The fighting had stopped during the lightning strike so that when the sizzling sound of electricity coursing through the metal ships stopped, only the sound of sails snapping in the wind and rigging banging against the wood rang out over the scene.

As if one, the metal Dragonoid ships began sinking into the sea. The Dragonoids who had boarded the cutters held up their hands in surrender. Other Dragonoids leapt from the sinking vessels—a very few—but most aboard the doomed vessels floated away in the rough seas, already dead as the ships sank beneath them.

The battle was won.

THEY RACED across the deck to the longboat waiting for them. General Lyren and General Bancrot each took one side, flanking Portia, while Archmage Vermeil trailed behind. Guards ran ahead and behind them. Their swords were up, and they were alert for any Dragonoid treachery. Most of the Dragonoids still on deck were already in manacles. Still, Portia's escort whirled around her for any sudden movements.

Mark came running up to join the group, but Portia waved him away. Blood ran down the side of his face, and he did not look well. Head wounds bled heavily, even when the wound was not serious, but Portia didn't want to take any chances. She didn't want to lose him now. Let him stay and have a medic look at his injuries.

Portia took her seat on the long wooden plank that stretched from edge to edge of the longboat. The others climbed in with her, and sailors cranked the lines to drop them down below.

"Wait!" a voice called from the deck above.

The sailors paused in their work with the lines. Magisend Lucy's head popped out over the railing and looked down at the longboat hanging in the air below.

"I have to tell you," Magisend said, pausing to catch her breath from running so fast. She bent over and then raised her body again and took a deep breath and swallowed, able to speak again. "There are too many notes—"

"I know," Portia said calmly, interrupting her.

They stared at each other, Magisend looking down at

Portia, and Portia, whose face was one face in a sea of faces of the highest commanders of the lands, stared back.

Their eyes locked for several breaths.

"Blessed be you in your journey," Magisend Lucy said finally, giving the traditional blessing for warriors going into battle.

"Thank you," Portia said gravely, meaning it.

HEALING the splinter did not take long, despite its massive size. It was so large that it took up half the horizon. They didn't dare let the longboat get too close for fear of the strong current pulling towards the splinter and drawing their boat into its massive opening. The few rowers on board would not be able to fight the current's increasing strength closer to the opening. But even at a distance, Portia was able to hear the low background sound of the music. It was the song as she remembered it—not the song as Magisend had written it.

Using her magic, Portia closed the tunnel between the two lands, first singing a healing song to the rift in the Dragonoid world, and then healing the Haulstatt side. The sea rose in a splash at the end and then fell back down, pulled up as the surface of the splinter grew smaller and smaller and finally popped out of existence.

Portia hung her head in exhaustion as the sailors rowed back to the *Pearl*. The scarred hull of the enormous vessel looked awful. The sailors on board were pumping water out of one discharge chute near constantly. But it had not sunk. What was damaged could be repaired.

All the splinters between the two different lands had been sealed. Thoughts of all those trapped on the wrong side weighed heavily on Portia as she gripped the side of the boat and let the cold seawater splash over her hand.

17

The ships sailed back to the harbor at Coverack, making time under the night stars, while those not on duty celebrated on the decks of the *Pearl* and the clippers around it. Mead and beer had appeared from deep within the ship's stores, and the sailors and soldiers alike took part, laughing and enjoying their victory. The occasional flares went from ships as rowdy sailors wasted the ship supplies. The good humor of the captains forestalled any admonishment of the excesses.

Portia sat alone at the prow of the *Pearl*. Her legs hung over the edge, and she kicked them as the breeze pushed back her hair. Pulling her cloak tight, she wrapped herself against the cool night air.

The decks below held chained captives, Dragonoids pulled from the cold waters after their ships had gone down and their only avenue of escape to their own lands destroyed. A shiver overtook Portia despite her woolen covering.

Tomorrow she would face them. Dread pulled at her stomach. No matter their crimes, they had family and a home—or they did. She, as Jack of Magic, had taken that from them. Her fists curled at the role she had been forced into. The pit in her stomach also mixed with rage. How dare they force the issue so?

Portia sucked in air and consciously breathed it out slowly through her mouth, forcing her hands to open. She placed her palms on her knees and rolled her neck, wishing her back would relax and the pain in her neck dissipate. Victory was not sweet in her mouth.

Mark appeared at her elbow and sat down next to her, handing her a glass of mead. He looked at her face, but she did not move her eyes from the horizon. He nodded and then gazed in the same direction.

"More orphans below," Portia said.

"A little old for orphans," Mark said, taking a sip of his own glass.

Portia stared down at the mead Mark had brought her. The sweet smell drifted up to her, but it did not entice. Her stomach stayed curdled.

"Does it matter?" she asked.

After a moment, he said, "No, I guess not. An orphan is an orphan."

They sat in silence for a few moments while waves washed up against the hull of the ship.

"I don't understand how that storm came up," said Portia finally.

"Iva did that."

Portia looked at him sharply. *All that time she traveled with Iva and had no idea.*

"No, she isn't here," Mark said.

"Then how?"

"Cecilia found out her father was a mage in Jukhnovo. That's how she knew magic even though they don't have an academy," Mark said, taking another drink.

"Lots of people know magic without an academy," said Portia. "You know that."

"True. But Iva knew of her father's storm magic. She told what she knew to Archmage Vermeil before we left. I don't think anyone thought it was even possible to do what she spoke of." He smiled at her. "Amazing what desperation can make possible."

"Who did it though?" Portia tried to think of all the mages on the voyage.

"The Academy mages pieced together wind and fire magic to make an approximation. It was enough to bring on the storms."

"Lucky us," said Portia after a moment.

"Indeed."

The waves lapped and echoed rhythmically underneath the sound of merriment around them.

"They want to celebrate with you. You're their Jack," Mark said.

Portia looked at him at the mention of her title.

He shrugged and took another sip of his glass. "You took care of me; why would it be so hard to believe you're to take care of the world?"

"Except—"

"Except nothing. No one is perfect. And you'd help no one if you were dead," he said.

Portia pursed her lips and looked down again. Mark's warmth against her side seemed to reach all the way into her stomach, helping the tight ball there relax. It was easier to breathe.

"Are you telling me to be kinder to myself?" she finally asked.

"Yes. Will you listen, please, because you know I'm too lazy to want to tell you again."

Portia turned to see a half smile on his face, almost a smirk. Both tears and laughter welled within her. She turned so he wouldn't see.

She took a drink of her mead and nodded. He rose to go and patted her on the back before turning and walking away down the deck.

After sitting for another hour, she was finally ready to go back to the tent and perhaps actually sleep. The celebrations had died down, and only a few groups stayed on deck speaking in low tones. Just as she was about to stand, a voice spoke out behind her.

"What, too good to celebrate with the rest of us, commoner?"

Portia turned. Magisend Lucy stood behind her, her hands on her hips, but her tone was not as confident as it normally was. There was a question within it; would Portia talk to her?

Waving to the spot next to her, Portia turned back to look

at the waters again. She heard rather than saw Magisend scramble and sit down. They sat together in silence.

So quietly Portia almost couldn't hear her, Magisend spoke. "I'm sorry."

"What?" Portia blurted out, turning to stare at her.

"You heard me. I'll not repeat it again to you, commoner." Magisend laughed, a self-deriding laugh that had a bitter edge to it.

Portia looked away again and tapped at her glass with her finger, considering her words carefully. "I guess I did know that. I never expected to hear you admit it though."

"It is not something I ever thought I would say, not to anyone, but especially not to you. I may be a noble, and I guess you are from a noble house too," the admission sounded painful in Magisend Lucy's words, "no matter how much you have stolen. For all that, you have given us so much more. I almost ruined that in my selfishness."

Portia waited, but Magisend said no more.

"What changed your mind?" Portia asked.

"Getting thrown from the deck of the *Pearl* and nearly killed by those I thought wanted an alliance. There is a time to be loyal to one's own people, and I nearly missed it. I'll not make that mistake again."

Portia turned to stare at Magisend.

"Would you like to make up for it?" Portia asked her tiny rival.

Magisend Lucy blinked back at her.

News of their victory traveled ahead of them by flag and by flare. The people of Coverack met them at the docks and tried to carry them to the palace. Celebrations filled the streets. Portia smiled and stiffly waved at the crowds from the open carriage she shared with the other students.

The royals, their advisors, and their commanders met the next day to decide how to move forward and restore their lands. Portia had not been invited but this time was able to gain admittance, the guards having heard all that she had done for the lands.

She curtsied before those meeting around the gigantic wood table.

"Your Majesties," Portia said.

"Our Jack," Queen Lorica said. "I thought you would be resting."

Portia's eyes flickered away briefly. Dark circles under them gave way to all that she was not sleeping.

"Urgent matters of retrieving our people weigh on me," Portia said. She did not speak of the Dragonoids she would like to return to their lands as well.

"They weigh on us too, that much you must surely know," said Queen Morgani, almost scolding. Queen Morgani's husband and king was still left in the Dragonoid lands.

Portia nodded, trying to find the words to speak next. Before she found the right phrase, King Consort Aldis interrupted her thoughts.

"Your concern is most heartwarming, but we must, as rulers, weigh the risk to all our peoples," he said with a smile, speaking slowly as if to a child. "If we were to open a splinter again and you perished, then there would be no way to close it again. All would be lost, and not just those on the other side. We have to trust in the blessings above that they will find their way over there, just as we will find our way over here."

"But that doesn't have to be the choice," Portia protested.

Queen Lorica tilted her head at Portia. "That is the choice. If you perish, who else may close the splinter?"

Portia looked down at her feet. She could think of no one.

"Perhaps another could be trained. Maybe Lord Fife knows of someone."

General Lyren gave a near imperceptible shake of her head to Portia. She refused to recognize it. There had to be a way, even if it wasn't clear now.

"When there is a second, and the plan can be safely executed, we will discuss it then," Queen Lorica said. She waved with one hand, both an acknowledgment and dismissal.

Portia nodded and stumbled out of the room. The sounds of talking resuming behind her were barely audible over the roaring in her ears.

A GRAND BALL was declared to celebrate the end of the war. The palace would be decked out and flooded with people invited to come dance. For those of the town not so lucky as to receive invitations, kegs had been sent around by royal guard, and silver and copper coins distributed to all citizens, right down to the children. All were to celebrate.

Looking in the mirror, Portia couldn't believe she was the same person she'd been when she'd arrived in this town years ago. A flowing gown of red velvet and silk had been crafted specifically for her by seamstresses working night and day for three days. The gown was near as complicated and beautiful as any that Lady Harper had ever worn. Portia plucked at one of the draped sleeves, and it occurred to her that perhaps Lady Harper had been the designer.

Iva, who had nearly suffocated her with hugs, also had a splendid gown and a title for her assistance in bringing back the Jack to their lands. More precious to Iva still was a small plot she had been granted in Jukhnovo and the promised support of the kingdom of Haulstatt in the rebuilding of the kingdom of Jukhnovo. Iva was staying for the ball, but even so, her impatience to return to her home was apparent. She paced even more than normal, swirling her gown around her as she turned.

"Portia, you look wonderful," Iva said. "Let's go and eat and dance!"

Cecilia came to the door of the room they had been granted within the palace to get ready for the ball. Her gown was a slightly darker shade of red that went well with Portia's. It was fitting that they should look similar, being the only surviving representatives of the house of Callac, the original royal house of the land. Despite Queen Lorica's misgivings about the house, she had extended all welcome to both of them. As splendid as she looked, Cecilia looked even more uncomfortable in her finery than Portia. They gazed at each other with their skeptical expressions and then burst out laughing.

"Shall we do this, young ladies?" Cecilia asked Portia and Iva.

"Not so young, but I accept the flattery," Iva said, curtseying to Cecilia.

The ballroom sparkled in a blaze of white magic and colored spots dotted along the wall and floating in bunches from the ceiling. It was already packed with nobles when they arrived. Mark came to the entrance as soon as they were announced, and after bowing to the three of them, held out his arm to Portia. He too was dressed splendidly, another gift from the royal seamstresses.

"There is dancing, and I hear two dinners are planned, and even a breakfast before the travelers go home to their own houses," he said to Portia as they walked into the crowded room and found their way to the punch table. He leaned in and spoke in her ear, "Before we get to that though, may I show you something?"

Portia pulled back and looked at him. His smile was broad and bubbled from within him. It was not a smile she had seen in a long time, not since he had been a small child in Valencia. As he grew older, his smiles had been more serious and more tinged with sorrow. She searched his face and found no anguish in it. She nodded.

"Excuse us, please, ladies," he said to Cecilia and Iva. "We will be just a moment."

They nodded their acceptance. Mark led Portia away towards a doorway that opened into a balcony on the outer wall of the ballroom. The stars were apparent above the heads of those in the room celebrating. A welcome cool breeze pushed into the room warmed by too many bodies wearing thick finery.

On the large balcony that ran the length of the ballroom, there was a cluster of chairs at the far end with people seated in the darkness there. Mark drew her closer to the group and Portia realized her mistake. They were not just people, but also elves and dwarves. General Lyren was there, as well as Archmage Vermeil, and even General Bancrot. Much to her surprise, sitting in the far corner of the group sat Magisend Lucy who stared back at Portia impassively with her eyebrows raised.

General Lyren rose at Portia's approach and pulled out a chair for her. After Portia and Mark were seated, General Lyren cleared her throat, and the small group looked at her expectantly.

"Mind you, young human, I am not here in any official capacity, and I would deny any knowledge of this if asked, but you are not the only one concerned about our people left behind."

Portia searched their faces, trying to understand what they were saying to her.

"Being too timid can also be a risk," General Bancrot said. She turned away when Portia stared at her, shifting in her chair as if the wood were uncomfortable as rocks beneath her.

"We are here to offer our assistance," Archmage Vermeil said quietly, almost too quietly for Portia to hear.

Assistance.

"You asked if I want to make up for it," Magisend Lucy said. "I do. I think your plan would work, and so do they." She waved to the rest of the group.

Magisend spoke of the plan to rescue those stranded on the Dragonoid world and return the Dragonoid prisoners to their homes—the plan Portia had shared with her on the *Pearl*. Portia searched the faces around her.

Each one gave Portia a nod as she met their eyes.

They were going to rescue their people.